The story of Jo Cox is as extraordinary as anything in her novels. Born in a cotton-mill house in Blackburn, Lancashire, she was one of ten children. Her parents, she says, brought out the worst in each other, and life was full of tragedy and hardship – but not without love and laughter. At the age of sixteen, Jo met and married 'a caring and wonderful man' and had two sons. When the boys started school, she decided to go to college and eventually gained a place at Cambridge University, though was unable to take this up as it would have meant living away from home. However, she did go into teaching, while at the same time running the administrative side of her husband's business, renovating the derelict council house that was their home, coping with the problems caused by her mother's unhappy home life – and writing her first full-length novel. Not surprisingly, she then won the 'Superwoman of Great Britain' Award, for which her family had secretly entered her, and this coincided with the acceptance of her novel for publication. She has now written nine novels which have all been widely praised:

'A classic tale . . . a born storyteller' *Bedfordshire Times*

'Tension and drama . . . a book to read at one sitting!' *Prima*

'A classic is born' *Lancashire Evening Telegraph*

Also by Josephine Cox

Let Loose The Tigers
Angels Cry Sometimes
Take This Woman
Whistledown Woman
Outcast
Alley Urchin
Vagabonds
Don't Cry Alone

Her Father's Sins

Josephine Cox

HEADLINE

Copyright © 1987 Josephine Cox

The right of Josephine Cox to be identified as the Author of
the Work has been asserted by her in accordance with the
Copyright, Designs and Patents Act 1988.

First published in 1987
by Futura Publications

Reprinted in this edition in 1992
by HEADLINE BOOK PUBLISHING PLC

10 9 8 7 6 5 4 3 2 1

All rights reserved. No part of this publication may be
reproduced, stored in a retrieval system, or transmitted,
in any form or by any means without the prior written
permission of the publisher, nor be otherwise circulated
in any form of binding or cover other than that in which
it is published and without a similar condition being
imposed on the subsequent purchaser.

All characters in this publication are fictitious
and any resemblance to real persons, living or dead,
is purely coincidental.

ISBN 0 7472 4077 9

Typeset by Keyboard Services, Luton

Printed and bound in Great Britain by
HarperCollins Manufacturing, Glasgow

HEADLINE BOOK PUBLISHING PLC
Headline House
79 Great Titchfield Street
London W1P 7FN

To two women:

my wonderful mother, Mary Jane – whose vitality
I hope has lived on in me and my stories.

Susan Watt; for her professional guidance and
unfailing belief in my writing; my unending
gratitude,

and

to friends and family for their unfailing
encouragement throughout.

Acknowledgements

Blackburn Daily Telegraph (Archives)
Darwen Library
Old Lancastrian folk for long-lost background
colour
The Brindles of Blackburn, for privileged
information

'In the morning'

'Awake! arise! my love, and fearless be,
For there are sleeping dragons all around'
John Keats

Prologue

He lifted his eyes to gaze on the grim determination
shaping her lovely face and he knew he would not
change her mind. Yet, as he slid his fist from beneath
her long caressing fingers, George Kenney felt the
urge to try just once more. And the method he used
was one of blackmail. Pushing the chair back, he got
to his feet and with a voice that betrayed his desperation, he threatened, 'I could force matters. I could go
and see Richard . . . and tell him the way of things.'

'He knows the way of things,' the woman's voice
gently chided, 'he knows that the child I'm carrying is
not his and, still he's begged me not to leave him. And
I won't! I can't desert him.'

'But you'll desert me quick enough, eh?' he
accused.

Rita Marsden looked up at his strong handsome
face and, in that split second of weakness, she might
have melted into his arms. But then she thought of
Kathy, George's long-suffering wife, also pregnant
by him. Steeling herself, she asked pointedly, 'And
what of Kathy?' Then without waiting for a reply, she
shook her head resignedly, saying, 'It wouldn't work.
I'm sorry, George.'

'To hell with Kathy!' George Kenney's frustration found expression in the vicious kick that rammed the chair under the table. 'And to hell with you!' he snarled, his final words being flung over his shoulder as be stormed through the door to the street outside.

Rita Marsden watched him go, her intent gaze following him as he thrust his way down the narrow winding alley, his heavy demob shoes angrily resounding against the uneven cobbles, the long khaki coat rippling out behind him like a mantle. And it struck her now, as it had so often done before, that here was a man of some stamp, a man of unusual handsomeness. But he was not for her. That much at least she had come to know. She took a last lingering look at his tall muscular figure, and that easy way he had of seeming to move without effort. She admired the thick fair hair which invariably fell across his deep blue eyes, causing him constantly to flick it back with a toss of his head. And in spite of the pain in her heart and fond memories of their time together she knew it was right that they should part.

George Kenney was as different from her own husband as chalk from cheese. George was wonderfully charming, with a certain style that had swept her into his arms without hesitation. These past few months of love and laughter had been unforgettable. Yet, lately, her deeper instincts had told Rita that her lover's heart still belonged to his wife, Kathy.

Rita Marsden suspected that beneath that smiling daredevil façade, George Kenney was a sad disillusioned man, made uneasy by the awful experiences of war. He was a creature of many moods and shifting loyalties, which she sensed would only bring her heartache. There was no future for them together; no peace of mind; and today had shown her a side to George Kenney that she had never seen before. It was not a pleasing revelation. His temper was vile.

Thankful that the little café was virtually empty, Rita Marsden returned the chair to its rightful place, paid the bill, and left in the opposite direction from George Kenney. And as she emerged from the cramped back alley, with its menagerie of colourful pavement stalls, marauding dogs and noisy children, her slim tight figure dressed in dark calf-length skirt with matching waist-fitting jacket drew more than a few admiring glances. But deep in thought as she was, Rita Marsden didn't notice. She was only thankful that she and her husband, Richard, would be leaving the area that very evening.

Her love for George Kenney had been a selfish passion, she could see that now. And she was sure that George too, must see the impossibility of it all. Rita also hoped that dear gentle Kathy, who idolized him in spite of his failings, might once again win the total attention of her wayward husband. With this hope came a measure of relief, because Kathy Kenney had weighed heavy on her mind for a long time now.

At that moment George Kenney, too, was thinking of Kathy. He hated her. He resented her smothering love and he despised the being he had spawned in her belly. If it hadn't been for that, he was convinced that he could have talked Rita round to his way of thinking. But the fact that Kathy was pregnant had only refuelled Rita's determination to end their relationship. In his blind anger he had stormed across the heart of Blackburn's narrow winding streets, along by the bombed-out buildings straddling the way up to the gaunt Victorian cottonmills, and now, halting beside the canal towpath, he hoisted himself up onto the remains of a wall where he tucked his knees up under his chin and let his tormented thoughts survey these past years. Strange, turbulent years they had been. He had been sucked into the war in October 1939, and during the years which followed he had seen the worst atrocities that man could commit against man. Some months ago, because of an injury that shattered his elbow, he had been medically discharged, and George Kenney was not sorry to turn his back on the bloody God-forsaken war. Oh, he'd done his bit, so they said. A man of courage and strength, they told him; a man who could take pride in himself. What bullshit! On the battlefield he'd been more afraid than he would ever admit. And what pride could be taken from slaughtering one's fellow men? There had seeped into his heart a hatred and utter hopelessness, which even now haunted his dreams. That bloody war was still raging, there were men and boys in their thousands being mown down like so many cattle, God! What a waste! And yet, was there any other way? Wasn't the evil of a tyrant like Hitler enough to justify such slaughter? In the agony of his mental torment, a twisted groan escaped from him. He didn't know the answer. He would never know! And if he dwelt on it, he knew it must take his sanity.

For a while, George Kenney directed his thoughts to another time, a time when the onset of a second world war had seemed unthinkable. Other matters at home had demanded concern, legacies of the *First* World War which ended in 1918 and which still plagued the nation, particularly the North. Housing shortages, unemployment and poverty, were rife. Was 1936 only eight short years ago, when two hundred desperate men marched from Jarrow to London to present a petition for work to the Prime Minister? And how many of those same men had marched again this time to fight for their country and were now lying somewhere under foreign soil; destined never to return to their homeland.

George Kenney's thoughts grew darker as he tormented himself with such agonies, but these agonies were as nothing compared to the rage instilled in him by the woman he had just left.

Images of Rita, with her soft golden hair and bright blue eyes, caressed his troubled mind. But then another image loomed up alongside her, and the picture that showed her in Richard's arms evoked unbearable frustration and jealousy in him. The black, heavy mood which had settled on him clung to him and fogged his reasoning like so many times before. For a while he gave himself up to it, disregarding the quiet murmurings of his conscience.

When the storm within him died down, so too had the images of Rita and her husband. He would have to let her go. Against her iron determination, there was nothing he could do. But the child! He had a right to claim the child, hadn't he? Well, no matter! Let it go with her, he thought, and good riddance to them both!

His eyes closed against the piercing daylight, George Kenney hadn't noticed how quickly the time was passing, and when some time later he shook off the melancholy of his thoughts it surprised him to see how the evening had crept up and how full with rain the sky had become. 'Bloody weather!' he moaned out loud, and he would have sprinted from his place on the wall but for the cramp that stiffened his legs. Instead he lowered himself down, painfully stretched his limbs and moved away towards town.

The pub was less than half a mile away, and George Kenney quickly made his way there. It was a place of laughter and noise, a place to lose your troubles and find your friends. The thought of it spurred him on and brought a defiant smile to his face. If Rita Marsden didn't want him, there was plenty of women who did!

It was only now that his mind dwelt on his wife Kathy, and the thought of that gentle loving woman who had never wavered in her love or loyalty brought a measure of deep shame to him. God knows he hadn't been easy to live with lately, what with his every waking thought reserved for another woman, and his inability to control those black unpredictable moods which even he failed to comprehend. It was astonishing that Kathy had put up with him at all. Ah well! Happen he'd find a way to make it all up to her.

When George Kenney swung open the door and entered the bar of the Navigation, all eyes turned in his direction. He was well known; extremely popular, and craved after by every woman who had ever set eyes on him. He was a devilish charmer at forty, as desirable and capable as a man half his age.

The next few hours were filled with booze, song and laughter. Only once was the revelry hushed, at the rumour that there had been a terrible happening on Victoria Street. It was said that a woman had lost her senses, taken to her husband with a kitchen knife and pierced his heart. They had taken her away and as far as folks were concerned, that was the best thing for her! But what of the poor little lad? His father murdered and his mother locked up for it. And the little fellow not but three years old. Aw, still an' all, the revellers decided. No doubt he'd be well looked after by the authorities. Oh yes, it was a bad business sure enough. But not one to keep them from their merriment for long.

The women who frequented this bar were not averse to joining in with what pleased the men, particularly with what pleased George Kenney. There was one woman, however, whose presence rarely graced the inside of a public house, least of all the Navigation which was renowned for its rough clientele. Biddy Kenney was no prude, always content to leave others to live their lives as they saw fit. But when it came to her brother, George, she often found occasion to intervene. It was just such an occasion that had brought her to seek him out this night.

Being a small spinster woman well into her thirties and of deceivingly ordinary appearance dressed neatly in a dark ankle-length dress with a grey knitted shawl about her shoulders, she might have gone unnoticed. But her air of authority and a certain quickness demanded attention. Now, as the whispers passed from one reveller to another, some supping at the bar, some seated and others crowded around the lively piano, the words, 'Why! It's Biddy Kenney!'

caused the laughter to subside and in its place evolved hushed murmurings, 'That rascal, George . . . what's 'e been up to now, eh, with Biddy 'ere to fotch 'im?'

George Kenney was quick to notice the stern condemning expression on his sister's narrow features. And the stiffness of her little body told him that a confrontation was imminent. At once, with a broad disarming smile, he disentangled himself from the arms of an over-amorous woman with carrot-coloured hair and sleepy eyes and negotiated the crowded room skilfully to reach Biddy's side.

Towering over her, yet still seeming the smaller of the two, he carefully took her by the arm and led her out into the night. Behind them came sudden gusts of laughter and cries of 'Music! Is this a bloody wake or what? Where's the music?' And immediately the quiet span that Biddy Kenney's appearance had created was forgotten in the upsurge of merriment and song, to the tune of a melodic accordion.

Outside, in the chill of a March evening, George Kenney's long capable legs barely kept him abreast of his sister as she hurried him away from the Navigation, past her own little terraced house in Duncan Street, and on to her brother's home where Kathy waited, well into the final stages of a premature labour.

'Is it Kathy?' George Kenney asked more than once, the night air mingling with the booze inside him and dulling his faculties. Breathless now from the hurrying, he began to grow angry at Biddy's silent condemnation of him, and he, too, fell into a dark brooding silence.

As they drew level with the front door of his home,

Biddy pinned him with an accusing glance, hissing, 'Shame on you, George Kenney! Unlike Kathy, I'm not blind to your gallivanting. Rita Marsden's left town, they say? Well, I hope to God she never comes back!'

In a quick characteristic movement George Kenney grabbed his sister into an embrace and, quietly laughing, he told her, 'Aye! 'Appen you're right an' all, woman. I expect I could do a great deal worse than my Kathy when all's said an' done, eh?' His words were devised to placate his irate sister, but the truth of them did not altogether escape him. Second best she may be, but Kathy valued and needed him. Well, the Divil go with the one who'd refused him! From now on, he'd treat his Kathy right, that he would! At that moment the door was yanked open from the inside and the large round figure of a woman hurriedly emerged. The resulting flood of light from the hallway caused a passing air-raid warden to issue a warning, 'Shut that bloody door! Unless you want a German bomb on the doorstep!' At which Biddy ushered them inside.

Ethel True was a neighbour from three doors down in whose charge Kathy had been left less than an hour ago. Now her anxious face told its own story and, ignoring George Kenney, she addressed herself to Biddy, her frantic words tumbling one over the other. 'Oh, thank God you're back! They've taken 'er to the Infirmary, and it's a bad 'un, Biddy! A real bad 'un.'

After calming the agitated woman and simultaneously coping with her brother's outburst of self-condemnation, Biddy learned that Kathy had lapsed into spasms of pain that were both erratic and vicious, and that when the doctor responded to Ethel's urgent summons, he declared Kathy to be haemorrhaging. Faced with such a serious complication, he had lost no time in despatching her to the Infirmary.

George Kenney and his sister lost no time either; boarding the late night tram from the nearest boulevard, they were transported to Blackburn Infirmary in a matter of minutes. In less than half an hour from the time that Ethel True had related the news, Biddy and her brother were seated on a wooden bench in the corridor outside Kathy's ward.

When Biddy had collected George Kenney from the Navigation, he had been numbed with booze. Now, he was numb only with shock; as stark sober as any Godfearing judge, and so afraid of his past ways that in his softly spoken prayers he pleaded desperately for Kathy's life and for another chance to be the husband he knew she deserved. Oh, he was in no doubt that he had caused poor Kathy a great deal of unhappiness, and all he craved now was to make it up to her. For, surprising to him as it now seemed, he could only think on how empty his life would be with her gone.

'You can go in now, Mr Kenney.' The nurse looked down on him as he raised his head, his haggard eyes searching her face for some sign of hope. She smiled now, a tight little smile that left her pretty eyes untouched. 'The doctor's inside, waiting for you.'

Biddy made to follow, but quietly resumed her seat when the nurse said kindly, 'Just her husband for now – sorry.' To Biddy Kenney, whose love for her wayward brother was as deep and fierce as her love for his wife, the next hour seemed like a lifetime. Her eyes followed the urgent movements of attending nurses, their faces encased in white masks, as they silently passed in and out of that little room. And as she watched and waited, Biddy Kenney's heart sank within her.

Her innermost fears were confirmed by the awful wail of grief which emanated from the ward, and then gave way to a most formidable silence. And when, on trembling legs, Biddy forced herself to go and push open the door whence the scream had come, the scene which greeted her was one she had hoped never to witness. Kathy's long tresses hung thick and loose down the length of the pillow, their rich dark sheen stark against the whiteness of the sheets around her. George Kenney, on his knees and as though in a trance, was repeatedly stroking her hair with his right hand, while with his left he clutched her long slim fingers to his mouth, his tormented cries protesting over and over, 'No! Please God, no. Not my Kathy . . .'

Biddy's gaze travelled the room, coming now to rest on the nurse standing nearest to her brother, and then on the newborn babe in her arms. Reaching down now, the nurse gently tapped George Kenney's bowed shoulder, and seeking to comfort, she said quietly, 'Mr Kenney, your daughter's beautiful.' She held the child out for him to see.

'No!' His vehement response caused the nurse to retreat and Biddy to step quickly into the room. 'I don't want it! I want Kathy – take it out of my sight, I tell you!' He was on his feet now and flailing his arms with such dangerous intent that the doctor intervened to restrain him. Biddy reached her brother's side at the same time and on seeing her, George Kenney fell to his knees before her, his sobbing pitiful to hear. Biddy caught him to her, cradling his head as one might a child's.

'All right . . .' she murmured, 'all right, love.' The swimming tears blurred her vision as she gazed towards the bed where Kathy lay, and, as though Kathy could hear, she whispered brokenly, 'I'll tek good care of them, lass . . . I promise.' Then she caressed the sobbing man's face in her hands, while drawing his gaze upwards towards her, as in a firmer voice she told him, 'George Kenney, the Lord in his wisdom has taken Kathy. And you must never blame that innocent little babby. Never! D'you hear?'

She watched his eyes dry to stone, felt his shoulders stiffen rigid and, in her heart, Biddy realized the hatred within him. She also knew that it would be up to her alone to give Kathy's daughter a measure of love. And she would, for as long as she lived.

Chapter One

'Get that little bastard out o' my sight!' As George Kenney's hard clenched fist struck the table-top with violent force, Biddy clasped the frail shivering girl to her and in defiant voice she rebuked her brother, 'Let the poor child be, George Kenney! When in God's name will you stop blaming the lass? Lord knows it wasn't 'er fault any more than it were yourn!'

As Biddy's words permeated the drunkenness of his befuddled mind, George Kenney rose from his seat with slow, threatening deliberation. His thick towering frame blocked the sun's rays from the window behind him, throwing the whole room into a darkness as evil as the hatred on his face.

The watery blue eyes glittered with a bright liquid reflection of the constant intake of booze which flowed through his blood, washing away any remnant of decency or self-respect. The thick lank hair tumbled about his heavy features like brown matted straw, and his wide bottom lip momentarily hung open. Now, it quickly tightened as he bellowed with rage, 'Do as I bloody tell you, woman! Get the brat out of 'ere!' At once, the jug he was holding left his hand in a propulsion of fury, to hit the wall just right of the woman and child. Its stinking contents splattered over

Biddy and the child Queenie, soaking them in its sticky boozy odour.

Small of stature but not of heart, Biddy took a bold defiant step forward and drew the child closer to her as she addressed her brother in a strong determined voice. 'There'll come a day, George Kenney, when you'll rue the divilish way you treat this child.' She paused momentarily looking at the creature before her; remembering the man who had returned from battle some seven short years before. Though the physical similarities were still evident, the change in his character was not easy for her to accept. Yet, if she was to admit it to herself, the signs might well have been inherent in her brother's make-up these many years – only in her love for him she had chosen not to see them. Now she waited for a sign of remorse. When none was forthcoming she held his eyes with hard directness, concluding, 'I'm thankful our Mam's not here to see this day. These past seven years since the Lord took Kathy, you've made this child's life a misery! And you with the weight of sin dragging you down!'

She raised a staying hand as George Kenney manoeuvred his great cumbersome body around the table towards her, his face hideously twisted as he hissed, 'Whatever sins I carry, woman! *I'll* be the one to answer for. So shut your mouth and take care . . . or face the consequences!'

The sight of Biddy's raised hand and the deliberate challenge in her slitted blue eyes seemed to hold him just a split second in caution. 'Your wicked tempers and blasphemous ways don't frighten *me*, George Kenney! You've sunk as low as any man could, and as far as I'm concerned, you're beyond the saving.'

With a growl, George Kenney lurched forward with intent to grab the cowering Queenie. '*She*'s the one as took my Kathy,' he cried. Then when Biddy yanked the girl from his reach his roaring fell into a sob of 'Kathy . . . oh, Kathy.'

''Taint "Kathy" as won't let you rest, George Kenney! 'Appen it's your own conscience, eh?'

'Evil bloody witch!' His narrowed eyes threatened tears as they raked Biddy's face, and all of a sudden he sank to the floor in a drunken stupor, deliberately bashing his head against the heavy table leg with repeated force until the skin split and the congealing blood stuck to his unkempt hair.

The scene was familiar to little Queenie. This was the father she had known since as far back as she could remember. There was nothing strange about seeing George Kenney crying like a baby, filled with self-pity, and raining blasphemy and damnation on her head.

Queenie was a frail seven-year-old and unnaturally subdued by her father's bullying. She'd long ago accepted the blame for her Mam's untimely death. Hadn't her father always insisted that it was so? It must be true! Because she had no mam to love her; only her Auntie Biddy. Queenie's tiny hand felt its way into the comforting strength of Biddy's fist, as she squashed closer into the brown calico skirt which always smelled of second-hand snuff and dolly-blue. Auntie Biddy was a hidey-hole; her one and only store of affection. And Queenie loved her passionately.

'Come on, lass!' Auntie Biddy propelled the child before her, 'I can't be doing with his snivelling threats!'

As Queenie's little legs hurried to keep abreast of Auntie Biddy's angry departure, she turned her head to glance back at her father. George Kenney's bloodshot eyes bored into hers with chilling dedication and the naked hatred in them caused the child to shudder deep within herself.

Auntie Biddy lifted the child easily, setting her against the big old pot sink in the back scullery, where she proceeded to wash the stale smell of booze from Queenie's clothes and face. Then, with the same urgency, she cleansed herself.

'Disgusting filthy stuff!' she muttered, pulling a tight sour expression. 'Don't know what's going to become of George Kenney.' She rubbed Queenie's face briskly with the wet flannel, her mutterings falling so low Queenie could hardly make them out. 'And that Marsden woman's interest in charity affairs fetching her in an' out o' Blackburn after all these years. Still an' all, I expect we should be thankful she confines her visits to church-bazaars an' the like.'

Assembling a sparse selection of vegetables ready for their evening meal, Auntie Biddy continued to mumble beneath her breath. 'My God, lass. I don't know! I just don't know!' She turned her full attention to Queenie. 'Look at you child! You weigh nowt but a feather! and the Lord knows I try.' She darted a scathing glance towards the cramped parlour where George Kenney sat slumped in a horse-hair chair muttering about this and that; his wandering mind too steeped in the past and booze to be sensible or coherent. A long deep sigh escaped her. 'Things is getting from bad to worse. And I gets less and less money to manage on. Just look at you! Poor scrawny thing you be.'

'I'm *not* scrawny!' Queenie's protest had immediate effect on Auntie Biddy, whose gaze grew tender.

' 'Course you're not, love,' she murmured, reaching out to tidy the light brown plaits across the child's head. 'I didn't mean to say owt to hurt you,' she assured her, adding: 'All the same, you could do wi fattening up a bit!' She squashed the child to her bosom. 'If only thi' Mam were here, lass. Oh, if only thi' Mam were here.'

Queenie sensed the sorrow in Auntie Biddy's voice as she threw her small arms around the slight pinafored figure to hug her comfortingly.

The little woman surreptitiously wiped the tears from her eyes and laughed. 'You're a grand lass, Queenie, a right grand little lass! Now come on then! I'm mekkin' a nice hot-pot from yesterday's leftovers – and just look here!' She picked up a small dollop of sad-looking meat. 'Yon blue-eyed Jack from the butcher's gave me this. By the 'eck lass, that'll add a bit o' taste.'

At this last remark. Queenie gave herself up to thoughts of Auntie Biddy's hot-pot, the best in Lancashire, according to some. Visions of squashy suet dumplings and all manner of diced vegetables bubbling in rich brown gravy swimming with little pockets of fat came into her mind. In the promise of that full, rich aroma permeating the air and filling her nose till the music in her stomach grew to a growl, Queenie could almost taste it, 'Ooh, Auntie Biddy,' she drooled, 'let *me* help, eh?'

And when the little woman thrust a small carrot and a knife into her hand, saying, 'Go on, then, get that scraped!' Queenie was happy beyond words. This special time when she was allowed to help was the best of all. Auntie Biddy would tell her made-up stories about dwarfs and goblins, and there'd be plenty of laughter at the unbelievable antics of these imaginary creatures. But even though Queenie tried to shut her father's face out of her mind it seeped into her subconscious, dulling the edge of her enjoyment.

Mealtimes themselves were a misery. If Queenie had any appetite before they sat down at the big old table, it quickly disappeared beneath the blatant hostility of George Kenney's glare.

It had never occurred to Queenie to ask questions. Her world was a small one, moulded by the need to survive and painted with resentment and hatred which she couldn't begin to understand. Yet she was not a discontented child, and her natural curiosity brought her a degree of happiness. Like Auntie Biddy, Queenie delighted in the busy life of Blackburn town. She had listened well to the stories which Auntie Biddy loved to relate with such vigour of the different people who lived in Blackburn; of the old ways that were fast disappearing, like the barge people who lived on the canal, and the muffin-men who plied their vanishing trade.

And oh, what a treat it was when she and Auntie Biddy took the walk into town on a market day! Happen they'd be carrying a pair of Auntie Biddy's boots which needed the holes mending. Old Dubber Butterfield would sit on his threelegged stool amidst the hundreds of boots, shoes and clogs which hung from walls and ceilings, then with the great iron hobbling-foot between his knees and with a practised flick of his wrist he'd fit the boots onto it, shape a fresh-smelling piece of leather over the holes and, taking the little nails one at a time from between his teeth, he'd tap-tap and shape until the worn holey leather on

Auntie Biddy's boots became a brand new sole.

Just occasionally, the two of them would go into Nan Draper's where every wall was piled high with shelves upon shelves of different sorts of cloth. Brown tweed; herringbone; flannel; winceyette, worsted . . . oh, there was no end to it. And here, Auntie Biddy would purchase her darning wool and thimbles, together with various sized needles. Queenie could remember the purchase of a measure of heavy brown cotton-material only once. Auntie Biddy explained that this rare luxury was necessary in the name of decency, as she was obliged to keep the two of them from 'falling into rags'. As far as Queenie was concerned, she was right glad Auntie Biddy had prevented such a thing. The idea of 'falling into rags' sounded a frightening prospect.

A dilly-dallying walk round the market, though, was something of a magic time for Queenie. Now and then they would stop at the liquorice stall and buy a threepenny bag of liquorice sticks and coltsfoot rock; then perhaps another time they might linger at Jud's corner stall, where amidst the colour and the shouting, the smells of roasting chestnuts and baking tatties, they would enjoy a glass of Jud's black frothy sarsaparilla. It all fascinated Queenie. And she had come to love Blackburn as fervently as did her Auntie Biddy.

Biddy's beloved Blackburn could never be described as a picturesque, green and fertile land. Too many deep scars of underground pits and towering gloomy Victorian cotton mills shadowed its natural beauty. No different from any other Lancashire town, its character was firmly stamped in the narrow alleyways and tightly packed terraced houses, familiar corner grocers and grubby pawn shops, which burst at the seams with paraphernalia of all kinds.

The sounds of Blackburn filled the air from early dawn to gas-lamp lighting. The sharp 5 a.m. rat-a-tat of the knocker-up's stick against the windows tumbled the bleary-eyed workers from their beds, and the persistent beckoning screech of the factory-hooters brought them out of their narrow doorways in droves of blue overalls, flat caps and khaki demob-coats, with billy-cans a rattling and snap-tins shaping their deep pockets into grotesgue proportions.

Every day started the same noisy, predictable way. And every evening, after a long back-breaking day, these same workers would laugh and sing in the pubs which held pride of place in every lamp-lined cobbled street.

It was an undisputed fact – which any real red-blooded Lancastrian would relate with chest-bursting pride – that there were more pubs, under the colourful names of Bells, Brown Cows, Navigations, and Jug and Bottles, than there were shops.

Next in order of importance came the betting-shops, picture-houses and slipper-baths; although it should be stated from the outset that rather than waste sixpence on a tub of hot water at the slipper-baths, the man of the house would much rather spend it 'wisely' on a swig of healthy ale. After all, there was always the good old tin bath hanging on its nail in the backyard.

The women of Lancashire were a race unto themselves. They experienced few luxuries, accepting hard work and domineering husbands as part of their unenviable lot. It was the men who claimed the upper hand and, when they converged in the Brown Cow or the Navigation, their women would abide unquestioningly by the unwritten rule: No respectable lass would ever be seen in a pub; unless rightly invited. And even then, they would know their place. So the women often preferred to stay at home and darn their mens' socks, bathe their countless offspring and count the dwindling brass which they skilfully hid from the 'old man' with his appetite for boozing.

This was the old Lancashire, steeped in a tradition of cotton and ale; a Lancashire unwelcoming and unresponsive to the gentle nudging wind of change which ominously murmured from the new generation of town-hall whizz-kids. The change *would* come, of that there could be no doubt. The old narrow houses with their steep unhygienic backyards, pot-sinks and outside lavvies, they wouldn't escape the cold relentless march of progress. But for now, Auntie Biddy's Blackburn remained relatively intact and contented and fiercely defended by every man, woman and child, who had never experienced any other way. They delighted in the open-topped rattling trams; the muffin-man's familiar shout as he pushed his deep wicker basket along the uneven cobbles, and the screech of the cotton-mill siren, starting another day. As long as one and all were left alone to make their own way, they bothered nobody and asked no favours. The children spilled out to all the streets, played with their skipping-ropes, hula-hoops and spinning-tops, their laughter no less spontaneous because of inherent poverty.

Auntie Biddy lay at the centre of everything little Queenie experienced and without question Queenie accepted the sparse existence they led. With each passing week George Kenney retreated more and more into his own twilight world of drink and memories and as he grew more pathetic and sullen, so Queenie grew strong and lovely beneath the protective wing of dear Auntie Biddy.

Auntie Biddy spent her days coping with the blubbering self-pity of her demented brother, whose financial contribution to the little household diminished rapidly in favour of his constant boozing; so much so that Auntie Biddy had resorted to taking in washing and ironing, in order to stave off the poverty and hunger that dogged them. Never once did her fierce loyalty to Queenie falter. Never again in Queenie's hearing did she refer to George Kenney's 'sinful ways'. Or his bastard child Richard born to Rita Marsden and by all accounts living in comfort in nearby Wigan. Biddy prayed the lad would lead a good useful life and never know the man who had spawned him. She was thankful that George Kenney had shown no inclination to seek out Rita Marsden. Often, Biddy spared a thought for Rita's husband and she wondered whether he knew he was not the boy's father. For if he did know then the burden of bringing up a boy conceived by his wife from another man was indeed a cross to bear.

Today, Friday, 12 September 1953, had spent itself like any other day. Queenie had attended St Mary's School, delivered to the door under the eye of Auntie Biddy, who had taken to seeing Queenie inside the gate because when faced with an alternative day of wandering Blackburn's canals and ginnels or helping Auntie Biddy with the laundry and mangling, Queenie never failed to opt for the latter. But there were laws, as Auntie Biddy quickly reminded her. Laws, such as 'The Eddycation Act' and creatures to uphold them, like 'yon sharp-eyed Truant Officer'.

Today, under distinct duress and displaying a heavy frown, Queenie had to suffer Miss Jackson, or Snake-Tongue as she was better known. Her tight weasel-face and sneck mouth drove the children into themselves, producing mountainous resentment and squashing any desire to learn. Miss Snake-Tongue Jackson hadn't a friend in the world. She was a pain, a moan, a blind mouth that spouted nothing but horrors. Queenie hated her, and when hometime bell clattered she was off to the safe and comfortable company of Auntie Biddy. Today, after having a warm all-over wash in the tin bath before the fire, and gulping down a bowl filled with dumpling stew, Queenie had helped to fold the day's considerable pile of washing. Auntie Biddy had watched her yawning. 'Sleepy are you, lass?' she'd asked gently. Queenie told her with fervent conviction that it was only that rotten school and Snake-Tongue as made her tired. Even so, she didn't put up too much of an argument when Auntie Biddy quietly but firmly ushered her up to bed.

It was well into the night when something jolted Queenie from her sleep. For a while she just lay there, a small still figure, lost in the span of Auntie Biddy's huge bed, which rendered her an insignificant speck in the deep folds of the chequered eiderdown. From above the line between the eiderdown and the head-bolster, two grey wide-awake eyes travelled the confines of the tiny room, taking in every detail and searching for the cause of her abrupt awakening.

The room echoed Auntie Biddy's strong Lancastrian character. There was a degree of warmth and splendid reliability in the stalwart green distemper, which reflected the half-light from the gas-lamp beneath the window. The big square wardrobe stood to attention in its disciplined uprightness, as it towered protectively over a short wooden-knobbed chest of drawers.

A small ripple of pleasure bathed the knot of fear in Queenie's stomach as her gaze rested on the kidney-shaped dresser. The shadowy dancing fingers of light crept in through the window where the dark brocade curtains hung open. There in the half-light were all the familiar things of Auntie Biddy's. A deep glass bowl filled with all manner of paraphernalia, hair-slides and bars, clips and fine mesh hairnets, all tangled together. Atop a pretty central lace doily stood a tall brass crucifix, which had belonged to Auntie Biddy's mother, Queenie's long-dead grandmother.

Standing in a silver frame, the cameo photograph of Auntie Biddy as a much younger woman smiled reassuringly. Queenie hoisted herself up to the height of the bolster in order to focus her direct gaze on the picture; in doing so, she wondered if the noise that had awakened her was Auntie Biddy. Had she gone downstairs to the outside lavvy? As she moved herself to settle down in the bed more comfortably Queenie's eyes alighted on the second, accompanying photograph. It was a wedding picture of George Kenney and his lost wife, Kathy.

Queenie had often sat on the wooden stand-chair in front of the picture, trying hard to come to terms with the confused whisperings inside her. Her fingers would travel an involuntary path along the contours of her dead mother's face; a hauntingly beautiful face, which brought about a great feeling of sadness in Queenie. But there was pleasure, too, in sitting by the dresser and comparing her mother's face with her own. The large dove-grey eyes were the same, as was the sensual mouth and attractive lean contours of feature, but while her mother's hair had been black as night Queenie's was of her father's colouring, light-brown with hints of fiery gold.

Lying in the half-dark, Queenie found it hard to settle. She sensed something was wrong. But what? After a while she dismissed the notion, and turned over to warm Auntie Biddy's side of the bed. But the uneasiness within her persisted. And slipping out from underneath the persuasive warmth of the eiderdown, she crossed to the window. For a change Parkinson Street was all quiet, save for the pitiful mewing of a frustrated tomcat, and the occasional dustbin-lid clattering to the flagstones beneath some scampering cat's feet.

Queenie looked along the higgledy-piggledy Victorian sky-line. The irregular pattern of chimneys reaching up like the fingers of a deformed hand traced a weird but comfortingly familiar silhouette against the moonlit sky. Lifting the window up against the sash, Queenie leaned out so she had an unobstructed view of the street below. Parkinson Street was home: No. 2, Parkinson Street, and Auntie Biddy, they were *hers*, her comforting world into which she could retreat when things became complicated and painful.

The street was long, but straight like the lines of a railway track, lit by the tall blue-framed gas-lamps, which winked and sparkled at regular intervals on either side. From No. 2, which was right at the neck of the street, a body could look along the continuous row of tightly packed houses and experience the same sensation as if standing at the mouth of a long meandering tunnel.

There were one hundred and four houses in Parkinson Steet – Queenie had counted them all with loving precision. And there were one thousand and forty flagstones; Queenie had hopscotched every single one. She hadn't finished counting the road-cobbles yet, but up to Widow Hargreaves at No. 16, there were nine hundred and ten; that was counting across the road to the opposite houses. When she'd finished them, she would start on the stained glasses in the fanlight above the doors. Queenie meant to learn all there was to know about Parkinson Street, because the more she knew, the more it was hers.

Stretching her neck, now, Queenie attempted to identify the dark figure approaching against the flickering gas-lamps. The tottering speck grew and grew, until it shaped itself into the towering frame of George Kenney. On recognizing it, Queenie involuntarily backed away from the window. As she quietly slithered the windowframe back into place she could hear his voice low and mumbling, rising occasionally in abuse of his 'bad fortune'. Peeking from behind the curtain, Queenie followed his ungainly progress until he entered the little house where Auntie Biddy was waiting to greet him with a few chosen words.

'Shut thi' bloody moithering, woman! Get off to bed!' he retaliated.

Biddy brushed his ill-mannered response aside, 'I'll

get off to bed when I've had my say, George Kenney! And not afore!'

Queenie knew they were standing in the passage at the foot of the stairs where Auntie Biddy had waylaid him, and from the ensuing scuffling and protesting she reckoned they were negotiating their way into the back parlour.

The door closed to the tune of Auntie Biddy telling George Kenney to 'Keep your noise down . . . Yon lass is asleep.'

Creeping across the narrow landing, Queenie quietly made her way downstairs until she stopped to seat herself on the narrow stairtread near the bottom. Here she could easily distinguish the voices of George Kenney and Auntie Biddy, raised in anger the like of which she had not heard before. Hardly daring to breathe, Queenie found no shame in listening.

'You've got to come to your senses, George Kenney.' Auntie Biddy's voice sounded strange to Queenie. The hard commanding authority which always characterized the chastising of her brother's cowardly behaviour had been replaced by a soft, almost pleading tone. 'Things are bad. I mean *really* bad. The few shillings I make at washing and ironing won't keep body and soul together. I'm telling you George, if you don't stop your drinking and wasting, we'll *all* end up on charity.'

Queenie could hear no response and assumed that George Kenney must be in a drunken stupor. It hurt her to hear Auntie Biddy saying these things. 'On charity' were words she'd only associated with poor folk, *really* poor folk who'd lost their man in the war. Could it be true that *they* were that poor now? A knot of anger fisted itself inside her chest. George Kenney, her father! *He'd* done this to her Auntie Biddy! It was him who'd made her take other folk's clothes in to wash and press, until her hands had grown swollen and red from the hard scrubbing and foul-smelling carbolic.

'George! Get up. You've got to listen to me for God's sake!' Tears filled Queenie's eyes at the anguish in Auntie Biddy's voice. 'George Kenney! I'll damn you in Hell if owt happens to that poor lass. Get up, I say!'

The scraping muffled sound which followed suggested that George Kenney was struggling to his feet. His voice, dulled by drink, grated loud and angry. 'I've told you afore, woman! I don't give a damn what happens to that little swine!' His voice was so filled with hatred it was almost incoherent, but to the listening child it was cruelly slicing.

'She's your daughter, George. You can at least do right by *this* child.'

George Kenney's protesting roar brought Queenie to her feet. 'Never! She's *not* mine! I don't want 'er. Do you understand that?' The shouting was intermingled with hurried clumsy movement and chairs being tumbled about. Then came the shout: 'Get out of my way!'

In her short life Queenie had known what it was to be frightened, but the sounds of violence which now filled the air struck terror into her. As the high-pitched scream emanated from the parlour she ran down the stairs to the parlour door and flung it open.

'Good Lord, child!' Auntie Biddy quickly brought her hand to her face, but not quickly enough. Queenie had seen the bright red weal which George Kenney's fist had drawn. And her heart grew cold at the sight of his body hovering menacingly over her Auntie Biddy, who in an instant was concerned only that Queenie should witness such a thing. She lost no time in ushering Queenie out of the room and back up the stairs to her bed.

Sleep came hard to Queenie that night. Long after Auntie Biddy had deserted George Kenney to his drunken ramblings, Queenie lay wide awake, nestled in the loving arms of her protector. Her course of action was clear. She would have to grow up quickly in order to take care of her Auntie Biddy and protect her from that man downstairs.

Chapter Two

'Rag-a-bone! . . . Rag-a-bone!'

The hoarse uplifted voice travelled the length of
Parkinson Street. Saturday was the day when colourful Maisie Thorogood stayed in her own back yard, so
to speak. She was a loud familiar figure, trudging the
lowly houses hereabouts, confident that in every
stairhole lay at least one article which she could
transform into hard cash. On this fine September
morning, she had high hopes of making enough brass
to buy her that new hat.

Maisie was a rattling, excitable character known
from one end of Blackburn to the other. Talk was that
she'd been 'a bad 'un' in her day, not particular about
the direction and volume of her strong language or her
constant stream of bedmates.

Whenever Queenie thought about Parkinson
Street, she invariably thought about Maisie. Nobody
could remember as far back as the day Maisie had
come to abide there. She'd *always* been part of it, like
the gas-lamps and the shiny worn cobblestones. It was
rumoured that, during the war, Maisie handed out her
favours to the grateful Yanks as freely and lovingly as
she swapped the children's rags for yo-yos and
coloured balloons from her familiar painted waggon.

She favoured everybody, and denied no one.

When the war finished, and the last of the Yanks went home, Maisie was left alone with the results of her generosity. Raymond and Sheila were twins, as different in looks and character as night from day. Fine healthy eight-year-olds now, they had long since learned to fend for themselves, as Maisie Thorogood set no great store by the tiresome duties of being a mother. She provided for her offspring, gave them a roof over their heads, and saw to it that their bellies were full. This, she was quick to relate at the onset of any awkward questions from concerned friends and neighbours, was enough.

'My kids are Thorogoods!' she'd state, with a proud shake of her peroxide head, then with a raucous guffaw which made folks wish they'd never asked, she would wink her eye and tell them, 'There might be a splash o' this, an' a dash o' that in 'em, but the richest blood as runs through their veins is mine! Make no bones on it! Them's first and foremost Maisie Thorogood's kids, an' they can tek care o' theirselves.'

After a while, folks just stopped bothering. Maisie was Maisie, and there wasn't a thing in the world to change her. The kids came to no harm; and who could help but love the brash woman who found herself their Mam? For all her loud vulgarity she was honest and genuine, with a heart of pure gold.

Queenie scrambled down from the table. 'Oh Auntie Biddy! It's Maisie! Can I give 'er some rags, eh?'

Auntie Biddy straightened up from the depths of the washing-tub, holding the small of her aching back as if to keep it together. Her cheeks were raspberry red from the rising steam and the physical exertion of scraping and rubbing the washing against the ribbed surface of the rubbing-board. The flailing wisps of grey hair had stuck to the sweat of her forehead, 'Nay lass, we've nowt we can give away.' She sighed wearily, running her finger and thumb along the length of her arm, to gather the frothy suds and plop them back into the dolly-tub. 'Nowt,' she repeated thoughtfully.

Queenie remembered an old pair of George Kenney's boots, which she'd seen not so long back in the stairhole cupboard. 'What about them old boots? *His* old boots in the stairhole?'

Auntie Biddy glanced down into the girl's wide-awake face and bright sparkling grey eyes. 'Aw . . . lass,' she sighed. Queenie waited patiently for what seemed an endless consideration. Finally came the words she wanted to hear. 'All right then lass, go an' get 'em. They're not much cop and I'd get nowt for 'em at Shiny's pawn shop, so you might as well . . .'

Before she'd finished talking, Queenie was already rummaging in the dark stairhole. In no time at all she'd unearthed an old Oxo tin stuffed full with old ration-books; two gas-masks with great bulging eyes and a long trembling red tongue; and from right up the back of the stairhole where it was blackest, a pair of George Kenney's old boots, hard and misshapen with age. Of a sudden Queenie poked her face from the stairhole and in a voice breathless from her scrabblings she shouted, 'Auntie Biddy, look what I've found. Can I take them to Maisie, eh?'

In the short time it took for Auntie Biddy to scan

first of all Queenie's pink excited face, then the Oxo tin and the gas-masks, made in Blackburn during the war, and shipped all over the country, and last of all the boots, she had decided. 'You can tek the boots, lass, but leave the other stuff. There's no tellin' when they'll fotch another war down on us . . . best keep . . .' There was no sense in her going on, because already Queenie was away out of the room and down the passage with the boots under her arm.

Maisie was lost to sight amid the small army of excited children who queued with their armfuls of odd artefacts: holey kettles, old lead-pipe, and anything else that might entreat Maisie to part with a yo-yo or a bright floating balloon. Maisie's waggon had always been a familiar sight standing unattended outside No. 41, stripped of all its treasures and tipped up onto the handles of its shaft. Folks had grown used to it, and it generated no particular interest or excitement in its dormant state. Now, dressed in bright bobbing regalia, it was suddenly real, alive.

Clutching George Kenney's old boots, Queenie hopped and skipped the few flagstones which separated her from the 'rag-a-bone' waggon. Its presence within the excited screeching throng of children was pinpointed by the numerous clusters of waving balloons. Every colour of the rainbow they were, dancing and jiggling towards the sky in erratic fits and starts, as the ticklish breeze played and teased the restraining strings.

There were sausage-shaped ones, round ones, egg-shaped and twisty ones; all wriggling and singing as they rubbed together gleefully. Queenie had often imagined Maisie sitting in her parlour blowing up the balloons. The magnitude of such an operation had prompted her on more than one occasion to ask Maisie where she kept all that wind, and if it took her all week to get the balloons ready. Maisie would roll about and scream with laughter. 'Bless your 'eart, Queenie darlin',' she'd shout, 'didn't you know I keeps a goblin in me shoe. It's *'im* as blows 'em up!' So frustrated and perplexed had Queenie grown at this regular answer that eventually she told Sheila, 'I think your Mam's as daft as a barm-cake!' Sheila had agreed most fervently.

The laughter and squeaky chatter of the delighed children filled the air, bringing the women to their doors to smile appreciatively at Maisie, with her rag-a-bone waggon and her little following army. Queenie muscled her way in, pushing and shoving with such deliberation that the deep barrier of small bodies reluctantly gave way to let her through. Not graciously though, judging by the angry snorts, sly sharp kicks, and loud abuse.

'Give over snotrag! Wait yer turn!'

'Hey! Who do you think *you* are?'

'Cor! Them bloody boots don't 'arf stink!'

Stink they may have done but Queenie didn't care! Not if that was why they'd all moved aside to let her in, she thought.

Her strong grey eyes widened in amazement as they lit on the appearance of Maisie's waggon!

The spill of bright colour and treasure fair blinded her. The low sides of the waggon were painted in Catherine wheels of gaudy reds, yellows and blacks; the big wooden-spoked wheels made a body dizzy as the zig-zag lines which wound about them screamed first in gold, then green and ended up in a delightful mingling of black and yellow blobs. The whole wonderful marvellous ensemble was entrancing. The inside of the waggon was filled to bursting and, at the shaft end, where the scabby little donkey tucked noisily into his oversized hay-bag, the piles of old rags and varying artefacts were stacked sky-high.

The remainder of the waggon was loaded down with penny-whistles; bundles of clothes-pegs; goldfish swimming about in little fat plastic bags; big blocks of white stepstone, and small tidy bundles of wood-stick for the fire. Around the rim of the waggon hung more cherry-red yo-yos than Queenie had ever seen in her life. Handmade they were, as Maisie was quick to point out; and polished as shiny as a still pond. They clattered against the clusters of metal-tipped spinning-tops, which also hung in groups of twenty or more from the crowded rim. Then all along the shaft arms dangled hundreds of coloured soft balls, gleaming and winking as the daylight caught the glinting lashing colours within. Finally, every spare inch of space was taken up by the myriads of brightly coloured balloons; so many that Queenie wondered why the donkey, waggon and all, hadn't been clear lifted off the ground to be swept away forever.

'Right then little Queenie! You've shoved your way afront o' these other brats, so what's it to be, eh?' demanded Maisie.

Queenie felt the boots being snatched from her grasp as Maisie examined them closely. That much at least she was quick to regret, as she recoiled hastily from the rising stench.

'By God! Them's sodding strong, Queenie!' With typical humour, she suddenly threw her head back to scream and chortle, causing one and all to step back a pace. 'Teks me back does that, Queenie,' she cackled in great enjoyment, 'I ain't smelled nowt like that since them bloody Yanks buggered off!' Such was her screeching and roaring as she hugged the size twelve boots to her ample bosom that everybody down Parkinson Street was infected with helpless laughter. The fact that they didn't know what they were laughing at didn't seem to matter. When Maisie started to screech and wail like she did, there was no telling when she was likely to stop. She laughed and roared until the tears ran down her face, then rubbing her hand across the rosy shine of her flabby cheeks she dabbed spasmodically at the blubber round her sparkling eyes.

'It's a bloody good job I ain't got no money to go to 'Merica,' she shouted gleefully, 'gi' them sodding Yanks a fright I would. Left many a warm package back 'ere in a lass's arms, eh? Randy sods!'

'Come off it, Maisie!' The shrill good-humoured voice shouting from a nearby house sailed above the noise, 'You loved every minute of it!'

'Too bloody true, I did!' Maisie peered through the sea of children to identify the voice. 'Med sure I got me fair shares, didn't I?' she laughed. 'Same as you, Florrie Dibble!'

With practised precision she launched the boots into the air and watched for them to settle on the pile of rags. Leaning forward towards Queenie, she lowered her voice to a whisper. Still spluttering and trying not to set off laughing again, she told the giggling Queenie, 'I reckons I'll keep them there boots under me bed . . .

just to remind me o' the good ol' days!' Queenie hadn't
a clue what she was talking about, but Maisie always
made her laugh and feel happy inside.

'They're George Kenney's old work-boots,' she told
her, 'Auntie Biddy said I could 'ave 'em. They've been
in the stairhole for years and years.'

Maisie ran her big capable hands through the bright
brassy mop of hair which stood out like petrified straw
across her head. 'Good for Auntie Biddy,' she said,
screeching again, 'I expect she were glad to get rid on
'em, eh? An' I'll bet she's 'ad no trouble wi' mice in 'er
stairhole? Not wi' them bloody boots in there!'

Composing herself as best she could she banged her
fist against the old tin bucket which hung in front of
her. There wasn't much cash in the bucket. Today's
trade had been mostly 'swappings'.

'What do you want from the waggon, Queenie?'

Queenie didn't need to think on it. She knew *exactly*
what she wanted, 'A yo-yo,' she told Maisie, 'a red
yoyo.'

Maisie reached up to unhook the yo-yo, which she
handed to Queenie. 'There you are then, one red yo-
yo.' She waved a chubby arm to beckon the next
customer. 'Come on then! Let's be 'aving you!'

Clutching her precious prize, Queenie squeezed her
way out of the pressing hordes of children who all
wanted to touch the yo-yo as she passed.

'Can I come with you, Queenie?'

Queenie turned towards the dark-haired girl who
had followed her. It was Sheila Thorogood, Maisie's
daughter. She was a pretty, brown-eyed creature, very
sure of herself and extremely fond of Queenie.

'Yes, come on.' Queenie wasn't one for making friends, because it had never come easy to her; but Sheila was different. You couldn't say no to Sheila. She was too much like her Mam.

The two girls made their way back to No. 2, where they promptly sat down on the kerbstones and took turns to play with the yo-yo. Sheila had inherited Maisie's loud guffaw, and every time the yo-yo spun neatly up the full length of string she screamed and hollered enough to wake the dead.

'Somebody's enjoying theirselves!' Auntie Biddy appeared at the door.

Queenie ran to her side, eager to show her what she had been clever enough to acquire in place of George Kenney's work-boots.

'That's grand, love.' Auntie Biddy rubbed her hands on her pinnie and smiled over at Sheila. 'Did *you* not get one, then?'

'No, I can play with 'em when I likes . . . so I'm not that bothered.'

Auntie Biddy smiled warmly, obviously amused at the youngster's dismissing remark. 'Oh,' she said simply.

'Is all the washing done, Auntie Biddy?' Queenie was quick and concerned to notice the pale tired face beneath two bright red patches marking Auntie Biddy's cheeks. She noticed, too, how the slight figure had leaned heavily on the door jamb. 'Are you tired?' she asked, her expression one of concern.

'Aye, I'm tired lass, if the truth be told. But there's still work to be done. Do you want to come with me, to take yesterday's pressing round?'

Queenie rammed the yo-yo up her sleeve, ''Ave I to get the pram ready?' She turned to Sheila, who was heeding this conversation with great care. 'Do you want to come with us?'

'Where?'

'To take all the clean washing back round to the folks.'

Sheila didn't have the same enthusiasm for work that Queenie had. Standing up, she shook her head, and made to follow Maisie who was just disappearing out of sight. 'No. I'll go an' ride on me Mam's waggon,' she shouted behind her.

Auntie Biddy chuckled. 'Maisie won't get much change out o' *that* one, I'm thinking!'

Inside the little scullery there was barely room to move. The stone floor against the back wall was lined with brown paper, on top of which was piled neatly pressed garments of all manner and design. The first pile was big Jack Rawtenstall's, a nice man who'd been widowed some ten years back. Queenie could always identify his particular bundle because of the bright red long-johns, which Auntie Biddy always set right at the top. 'Won't mistake *his*, will we lass?' she'd say stoutly, with a little blush; wryly reminding Queenie at the same time that it wasn't considered ladylike to snigger at a gentleman's long-johns. There was no doubt but that Big Jack was indeed a gentleman. He was the butcher round these quarters, and his fancy for Auntie Biddy had long been common gossip. It was all greatly entertaining to Queenie, who wasn't really sure what to make of it all.

Next came Nosey-Parker Hindle's pile. There was nothing fancy or colourful about this awful little busybody. More often than not, she'd set to and rinse out her own undergarments. 'Nothing personal,' she had assured Auntie Biddy, 'it's just that I don't fancy my corsets fluttering on someone else's line, you understand?' Auntie Biddy had politely satisfied her that it made not the slightest bit of difference. She'd just be glad to do what pleased her most.

Queenie didn't hold much truck with this dreadful woman, who sent all her heaviest washing and moaned endlessly if it was so much as a minute late. And as for them heavy clanging corsets 'fluttering' on the line . . . 'twas more likely *them* as had broken Auntie Biddy's line on the two occasions she'd been honoured with the washing of them! Her pile was by far the biggest; thick blankets and bolster cases; and a crocheted shawl which lined her spoilt pooch's wicker basket. Queenie reasoned that at least Nosey-Parker Hindle might have spared Auntie Biddy the washing of *that*! That woman was just like her snappy pooch, spiteful and petted. But Auntie Biddy had no choice in the matter. Nosey-Parker Hindle paid her good money, money that Auntie Biddy could not do without even if it did mean her having to submit to that dreadful woman lording it over her!

And what of the clothes themselves? They were so worn and stretched that Queenie fancied it would be an improvement for the tyrant to clothe herself in some of the barrow-boy's hessian tater sacks. Even *they* weren't so shabby. Not that Nosey-Parker Hindle wasn't always dressed for showing off when Auntie Biddy was due. Queenie knew Auntie Biddy couldn't be doing with the woman's endless questions. It was always the same. Every time the washing went back, she peered into the pram to see whose washing was worth a mention, then: 'Been to Widow Hargreaves 'ave you? They tell me she's bought herself a fancy radiogram. Still got that glass cupboard full o' silver, has she?' On and on it went, and Auntie Biddy was obliged to stand there pretending to take an interest; because she never got paid till Nosey-Parker Hindle had questioned her fill, about everybody and everything. It didn't matter that she never got any answers, for if Auntie Biddy *had* satisfied her curiosity, whatever would there be left for her to think on? She wasn't short of a bob or two neither. She rarely bought anything new, because, 'I don't believe in squandering money! Always let it bide and grow, my dear ol' dad used to say . . . let it bide an' grow.' It was rumoured that she was rotten rich. But even she had made mistakes with her precious money, which gave Queenie a deal of pleasure. According to Auntie Biddy, Nosey-Parker Hindle had been the very first person in Blackburn to purchase a television. That had been some five years back, in 1952, the year King George VI had passed on.

Nosey-Parker Hindle had invited all the neighbours to come along and see this new acquisition. 'There'll be lardie-cakes and plenty o' tea.' She persuaded them, never being one to pass up an opportunity to show off. As it was, the parlour had filled to bursting, more from the promise of a lardie-cake and a few hidden in the shawl for tekkin' 'ome, than to 'ear Nosey-Parker Hindle's tiresome boasting, so Auntie Biddy had related. Anyway, the upshot of it all was that the entire gathering had duly settled down to see this wonderful picture-box when, without any warning whatsoever, there had been an almighty bang and spurts of smoke, followed by the picture turning in a fit of somersaults, before disappearing altogether . . . along with the startled company and every last one of the lardie-cakes!

The very next day, Nosey-Parker Hindle had marched down to the shop with the offending article wrapped in a coat; and even in the face of the manager's protest that television had been successful throughout the country since the resumption of broadcasting in 1947 she managed to secure a return of her money.

Under Queenie's insistence, Auntie Biddy had related this same story to her many many times. And the telling of it never made it any the less amusing. But when the laughter died down, Auntie Biddy would shake her head as always and say in a tired little voice, 'Aye, lass, it were a sad year for us all when we lost our King . . . 1952, not a time to forget, lass.'

Queenie knew of King George VI, because one evening a time back, when Auntie Biddy and she had been cutting up newspaper squares and threading them onto a length of darning wool to hang in the outside lavvy, there had been a particular article which Auntie Biddy had seized upon, and which was now lovingly pasted into a scrap-book.

It was an excerpt printed by the *Blackburn Telegraph* and taken from an American paper, *The Washington Post*, and it read:

'If courage was the test of greatness, Britons of the reign of King George VI had it in supreme measure, for they endured terrors and beat back

45

dangers as none of their ancestors had faced in modern times.

If character is the test, the late King and all his people showed it through the hardships of the War and post-war years.

And if statesmanship is the test, then the Britain of King George VI had it too . . . we submit that more greatness was packed into the fifteen years of George VI, than into all the sixty-three years of Queen Victoria!'

Queenie didn't fully understand its sentiments but when it had reduced her Auntie Biddy to tears of pride she sensed it was something of particular value.

The last pile of clean washing in Auntie Biddy's scullery was full of frilly, dithery things. Little lace doileys and precious crocheted bedspreads, backrest covers, bright yellow knitted bedsocks and dainty bedjackets.

There was no mistaking *this* washing. Queenie knew it just had to belong to the two old spinsters, Miss Tilly and Fancy Carruthers. She always made a little bet with herself before ever going to their house, that both of them would be perched upright in the great big brassknobbed bed which filled the tiny parlour, wearing their frilly green caps, a' smiling and a' nodding. And sure enough, they always were!

Queenie collected the old pram from the stairhole, after which she wheeled it into the scullery, where Auntie Biddy had filled the big tin bowl with the freshly washed clothes. 'I'll put these out, lass. You load the pressing into the pram. Do it careful mind! I don't want 'em creased.'

Queenie wished with all her heart that they were rich. She didn't know of anybody else in Parkinson Street who had to wash and press other folks' clothes, an' it didn't seem fair that Auntie Biddy should 'ave to do it. 'Don't supppose she *would*, if it weren't for that rotten ol' George Kenney!' she grumbled fiercely, throwing the clothes in as carefully as her anger would allow.

Closing the door quietly, for fear of waking George Kenney, Auntie Biddy set off down Parkinson Street, the pram loaded high, and Queenie hanging onto the side; her little legs hurrying in an effort to keep pace with Auntie Biddy's determined strides.

'Where are we going first?'

'Well, it makes sense to unload the *nearest* first, so being as Big Jack Rawtenstall's is lying atop, we'll mek for there.'

Big Jack's butcher's shop stood between the Navigation and Widow Hargreaves', at the very end of Parkinson Street.

'As the two are right aside of each other, we'll do them both quick,' declared Auntie Biddy, beginning to puff and wheeze just a bit.

As they drew up outside the shop-window, Big Jack caught sight of them. No matter that he was halfway through serving a customer, he wiped his bloody hands on his white apron and hurried out towards them. He was a giant of a man, a bumbling mountain of gentleness. The black hair and bushy 'tache which spread between his prominent ears set a sharp contrast against the vivid blue eyes, which lit up luminous at the sight of Auntie Biddy.

''Ere! I'll lift that.' With no further ado, he hoisted

his pile of clothes out of the pram and ambled clumsily inside.

Auntie Biddy followed while Queenie stood with the pram, her observant grey eyes piercing the shop-window and admiring the considerable width of Big Jack's toothy smile as he placed five shillings and a succulent pig's trotter into Auntie Biddy's out-stretched hand. When she came back out, her dear face looked just a shade pinker and her need to depart seemed to Queenie perhaps a measure too hasty.

Nosey-Parker Hindle was an ordeal Queenie detested. And as they drew closer to the woman's house, Queenie felt her heart sinking into her knees.

'Oh, it's *you*!' came the anticipated retort as the door was flung open in answer to Auntie Biddy's knock. 'Been watching for you! And I must say it isn't like you to be late!' She wasn't at all pleased, at once tripping smartly out of the front door and down the step. In her frantic haste to dive into the pram and survey other folks' washing, she almost crashed headlong into Queenie. 'Oh!' she cried, her quick scathing glance at Queenie reflecting the well-known opinion hereabouts that Nosey-Parker Hindle did not approve of children in any size, shape or form. She had made a deliberate choice many years before, never to sanction her marriage with 'bothersome kids'. It had struck Queenie of late that maybe the reason for her husband's unexplained disappearance was that he wanted 'bothersome kids', which was also the opinion of her Auntie Biddy.

Sweeping her piggy eyes over Queenie's delicate figure, she met the forthright stare with disapproval. 'Brought *you* today, has she? Hmph! Can't see as how a mite two-penn'orth like you could be of any use nor ornament! More trouble than you're worth, I shouldn't wonder!'

Queenie could gladly have stomped on the great fat feet. Instead, when faced with that woman's shrivelling stare, she instinctively moved behind Auntie Biddy whose flared nostrils and angry face betrayed a side not often seen.

'I'll thank you kindly to guard that tongue o' yourn!' Auntie Biddy reached a comforting hand behind her, to grasp Queenie's shoulder and draw her out. 'If you insult Queenie. . . well then, you insult *me*!' She stood her ground, the weariness mysteriously gone from her thin defiant features. 'Well!' she demanded, 'I thought you 'ad summat to say?' Queenie had never heard Auntie Biddy speak in the grip of such anger; and by the expression on Nosey-Parker Hindle's face, neither had she.

'Good Lord, child!' Nosey-Parker Hindle levelled a wide surprised look at Queenie, who could feel the fires of Hell blazing from the woman's eyes. 'I meant no insult. Come away in!' she instructed, standing aside and ushering them both in, content to let the thin wasted woman and the scrawny child struggle beneath the considerable weight of her sparkling, neatly pressed washing. 'I just have to say, Miss Kenney – you really do know how to turn out a good laundry.' Her face crushed itself into a self-pitying grimace. 'I'm so terrible helpless . . . what with my arthritis an' all.'

'Terrible lazy, more like,' Queenie mused resentfully. She tried not to look at the woman, whose thick sweet smile made her skin crawl and her stomach churn.

'There,' Nosey-Parker Hindle waved a hand towards the open fireside cupboard, 'just stack them in there, would you?' Her tiny darting eyes followed their every move.

'Thank you.'

Queenie rammed the blankets hard into the shelves, concerned now that Auntie Biddy didn't look well at all. And there was that squeaky-voiced woman, arms folded and a false smile screwing up her awful face, 'I'd give you a hand,' she piped, 'only I've been plagued with this sharp pain. All week it's gnawed at me . . . it's my leg you know, dreadful! Just dreadful it is! Nobody knows how I suffer.'

'That's all right,' Auntie Biddy told her, 'we can manage.' She smiled down at Queenie, whose short arms were struggling to reach the heavy blanket up to Auntie Biddy's grasp, 'Used to it now, aren't we, lass?'

The dog came from nowhere; snapping and causing Queenie to scream out, her heart jumping in fear at the sudden unprovoked attack. As the dog dived at Auntie Biddy's legs in a fit of noise and hurry she let out a sharp startled yell, dropping the crocheted shawl into the empty fire grate.

Nosey-Parker Hindle's leg seemed to have healed miraculously as she surged forward to retrieve both the dog and the shawl; totally oblivious to the fact that Auntie Biddy was clinging fearfully to the cupboard door.

'Oh poor little Sweetie,' she fussed and petted the panting dog, before turning her attention to the shawl. 'This is Sweetie's bed rug, you know! Lucky the fire's not lit . . . can't see any dirty marks on it though. I would have been quite within my rights to ask you for a second wash – without charge!' She dug into her purse and paid Auntie Biddy the five shillings, at the same time leading towards the parlour door, eager to be shot of the two of them. 'No real harm done.' She kissed the snarling dog repeatedly. 'Fetch the washing next Friday you can, as usual.' Smiling them all the way down the passage, she shut the door firmly behind them.

'I don't like her!' Queenie was surer of that now, than she had ever been.

Auntie Biddy sighed, a deep slow sigh which filled her eyes and quivered her mouth. 'Don't say that, Queenie.' She bent down to kiss Queenie's upturned face. 'She's a lonely old woman. That surly dog is all she 'as. She's not lucky like me. I've got *you*. Besides, we must be grateful for what we get from 'er.' She clasped her hands round the cold shiny pram handle. 'Come on, lass. We've to mek us way round Queen Victoria Street yet!'

Queenie felt miserable. Why did they need to be grateful to that rotten ol' creature? But it was only the fresh anger inside her, and the concern she felt for Auntie Biddy, that made her question these things. She knew in her heart, her wise old heart, that Auntie Biddy was doing it for her even though Queenie would have given anything for it not to be so. Her troubled thoughts materialized in the deep frowning lines which etched her forehead. She had to accept that there was nothing she could do about any of it, for she was only eight and not yet growed.

She had observed that the whole episode had almost proved too much for her Auntie Biddy. For the dear little woman had visibly *shrunk*, sagged heavily into her little pointed boots; the haggard look on her face was frightening to see.

Quietly reaching out to slide her hand into Auntie Biddy's, Queenie pleaded, '*I* can take the washing to Miss Tilly's and Fancy Carruthers. You can go 'ome, Auntie Biddy.' She was aware that the tears had toppled over the rims of her eyes, to hurtle down her cheeks. But she didn't care! She only cared about her Auntie Biddy . . . her darling Auntie Biddy!

The woman's pale face suddenly brightened at the girl's heartfelt concern, and when she gazed down on Queenie, Auntie Biddy's voice was gentle with love. 'No lass. I'll not put on you to take my responsibilities to yourself.' She murmured low, 'Lord only knows that'll 'appen soon enough.' Squaring her narrow shoulders, she leaned against the pram handles to push it into motion. 'One more stop, lass, then we can *both* be off 'ome!'

Queen Victoria Street was more of a back alley than a street, consisting of six houses on either side and the Foundry pub on the corner. There were only two gas lamps, one at each end. The pride of Lancashire was lovingly embedded in each and every gas-lamp in every street, square, and back alley, in the shape of a Lancaster Rose, carved deep and clear beneath the mantle-holder where the jutting arrn protruded, as if in perpetual salute. It was common acceptance that the importance of a street was measured by the number of gas-lamps lining the flagstones; so Queen Victoria Street was not reckoned to be anything special. Queenie had already decided that it didn't hold a candle to her beloved Parkinson Street. But Queen Victoria Street or Parkinson Street, there were enough poor folks biding in *both* to shame the pride that had carved the Lancaster Rose; and after all, mused Queenie, it were *folks* as were important, not gas-lamps, or bricks and mortar.

She twitched her nostrils at the odd mingle of smells which pervaded the air. She couldn't rightly put her finger on it. There was the lingering smell of stale ale from last night's boozers; the strong tang of fresh horsemuck from the milkman's early round; and something stinging, like a leaky gas-lamp; then she thought wryly, mebbe it was the sweet, thick pong of decaying sick, spewed along the gutters by marauding drunks.

'Here we are then, lass,' Auntie Biddy's words gathered Queenie's scattering thoughts.

The front door was open into the passage. It was *always* open. Miss Tilly and Fancy Carruthers loved nothing more than to have visitors. They were always welcome, any time of the day or evening. 'Go and tap on the parlour door, Queenie. Tell 'em we've fetched their washing.'

Queenie skipped along the passage, making the very same bet with herself that she had made on every single previous occasion: that the two old ladies would both be abed and wearing their frilly green caps.

Sure enough, on command of the thin piping voice which urged them to 'come in', the same peculiar scene awaited. The tiny parlour reeked of snuff and something suspiciously like George Kenney when he'd been boozing. The big bed which reached right up to Queenie's shoulders nigh filled the room. The top and bottom of it were like the bars of a jail, and each tall corner was conspicuously marked by huge shiny brass bells, which distorted Queenie's face whenever she looked into them. It would stretch wide and misshapen, then it would squeeze into itself like a concertina, shaping Queenie's mouth into a long narrow 'O', which quickly vanished into her sucked-in-cheeks.

There was *real* carpet on the floor, and big soft flowery armchairs which could swallow a body whole. Plants reached out from everywhere – from the tiny sideboard, the whatnot, the slipper-box, and even from the shelves on the wall.

'Hello Queenie love. Go and fetch your Auntie Biddy – tell her to push the pram down the passage. It'll save her a few steps carrying the washing.'

Queenie had never seen Miss Tilly out of that bed so she wasn't rightly sure what shape she was, or even if there was any more of her than peeped above the bedclothes. But a good guess, calculated by the tiny pointed face sticking out from beneath the green frilly cap, and the small straight shoulders draped over with a pretty white shawl, told Queenie she was probably right little. Her eyes, though, were huge. Bright blue and stary, with long ginger lashes which looked as though they did not belong to the smiling wizened face.

Sitting next to her, as always, was Fancy Carruthers, nodding and agreeing with everything Miss Tilly said. 'That's right dear,' she kept saying, 'that's right.'

Her features were very grey and very wrinkled, and her eyes had sunk away into deep bony caves, which prompted Queenie's silent comparison of her to a skeleton. From the brow of her frilly green cap a strand of thick grey hair hung down the wrinkled forehead. Queenie liked them both. She didn't fully understand their strange goings-on, but she liked them well enough.

It was hard, though, for Queenie to reckon on how it was that the teapot, on the firebrick in the hearth, always contained a hot brew; and the cake-tin on the sideboard was never empty of delicious home-made cakes. They must get out of bed *sometimes*, she reasoned. But 'twas an odd thing, a very odd thing!

With Auntie Biddy settled down to a mug of tea and a wedge of cake, Queenie felt much better.

'Climb up here, young 'un. Let's get a closer look at you.' Miss Tilly patted the bolster beside her.

'Yes, climb up, young Queenie.' Fancy Carruthers screwed her face into a peculiar shape of concentration as she seconded Miss Tilly's request.

Queenie looked round at Auntie Biddy, as if to seek her approval. Upon receipt of Auntie Biddy's reassuring smile, she quickly wolfed her cake down and proceeded to hoist herself up on to the cream-coloured eiderdown. It was no easy task, for the bed was high and the soft eiderdown gave way beneath her grasping fingers.

'Come on,' Miss Tilly encouraged.

'Yes, come on,' repeated Fancy Carruthers. Finally, Queenie clasped both her hands round the big brass ball and climbed up along the top. Scrabbling to where Miss Tilly had indicated, she felt as though she'd just climbed a mountain. Sinking into the squashy depths of the bolster, she looked hard into Miss Tilly's eyes, and waited politely.

Miss Tilly grabbed her by the hand, squeezing it affectionately. 'Been helping your Auntie Biddy take the pressing round, 'ave you lass?' Her features gathered themselves into a tight pointed smile as she looked down at Auntie Biddy contentedly supping her tea. 'Fair worn out she looks, bless 'er.'

'Yes,' Fancy Carruthers muttered, her head nodding in fervent agreement, 'fair worn out.'

Auntie Biddy reached her tired eyes up towards the threesome atop the bed. 'I'll be right as ninepence once I've rested me feet an' supped me tea.' She smiled determinedly, watching to make sure Queenie heeded her words. 'There's nowt wrong wi' me! I just 'ad a broken night, that's all.'

Miss Tilly could understand the wisdom of *that*. 'Aye well, a broken night *will* pull you down sooner than owt!'

Leaving Auntie Biddy to finish her tea in peace, Miss Tilly swivelled her attention to Queenie. 'How's thi' getting on at school then?'

Queenie pulled a small face. She would much rather have talked about *anything* else; but since the question had been put, there was no option but to answer it,

'All right I suppose, Miss Tilly. Thank you.'

'All right! Good God, child, that tells me nowt! What sort o' things do you *do*, lass?' Miss Tilly insisted.

'Aye! What sort o' things?' echoed Fancy Carruthers.

Queenie wondered what she could tell them. Truth was, she was never at school. Even the Truant Officer had grown tired of fetching her from her various hidingplaces around Blackburn and there weren't many o' *them* now that he didn't know about. But he was a kindly man. Queenie suspected that half the time he didn't report her. She'd have been hauled up afront o' the authorities afore now, if he had! She screwed her face up, stuck for an honest answer to Miss Tilly's question. 'Well . . . we sometimes do sums and singing . . . and sometimes we write stories.'

'What do you like to do best?' Miss Tilly seemed downright insistent.

'Oh, I like stories best! I likes writing stories and sometimes we get telled stories, and it's really grand, Miss Tilly.' Her face clouded over, and her eyes fell into thought. 'Only we 'ave Snake-Tongue Jackson most o' the time, an' I don't like '*er*!'

'Snake-Tongue Jackson! That's a rum sort o' name!'

'That's not 'er *real* name! We all call 'er that because she's got this sharp quick voice . . . an' she's allus nagging . . . nag! nag! nag! All the time.'

'Aye well,' Miss Tilly smiled, 'I expect it's you kids as make 'er nag!'

'It's not,' retorted Queenie, quite taken aback, 'she *likes* nagging!'

Auntie Biddy got to her feet, obviously rested and raring to go. 'Right then Queenie. Let's be off.' Then as an afterthought, 'An' that's no way to talk about your teacher!'

Queenie clambered down. 'Nobody likes 'er! Not even the other teachers.'

'You know where the money is, Biddy.' Miss Tilly pointed a small bony hand in the direction of the sideboard. 'Help yourself, love.'

'Yes, help yourself,' Fancy told her firmly.

As they were leaving Miss Tilly called out, 'You haven't caught sight o' Maisie Thorogood, have you? Only she promised us a stone-bottle for the bed. Can't seem to keep us feet warm.' She turned to Fancy. 'Can we, love?'

'No, can't keep 'em warm at all . . . not at all,' Fancy confirmed with a shake of her frilly green cap.

'We saw 'er afore we started out,' returned Auntie Biddy, 'I expect she's on 'er way. Goes on a right lengthy trot of a Saturday, does yon!'

'Aye well, leave the door open lass, and if you see 'er on the way, perhaps you'll remind her?'

'We'll do that, Miss Tilly. Thanks again for the cake and tea.'

'Tata,' the two frilly green caps called out together, as Auntie Biddy bumped the pram over the iron rim of the doorstep.

They didn't see Maisie, or anyone else come to that. 'All doing their washing, I expect,' Auntie Biddy speculated, letting Queenie push the empty pram. 'An' I expect the men are off to the pubs.'

What with Auntie Biddy not looking so well, and knowing that George Kenney would be out by now, Queenie felt relieved when they reached their own front door.

She minded the pram while Auntie Biddy opened the door and went ahead. Then manoeuvering the pram up the narrow passage, she fished the bulky yo-yo from her sleeve. The enjoyment she felt, just knowing it was hers, shone from her face; and the cosy glow at being back at No. 2 Parkinson Street, with her own Auntie Biddy all to herself, warmed her heart. 'I'm not playing out just yet,' she told Auntie Biddy, 'I'm staying in, wi' you!'

Chapter Three

Father Riley was a kindly enough man, and he meant well. But for all his regular visits and tireless involvement in the care of his 'poor folks', Auntie Biddy had never allowed herself truly to confide in him.

'Oh, he does his level best to help the folks hereabouts,' she'd tell Queenie, 'but what can the dear soul *really* know about going to bed hungry, or waking up of a morning and wondering how to get through the day? He has his grand big house and old Katy Forest to tend his every mortal need. Aye! and the good Lord to see to his soul.' Then, shaking her head, she would decide, 'Nay, lass, we shall just have to sort us-*selves* out.'

But Queenie, who grew in resolute strength daily, had other ideas. She had not forgotten that awful night when George Kenney had first raised his fist against her Auntie Biddy. He hadn't done that in these many months, but in other ways their lives were no easier; if anything, they had worsened. Queenie often lay awake in the darkness of her bedroom listening to the endless rows, each one more disturbing than the last. Strange though, Queenie thought, how she didn't seem to hate her father any more; at least not in the way she had done, when every nerve in her young body would scream for revenge, and the blind hatred swept every other emotion away until she thought she couldn't stand to be near him.

Since George Kenney had lost his job with the Corporation, Queenie had found a degree of solace in watching his accelerating downward spiral. Seeing him deteriorate both physically and mentally seemed to have sapped some of the raw hatred she had felt. He didn't hit Auntie Biddy any more, but that was the only improvement in him. In every other way, George Kenney had gone from bad to worse.

His new-found friends were undesirable people who arrived home with him at all hours. Their drunken shouts and coarse laughter would echo round the little house, until Queenie wondered whether the whole of Parkinson Street were up from their beds. She had discovered a new word to describe them. 'Scum!' she'd tell Auntie Biddy, 'they're all scum!'

'Ssh child . . .' The dear old face would twist in quick concern. 'Keep away from them, lass. They've nowt to do with us!' Queenie didn't worry Auntie Biddy about it again, but scum was how she privately continued to think of the unwelcome intruders.

Today was a special day, Queenie's birthday; heralded by a spherical object carefully wrapped up by Auntie Biddy and left on Queenie's pillow that morning. It was an orange, a big Jaffa with thick pocked skin which shot out gas and juice as Queenie greedily tore it away from the segments. She had delighted in sucking into those fat segments when the bitter sweet juices flowed into her mouth, making her nose sting and twisting her features into such protesting grimaces that might have frightened the devil himself!

Queenie had thoroughly enjoyed her birthday treat and she was quick to tell Auntie Biddy so. Now, she intended to make a special effort to forget about the drunkards who invaded their little house all too often of late.

Only two nights ago there'd been a right shindig. Auntie Biddy had allowed Queenie to sit up with her. They hadn't talked much because Auntie Biddy had busied herself doing the mending and darning, and Queenie had sat entranced at the quick fingers which wove and darted about until the gaping holes vanished from the socks and cardies, and in their place appeared a whole new garment as if by magic.

George Kenney's noisy fumblings at the front door had alerted Auntie Biddy and Queenie to the fact that not only was he blind plaited drunk again but he had company. With practised speed, the two of them had whispered away up the stairs before the whole drunken party fell through the door and rolled into the passage. Peeking angrily from the top of the stairs, the fugitives had recognized at least two of the men.

There was Fountain Crossland, a burly pitworker, who had fists the size of sledge-hammers and a head like a stud-bull. Then there was little Tommy McAbe, who never stopped laughing, and who, according to Auntie Biddy, was daft as a bent nail, and just about as useful.

The other three men were comparative strangers. 'From another part o' town,' whispered Auntie Biddy from their hidey-hole, 'met for a game o' dominoes I expect! Drunken no-goods!'

She had fair cause to curse again later, when she and Queenie were rudely awakened from their sleep. Fountain Crossland had somehow managed to locate and violate the privacy of their bedroom.

It was an adventure that he would never look to repeat drunk or sober, thought Queenie. With the unexpected strength of the indignant, Auntie Biddy had pushed and shoved him to the top of the stairway, where with a mighty heave she hoisted him through the air to land in a disgruntled heap at the bottom of the stairs. 'You forget your place, Fountain Crossland!' she told him with disgust. 'It's *ladies* you're dealing with in *this* 'ouse, and don't you forget it!'

Queenie didn't doubt for a moment that he would heed Auntie Biddy's words. But unknown to her Fountain Crossland had other ideas. The sight of Queenie in her long flowered nightie, with her large grey eyes and sweeping burnished hair, had triggered an insatiable need in him.

All she could think about, by contrast, was that today she had graduated into double numbers. She smiled at herself in the mirror, her grey eyes dancing as she surveyed her reflection with satisfaction, 'Queenie nobody,' she told herself, 'you are *ten* years old!' Oh, she wanted to grow up so quickly it made her ache. Of a sudden, a frown cut deep into her smile causing it to fade away and in its place there came a look of impatience, as she thought how strange it was that George Kenney could infiltrate her happiness, leaving her feeling deflated even on a wonderful day like today. He had denied her a name, *his* name . . . and now she did not want it, ever! When anybody asked her name, she would tell them, 'I'm just Queenie.'

Queenie had inherited her mother's striking beauty and gentleness; but over the years she had also acquired her father's dogged stubbornness.

'Come on, child!' Auntie Biddy was growing impatient. 'Father Riley hasn't got all day, you know.'

Queenie skipped down the stairs two at a time, excited and optimistic that being ten heralded a swifter transition into adulthood. Soon she would be able to take more of the load from Auntie Biddy's shoulders. For a long time now, Queenie had sensed that something was very wrong with her darling Auntie Biddy. She sensed it now as the little woman came into view.

Constant worry and the back-breaking work she slaved at had finally begun to take their toll of George Kenney's sister. Gone was the air of authority which had cloaked her small figure; gone was the gentle glow of her light brown hair, which was shot through now with a growing blanket of dull lifeless grey.

More and more these days Queenie had to accept that Auntie Biddy was ill, wom out by the never-ending struggle to 'keep our heads above water'. The slight irritating cough she'd contracted some months before had developed into sudden unexpected bouts of racking pain when she would lock herself in the outside lavvy anxious that Queenie shouldn't witness the ever-increasing expulsion of blood. Queenie's suggestion that she should fetch the doctor had been swiftly refused. Auntie Biddy didn't need no doctor! Hadn't her own Mam gone through the self-same torture? She didn't need to fool herself either; this consumption had been creeping up on her long enough now. Only the whitewashed stone walls would echo the prayer she constantly whispered: 'Dear God, don't take me yet. I've got to see our little Queenie right.'

Queenie's concern over Auntie Biddy started and ended her every day; but such things were outside her experience, and she couldn't rightly tell what it was that moithered her so. She only knew that something awful might happen so that nothing she could do would be powerful enough to stop it.

'Queenie! What d'you want to go clattering down them stairs like that for?' Auntie Biddy's pale blue eyes shot a narrow disapproving glance in the upward direction of the back bedroom. '*He's* up there! Saturday morning, and he's lying up there half-dead, still full o'booze.' She buttoned up her old tweed coat, wrapped a scarf around her head, and made her way to the front door. 'I can do without him down 'ere shouting and swearing! Come on, lass. Let's be off to Father Riley.'

Queenie grabbed her blue school-mac from behind the door and raced after Auntie Biddy, who was already on her way down Parkinson Street.

Queenie knew it was George Kenney who had caused Auntie Biddy to be ill. She'd convinced herself long ago that all their troubles stemmed from him. Her lovely face grew thoughtful as she ran along, murmuring the words dearest to her young heart. 'I wish he'd die! I wish one morning we'd wake up and never have to see him again.'

For just a second her heart grew cold and dead as thoughts of her father and his awful drunken friends filled her mind, but they occupied no more time than it took to dismiss them. The bubble of happiness with which she'd started her day refused to burst. She was ten years old; almost grown! A whispering smile lit up the magnificent grey of her eyes until specks of sparkling blue charged them with a rich excitement. Catching up with Auntie Biddy, Queenie slipped her small hand into the responding clutch of bony fingers. 'What's my surprise, Auntie Biddy?'

'If I was to tell you that, lass, it wouldn't be a surprise no more, now would it?'

Queenie laughed. 'No . . . don't suppose it would.'

'There you are then! Mind your own business; you'll just have to wait and see, won't you?'

As the two of them travelled the considerable length of their beloved Parkinson Street, they heard many a cheery 'Good morning' and many a 'Happy Birthday, lass', as Queenie told one and all that it was her *tenth* birthday. Nosey-Parker Hindle crossed the road to remind Auntie Biddy, 'You won't forget to darn all the ravels in Sweetie's bed-shawl . . . he will keep catching his dear little nails in it.'

'I'll not forget,' Auntie Biddy promised with a smile, side-stepping skilfully as Sweetie dived for her legs.

'Seems to have taken to you,' Nosey-Parker Hindle said in a proud patronising manner.

Queenie could have gladly belted that mongrel. She had nothing against dogs. But this one had taken a dislike to her Auntie Biddy, so it had better watch out!

'Our Sheila's been looking for you, Queenie lass!' Maisie Thorogood hung out of her upstairs window like a rag-doll losing its stuffing and looking set to dive headlong onto the flagstones below. Brandishing a chamishine, she stretched dangerously to the bottom corners of the window, everything decent hanging indecently out of her low-necked blouse. 'Keep yer eye on 'er, Biddy love! That lass is a right good-looking piece o' stuff . . . won't be long afore the lads come a-sniffing!' With an extra loud guffaw, which very nearly tipped her out of the window altogether, she finally managed to gather her disjointed carcass together to squeeze back through the vdow and out of sight.

Queenie wasn't too sure about being referred to as a 'piece o' stuff' but she paid little mind; Maisie meant no harm, she knew that.

Old Mr Craig from No. 46 thought that a *tenth* birthday warranted special attention. 'Just you 'ang on a minute, lass,' he told Auntie Biddy, his weak old eyes screwing up to focus on the child, 'I've got just the thing for a bright young lass who's ten today.'

Auntie Biddy and Queenie exchanged amused glances as Mr Craig's stooping figure scurried back inside. Queenie liked Mr Craig, who spent long lonely days sitting outside his little house. The rickety stand-chair had a permanent place on the flagstones by the front door. Folks had long ago stopped asking questions or wondering why it was that a stand-chair should be left outside in all weathers year in year out. They'd gotten used to the old fellow sitting there, happy to pass the time of day with anyone who could spare it. From early morning to last thing at night when the biting chill of evening forced him in, he'd just sit there smiling and chatting to one and all, and generally watching the world go by.

During her flag-counting sessions, Queenie would often run errands for him, or come and set herself on his step, where she'd listen enthralled to exciting stories of his daredevil days and frightening accounts of the war he'd fought in as a young man. He'd always lived in Parkinson Street like his Mam and Dad afore him. He was born in the little house he treasured, as were his two sons and daughter. Since his beloved wife had died some twelve years ago, none of his children came to see him. But he never complained. 'Got their own lives to live,' he'd tell Queenie, trying to suppress the heartache she knew he felt. He might have forgiven them . . . but Queenie never could.

Queenie looked up from her thoughts as old Mr Craig returned. Reaching his long unsteady arm towards her, he opened his gnarled hand to reveal her birthday present. Queenie's eyes grew wide and dark with admiration, for nestling in the etched lines of his palm was a necklace! It was the most beautiful thing Queenie had ever seen. Shaped in the image of a golden heart, its centre was encrusted with shining stones which flashed darting arrows of breathtaking colours. The golden chain which held it was long and delicate, like the fine strands of a cobweb.

'Nay, Mr Craig! The lass can't accept that.' Auntie Biddy voiced the words which were already forming on Queenie's lips.

Her words fell on deaf ears as old Mr Craig shuffled forward and slipped the golden necklace over Queenie's head. 'You wouldn't deny an old man a bit o'pleasure, Biddy Kenney, would you?' His eyes never left the golden heart which Queenie was examining rapturously. 'Fifty year old is that.' His sad eyes glazed over. 'That were my Annie's. I gave 'er that necklet the day we wed,' the old man's voice trembled with emotion, 'and she said she'd wear it all 'er days as a symbol of our love.' He lifted his moist old eyes to Auntie Biddy, 'Them words is lovely . . . just lovely.'

He drew on the clear grey innocence of Queenie's gaze, a quiet smile whispering about his mouth. 'My Annie wore that there necklet every day of her life, bless her . . . right up to the day I laid her to rest.' It seemed as if the old man's thoughts were too far in the past to focus. 'All through the War as took me away from 'er . . . she wore that necklet as a charm for me to be looked after.' With a sudden movement he grabbed the unsuspecting Queenie, pulling her close to him. 'Queenie lass, you're the only one who's shown a lonely old man a bit o' love and regard, and my Annie knows. We both want you to have yon necklet, and wear it with love and pride.' He pushed her away just as suddenly as he'd grabbed her, before sitting down in his stand-chair as though it had all been too much of an ordeal. The tears which he'd so bravely fought to suppress now ran unheeded down the deep crevices of his aged face.

Queenie could hardly talk for the tight sorrow which gripped her throat, at the sight of old Mr Craig bowed in memories too painful to bear. Lunging whole-heartedly at the dear old man, she hugged him fiercely, 'I'll *always* look after Annie's necklace,' she promised fervently, 'I'll wear it forever; and I'll love you forever!'

The old man held her at arm's length, 'God bless you little Queenie. We all knows what you've been denied . . . but God'll have revenge on yon George Kenney!' He smiled up at Auntie Biddy, whose blue eyes were filled with tears for this sad old man. 'Your brother's a sinful man, Biddy; he's *never* deserved you and this lovely child.' Turning to Queenie, his voice tired and failing, he urged her, 'Don't ever let George Kenney see that necklet. Never part with it to anyone, lass. It'll keep you safe.'

'I won't! I won't Mr Craig. I'll *always* keep it next to me.' And she did. Queenie wore the golden heart against her skin, taking it off only on bath nights on strict orders from Auntie Biddy, who would lay the necklace carefully over the big tin bath where Queenie could see it. And never once did Queenie forget to say a little prayer for the old man and his departed darling.

When six months later the old man was found dead one evening sitting on his stand-chair, the look of contentment across his peaceful old face suggested that at long last he and his Annie were together again. Queenie *never* forgot him or the day he had given her the necklace, and how all the way to Father Riley's she and Auntie Biddy had been subdued by the lovely gift.

Father Riley was young, energetic, and totally devoted to his parishioners. He had a special spot for Auntie Biddy and Queenie on whom life had seemed to frown more unfavourably than on most. He was well aware that they often went hungry, but Auntie Biddy's pride wouldn't allow her to ask him for help. He respected her for the proud stubborn woman she was, a woman who'd protect her niece against anyone and anything even to the extent of sacrificing herself. It was only her accelerating illness, he was sure, that had finally prompted her to come here at all if only for Queenie's sake. Queenie smiled up at him. She always felt comfortable in his presence, and was always pleased to see him on visits to their home, or her school. He had kind dark brown eyes and a strong laughing mouth which always had a kind word for everybody. Today he was eager to share her joy.

'Well, our little Queenie – ten years old, and all grown up.'

His eyes appraised the small straight figure before him. The long golden-brown hair plaited across her head shone like silk, her stance was proud and defiant. Her honest grey eyes held his gaze with such surprising strength that he was amazed at her maturity of outlook. He knew that this child, little Queenie, would leave her mark wherever she went, whatever she did. Adversity would never be *her* master. Her deep love for the woman by her side was clear and unmistakable. The loyalty of one for the other was something uniquely satisfying.

'I'd nearly given you both up,' he told her.

'Aye,' Auntie Biddy confirmed, 'we *are* late. Old Mr Craig stopped us on the way, poor old soul. Gave Queenie a beautiful present for her birthday. It meant a lot to him.'

Father Riley often visited old Mr Craig. He was another stubborn character, 'Oh . . . a birthday present, eh?' He waited, just long enough to realize that Queenie wasn't going to show it to him. She obviously cherished it too much. 'That was kind of him. He doesn't have much apart from his precious memories.'

Queenie looked around the Mission Hall. She hadn't been here before; Auntie Biddy always changed the subject whenever Queenie mentioned it. It wasn't too difficult to understand why. Recognizing the existence of the Mission Hall meant recognizing its prime purpose. Years ago it had been merely a meeting place, a central prayer-raising gathering point for Christian folks from the lower levels of society. Now, however, it served a very different purpose although the folks who still gathered there continued to come from the lower, now much poorer, homes. It was this very fact that had cultivated Auntie Biddy's stubborn resistance to ever entering the premises. As a child, she had always been well provided for. She and her brother George never knew what it was to go hungry. Their father, old Robby Kenney, owned a butcher's shop. He was a well-liked and respected man . . . as was George, until Kathy's premature death.

Queenie's roving eyes alighted on the large wooden plaque high up on the far wall. It read:

'BLACKBURN RAGGED SCHOOL'
Founded in the Cause of
Christian Love and Fellowship
Opened by Mayor John Truman
July 15th, 1942.

Queenie turned the words over and over in her mind. 'Blackburn Ragged School'. They had a sad ring about them, and their implications frightened her. She refused to dwell on the matter, thankful that her hand stayed well and truly fast inside the security of Auntie Biddy's.

She looked up now at the mention of her name. 'Queenie! Pay attention, lass.' Auntie Biddy shook her gently by the hand. 'Father Riley's after telling you about your birthday surprise.'

Father Riley led Queenie and her Auntie Biddy

over to one of the long wooden tables, where he gestured for them to take a seat on the accompanying bench. 'Now then, little Queenie, do you want a glass of sarsaparilla, or a nice cup of Sarah's tea?'

Sarah beamed at them from her place behind the serving-hatch. Queenie, momentarily fascinated by the odd face-twitching way Sarah had of hoisting her rimless glasses up the considerable length of her nose, said smiling, 'A glass of sarsaparilla please.'

Father Riley swept away to collect the refreshments. Queenie's observant eyes travelled the length and breadth of the Hall. She didn't think it a very impressive place at all, more like a big tram shelter, she decided. The woodblocked floor was dull and considerably worn, especially in the immediate vicinity of Sarah's serving-hatch. The high daunting walls were distempered the most nauseating shade of shiny purple, and the few narrow slitted windows way up towards the ceiling were so grubby that even the bright filtered rays of watery spring sunshine lost their natural exuberance on struggling through.

Queenie thought it too depressing for words. She began to wish they hadn't come.

'All right, love?' Auntie Biddy looked so anxious and uncomfortable that Queenie had no choice but to grin and bear it for both their sakes. Her heart went out to the kindly face looking down on her, waiting for reassurance. Queenie's responding smile wrapped itself around Auntie Biddy's tired face, and, disguising the dull disappointed feelings inside, she said stoutly, ''Course I'm all right.' Then, quick to change the subject, she added, 'Sarah looks nice, doesn't she?'

Auntie Biddy's voice emerged as a sigh, as she squeezed Queenie's hand lovingly. 'Yes lass. She looks right pleasant.'

'Here we are then, one extra large glass of sarsaparilla,' Father Riley slid the drink across the table to Queenie, before handing Auntie Biddy a cup and saucer, 'and one of Sarah's specials.'

Queenie paid little mind to the grown-ups' conversation as she was kept occupied by the increasing activity around her. It was the start of the State schools' Easter holidays, and seemingly every pupil from miles around had congregated here in the Ragged School. As the Hall began to fill up with all kinds of lads and lasses from tiny tots to great lumbering youths, Queenie began to feel desperately closed in. Moving involuntarily back towards Auntie Biddy, she felt fascinated yet frightened by the increasing volume of noise and generated excitement which bounced threateningly off the walls. Father Riley sensed her impending distress. 'There's so much noise in here, Biddy! Perhaps we could talk better in Sarah's kitchen?'

Sarah's kitchen was bigger than the whole of Auntie Biddy's house. Queenie thought it grand and fascinating. Great black iron pans of enormous dimensions littered the endless array of shelves and benches. Three huge cooking ranges, blackleaded and polished till you could see your face in them, stretched away down the centre of the room as far as the eye could see. The red quarry-tiled floor shone with loving care and elbow grease.

Queenie felt pleasantly secure in this kitchen, and it heightened the immediate liking she had taken to the

homely Salvation Army officer, Sarah, who plied her
constantly with glasses of sarsaparilla, and gave her
reassuring glances occasionally brightened by the
cheekiest of winks. By no stretch of the imagination
could Sarah be described as pretty. Queenie tried so
hard not to stare at the bulbous warts which festooned
the plump smiling face but somehow her eyes were
constantly drawn back to them.

'Not very pretty lass, are they?' When Sarah smiled,
as she did now, her white even teeth shone like pearls,
and her whole face lit up. From behind the spectacles,
her fair eyes danced cheekily. 'Haven't *always* re-
sembled a wart-hog,' she laughed, putting the squirming Queenie instantly at ease, 'one o' these days, I
might see what can be done about 'em; but they're
no bother! I'm not out to win any beauty contests.'

Queenie decided she liked Sarah almost as much as
she liked Auntie Biddy.

Father Riley's quiet voice addressed itself to
Queenie. 'Auntie Biddy thinks, and so do *I*, that it
would be nice for you to have a few more friends of
your own age.' Queenie knew what he meant. She had
no friends really, except for Sheila, and that had long
been a source of concern to Auntie Biddy although it
had never bothered Queenie. But she listened politely
to Father Riley. He was a nice man, a caring, helpful
person; in fact Queenie had already adopted him as
one of her dearest people. 'Every Easter,' he went on,
'the Ragged School children have a special surprise
treat. It isn't very often that we can afford to go to the
seaside; but *this* year,' he smiled knowingly at Sarah,
'thanks to help from our Salvation Army friends,
we've been given the use of a coach and we're all off

74

to Blackpool – only for the day mind. Now then, Queenie, how would *you* like to come?'

Blackpool? The seaside! Queenie had always longed to go to the seaside, but she'd kept the dream simmering deep in her heart. She knew Auntie Biddy couldn't take her, so she'd accepted that it would have to remain a dream probably for a very long time to come. But *now*! 'The seaside? The real seaside, for a whole day?'

Father Riley took hold of Queenie's small hand. 'Yes, lass. The *real* seaside, with shells and crabs, and golden sand. It'll be grand, won't it?'

Queenie's first reaction was as always, to share her joy with Auntie Biddy. Reaching her small arms up and around the scrawny neck, she pulled Auntie Biddy's head down to smother it in kisses. '*You're* coming too, aren't you?'

Auntie Biddy held her tight, the two of them laughing. Until, of a sudden, a spiteful coughing fit engulfed the little woman. Queenie watched helplessly as Auntie Biddy groped in her bag for the cotton square she always carried with her, and when Father Riley took Auntie Biddy gently by the shoulders and led her towards the open window, where the light breeze offered small comfort, Queenie followed their every move. A great sadness flooded her heart as she waited and watched, while Father Riley supported Auntie Biddy's thin delicate figure against the racking torment of her accelerating illness. Queenie noticed too the specks of red which stained the cotton square and she hadn't missed the look of sympathy and resignation which passed between Father Riley and Sarah.

'Queenie,' Sarah had moved between Queenie and the two figures by the window, 'would you like another sarsaparilla?'

Queenie thanked her . . . but no. She didn't want anything. A persistent horror that Auntie Biddy was going to leave her grew into a tight band of fear across Queenie's throat, until she felt sure she would choke.

Auntie Biddy returned to pat her reassuringly on the hand. 'That darned biscuit went down the wrong hole, lass,' she told the frightened child, painfully conscious that although Queenie *was* only a child, she had already been subjected to many harmful experiences. Sadly they seemed to have robbed her of that trust and innocence special to childhood.

Queenie knew instinctively that Auntie Biddy was trying to deceive her, and she felt a degree of resentment. But it was short-lived as her worried grey eyes scanned the rapidly changing features of her Auntie Biddy. Of late, the cheekbones jutted out like chiselled marble and the blue eyes which had once shone as bright as new pennies were dim and scarred.

Queenie's fear did not show as she clung tight to Auntie Biddy's hand. She had made up her mind. 'Thank you, Father Riley,' she said with a disarming smile at the priest, 'it was kind of you to invite me on your trip – but I don't want to go.'

'Oh?' Of a sudden, Father Riley's brown eyes had grown sad. 'You're sure?'

Queenie nodded. She was sure. Somehow she was convinced that her time with Auntie Biddy was even more precious, and she wanted to be near her. From now on *nothing* would take her from Auntie Biddy's side. No amount of persuasion would convince her to change her mind. So, a few minutes later, it was a sadder but wiser priest who watched Queenie and Auntie Biddy walk away down the street.

Sarah dabbed behind her glasses, making a poor job of disguising her tears. 'God help that poor little lass, made to grow up afore 'er time,' she said in a croaky voice.

'Sarah,' said Father Riley, 'God *will* help her; but she'll also help herself. Queenie has all the strength she needs to get through. I hope God in his mercy doesn't let Biddy suffer too long. She's devoted her life to little Queenie, with nary a thought for herself.' His eyes sad, he took Sarah's arm, turning her gently with him as he went back inside. They entered the Hall in reflective silence.

Auntie Biddy and Queenie walked home together, each lost in her own thoughts. Queenie held on fast to the gnarled fingers which clutched protectively around her hand. A burning sensation filled her tight throat as the tears rose to blur her vision. Determined not to concern the dear woman walking slowly by her side, Queenie blinked the tears back. 'You aren't angry are you?' she asked tremulously. 'About me not going to the seaside?'

Auntie Biddy stopped to take a breath, squeezing Queenie's hand lovingly. 'No lass. I'm not angry. I just want you to do what pleases *you*.' She looked deep and searchingly into the child's face. 'You're a funny little thing an' no mistake. But if my Queenie doesn't want to go . . . that's good enough for me!'

On reaching home, Auntie Biddy admitted that she was 'fair worn out'. Queenie, relieved that there was no sign of George Kenney, packed her off to bed.

Later, when she crept into their bedroom with a hot drink, Auntie Biddy was already hard and fast asleep.

When George Kenney finally arrived home hours later Queenie had also gone to her bed. She lay awake close to her darling Auntie Biddy, watching her sleep. At first her sleep had been fretful, when she had called out in strange broken phrases, the name 'Richard' standing out clearly from the jumble of words. Queenie breathed a sigh of relief when the ramblings subsided and a faint tinge of colour slowly infiltrated the pale gaunt cheeks. The rapid breathing gradually gave way to a soft even rhythm and Auntie Biddy became peaceful. Now and again, Queenie would lean over ever so gently to place a gossamer kiss against the beloved face. She tried to put certain things out of her mind, but the questions rampaged about her thoughts. Who was Richard, the lad that Auntie Biddy had talked about; and what dreadful thing had George Kenney done that should play on Auntie Biddy's mind so? Queenie deliberately closed her mind to it all and settled to go to sleep.

George Kenney was as usual creating havoc downstairs, calling loudly for 'that bloody woman!' and clattering things about in his mindless state of drunkenness.

Alarmed that all the noise would disturb Auntie Biddy, Queenie got out of bed and stealthily picked her way down the stairs. As she pushed open the parlour door George Kenney was mumbling and swearing to himself. Suddenly aware of Queenie's presence he turned, peering through half-closed eyes in an attempt to distinguish the shadowy figure by the door. 'Who the 'ell's that? Eh?'

Disguising the revulsion she felt at the sight of her drunken unkempt father, Queenie told him, 'It's me . . . Queenie.'

George Kenney turned too sharply. Losing his already ungainly footing, he staggered backwards, landing half in and half out of the horse-hair chair by the fireplace. 'What the bloody 'ell do *you* want? Where's that lazy, sodding woman!'

The sight of him, the smell of him, filled her with sick disgust; but none of these driving emotions showed in the flat tone of her voice as she answered, 'Auntie Biddy's been poorly today. She went to bed early.'

'Poorly, you say!' His face twisted sneeringly. 'Bone idle more like! Bloody bone idle! She's too old . . . getting useless!' Suddenly aware that Queenie's critical eyes were burning into him, George Kenney lunged forward at her; the force of which triggered off an eruption of the enormous reservoir of booze inside him. Without any self-restraint whatsoever he brought up the entire contents of his stomach, spewing them across the oilcloth and furniture. Then he promptly fell back into the chair in a deep stupor.

Queenie thought he'd be better off dead. They'd *all* be better off without him, because he was no good! She set about cleaning up the thick stinking layer of sick. That done, she took the paper packages down to the bin, scrubbed the oilcloth, washed her hands under the icy cold water from the tap and went back to bed.

As she lay quiet between the prickly winceyette sheets, snuggled up carefully to the thin wasting figure beside her, Queenie hardly dared think about a world without her Auntie Biddy and of a sudden, a strange sensation strangled her heart. The stark realization came to her that as everyone around her grew weak and helpless, it would be brought upon her alone to emerge strong and capable.

Wrapping her small cold fingers around Auntie Biddy's hand, she caressed the warmth back into it and quickly fell asleep.

The next day was Sunday. Queenie could still remember when Sunday meant a special dinner of meat and potato pie and small tasty carrots. Not any more though! Not since George Kenney had lost his job and Auntie Biddy had got too poorly to take in washing and pressing.

Queenie had done her best, but she was not capable of providing for all three of them on what few clothes she could launder. It barely paid the rent. Nobody seemed anxious to help, not even the Truant Officer, who thankfully turned a blind eye to Queenie's consistent absence from school. He had failed in his promise to send the Welfare round. And Queenie hated the prospect of going begging to them.

The onset of poverty, real degrading poverty, had crept up on them, in the guise of false hopes. Now optimism was a luxury; yet Queenie could not be daunted. While she had Auntie Biddy the world was bearable, and she had become used to being hungry and wearing cast-off clothes. Many times when she'd seen Auntie Biddy trying hard to hide her tiredness, Queenie would finger old Mr Craig's beautiful locket, and into her heart would creep an awful temptation.

It would be an easy thing to shove the golden heart over the pawn shop counter in exchange for half-a-crown . . . But the half-crown would be gone in no time, and along with it any hope of ever getting Mr Craig's precious locket back. In these times of temptation, Queenie was forced to remember the promise she had made to the old man and she would swiftly reproach herself. 'Twern't the answer, she decided. Old Mr Craig would think badly on her for having done such a thing. So, thrusting the temptation away, she found diversion in working twice as hard at the washing and pressing, consoling herself with the satisfaction of having eased the workload from Auntie Biddy's shoulders.

Auntie Biddy was still sleeping quietly as Queenie slipped out of bed and got dressed. The town-hall clock was striking eight as she entered the back parlour, and there was no sign of George Kenney. 'Dragged himself off to bed, I expect,' Queenie decided with a sigh of relief.

Some ten minutes later found Queenie on her knees by the firegrate. The fire was well underway now; its warmth had caressed her face to a rosy pink and brought an attractive shine to her eyes. It was a pleasing picture that greeted Fountain Crossland when George Kenney's daughter opened the door to his tapping.

'A sight for sore eyes, that's what you are, young Queenie,' he said quietly. Then without waiting to be asked he stepped inside and proceeded down the passageway towards the parlour. Queenie closed the door and followed. 'He's still in bed,' she said, leaving the parlour door open as she came in from the passage. 'No need fer that,' Fountain Crossland told her, his face crooked into a half-smile.

Queenie had already turned away with the intention

81

of rousing George Kenney but now the big man came to block her exit. Putting his finger across his lips he leaned towards her, at the same time reaching out behind her to push the door to. 'Ssh . . . we don't want to fetch 'im from 'is bed, do we? I've seen what 'es like on wakkening!' He stretched his face into an ugly grimace, and it was such an accurate mimicry of George Kenney in a foul temper that Queenie found herself laughing out loud in spite of herself. Auntie Biddy had no liking for Fountain Crossland, Queenie knew, but he could be so funny, and a great deal nicer than George Kenney.

'Auntie Biddy abed too is she?'

'Yes . . . she's been badly.'

'Ah! Works too 'ard does Biddy.' Fountain Crossland seated himself in the horse-hair chair by the fireside, all the while regarding Queenie through careful eyes. 'I'll tell you what, lass,' he said quietly, 'let's you an' me 'ave a little talk eh?' His broad smile was disarming, and when he stretched out a hand Queenie went to him.

At once, he pulled her on to his knee and Queenie was quickly enthralled by the stories he told her . . . funny stories about little creatures called Shenagins who lived in folks' mattresses and who had the most marvellous adventures.

It seemed that Fountain Crossland, too, got carried away in excitement at the little creatures' antics, because once or twice Queenie found herself being violently jiggled up and down on his lap. And when at one stage Fountain Crossland took to acting out a scene where he took off his trousers and put on Auntie

Biddy's pinafore he looked so silly that Queenie fell about laughing.

It was this scene that Auntie Biddy came upon when she brought herself down from the bedroom to investigate the noise. It took her but a moment to see Fountain Crossland's real game and with a cry of 'You fornicating old sod!' she grabbed up his trouser belt and whacked it hard across his bare legs. 'Out! Get out and don't show yourself here again!' she told him. Even when Fountain Crossland took to his heels and ran off up the passage without his trousers, Auntie Biddy would have followed him if it hadn't been for the fact that the bubble of energy she had summoned was now depleted. Falling into the nearest chair, she told the gaping Queenie, 'Throw 'is old trousers after him, lass.'

This Queenie did, firmly closing the front door after both Fountain Crossland and his trousers had disappeared through it, only to be tripped head over heels by Mrs Farraday's terrified ginger tom. When she returned to the parlour, Queenie was uncertain as to whether she would be blamed for letting Fountain Crossland into the house, and looked into the little woman's face with a sheepish expression.

'I'm sorry, Auntie Biddy,' Queenie said. For a moment there came no response. Then, just as Queenie began to think she would not be forgiven, she noticed a twinkle which spread into a smile and the smile erupted into laughter, Queenie ran to her Auntie Biddy and together the two of them rocked helplessly at the memory of Fountain Crossland fleeing up the passage in a pinnie, after having his buttocks well and truly thrashed by Auntie Biddy. 'I don't think we'll be bothered with Fountain Crossland again,' she laughed. Queenie vowed he would not come into this house again by *her* hand.

'I'll get some breakfast, Auntie Biddy,' Queenie said, shivering as she went into the scullery. It was one of those places that always struck cold whatever the time of day or year. In the cupboard she found a small hunk of bread, a little margarine and a couple of spoonfuls of jam. She prepared two helpings, one for Auntie Biddy, and one for herself, leaving the crust-end for George Kenney. It amused her to recall how difficult it was for him to negotiate the crusty ends.

Auntie Biddy glanced at the clumsily cut hunks of bread and jam. 'You've left some for your dad, haven't you?'

'Yes. Don't worry!' Queenie said nothing about George Kenney having been sick all over the place.

'You might not prepare the daintiest of slices,' Auntie Biddy laughed, 'but you make a grand cup o' tea.'

'Do you feel better today, Auntie Biddy?'

The woman looked deep and searching into the soft beauty of the strong grey eyes which scrutinized her face. A look of sadness fleeted like a dark shadow over her features as she cupped Queenie's small face between her hands. 'You haven't plaited your hair, lass,' she remarked as her thin fingers ran through the thick fair locks which hung across Queenie's shoulders and reached down to her waist: 'I'll do it when I've washed up.'

Queenie wanted an answer to her question. '*Are* you feeling better?' she insisted.

The hands released her, and as Auntie Biddy stretched out to retrieve the half-filled mug from the firegrate, she sighed, 'Aye lass . . .' The smile in her voice lifted the corners of her mouth, and crept into her blue eyes, as she went on, 'Aye I'm feeling a whole lot better . . . and I'll tell you what! You and me's going out today.' Her voice was suddenly pitched with an enthusiasm which infected Queenie, momentarily erasing the worried frown from her forehead.

'Going out? Where we going, Auntie Biddy?' Queenie felt lighter of heart; perhaps after all she'd been worrying for nothing. And now, with Auntie Biddy unexpectedly infused with new life, she'd indulge herself in this rush of happiness, which had suddenly coloured the world a brighter place.

'We're going to pay a call on some of Father Riley's old friends.'

'We're not going back down to the Ragged School, are we?' Queenie asked fearfully.

'No, lass. It's a *special* journey for you, because I'm tekking you farther afield than you've ever been! You'll see broad green fields, stretching that far afront o' you, they could be the ocean itself! Oh aye, thar in for a treat, my gel!' Auntie Biddy thought it would partly make up to the child for missing the Blackpool treat.

At this Queenie was on her knees, her eyes wide with wonder as they met Auntie Biddy's smiling gaze. '*Outside* Blackburn, Auntie Biddy? Are we going outside Blackburn?'

'You'll see!' Auntie Biddy told her. 'Now get a move on, we don't want to miss the tram. I've enough coppers in my purse for that.'

Half an hour later, after they had left behind the grimy buildings of industry and the grey damp alleys of Blackburn Town, Queenie found herself being transported through little villages of tiny cottages with stretches of grass at the front door instead of yards made up from drab flagstones. And they had little winding paths with clusters of flowers alongside . . . all the colours of the rainbow. Everything was open and spacious; even the sky looked bigger and brighter. It was all a wondrous revelation to Queenie's eager eyes.

Throughout the entire journey, Queenie gasped and laughed, calling out for Auntie Biddy to look at this or that. And such delight in her child did the frail woman more good than all the medicine in the world.

The only time a frown appeared to mar Queenie's enjoyment was when she had grown excited at the sight of a small herd of cows. Somehow, it had never occurred to Auntie Biddy that cows grazing in a meadow were beyond Queenie's experience. She explained, the only way she knew how, that these were destined to be the carcasses hanging in Jack Rawtenstall's butcher's shop, and in such-like premises everywhere.

Queenie's reaction was not the one Auntie Biddy had anticipated. 'You mean people *eat* them! They're chopped up for hot-pot and things?' The thought filled Queenie with horror and for a while she was silent, her bubble of enthusiasm cruelly burst. Auntie Biddy chided herself for being so insensitive to the child, and with all the enthusiasm and energy she could summon she set about wiping the upset from Queenie's mind; drawing attention to the brooks, the trees and the folks fishing.

An hour later the two of them alighted from the tram, Auntie Biddy all spick and span in her black Sunday coat, and Queenie scrubbed and polished, with her long hair secured in crossover plaits. Cherry-Tree seemed a million miles from Blackburn, with its expanse of green grass and enormous spreading trees. Queenie stood open-mouthed at such beauty.

'Why haven't we been here before?' she asked.

'Because we've had no call to,' was the curt reply, delivered in a manner which thwarted any further questions.

As they walked down the tree-lined avenue, the width of the road gradually narrowed down to a leafy lane. 'Just a bit farther lass . . . then we're there.'

Almost at once they rounded a crook in the lane, and directly before them was a wide open gateway bearing a board which read:

THE CONVENT OF
NAZARETH HOUSE

To the left of the broad gravelled driveway, a narrow footpath followed the winding bends up the bank to the convent. Queenie trailed behind Auntie Biddy, her excited chatter temporarily silenced by the awesome solitude and magnificent sights all around her. The whispering willows touched and teased them as they passed by, and the bright songs of birds filled the air with happiness. Queenie felt as though this day she'd been whisked off to paradise.

On reaching the top of the winding footpath, Queenie and Auntie Biddy found themselves entering a kind of open courtyard, surrounded by sweeping lawns and colourful shrubberies.

'Oh, Auntie Biddy!' Queenie could hardly believe her eyes. 'It's beautiful!'

'Aye lass,' Auntie Biddy was slow in recovering from the steep climb and her words were strangled, 'it is that. But I still wonder how folks living in such luxury can ever understand folks like us. It don't sit right in my mind!'

Nazareth House stood proudly before them: a great sprawling mansion of grotesque proportions. Its Victorian origin was evident in the additions of ugly haphazard extensions, jutting out at most peculiar angles from both wings of the house. At either side of the central oaken door, wooden-slatted benches rested beneath towering golden conifers.

Queenie's eyes were drawn to the eccentric-looking figure seated on the right-hand bench. The tramp looked up to meet her gaze. 'Morning, young missie,' he said. He was dressed in a long, heavy black coat which reached right down to the floor, all but covering his thick mud-spattered boots. Around his waist, from the frayed string which secured his buttonless coat, hung various artefacts including a white enamel mug covered in dark chipped patches, and a collection of eating tools tied round the ends by a thinner piece of string.

Queenie walked slowly towards the bench, never once taking her eyes off the man even when Auntie Biddy told her, 'Go and sit yourself down, lass. I'll ring yon doorbell.'

The tramp carried on devouring his thick wedge of bread, 'Come on, missie. Come and sit aside o' me.' His long grey beard, which seemed to spread right across his shoulders and down to his knees, waggled and danced as he ate and spoke at the same time.

Queenie sat down beside him, hoping she could dodge the bits of chewed bread which shot out of his mouth in a spray of words. She couldn't see his eyes, because the black felt trilby was so battered and old that the brim had grown limp: it hung over his eyes in a comical, yet sinister fashion. Tearing at a chunk of bread, he offered some to her.

''Ere you are missie . . . you look 'ungrier na me!' He lifted his face in order to fix her in his sight more comfortably. Queenie was taken aback at the un-expected beauty of the tramp's eyes. Black as night they were, and shining liquid beneath the long dark lashes.

'Go on,' he urged her impatiently, 'take it then!'

She took it and thanked him. Then breaking the piece of bread in half, she tucked one piece into her lap. 'That's for my Auntie Biddy,' she explained.

The tramp nodded his head in the direction of the doorway, where Auntie Biddy was engaged in hushed conversation with a black-frocked nun. 'That your Auntie Biddy, is it?'

Queenie turned to look, then swivelled back in her seat and nodded.

'Well! I must say. You look a right pair o' scarecrows an' no mistake!' The thick grey foliage parted to reveal a set of blackened uneven teeth, and Queenie took the movement to be a smile. 'Never mind. They'll look after you 'ere,' he told her.

The old tramp and the young girl deep in conversation presented a strangely disturbing picture to the watching Auntie Biddy, who was experiencing some embarrassment in answering the nun's pointed

questions as to how they had found need to come to
Nazareth House.

Now and again, Queenie's laughter at the tramp's
humorous revelations on life on the road filtered
through the air, bringing a gentle smile to the attentive
face of the listening nun. Auntie Biddy's obvious
concern for Queenie prompted the nun to assure her
gently, 'There's no need to worry about the child . . .
Old King wouldn't harm a soul. He used to be a man
of considerable means – a high-born gentleman.'

'Have you *never* lived in a proper 'ouse?' Queenie
was completely entranced by this stange apparition
before her.

'Got no time for walls and doors!' he told her,
tearing at his bread with the practised skill of a wild
animal. 'But I had a house once . . . and a mother.'
His voice grew soft and distant and his eyes melted
beneath his brows, then with a sharpness which took
Queenie by surprise he demanded of her, '*You* got a
mother, have you?'

Queenie had to search within the hidden pockets of
her heart, where everything precious was securely
stowed away. Nobody had ever mentioned her mother
like that before; all the hurtful questions had only ever
come from within herself. 'No, only my Auntie Biddy,'
she answered, remaining surprisingly in control.

The tramp fixed her hard with the wet blackness of
his eyes. 'Oh,' he said in a sharp pointed voice, finally
looking away to concentrate on his food.

Queenie waited. She sensed he had something more
to say, but suddenly she wanted him to know. 'My
Mam birthed me . . . an' then she died.' Queenie could
hardly believe that was *her* talking! Saying things

out loud which had never seen daylight.

'That's a sadness,' he nodded and waggled his head about, obviously thinking hard on it, 'oh aye, I'd say that was a terrible sadness.'

Suddenly, as if afraid that the conversation was getting to him, he sniffed hard and wiped the back of his hand along his dripping nose. 'That might account for your being an old-fashioned body! No mam to make a childhood for you eh?' He stood up as if to go, but then he turned and looked down on her. 'Don't let folks ever tell you that material things are best! I've had them all . . . money, riches, a fine big house and everything. But it's all empty fashion! When *my* Mam died, I gave everything to the church! Church demands *nothing* in exchange for the care of poor lost souls! Church and God's lovely world! That's all that matters!'

He finished the last of his bread in noisy enjoyment, then cheerfully ambled off towards the footpath. The clattering of his cup and other jangling things hanging from his belt of string sent the birds soaring above the trees in loud protest. As Queenie's gaze followed his departing figure she couldn't help but wonder about him; about those black eyes that looked as if they were crying. She had sensed his unhappiness, and she began to wish he'd stayed just a little longer.

'Sister Magdalen wants us to wait here, Queenie. She'll be out in a few minutes.' Auntie Biddy sat beside her.

Queenie slipped her hand through the crook of Auntie Biddy's arm. 'Why have we come here, Auntie Biddy? Who's Sister Magdalen?'

The embarrassed blue eyes struggled against

Queenie's direct questioning gaze. 'I told you. They're friends of Father Riley's.'

'Yes, I know. But what are *we* here for?' Deep down in her innermost heart Queenie had already guessed, but she wanted so much to hear Auntie Biddy deny it.

'Queenie! Don't ask so many questions, lass. What does it matter *why* we're here? We're among friends.' Her voice trembled and Queenie felt guilty at having asked her. Yet in spite of telling herself that it didn't matter why they were here, the deep shame she felt told her otherwise. It *did* matter. Very much!

Later, Queenie told Auntie Biddy that the huge wedges of bread and dripping, and the enormous tin mugs of hot tea brought to them by Sister Magdalen, were the best she had ever tasted. What she did not say was that every mouthful stuck in her throat. When Auntie Biddy graciously thanked the nun for the two half-crowns slipped into her hand, Queenie was forced to look the other way.

On that lovely spring morning Queenie made herself a fervent promise born out of deep undying love for Auntie Biddy and such frustration that made her want to cry. She would do anything, *anything* to ensure that she and Auntie Biddy would never again have to accept charity.

In the making of it, she inevitably ostracized herself from childhood. She knew that looking after Auntie Biddy was a grown-up's job. And a grown-up was what she would have to be.

Chapter Four

Life was hard. Although Queenie had taken on a much greater workload in order to ensure their independence, the pittance acquired from washing and pressing endless baskets of other folks' laundry provided no luxuries above day to day survival. But Queenie had kept her self-promise in view. They had never since been forced by hunger to seek charitable handouts.

'How's your Auntie Biddy, lass?' the chubby-faced shopkeeper enquired as she held out a large packet of soap-flakes. 'Been right bad, I 'eard tell.'

Queenie counted seven pennies out of her purse, placing them on the counter. She knew old Mrs Farraday was genuinely fond of Auntie Biddy and the gratitude she felt showed in her warm smile as she responded, 'She's fine, Mrs Farraday, just fine.' Then the shopkeeper launched into a volley of complaint regarding all manner of things from the controversial launching of the first Sputnik satellite some months back – it had horrified old folks hereabouts, causing them to warn of God's vengeance at having his heavens invaded – to the prospect of Britain's first motorway, due for opening any time now. 'If that's what they call progress, then the sooner I'm six feet under the turf the better!' she declared, adding with renewed vigour when she spied Queenie glancing through a magazine from the counter, 'and though I say it as shouldn't, being the poor unfortunate as tries to sell them magazines as a bob's worth, they're full o' nowt but blessed adverts! Same as the television these days. Two years now since they first started adverts on the television and it *still* aggravates me the very divil!' She paused, taking a great billowing breath which blew her face into a broad smile. 'Ey, lass! I can remember not so long back when thi' Auntie Biddy 'ad a few sharp words to say about yon magazines, eh?'

Queenie returned the smile, for she too remember-ed. And though it had been some three years back, it seemed like only yesterday when Auntie Biddy had firmly replaced a magazine which Queenie had picked up in this very shop. 'Don't you be bothering yer 'ead with such luxuries!' she'd told Queenie. 'Such things aren't for the likes of us!'

Funny how things like that have stuck in my mind, thought Queenie, realizing with small resentment that her curiosity thereafter had been effectively curtailed. To pay out precious money on such reading matter now would seem something of a betrayal to her Auntie Biddy, especially in the face of Mrs Farraday's gloomy comments about all the advertisements.

Mrs Farraday folded her arms, a signal that she had said her piece. Then, with an acknowledging nod of the head, she watched the tall graceful figure of the thirteen-year-old girl as she moved towards the door. Queenie had grown taller, more self-assured, and, if possible, more beautiful than ever. In spite of the lack of nutritious foods and always having to make do, Queenie positively glowed. Her hair, grown down to the small of her back, was dressed as usual with its length crossing twice over her head in rich thick plaits of honey-coloured silk. Her eyes, while still the soft-grey of a dove, were stronger and more striking, as were her fine proud features, which betrayed nothing of the conflict ever within her.

Mrs Farraday turned as her husband emerged from their living quarters. 'That were young Queenie,' she told him, shaking her head and tutting, 'the lass still can't bring herself to admit her Auntie Biddy's at death's door.'

Mr Farraday was genuinely sorry. 'Aye . . . she's a grand lass, is that. Poor little thing's 'ad a cross o'er 'er back sin' the day she were born. God 'elp 'er when she's left to cope wi' George Kenney on 'er own!'

Mrs Farraday set her chin into the width of her neck, her small eyes bright and angry. 'Wants whipping, does that one! I'd do it meself for nowt!' she snorted angrily.

'Weren't there talk o' Queenie 'aving a brother somewhere?' said Mr Farraday as he rubbed his bald head.

'Aye, it has been said as George Kenney's got a lad hereabouts. There's all manner o' speculation but Biddy won't let the truth out, an' that's a fact!'

'Well . . . 'appen it's just as well. There's nowt to be gained from raking up old cinders.' He looked questioningly at his wife, but she gave no reply. No more words were exchanged on the matter, although their thoughts were alike. This lad of George Kenney's was reckoned to be fetched up amongst wealthy folk – surely he would want to see his sister looked after?

Queenie covered the flagstones along her beloved Parkinson Street with brisk business-like steps. The thick heels of her practical brogue shoes resounded against the concrete paving slabs. Many was the time she had seen and envied other girls of her own age. No practical brogues for them! They'd be all stockings and smart slender-heeled shoes. The run of her thoughts brought a smile to Queenie's face. Oh, and what about their boyfriends? Hair all larded down, and swaggering full of their own importance.

There were plenty of boys who would have fancied Queenie's company. She knew that, from the way they ran after her and ogled her with brazen eyes. But Queenie had no patience with their loud remarks and silly whistling. A faint blush crept its way up her neck and into her cheeks to set them on fire as the image of a particular boy came into her mind. A quiet boy with fair hair and serious brown eyes, he was a friend of Father Riley's. He would often accompany the priest on his regular visits to the house although Queenie never gave Father Riley the satisfaction of accepting his offers of help. She would tell him quite firmly that they were 'managing very well and thank you all the same, but there must be folks more deserving of his charity'.

Father Riley would always smile resignedly and shake his head. He had lately thought of giving up trying to persuade this slip of a lass to accept any help. He respected her for the determined child she was. His thoughts on the matter were invariably confided to his young companion, Rick Marsden, who had long been of the opinion that Queenie was a lovely girl of exceptional character, and one of whom he found himself growing increasingly fond.

Young Rick Marsden came of a good background. His mother, Rita, did a great deal for charity. His father was a mill-owner among other things, and the family were reputed to be very well off. Queenie had often reproached herself for admiring Rick and presuming that the admiration was mutual. A young man of Rick Marsden's stature was not for the likes of her, she knew that. But she could not help her own feelings, however successful she might be in suppressing them. And now it seemed as though her Auntie Biddy had perceived the way she felt towards Rick Marsden, because, against the little woman's kind nature, she had never failed to give him a cool reception. That was a painful thing to Queenie.

Rick Marsden told Queenie that he had thoughts of entering the priesthood, and although Queenie told herself that it was none of her business, she secretly hoped he would change his mind. Father Riley was of the opinion that as Rick was only sixteen, there was time enough for him to do just that.

Queenie cherished wonderful memories of the party for the Ragged School children last Christmas. Auntie Biddy had not been keen to go, but Father Riley would not take no for an answer. 'Just to help,' he assured Queenie, knowing that any other approach would have resulted in a polite refusal.

Queenie had loved every minute of it, and it did her heart good to see Auntie Biddy absorbed in the preparations, because lately the little woman had been so down and fretful. Queenie and Rick had been put in charge of the toy-chests. On Christmas Eve all the well-off folks had brought along all manner of toys and games. Dolls and teddy-bears went into the girls' chest, while the boys' chest quickly filled with trains, lorries, footballs and other exciting treasures. Rick's attractive mother, of small build and elegant dress, had turned out all of Rick's old toys to help swell the gifts for the poorer children. Queenie had felt very much in awe of Mrs Marsden, who seemed to show a particular interest in this young girl whom her son never stopped talking about. But if she occasionally glanced across at Queenie, she made no effort to enter into conversation, except for a kindly word on introduction.

On Christmas morning all the children lined up to choose a toy from the heaped-up chests; Queenie thought that as long as she lived, she would never forget the expressions of delight on their small faces as they went off clutching some second-hand one-eyed teddy or threewheeled lorry. The sadness and anger she felt at their plight was tempered with a feeling of satisfaction that she had at least helped to bring them a small measure of joy.

That night, Queenie had thanked God for her own blessings; especially for her darling Auntie Biddy. She cherished her friendship with Rick, and she remembered how marvellous he had been with the children, and how they seemed to sense his very real affection for them. Since she had first seen Rick at Mass some two years before, Queenie had known that he was very special. He had been at the front of the church, in the pews before the altar. Standing amidst the sea of choir-boys he had sung in solo, and so magnificent was his voice that Queenie had felt herself rooted to the spot.

Twice their eyes had met across the church, and each time Queenie had been unable to stem the fierce blush which coloured her face. She had tried to look away, to concentrate on the twelve steps of Calvary around the church, but the only image she could see was his face, and those hypnotic eyes . . . one moment smiling, the next as deep as a mighty ocean. One bold glance from them and Queenie was lost to all else.

Rick Marsden had since visited their little house with Father Riley, and Queenie was thankful that each time bar one, it was in George Kenney's absence. On the one occasion when George Kenney had been present he had been sprawled in the chair, half drunk. This was the first time Rick had come to the house, and Queenie had been confused by the strained atmosphere he appeared to have created. It was certainly strange that Auntie Biddy greeted Father Riley with less than her usual friendliness, and in a great hurry she had hustled George Kenney up to his room. Queenie put the whole situation down to the fact that the sight of George Kenney, unshaven and drinksodden, had brought shame on Auntie Biddy. Queenie could understand that, for she would have given anything for Rick not to have witnessed such a sorry spectacle.

Since that day, and in spite of Auntie Biddy's inexplicable resistance to their continuing friendship, Queenie and Rick had become firm friends, easy in each other's company.

'I think I want to be a priest,' he'd confided in Queenie, 'but I'm not really sure.' Then, as if to test the quality of what he would be denying himself forever, he had kissed her full and passionately on the lips before making a hasty retreat down the road, leaving Queenie breathless from the intimate contact, and Father Riley wondering why the lad had made off in such a hurry.

Later, when Queenie had told Auntie Biddy about the kiss, her face had grown hot under the ensuing scrutiny. For the first time ever, Queenie found herself wishing she had said nothing. Could George Kenney's obnoxious behaviour be at the root of the little woman's anxieties?

Returning from the shop the next day, Queenie was brought to a rude halt by Mrs Aspen's cheery greeting, 'Well now! You're looking pleased wi' yoursel', an' that's a fact.'

'Oh . . . hello Mrs Aspen,' Queenie replied, keeping her gaze fixed on the front door-lock, thankful when out of the corner of her eye she saw Mrs Aspen go waddling away down the road. The old dear meant well, but Queenie did not feel up to answering her questions today.

Turning the key in the lock, Queenie pushed the door open, stepped into the passageway and closed the door behind her. Pausing for just a moment, she let herself indulge in the memory of Rick's kiss, which still burned on her mouth. As her fingers came up to brush against her lips, she chided herself for imagining that it was anything other than an impetuous action, which Rick had no doubt later regretted.

'Took you bloody long enough!' The familiar cutting voice pierced Queenie's pleasant mood, shattering the warm feeling inside her. 'A body could be sodding well dying, for all you care!' George Kenney's bloated face leered at her accusingly as he snarled, 'Get me fags did you?'

Over the years Queenie had learned not only to endure his cruel taunts and spiteful tongue, but to dismiss them. Crossing the tiny parlour she drew out a thin pack of five Woodbines from her basket and threw them scornfully onto his lap. 'You'll get no more this week!' she told him. 'And if there's no money coming from you again you'll get no food neither.'

George Kenney slung the pack of Woodbines back across the room, laughing cruelly as they skimmed sharply into the corner of Queenie's lip, drawing a bright sliver of blood.

Queenie stooped to collect them from the floor where they fell, and unfussily wiping her mouth, she put the cigarettes back into her basket with a flourish which belied the anger she was feeling at his predictably childish behaviour. 'Please yourself!' she told him flippantly. 'I can always ask Mrs Farraday for the money back.' Then, going out into the passage to hang up her coat, she sneaked a backward glance and smiled knowingly as she saw George Kenney slyly retrieve the pack of Woodbines.

Nothing more would be said about the incident, which Queenie stored away with the many other farcical scenes they had enacted for so long. At first, George Kenney's blatant hatred of her had seared painfully into her young impressionable heart. There had been hatred in her retaliation, and bitterness at having been deprived of a father who might cherish her, as her schoolfriends were cherished. But now – Queenie sighed deeply as she made her way up the narrow stairs to Auntie Biddy – *now*, it didn't matter. There was little hatred or bitterness left in her, only a deep sense of loss. The only light in her life, and the only person who filled her days with meaning, lay upstairs.

Queenie tiptoed into the bedroom. If her Auntie Biddy was still asleep, then Queenie's exit would be just as silent. But Auntie Biddy's fitful bouts of coughing constantly woke her from the rare spasmodic nap. Even during these infrequent naps, she seemed to be denied restful sleep as her mind churned over and over, delving into the past and crying out in deranged mumbles of which Queenie could make neither head nor tail.

'Is that you, Queenie?' she called out now.

Queenie entered the room and crossed to the window. 'Yes, Auntie Biddy. I thought you might still be asleep.' She raised her arms and drew back the curtains, pausing for a moment to gaze fondly across the familiar skyline over Parkinson Street. A skip of pleasure fleeted through her thoughts as the sun alighted on her young features. 'Oh Auntie Biddy, it's going to be a beautiful day,' she murmured. There was no reply as Auntie Biddy slipped again into drowsiness and a painful expression scarred Queenie's grey eyes as her thoughts were drawn back over the last twenty-four hours.

Yesterday had been her fourteenth birthday. It had arrived and departed with no special sense of significance. Auntie Biddy had been too ill to remember, and it would have broken her kindly heart had she realized. George Kenney, though, had remembered. It was a date he would never let Queenie forget because of the fact that Kathy had been taken from him, and in her place was this girl Queenie, who tore at his conscience mercilessly. For Queenie, it had been a day of mixed emotions. She had finished the housework and laundry chores, then after settling Auntie Biddy to sleep, and watching George Kenney negotiate his way painfully down Parkinson Street towards the Navigation, she had gone quietly back upstairs to seat herself in wistful thought at the dresser.

Here, the picture of her mother had smiled back at her, and Queenie had been lost in speculation over what might have been. The dark stunning beauty of the woman who had died giving birth to her held Queenie captivated, as she wished with all of her heart that she could have known her mother. With her arms around the picture, Queenie had given vent to the heartache which had been suppressed for so long and the sorrowful sobs permeated the air with such distress that Auntie Biddy was awakened. She had seen and stayed silent. There was nothing for her to say . . . nothing that she could do to relieve the child's heartache. Unable to stem the tears, Auntie Biddy had whispered a heartfelt prayer.

'Dear God above,' she asked, 'oh, please help her, for she's only a child and she'll soon be alone.'

Now, the morning after, Auntie Biddy had watched Queenie, her poor dying eyes pained by the quick rush of light which infiltrated the room. 'Are you all right, lass?' she asked.

Queenie shrugged off the lingering thoughts of her birthday. It was gone . . . and what did it matter anyroad? Pushing the window up just far enough to allow the merest suggestion of a light breeze into the room, she told Auntie Biddy in a cheerful voice, 'Don't want no draughts in here, do we, eh?' She moved towards the bed as she went on, ' 'Course I'm all right, why shouldn't I be?'

'Oh, you just seemed lost in thought, that's all.' Then changing the subject, Auntie Biddy asked, 'Where's your dad?'

Queenie had long ceased to regard George Kenney as her 'dad', even though her sense of loyalty demanded that he was her responsibility, and in spite of the fact that she had been unable to rid herself of the guilt for her mother's absence.

'He's gone off to the Navigation,' Queenie explained, adding with a little smile, 'with a packet of Woodbines in his pocket.'

'Been buying 'is fags again have you, Queenie?' Auntie Biddy groaned. 'Lord only knows what's going to become o' that one!'

Queenie sat down on the bed, reaching forward to kiss the yellowing face. 'Oh, he'll not come to any harm. He's craftier than a waggonload of monkeys . . . you know that.'

Auntie Biddy grasped the slim hand which stroked her forehead lovingly. 'No, he won't come to no harm, lass, because he's lucky enough to have you for a daughter – though God knows he's never deserved you.' She squeezed Queenie's hand as her voice fell away in embarrassment. 'He hasn't fotched any more o' them . . . women home, has he?' she enquired.

Queenie smiled reassuringly, 'No, he has not.' She omitted to state her belief that it was only a temporary reprieve in view of him probably not being able to find one that could fancy him. The George Kenney they once knew was no longer the pivot of attention, leastwise not in the way he would have preferred. He had taken to muttering to himself more and more, and once, when he'd filled his insides to overflowing with booze, even his natural functions had gone beyond his control. The story had been spread by Fountain Crossland who, since his undignified ejection from the house by Auntie Biddy, had taken great delight in slandering George Kenney at every opportunity. 'Stood agin that bloody bar like a 'elpless babby,' he would impart to the eager listeners, 'all down 'is sodding leg it were! Pissed 'isself 'e did – ran out 'is trousers and down 'is leg like a bloody river!'

Queenie had kept it all from Auntie Biddy, who entreated her now, 'Finished with them kind o' women is he? That's good, lass, there's still a spark o' decency in 'im then?'

'Must be,' lied Queenie.

The only breakfast Auntie Biddy could manage was a softly boiled egg . . . she couldn't even finish her treasured mug of tea. As a result Queenie moved about all day in a state of increasing anxiety. She'd always had this fixed notion, due no doubt to Auntie Biddy's upbringing, that lost appetite was lost health. The thought nagged at her as she went about her chores.

'How's your Auntie Biddy then, lass?' Grey-haired Mrs Aspen kept a wooden box by the back yard wall. Whenever she noticed Queenie hanging out the washing, she'd hoist her fat little form onto the box and stretch her short neck to peep over. Queenie found it amusing; although she was utterly convinced that one of these fine days, there'd be an almighty clattering and crashing as roly-poly Mrs Aspen fell off her rostrum.

Queenie halted the great mangle roller, leaving Mr Eddies' long-johns squirming half in and half out. Then walking over to the wall, she told Mrs Aspen in a small voice, 'Oh, she *says* she feels all right . . . but she'll not eat anything! I'm that worried, Mrs Aspen.'

'Is she still coughing, lass?'

Queenie could not deny it. 'The coughing's worse,' she admitted, 'a lot worse.'

'Look, lass, I knows 'ow you feel, an' if there's owt I can do you've only to let me know,' she said as her eyes glanced nervously towards the back door, 'but I'll not come nowhere near that black divil, George Kenney! Oh, but never you worry, lass. Yon Dr Noel is as good as they come. One o' the best welfare doctors there is, I'm telling you!'

Queenie smiled. She knew that and she also knew that Mrs Aspen was a genuine friend to her and Auntie Biddy. Right now Queenie needed a favour, and much as she hated to put on this dear little soul there was no real choice. 'Mrs Aspen . . . would you please sit with Auntie Biddy for an hour? I've to take the pressing round and I'm afraid to leave her.' She perceived Mrs Aspen's hesitance, and promised, 'George Kenney's out and he'll not be back afore me.'

Satisfied that Queenie would not claim such a thing if it were not so, Mrs Aspen nodded and disappeared. Five minutes later she reappeared at Auntie Biddy's front door. 'Go on then, lass,' she told Queenie, 'but be as quick as you can. I don't want to be faced wi' that George Kenney!'

The laundry round was not as considerable as it used to be. Nosey-Parker Hindle, for one, had shown her faith in Queenie by sending round a note:

I'll not be needing your services any more.
I don't want no slip of a girl doing my washing.
I'll make other arrangements.

Mrs Hindle

In a way, Queenie was glad. She had never seen
anybody rile Auntie Biddy like that woman had. But
the few shillings got from her were sorely missed.

Big Jack Rawtenstall had grown weary from the
waiting for Auntie Biddy, and a couple of months back
he'd taken on a wife who had persuaded him to indulge
in what Auntie Biddy and folks hereabouts described
as 'one o' them newfangled washing tubs as dance and
agitate the clothes to shreds'.

It was a sad fact, and one which affected Queenie
and her heavy responsibilities, that the few folk who'd
got money to pay for their washing to be done were
slowly but surely getting caught up in the novelty of
these new inventions. Widow Hargreaves of course,
had one standing in her scullery, all bright and shiny.
But she was downright scared of it. That didn't bother
Queenie none. If stuck-up Widow Hargreaves had so
much more money than sense that she could buy a
machine just to show off to one and all, then it was all
the better for Queenie! It seemed that for a while at
least Widow Hargreaves' money could be counted on.

Then there was old Mr Ambler, residing on the
corner opposite Mrs Farraday's. He was too bent and
crooked to do for himself, so his sister, who lived two
doors away, paid Queenie six shillings to fetch and
carry his washing. Mr Ambler was an old misery,

always at his happiest when moaning and groaning. So Queenie never stayed long. He seemed to have the power to depress her . . . and she could do without that!

As Queenie pointed the pram into Queen Victoria Street she recalled with pleasure the many times she and Auntie Biddy had trundled down here. The pleasure she felt was interspersed with pangs of sadness. There she was, following in Auntie Biddy's footsteps, washing and pressing other folks' washing as she had vowed never to do. And there was her Auntie Biddy lying in bed weak and wasted.

Queenie's grey eyes reflected the sorrow which pierced her heart and dragged her step. She had promised Mrs Aspen that she'd get right back, and with that in mind, Queenie hastened towards the last familiar house.

Fancy Carruthers had died some twelve month back now; just gone off to sleep and never woke up again. Miss Tilly had left her friend resting on the pillow for two whole days before she had decided to catch the milkman's attention and ask for help. It was said that she cried for a week after they'd taken Fancy away and nobody nor nothing could persuade her to go to the funeral.

For a long time afterwards, Miss Tilly would not speak. She just smiled vacantly, nodding her green frilly cap and sighing, until everyone felt sure that she would not be long behind her little friend.

'Miss Tilly!' Queenie raised her voice to pierce the old dear's deafness, 'Are you there Miss Tilly? It's only Queenie come wi' the washing.'

'All right Queenie, lass,' came the thin reply.

Queenie hurried down the passage to the parlour door. Pushing the door open with her elbow, she edged in and placed the pile of clean pressing on a stand-chair.

Miss Tilly was propped up against a bolster. Her huge watery-blue eyes were now drained of the vivacity which Queenie had always admired so, and their size, which had always been considerable, seemed even more prominent in the shrinking folds of her aged face. It struck Queenie that the smile which had always been perpetual on Miss Tilly's face had developed into a peculiar fixed grimace. A feeling of overpowering helplessness engulfed Queenie as she moved towards the old woman.

Miss Tilly swivelled her enormous eyes upwards to focus squarely on Queenie. 'Hello little 'un,' she piped in an odd shrill voice, lifting a hand for Queenie to grasp, 'Oh, I miss her you know.' She glanced at the pillow beside her, then looked away quickly as though afraid of what she might see. 'Took her away, they did, Queenie, been my darling friend for sixty-odd years . . .' Her wrinkled mouth lifted ever so carefully at the corners and a big pear-shaped tear fell out of one eye. 'Oh, Queenie lass,' she croaked, ''taint the same no more wi'out her.'

Queenie bent to wipe away the solitary tear. Then settling down beside her, she lay back into Fancy's pillow, her arms around Miss Tilly's frail shoulders. 'I know,' she murmured comfortingly, 'I miss her too.'

For a while until Miss Tilly lifted her head from Queenie's shoulder, the two of them lay still in each other's arms. Eventually, on Miss Tilly's insistence, Queenie collected her shillings from the sideboard, after which she busied herself to leave Miss Tilly with a bowl of hot soup and a wedge of bread to soak in it. As she wended her way back along Queen Victoria Street, Queenie's concern for Miss Tilly was tempered by the knowledge that the welfare did apparently send someone round on a regular basis, to keep an eye on the old dear.

Heading the empty pram over to the far side of Queen Victoria Street, Queenie hurried as she thought of Auntie Biddy and Mrs Aspen waiting at home.

At the corner of Pump Street and Waterfall Mill, there stood a monstrous monument known as the 'Cob o' Coal'. It stood proud over the wooden cobbles, towering over the two horse troughs on its either side, and filling the little square with its awesome dimensions. Nine feet tall with a skirt dimension of twenty feet or more it was, raw and shiny black hard as the day it was wrestled out by the miners from its long resting place beneath the ground.

The respectable body of coal-merchants had proudly transported it through the town on a flat-waggon, to the tune of a playing band and the happy singing of following armies . . . young and old alike. It was skilfully erected on the site, cordoned off by a spiky iron fence, then adorned with a shiny brass plaque which boasted of the virtues of the coal-merchants and the quality of their coal.

That was six years ago. Since then, the raging poverty and slacking pride of Blackburn's deprived folk had seen the proud hulk of coal disintegrate until it had shrunk into a hump-backed deformity of which no one could be proud, least of all the coal-merchants. It was raw rock-coal, unrefined and unsuitable for domestic fires because of the spitting sparks which resulted from the burning, together with the pungent smell it emitted. But that never bothered the poor folk, least of all Queenie. In the pitch black of a cold January night some two years back, Queenie had found herself sneaking through the back streets like a common thief to fill her bucket with a chunk of that precious monument, more scarce than gold. It eased her own conscience somewhat to find that at least a dozen other folk had travelled the self-same path and were all quietly chipping and picking away to fill their little galvanized buckets. Hardened by necessity, they did it all openly, without shame or fear of reprisal.

Queenie was certain that it would not be long before the eyesore was removed altogether by the authorities. Picking up the loose scaly stuff which had fallen from the crumbling heap Queenie laid it carefully in the bottom of her pram, then headed for home.

Full of thought and reflection on the issues of life, she had not been alert to the fact that her wandering feet had carried her down the narrow ginnel which led to Carter's Brook. As her path became less smooth and increasingly difficult to negotiate, Queenie realized with a stab of surprise that she and the coal-laden pram were meandering along the footpath which ran alongside the brook.

Smiling quietly at her foolish daydreaming, she swung the pram round towards the next ginnel which would take her back onto Parkinson Street. As she did so her eyes swept the far bank, and what she saw astonished her, drawing her gaze like a magnet; although she would have preferred to run from that place without seeing anything.

It was Sheila who spoke first, seeming surprised and amused by Queenie's unexpected intrusion. 'Queenie! What you doing down the Brook?' Stepping away from Rick Marsden, she gave a loud and vulgar laugh which echoed across the narrow span of water. ''Taint no place for angels!' she called.

When Rick Marsden glanced directly at Queenie's blushing face, she wished herself a thousand miles away. Rick, of all people . . . here with Sheila. But of course, Sheila was everything *she* was not: confident and carefree, there was no man to whom she wasn't attractive. And if she'd decided to set her cap at Rick Marsden, there was very little that could be done to stop her. If Queenie had been aware of it before, there was now no doubt whatsoever that she loved Rick so much that just to look at him caused her pain. As they stood, each intent upon the other, Queenie was persuaded that Rick's initial look of surprise had dissipated into a reflection of what she herself was feeling at that moment. Sensing that his quiet eyes were asking her to understand more than she was capable of, she lowered her gaze to the ground and disappeared hastily down the ginnel.

After a long hard day collecting and returning laundry, the utterly exhausted Queenie crawled into bed before ten o'clock. She had spoon-fed Auntie Biddy with a cup of warm broth, and made her as comfortable as could be. Now she lay in bed, unable to sleep, her thoughts disturbed by many things, not least the memory of Sheila and Rick arm in arm down the brook today. But most of all Queenie was disturbed by the doctor's parting words this evening, after he had seen Auntie Biddy.

'You know your aunt's very ill, don't you, Queenie? It's best that you prepare yourself for the worst . . . fetch me at once.'

The tears burned hot beneath Queenie's closed eyelids as she reached out to take Auntie Biddy's hand in her own. She squeezed it tight, as though willing her own strength into it, but the small fingers were cold, and life seemed already to be ebbing away. All manner of pleas to God, to this little woman she loved and to the forces of good which she believed did exist – rose into Queenie's throat, only to gather there in such a great tight lump that she could utter none of them.

Finally, in spite of the fearful thoughts careering through her troubled mind, Queenie gave herself up to sleep.

It seemed to Queenie that almost as soon as she had closed her eyes she was wide awake again, feeling instinctively that something was wrong. 'Auntie Biddy?' she called softly as she lit the night-light. A glance at the bedside clock told her that she had been in bed just over an hour. Eleven o'clock! And George Kenney wasn't home, because she would have heard his fumbling and cursing. So what had woken her?

She looked across at Auntie Biddy, sleeping peacefully. Crossing to the window, Queenie opened the curtains; Parkinson Street was quiet. The only sign of life was the flickering flame in the gas-lamp a few doors away. Opening the window as quietly as she could, Queenie leaned out. Mrs Aspen's light was still on. 'Sewing, I expect,' muttered Queenie . . . Mrs Aspen did some lovely embroidery. She looked hard and long down the length of Parkinson Street. Funny how folks seem to clutter a place up and spoil it, thought Queenie, her agitated mind somewhat calmed by the serenity of the street at night.

Even the air, usually thick black from belching factory chimneys, tasted thin and sweet. The quietness was almost overwhelming. And with that realization came another, causing Queenie to freeze in horror as her mind fought to reject the obvious. She had not heard the persistent cough which plagued Auntie Biddy even while she slept. Queenie prayed that she was wrong, but even as she turned from the window and crossed to the bed, she knew.

Next door, Mrs Aspen jumped with fright, dropping the needle across the tapestry on her lap as the griefstricken wail filled the air. 'Jack! Jack!' she cried, prodding the dozing man in the chair, 'Lord help us, I think it's Biddy.' Without waiting for an acknowledgement, she rushed next door. 'Queenie! Queenie, lass,' she called through the letter box. 'Let me in, gel.'

Muffled sobs and the sound of slowly descending footsteps filtered down the stairs as Mrs Aspen straightened up, and after a moment the front door opened to reveal the painful drawn face of Queenie. For what seemed an eternity to Mrs Aspen the girl stood staring at the little figure before her, unable to see for the moving river across her sight. After a while Mrs Aspen reached out a hand, her sharp piggy eyes bright with trembling tears at the look of terrible grief on Queenie's face. 'Is it your Auntie Biddy, lass?' she asked, her voice a thick whisper.

With a desolate cry Queenie crumpled to her knees and fell into the outstretched arms. 'Oh . . . please say she's not dead. . . say she's not, oh, Mrs Aspen . . .'

The broken words tumbled out incoherently, and murmuring words of comfort Mrs Aspen manoeuvred herself and Queenie into the passage, when of a sudden she was taken unawares by Queenie wrenching away to run back up the stairs, her voice pitched with hysteria, 'It's not true! I won't let it be.'

It was the first time Queenie's small world had been touched by the cold fingers of death, and they clutched cruelly at her heart. Now, as she looked on the dearly loved and familiar face of her Auntie Biddy, Queenie suffered such emotions of plunging depths and powerful magnitude that every sense in her body was taut with agony. There was nothing to console her . . . no one to whom she could turn. Anger, frustration and awful helplessness racked her being, and she was hopelessly lost. Through a tortuous mist, she looked down on the quiet still face. 'Why did you leave me?' she asked gently, but in her voice there was an element of accusation. 'Why have you left me all alone, Auntie Biddy?'

Mrs Aspen looked on helplessly, furtively dabbing at the tears which toppled down her chubby face in a steady stream.

Queenie tenderly gathered her Auntie Biddy into her arms. 'Where have you gone?' she whispered, raining gentle kisses on the small wasted face, free now from earthly pain and suffering. 'Oh Auntie Biddy, why didn't you take me with you?' Clasping the small figure to her heart, Queenie buried her head in the sleep-bedraggled grey hair. Unable to see now for the thickness of the tears which clouded her eyes and ran down her face into her mouth, Queenie traced a loving finger around the features of that adored face that would never smile at her again. She felt strangely alienated from all around her and the grief within her became a madness as she whispered, 'I won't let them take you, my darling . . . you'll stay here with me, in our room.'

Mrs Aspen was not known for her softness, but now she wept unashamedly at the tragic sight before her. 'No more, child,' she said softly, 'no more.' Then gripping Queenie by the shoulders, she told her, 'You mustn't punish yourself no more.'

Queenie turned her tragic grey eyes up towards the voice. What did she want? What was Mrs Aspen doing in her Auntie Biddy's room? Of a sudden Queenie was made to think, and reason prevailed. It was as though she had just awoken from a dream, a kind of jigsaw nightmare where all the pieces had become disjointed; but which had now begun to form a grotesque pattern which she finally had to recognize. 'Auntie Biddy . . . she's . . . ?'

Mrs Aspen's face crinkled into distorted folds, as though she was suppressing a weight behind it. 'Aye, lass . . . she's gone,' she sobbed.

The words were slow to sink in even now and Queenie's mind played around with them before allowing them into her heart. Turning back towards the bed, she laid her Auntie Biddy back into the pillow with the greatest reverence. The pain inside her was all-consuming, devouring her until she thought she must scream out, and throwing herself across the thin gaunt form in the bed she wept as never before, her tears running into Auntie Biddy's hair and face.

Mrs Aspen let the child sob – better out than in, was her heartfelt belief. After a while Queenie knelt by the bed, her hands folded in prayer as she begged the Good Lord, 'Please take care of my Auntie Biddy . . . and tell her that I'll love her for as long as I live.'

She did not hear Mrs Aspen depart to seek assistance. She only knew that her world had suddenly become a very cold empty place. How would she ever get through the days without her Auntie Biddy there? The thought of living in this house with only George Kenney for company froze her heart to stone.

Chapter Five

For weeks after the light of her life had been laid to rest, Queenie wandered about in a daze. Any slight sound or movement outside the house brought her rushing to the door, convinced that her darling Auntie Biddy would be waiting on the flagstones. Then gradually, as the long unbearable weeks ran into months, and the months accumulated into a year, she found she could think retrospectively without the deep despondency which had hitherto followed.

The night Auntie Biddy left this world, several of the neighbours had helped Queenie to bathe and lay out the poor thin remains. After which, Queenie and the women had sat silent and respectful by the flickering night-lights, keeping watch while Auntie Biddy slept her final sleep. It had been well into the early hours when George Kenney had staggered home, hopelessly befuddled.

Queenie thought she would remember the bitterness of his sobbing for as long as she lived. She had never heard him cry that way before and, somehow, his tears of grief and remorse helped Queenie to forgive him for the way he'd treated the sister who had never wavered in her love for him.

But he wouldn't . . . couldn't face Biddy. He sat

huddled downstairs all night; as sober in an instant as Queenie had ever seen him. Not once did he make any effort to climb the stairs to where his sister lay and not once in all that long night did he speak of her to anyone. During the church ceremony, he had sat right at the back: 'As if to stay near an escape route from God's wrath,' thought Queenie wryly.

In the following weeks, it had seemed to one and all that George Kenney had finally mended his ways. He begged booze money from no one, and he even tramped about looking for work. He treated Queenie in the same uninterested manner, with the occasional verbal atack but the lashings of his spiteful tongue didn't seem as sharp to Queenie; or maybe, she thought, it was because he didn't have the power to hurt her like he once could. His abstinence from booze did not last, though. It couldn't! His way of life was too steeped in it. He did not get a job; there were plenty who claimed that he had not looked hard enough nor wanted one badly enough, and Queenie didn't know what to believe. Within six months of the funeral, it was however plain to her that George Kenney was rapidly slipping back to his old habits.

Queenie was fifteen now, and the promise of beauty which had filled her formative years blossomed and glowed. Her expressive grey eyes had deepened, perhaps by the sorrow she had borne, and her figure was as fine and graceful as a willow sapling. The honey-gold hair sometimes hung long and free down her back, but more often than not she wore it the way Auntie Biddy had liked, crossed over the top of her head in thick silky plaits.

The insistent tapping on the front door disturbed her

concentrated efforts to weave the same magic over a pair of George Kenney's holey socks as her Auntie Biddy always had. But somehow, the ravelled threads she painstakingly drew together seeemed bumpy and misshapen by comparison. The tapping grew impatient. Queenie sighed and lifted her lovely head, squeezing the half-darned socks and skein of wool back into the tin at her feet.

Making her way to the front door, she speculated as to who it might be. George Kenney was out like a light upstairs and she hoped it wasn't one of his cronies. An angry expression darkened her features as she thought on the night before, when they had fetched him home drunk as a lord.

'Oh . . . it's you.' Queenie's voice registered both surprise and pleasure as she swung the door open and Sheila pushed past to wend her way into the parlour.

''Course it's me!' she retorted. 'You ain't got no secret lovers, 'ave you? Rick Marsden wouldn't like that!' She disappeared into the parlour with a backward wink.

Queenie found her rubbing her hands together to warm them in front of the fire. 'I'll make us a brew,' she told her, going immediately through to the scullery.

'It's enough to freeze the balls off a brass monkey out there!' Sheila's words collapsed into a noisy shudder as she took the mug of tea from Queenie. 'I'm bloody stiff wi' cold!' she said shivering, wrapping her hands around the mug and touching her face with it. 'Aw . . . that's great.'

'Pull the chair up to the fire,' Queenie instructed her, at the same time inching her own nearer. Sheila had given her the goose-pimples. Just for a moment she watched as Sheila clumsily dragged the chair across the oilcloth, her tea plopping and dripping from the mug in her hand. Then placing her own mug on the mantelpiece, Queenie went to her assistance, where the two of them made light of the task.

'Sloppy bugger, ain't I?' Sheila said as she glanced at the small circular pools of tea on the oilcloth. 'Never mind,' she laughed, bending down to use her coat-cuff as a floorcloth, 'worse things 'appen at sea, they say!'

Queenie laughed out loud, 'Yes! You *are* a sloppy bugger!' she agreed. But she was always glad to see Sheila, sloppy or not. How like her mother she grew day by day – in another twenty years, thought Queenie, there'd be no telling the two of them apart, as Maisie was now, so Sheila would be. Taking stock of her now, Queenie was not surprised to see that the girl's features had taken on the same thick-set attraction of her mother's. The short hair might be dark, but then so was Maisie's under the brassy peroxide.

Sheila's weakest features were her eyes. A sort of shadowy speckled colour, they lacked strength and character, always shifting beneath another's gaze, something Queenie found slightly unnerving. Although Queenie was unaware of it, Sheila envied her quiet friend's deep grey eyes which, steadfast and honest, spoke volumes on their own.

'Went to the flicks last night, gel,' offered Sheila in between slurps of tea.

'That's three times this week!' Queenie laughed.

'Oh, I know! And I'd be there *every* night if I could tap me Mam a bit more often. She's getting to be a bit of a skinflint . . . I 'ad to satisfy myself with sitting in the one and threepennies last night. Imagine – *me* in the bloody flea-pits!' Her face was a picture as it related to Queenie the horror of such a thing. 'But ooh, that Tyrone Power! I could do 'im a good turn, I'll tell you! That Virginia Mayo wouldn't stand a chance aside o'me!'

'Oh, it's Tyrone Power now, is it? Last week it was Errol Flynn,' teased Queenie.

'True gel . . . but they do say as variety's the spice o' life, eh?'

There followed much laughter, with Queenie being treated to every detail of the film. Then the subject exhausted, Sheila asked, 'Lordship in bed, is 'e?' She slipped her shoes off and stretched her toes in front of the fire. 'Me Mam were down the Navigation last night early on. She said as 'ow George Kenney got into such a state that 'e 'ad to be fotched 'ome . . .' Without waiting for confirmation of this fact she chattered on, 'Sick as a parrot 'e were! Me Mam says 'e's not half the man 'e used to be . . . pisses 'isself an' all!' She wrinkled her nose in disgust. '*You* don't 'ave to clean 'im up an' wash them pissy dothes, do you, Queenie?'

Queenie could understand how Sheila must feel. She had felt that way herself at first, but now she'd learned to knuckle down and get it over with. 'Yes I have to clean him up, Sheila. If I didn't, who would, eh?' As the humiliation rose in her, her voice took on an angry edge.

Sheila could see that she had touched on a sore spot. 'Tek no notice o' me, gel! All the same though, I'd get the welfare round if it were me . . . 'e's bloody senile! Wants looking at! Them bloody welfare they're not daft, are they? It suits 'em to let *you* take all the responsibility! Me Mam says that's why they've turned a blind eye to you not going to school. Crafty buggers! You get some 'elp, gel . . . shake the buggers up!'

Queenie didn't expect her friend to understand; not really. For Sheila had not lived with George Kenney all these years. She had no way of knowing how it was and no words that Queenie knew could ever explain. 'The welfare? Well, they would just smile and nod, and report that George Kenney was doing all right in the capable hands of his daughter . . . then they'd disappear back into their hidey-holes.'

Sheila was surprised at the cynicism in Queenie's voice. But she was *not* surprised when Queenie added, 'No. I'll not ask the welfare for help, Sheila. Auntie Biddy left me to look after George Kenney, and I'll see to it on my own.'

There were times when Sheila felt unusually humble in Queenie's presence, and this was one of those times. 'I expect *you* will cope, Queenie,' she told her, 'but I'm buggered if *I* could! Me, I'd turn the old sod out onto the street an' bolt the door agin' 'im!'

Having said her piece, she got to her feet and promptly changed the subject. 'I'm going to Teddy's for a sarsaparilla. You coming, are you? Rick'll be there.' A devious smile spread over her face. ''E fancies you some'at rotten does Rick,' added Sheila slyly.

Queenie's heart leapt at the mere mention of Rick Marsden's name, and her face grew bright pink as she tried to hide it in the depths of her tea-mug. 'Don't be silly, Sheila,' she murmured.

'I'm telling you, Queenie! Remember that time when you saw us down Carter's Brook?' She waited

for Queenie to confirm it. Queenie gave no acknowledgement, but she remembered with every fibre of
her being. 'Don't tell me you've forgotten, Queenie,'
teased Sheila. 'Anyways I 'ad me sights on that one.
But I might 'a been a bloody chimney for all 'e could
see! It were "Queenie this" and "Queenie that".'
Winking knowingly, Sheila went on, ''E pumped me
about the fellas in your life. I told 'im there weren't
none, 'acause you didn't give the poor sods a look in!'
Throwing her hands up in the air, she gave a great sigh
and said, 'Now get yourself ready. You're coming
down Teddy's wi' me!'

Queenie regarded her drab clothes, and she thought
on all the darning to be done. Oh, she wanted to see
Rick more than anything, but she felt so ashamed of
her appearance. Auntie Biddy's clothes, even though
painstakingly altered and extended, were nothing to
be proud of. Even so the thought of his eyes on her
charged Queenie's heart to race.

Sipping her tea, Queenie feigned interest in Sheila's
incessant chatter but all the while her mind was on Rick
Marsden, only vaguely aware of Sheila's vivid
description of an argument which had taken place
between herself and her mother. 'Chucked me out, she
did, rotten ol' cow!' exploded Sheila. 'All 'cause she
caught me spying through the bathroom key'ole at our
Raymond.' She threw her head back and let out a roar
of laughter. ''Taint as though 'e 'ad owt worth spying
on! Like a bloody twopenny-halfpenny winkle it
were,' she screamed.

Queenie was all attention now. She could easily
imagine the irrepressible Sheila on her knees by the
bathroom door and it took only a small stretch of the

imagination to appreciate the scene which would have followed between Maisie and her daughter. As always, Sheila's infectious laughter lifted her spirits, 'Sheila Thorogood! You're a right shocker,' Queenie told her.

Sheila thought how beautiful Queenie was, and it hurt her to realize how lonely she must be since Auntie Biddy had been gone. 'Right then,' she declared, 'there's no argument! You're coming to Teddy's with me.' Stretching herself to yank Queenie out of the chair, she ordered her upstairs to put a frock on.

Ten minutes later Queenie returned to present herself for Sheila's inspection; with her brown pinafore dress over a high-necked black shirt, her face scrubbed shiny and her glowing hair nestled into thick soft plaits, she waited for Sheila's judgement.

Sheila eyed her up and down. 'Bloody Nora! Is them your best clothes?'

Queenie had grown impatient at the prospect of seeing Rick again; but now her sense of excitement deserted her and even though she was used to Sheila's forthright tongue, she felt miserable and deflated. 'I've got no more,' she replied, trying hard not to show her disappointment, 'perhaps I shouldn't go, Sheila. I don't want to show you up.'

Sheila laughed disarmingly. 'Oh, kid! I were only joking. You look smashing . . . really! Anyroad, you're so bloody gorgeous nobody'll notice what you're wearing.'

It was only a ten-minute walk to Teddy's shop, off the High Street and down a cobbled alley. Teddy was a twisted dwarfed figure, with huge pink eyes and a bald head. His little shop, well known throughout

Blackburn, sold the finest herbs, spices, Woodbines and snuff. It was a delightfully quaint old shop, with layers of deep shelves from floor to ceiling. Each shelf was crammed with jars containing green rosemary, black liquorice, wood sticks, brown snuff, pink and yellow barley-twists and hundreds of other colourful herbs and remedies of all shape and description. It was said that he knew how to cure everything from a toe-ache to a broken heart.

The deep glass-fronted counter where you paid for your purchases was filled with spacious tubs of different-coloured Khali, a kind of fizzy sherbet powder; along the floor against every wall stood enormous stone bottles of sarsaparilla, a delicious tar-coloured liquid which stung your nose and brought tears to your eyes. A long narrow glass of sarsaparilla was a real treat and was usually drunk in comfort and leisure on the 'staying seat'. The staying seat was tucked away out of sight behind a green curtain. Anyone fancying a measure of sarsaparilla just sat themselves down on it, and waited for Teddy to serve them.

As Queenie rounded the green curtain her every nerve was leaping with anticipation at seeing Rick. When she saw that he was not there her heart sank. The staying seat was empty, and the cubicle felt cold as she followed Sheila in and sat down alongside her. Teddy poked his head round from behind the counter. ''Ow do, young 'uns,' he said, his mouth stretching back across his face to give him the look of a surprised goblin. 'That's it. Just you set yourselves down there. I'll be nobbut a minute.'

No sooner had Teddy brought the two girls their

sarsaparilla than the shop door opened to the sound of the bell overhad, and even before she heard his greeting to Teddy, Queenie knew that it was Rick.

'There you are,' Sheila whispered, 'didn't I tell you?' Swinging the green curtain back to reveal their whereabouts, she shouted, 'We're in 'ere, 'andsome!'

If Queenie could have melted away into the bench, she would most certainly have done so. Sheila had a way of relaying things that made Queenie feel as though the whole world and its mother was looking at her. 'Sheila . . . don't embarrass him,' she urged her giggling companion.

'Give o'er!' Sheila retorted as she dug her elbow into Queenie's side. 'That's half the fun, love.'

As Rick bent his head to enter the cubicle his gaze fell on Queenie, and when he murmured her name it was with an intimacy that shut out everyone else.

Certain that he must hear the violent antics of her heart, Queenie breathed in and forced herself to greet him with a calm that she was certainly not feeling. The four walls seemed to close in on her as he continued to search her face with those fathomless dark eyes. All the while, Queenie could feel herself growing hotter and hotter beneath the intimacy of his gaze. Only now did he step forward, and as he straightened up the whole cubicle seemed to diminish. 'Sheila,' he nodded in greeting and at once his eyes were drawn back to Queenie.

'Like a pair o' bloody love-birds!' Sheila shouted, tainting the situation with her own special brand of vulgarity. ''Ere, Teddy! Fetch what you like. It won't matter if it's poison . . . thse two won't know the difference!' The raucous laughter echoed round the shop, and it struck Queenie that there seemed to be a measure of malice in Sheila's voice that she had never heard before. It came to her that Sheila, too, was deeply in love, possibly for the first time, with Rick Marsden. So, all that bravado and match-making was a cover-up for her real feelings? What a blind fool she'd been not to have realized it earlier.

Queenie's shame quickly deepened the blush of pleasure on her face into the heat of embarrassment as she saw things for what they really were. For some reason, Sheila had deliberately made a fool of her. It was obvious that if a man like Rick was about to choose between herself and a lively attractive girl like Sheila . . . well, there was no doubt in *her* mind as to what would be the outcome.

'I'm sorry,' she blurted out, getting to her feet with self-conscious awkwardness, 'I have to go.' She hated the way the two of them stared at her, Sheila with her mouth open. And she was painfully aware of her dowdy clothes, and the foolish notion she had entertained that Rick could ever feel the same way about her as she did for him.

Of a sudden, Sheila threw her arms possessively about Rick's neck, teasing his thick fair hair with the touch of her lips, and without looking at Queenie she asked, 'Oh, Queenie! Do you 'ave to go?'

Somehow Queenie was now not surprised by the depth of Sheila's cruelty. 'Yes,' she said quietly, hoping desperately that her voice did not betray the trembling hurt inside her, 'I've too much work to do at home without gallivanting about.'

Did she imagine the warmth and concern in Rick's voice as he firmly pushed Sheila from him and asked,

'Queenie! You're not going because of me?'

'No! Of course not.' Her answer was too quick, too emphatic. She knew that and felt all the more awkward because of it. 'I'll see you,' she told them both, quickly stepping beyond the curtain and breathing a sigh of relief when it fell into place behind her.

As she lifted the front door sneck to let herself out, Teddy called out, 'Queenie! You used to do Miss Tilly's washing and pressing, didn't you?'

The mention of Miss Tilly brought a warmer glow to her aching heart. 'Yes, and my Auntie Biddy afore me, until they put Miss Tilly in that gentlefolk's home.'

'Aye well . . . seemed she didn't fare none too good after Fancy passed on. Give up, they said, she just give up! Buried 'er yesterday, poor old soul.'

At that moment the curtain was lifted and Queenie could feel Rick's gaze on her as she expressed her sorrow at Miss Tilly's demise. Defying all her instincts, she turned at the door and looked towards the curtain where Rick's eyes were following her every move. As she did so, Sheila dropped her head on Rick's shoulder and smiled sweetly at Queenie as she said, 'Be seeing you, Queenie . . . I'll come round, eh?'

Queenie nodded, and left the shop without a backward glance.

She didn't feel like going straight home . . . this last year home was a cold empty place with nothing to warm her but pictures of people long gone. Dancing images of Fancy Carruthers and Miss Tilly kept flitting in and out of her tortured mind, the hopeless love she bore for Rick weighed heavy and uncomfortable in her bruised heart.

A bitter determination gripped her. A job! She had to get herself a proper job, something to fill her days and take her mind off other things. If George Kenney didn't like the idea, he would just have to do the other. As she set off in pursuit of her goal, Queenie's steps seemed brisker now that they had a purpose.

'A job, you say?' The little wizened man tipped his neb-cap back and scratched the thinning thatch beneath, spreading it across his head in such chaos that he might have been hit by a hurricane. 'Well, I don't know, lass. There doesn't appear to be much of you . . . we usually take on strapping great lasses, wi' a bit o' meat about 'em. It's a hard job! You 'as to do all yer own fetching an' carrying.'

'I've done hard work before, Mr Tomlinson, and I'm used to it. I'll need no one's help.'

Mr Tomlinson's direct scrutiny pierced the steadfast grey eyes, a look of recognition causing his gaze to narrow. 'I've seen you afore, young lady. You're George Kenney's lass, aren't you? Queenie?'

'I'm my own lass, Mr Tomlinson,' Queenie replied, her chin high. It was her turn now to disown the name she had always been denied. 'Folks just call me Queenie . . . and you needn't worry that George Kenney will come bothering me at work. We don't concern one another.'

Mr Tomlinson stroked his chin thoughtfully. So this was the lass his wife was always on about, the one as kept George Kenney from ending his days in the gutter. Oh aye, he'd seen her himself, fetching her dad from the pub and guiding his steps the long way home. Well, it were true what they said . . . you should never judge a book by its cover, for this lass afore him who looked slim and fragile as a gossamer cloud was a strong 'un all right and far too good for the likes o' George Kenney as a father.

'We'll give it a try,' he told her, 'tomorrow morning . . . six o'clock sharp mind.' He waited to see whether reporting at such an ungodly hour might put a young girl off; but the stubborn set of her jaw persuaded him otherwise. 'Fair enough! Nineteen pounds a week and full shift rota like everybody else,' he concluded reluctantly.

It didn't take long to iron out the details. She was to work six a.m. to two p.m. this first week; then alternate shifts of two till ten. Queenie was happy enough. Nineteen pounds a week – she'd be able to manage right well on that. It was with a lighter heart that she made her way home towards Parkinson Street.

'Tomlinson's Distillers!' Mrs Farraday's eyes hardened like marbles and threatened to pop out of her head. 'You can't work *there*, lass!'

Queenie had expected just this reaction from Mrs Farraday, but she was determined not to be swayed. 'Why not?' she asked.

'Why not indeed! Well he's a slave-driver for one thing, and the place stinks o' vinegar and booze . . . and what about the rats as run loose round yon sheds? Nay lass, can't you find nowt else?'

Queenie did not see any point in telling her that Mr Tomlinson's had been her last hope. She'd covered the length and breadth of Blackburn, but nobody wanted a 'slip of a lass only fifteen'.

'No. There's nothing else Mrs Farraday,' Queenie said, her heart warmed at the genuine concern on the kindly woman's face. 'Don't worry. I'll be all right.'

'It's that lazy drunken father o' yours as should be out working! Don't seem right that you should 'ave to keep him!'

'I'll be off then.' Queenie didn't want to get involved in a conversation about George Kenney's shortcomings. She knew them only too well. Auntie Biddy had often said he was how the Good Lord had made him . . . and it wasn't for the likes of them to question.

'You're too easy put on, lass,' Mrs Farraday's voice called after her, 'but by God you make me feel ashamed.'

Queenie was glad to get home. It had been a wearying sort of day, and that was a fact. Stacking the jar of blackberry preserve and small wedge of cheese into the cupboard, it crossed her mind that George Kenney would not be back for hours yet. He followed a regular pattern: sleeping till midday, then down for a pint mug of tea, and straight off to the boozer for a few glasses of something stronger. If he wasn't back by three, it meant he'd gone on to one of his crony's houses with a fresh crate of booze and, like as not, an armful of floozy.

Glancing at the mantelclock Queenie noticed that it was way past four o'clock, indicating that she needn't expect him till midnight now. The thought of a few more hours alone without his odious presence found Queenie humming to herself as she polished the furniture. Queenie loved polishing Auntie Biddy's furniture, loved every old worn-out stick of it. It brought her back to the times they had shared each other's company. The photograph of Auntie Biddy as a young woman had been brought downstairs and given pride of place on the mantelpiece; Queenie had developed a habit of talking to it while she polished. 'Lord knows,' was her justification, 'that I've got no one else I can talk to, not properly.' She frowned heavily and paused in her rubbing. 'Thought I could talk to Sheila . . . but I'm none too sure of that, now.'

Everything was just as Auntie Biddy had left it. The old wireless still stood on a table in the corner, resting on a lace doily which had been a present from Mrs Aspen. The heavy wooden sideboard swallowed up the whole of the back wall; its once-bulbous wooden drawer-handles nigh worn thin by the constant rubbing and polishing. The rolled arms on the horse-hair settee were as hard and prickly as they ever were.

Collecting Auntie Biddy's picture from the mantelpiece Queenie sank into the settee, a little smile fleeting across her face as though she was about to impart a secret, 'Got a job today, Auntie Biddy . . . a *real* job in a factory! Nineteen pounds a week, if you ever did! The first thing I'm going to do is to have a "Sacred Heart" statue put on your resting-place, the best "Sacred Heart" in the whole world.'

The sharp rap on the front door momentarily startled Queenie. 'Must be our day for visitors,' she muttered to the picture, jumping up to replace it on the mantelpiece. Then, hoping her visitor was not Sheila, she hurried to the door.

It was Father Riley. Queenie was embarrassed to see Rick Marsden hovering in the background as well. She could not bring herself to look at him, so smiling quickly at Father Riley she invited them in and with her eyes deliberately averted from Rick's searching gaze as they passed.

Once inside the parlour, Queenie could not suppress the deep flush of excitement she felt and surreptitiously sneaked a glance at Rick whose back was towards her as he found his chair. What was he doing here – and where was Sheila? Set in the homely ways of her Auntie Biddy, Queenie lost no time in bustling about to brew a fresh pot of tea. Soon they were all seated facing each other and enjoying a strong brew.

Father Riley had chosen to seat himself on the tall hard stand-chair by the dresser. He faced Queenie squarely as she shyly edged herself onto the armchair, opposite where Rick had spread himself across the horse-hair settee, his awkward torso into one corner, legs akimbo and arms straddling the back and side of the settee in what looked to Queenie to be a most uncomfortable fashion.

The sight of his long cumbersome figure seeking to settle inconspicuously into the needle-sharp aggression of the horse-hair upholstery sent a delicious little shiver of warmth and protectiveness through Queenie's senses. How handsome and grown-up he is, she thought. His fair hair fell across his forehead in tumbles of thick wayward strands, and when he caught her peeking at him, Queenie was so surprised she nearly choked on her tea. 'Good heavens, child!' Father Riley exclaimed, stepping forward. 'Take your time.'

Queenie had quickly composed herself and now she smiled foolishly at Father Riley, saying, 'I'm sorry . . . I didn't realize how hot it was.' In an effort to relieve the situation, Queenie asked, 'Would anyone like a paste butty?' realizing at once that far from easing her embarrassment, she had only served to compound it.

Rick had perceived Queenie's agony, and he came to her rescue. 'No thank you, Queenie,' he told her with a strong reassuring smile, 'you just relax and enjoy your tea.'

Queenie's attention was drawn to Father Riley, who was now addressing her. 'What we *really* came for, Queenie, was to ask you a favour.'

She was at once curious. What on earth could Father Riley want from her? 'I'd be glad to do you a favour if I can, Father Riley. You know that,' was her prompt reply.

'Ah! Good.' Turning to Rick he said, 'Perhaps you'd like to explain?'

Rick Marsden carried a gentle maturity far older than his approaching eighteenth birthday signified. Queenie had long admired his ability to present his thoughts in a calm ordered fashion, giving the impression that everything he said had been carefully gone over first. When he spoke, the richness of his low voice set off an uncomfortable palpitation across her chest, and she found herself forced to concentrate on his blue tie which she thought suited his colouring very well.

'Queenie,' he murmured, and she found herself gazing into those brown smiling eyes which held hers fast so that she could not tear them away. 'You remember last Christmas and helping with the distribution of the children's toys?'

Queenie felt disappointed. Surely he was not about to discuss *next* Christmas? She had hoped the matter would be a little more immediate than that, but she replied simply, 'Yes . . . I remember.'

Rick sat up and leaned towards her, 'We've got a summer outing planned, to Blackpool. Sarah was to help out, but her mother's been taken ill, and she's had to go off to Chorley for a while.' He hesitated, then his voice charged with excitement, he finished, 'Would *you* come with us, Queenie? Help with the young ones?'

Blackpool! Queenie's thoughts rode the years, back to when Auntie Biddy had first taken her to the Ragged School and she did not even have to think on her answer. 'Oh, yes! I'd love to,' she said.

The look of relief on Rick's face thrilled her, provoking teasing questions best ignored. He was just glad of the help, she supposed, glad to find a replacement for Sarah. Oh, but Blackpool!

Father Riley laughed out loud. 'That's very good!' His voice took on a serious note as he went on, 'Those children deserve all the help we can get and I know you'll enjoy it, Queenie. But there's another reason why I'm here.'

Queenie was caught unawares at the accelerating turn of events. '*Another?*' she asked, this time apprehensive. 'Well, I really ought to be discussing this with your father first,' Father Riley said as he looked around for any sign of George Kenney's proximity. 'He's out is he? Not in bed?'

Queenie smiled at Father Riley's diplomacy. So George Kenney's relapse into his drunken layabout habits had even reached the ears of Father Riley? 'No, he's not abed, Father Riley. He's off with his cronies, swilling booze and gambling, I expect.' Queenie knew it was not quite the enlightenment Father Riley preferred but it was no less than the truth.

Father Riley cleared his throat and grunted, 'Hmph! Well now, the thing is, Queenie, as you're turned fifteen,' his voice hollowed to an angrier pitch, '*and* you might say, the only breadwinner in the family! I thought I'd come looking to you, before looking in other quarters.' Gathering his long black frock in one hand, he got to his feet and proceeded to pace the floor anxiously. 'You know old Katy Forest, don't you, Queenie?' Without waiting for a reply or noticing Queenie's nod, he went on, 'She's getting on a bit now, you know. Should have retired long ago, but she looks on the Church-house as her home. But now, I'm afraid, it's all getting too much for her – although she'd never admit it. Bit of an old tartar, she is! Now, I'd very much like *you* to come and help out. You'll get regular pay, and the odd occasional tit-bit from the kitchen, to fetch home for your Dad.'

Queenie chose to ignore the constant references to her Dad. He had never been that, not all these years, and it wasn't likely that he was about to start now even if she wanted him to. But Father Riley's words began to sink in with their real implications, and Queenie felt as though a new life was opening up to her even if in the realization of such a possibility she felt unsure of her own ability to make the right response or the best decision. Seeing Rick more often might only serve to hurt her, apart from the fact that there was this Katy to contend with. Auntie Biddy had once described her as a right battleaxe. Oh, if only Auntie Biddy was here now. Queenie's troubled eyes travelled upwards beyond Father Riley's questioning face towards the picture on the mantelpiece, and as her gaze rested on the dear familiar features, a calming sense of peace settled her confused thoughts. Things could hardly be worse than they were, could they?

'Come on, Queenie!' Rick prompted an answer, at the same time leaning forward to cover Queenie's hand with his.

The small rush of pleasure that tingled through Queenie showed in the soft blush which highlighted the gentle beauty of her face. Lifting her eyes to meet his gaze, she smiled and withdrew her hand lest her feelings gave her away. Then turning to Father Riley, she told him; 'Thank you. I'd love to come to Blackpool as I said but,' her eyes clouded to a quieter shade, 'I don't know that I can take up your kind offer – much as I would like to. You see, I've given my word to Mr Tomlinson that I'll start in tomorrow.'

'Tomlinson!' Rick exclaimed, horrified. 'You can't mean Tomlinson's the distillers?'

Queenie had taken no mind to Mrs Farraday's similar reaction, but Rick's obvious disapproval made her heart sink with its condemnation. A spark of anger trembled in her voice as she replied, 'Yes, I traipsed *all over* Blackburn looking for work; and he was the only one to take me on!'

Father Riley came forward and stooped towards her, his eyes drawing her attention. 'I know how you feel, Queenie, and you're right – it *was* kind of Mr Tomlinson to offer you work, but you're not cut out for labouring in a distiller's. Oh, I'm not after telling you what to do, Queenie, but you'd not be happy there, not happy at all.'

Queenie knew it, without having to be told. She had

known Mrs Farraday was right too, but there had been no other choice. Yet now she heard herself saying, 'I would *rather* work at the Church-house, Father Riley.' And the truth of her statement settled matters at once for the two men.

'Then that's what you must do!' Father Riley declared, with Rick murmuring support of such a decision. 'Mr Tomlinson isn't so badly in need of labour that he needs a fifteen-year-old girl on his staff . . . Now, would you like *me* to tell him? I could kill two birds with one stone, so to speak. It's been a long time since I've seen Mr Tomlinson set foot in the Church.'

'No thank you, Father Riley,' Queenie said firmly, 'it were me as asked him for work and it'll be me as tells him otherwise.'

'All right . . . but it's a shame,' conceded Father Riley.

'Ah but this time,' interrupted Rick, moving so close to Queenie that she began to panic, '*I'm* coming with you.' As he remembered her passion for independence he added, 'That's if you'll let me?' His voice had dropped to a mere whisper which set Queenie all a tremble. 'Seems to me you're in need of someone to watch out for you.'

So it was settled. Rick would accompany Queenie to tell Mr Tomlinson; although Queenie was adamant, 'If he's relying on me now, I'll not let him down!' Afterwards, she and Rick were to report to the Church-house, where Queenie was to be introduced to old Katy Forest.

It was some hour and a half later when Rick and

Queenie arrived at the Church-house. Queenie felt positively light-headed, her heart still pounding uncontrollably. How privileged she'd felt at having the tall handsome figure of Rick by her side as she had walked down Parkinson Street and all the way to the distiller's. The overwhelming feeling of pride as they had passed the time of day with various neighbours – including Mrs Nosey-Parker Hindle – was something she wasn't ever likely to forget. The occasion would go down in her carefully preserved store of precious memories.

'Here we are then, Queenie,' Rick said as he guided her in through the narrow side-gate alongside the driveway entrance, 'I expect Father Riley's impatient to hear what happened.' As she brushed past him, the slight contact between them triggered a strange hush, and in that small space of a heartbeat their eyes met and intermingled, and it seemed to Queenie that they were as one. As Rick gazed down on her, she wished with all her heart that he would wrap his arms about her and whisper the things she had only ever dreamed of. But there was a seriousness on Rick's face which told her of her foolishness so that she was forced to chide herself, thinking how he would smile if only he could read her mind.

Rick too, had sensed something in Queenie that was alive in his own thoughts. Was it possible that she could love him? Did she lie awake at night as he did, thinking of what might be? The urge was strong within him to ask her, but he was afraid of her answer, afraid that she would reject him. If she did, this magic he felt whenever he came into her presence would be gone for good. Suddenly ashamed of the coward she made him, he summoned courage enough to murmur her name. He would at that moment have spoken what was in his mind, but when she began to walk on the moment was gone and, with it, his courage.

Not having heard him speak her name, Queenie concentrated her attention on the house before her. It was a lovely old house, its wide spacious dimensions spreading regally across a vast area, surrounded by velvet lawns and spills of colour. 'No wonder old Katy Forest doesn't want to leave here,' Queenie mused as she gazed in admiration. Jutting bay-windows criss-crossed with shiny black leaded strips gave the house a rich appearance, and the bright green ivy creeping up and along the brickwork seemed like a thousand arms caressing it.

Queenie's astonishment and sense of awe vented itself into a cry of, 'Oh! It's beautiful!' She felt almost moved to tears and wondered how anyone could ever take such beauty for granted. 'Oh, Rick . . . what a wonderful, wonderful house,' she enthused.

Ric looked down on her, his heart moved by the childish excitement lighting her lovely face, and for the first time, he realized how condemning Queenie's existence had been. 'A house is just a house, Queenie,' he smiled, 'it takes someone very special to turn it into a home.'

'Ah! There you are!' Further conversation was thwarted by Father Riley's flurried approach from the front porch. 'I'd just about given you up for lost.'

Cupping her elbow in his hand, Rick eased Queenie forward, 'We haven't wasted any time – as a matter of fact, I thought we concluded our business with Mr Tomlinson rather quickly,' he said, negotiating himself and Queenie through the oaken front door. 'To be honest, I think he was relieved.'

'And so he should be!' commented Father Riley.

Everything she saw was a brand new experience for Queenie. While Rick and Father Riley went on to discuss Mr Tomlinson and the matter of her withdrawal from his employ, Queenie stood inside the spacious hallway, her wide eyes taking the measure of everything around her. The floor on which she stood was a myriad of mosaic patterns, sweeping and swirling profusely in arrays of splendid design and colour, whose coolness lent sophistication to a warm summer's day. The walls were panelled with rich honey-coloured wood polished to a deep glowing shine; all around tall arched windows with stained-glass pictures reflected multitudes of unbelievably brilliant colours. On the far side of the spacious hallway, the stairs swept up in a flourish of wide inviting crescents; each twisting platform adorned by gigantic trailing plants which sought to escape their confines by sending out tendrils from the huge brass jardinières to run down the base pedestals and probe their way along the deep red carpet.

Queenie had never seen anything like it. The stairs alone took up enough room for *two* of Auntie Biddy's house! A kind of sadness, some strange emotion which cradled the past in its midst, took hold of Queenie. It was not for herself that she felt this uncomfortable emotion but rather for Auntie Biddy, who had lived such a hard life. All this beauty, and none of it to be shared with the one person to whom she could open her heart. Queenie knew that never again would she be able to share anything tangible with Auntie Biddy, yet her *heart* still had to be convinced. The small sigh which now escaped her lips caught the attention of the two men; and Father Riley, misinterpreting it, was at once attentive.

'Fed up waiting, are you, Queenie?' He swept towards her, with Rick following. 'Sorry. I was just asking Rick to fetch Katy from the kitchen . . . she's been in there sulking, ever since I told her she was going to have some help – like it or not!'

Queenie began to have second thoughts. She had no wish to intrude on the old lady's territory; and she certainly didn't want to make any enemies, 'Oh dear,' she said, quite prepared to leave here and now, 'perhaps I should have gone to Mr Tomlinson's after all?'

'Stuff and nonsense! Katy's just a bit strong-minded . . . and needs to be put in her place now and then, and you're just the person to do it!' He gave Queenie a cheeky wink.

Queenie wasn't so sure. She was an outsider and bound to be resented by Katy. Rick nudged her as he brushed past, 'Don't worry, Queenie. Katy'll love you . . . she'll fall under your spell, just like we all have.' The intimate look he gave her told Queenie that she would not be short of allies. She watched him stride across the hallway to a closed door, which she assumed must lead to the kitchen; and she felt that soon he would be gone from her. No doubt he would have to embark on his chosen career quite soon, maybe go away to college, where he would meet all sorts of girls from a similar background as himself? The thought frightened her, and she pushed it from her mind.

'Come on, Queenie,' Father Riley took her by the

arm, 'we'll get settled in the library. I always execute my best battles in there.'

Queenie did not want to do 'battle'; but she knew that the only course open to her at that moment was to go along with Father Riley. After all, she and George Kenney couldn't live on fresh air.

The library was a welcoming room; but such a room as Queenie had never entered before. Every wall was a mass of leather-bound books packed tight row upon row. The furniture was solid and attractive, not horse-hair like Auntie Biddy's but real leather, smelling of polish, and so slippery that when she sat on the edge of an armchair she had to push back quickly into its folds, for fear of landing at Father Riley's feet in a most undignified manner.

Reaching up to collect a pipe from the mantelpiece, Father Riley proceeded to pack it tightly with strings of tobacco from the wad in his pocket. 'Even priests have their faults,' he laughed, catching sight of Queenie's surprised expression.

There came a light tap on the door, before it swung open to admit Katy Forest and Rick. At once, an air of authority filled the room, bristling the atmosphere as all eyes turned to rest on the defensive stance of Katy Forest. Queenie felt herself shrinking inside beneath the piercing black eyes of the old woman as they darted from one to the other in the room. 'Well!' she spat out, and Queenie found herself incapable of remaining seated in the presence of such an overpowering being. She slid forward out of the sucking depths of the armchair, and as she struggled to get to her feet she turned an angry shade of pink with embarrassment.

The girl and the woman faced each other, each

waiting for the other to make the first move. Queenie knew that Katy Forest was taking stock of her, and the exercise was mutual.

Katy was a big bumble of a woman. Thick-set and adorned with strong capable muscles, she looked as full of fettle as Queenie had ever seen. Her short hair, rolled into a thick halo round her head, still retained traces of coarse bleach, which was now overpowered by the pursuing strands of grey. It looked to Queenie as though she had given up the struggle to restrain the symptoms of advancing age. Adorned in a white wrap-around pinnie, she could have been one of those people Auntie Biddy often threatened George Kenney with. 'Go on the way you are,' . . . she had told him, 'an' them folks in white coats'll be coming for you!'

Katy's eyes darted about, intent on missing nothing; but for some reason, Queenie thought they could soften to a warm brown in the right moment. She watched Katy now as the tight thin lips began to move. 'Are we to stand 'ere all day? I've work to do!'

Rick closed the library door and stepped forward. 'This is Queenie,' he offered, propelling her closer to the old woman, 'Queenie, this is Katy Forest.'

Queenie felt extremely uncomfortable as the black eyes swept her from head to toe, seeming to be taking microscopic measurements. 'Why! There's nowt but twopenn'orth of 'er! What use will the lass be to me?'

It was all Queenie could do not to turn tail and run for the sanctuary of the outer hall. She wouldn't stay where she was not wanted! She was no beggar off the streets to be humiliated! A great surge of anger and pride flooded her veins. Father Riley was right: the woman *did* need putting in her place. Queenie's lips tightened as she proceeded to have her say. 'Mrs Forest! None of this was my idea . . .'

Father Riley stepped between them, his face wreathed in amusement; but before he could say anything Katy Forest had visibly relaxed, her broad face crinkled up in surprise. 'Well I never!' she said as she turned to Father Riley. 'She's got some hot blood beneath that cool exterior, I do believe! Now, was she about to tear me off a strip, I ask myself?'

Rick took up position beside Queenie, who was still seething with irritation at the woman before her. 'Oh our Queenie's got a fair share of fettle all right,' he laughed, his expression one of pride.

'That's right, Katy,' confirmed Father Riley, 'and yes, I'm of the mind that she *was* about to tear you off a strip.' He eased himself into a chair, sucking on his pipe while gesturing for the others to sit down. 'Queenie's as straight as the day's long . . . you can rely on her to speak her mind. A bit like yourself, I'm thinking?' he laughed.

Queenie relaxed as the ensuing laughter smoothed away any remaining traces of anxiety. And now, Katy sat beside Queenie and patted her hand reassuringly. 'Mebbe you'll do after all, young 'un,' she laughed, 'but if I'm honest I 'ave to tell you that I'd rather not 'ave anybody!' She got to her feet, and, much to everyone's amusement, proceeded to flex her muscles. 'Look at that!' she said. Queenie had to admit that Katy's upper arm measurements presented an awesome spectacle. 'Now then! Just show me a man wi' muscles the like o' that, eh?'

'Now then, Katy,' Father Riley was obviously

enjoying the whole procedure, 'nobody's saying there's anything wrong with your muscles.'

'What then?'

Rick came to his rescue. 'Perhaps you're just not as speedy as you once were?'

Katy Forest smiled, endorsing his statement with reluctance. 'Mebbe! Aye, mebbe. But I'm not ready for no knacker's yard yet! I'm only sixty-eight,' she eyed Father Riley accusingly, 'so you just think on *that*!' In a flash, she turned and grabbed Queenie by the hand, yanking her unceremoniously out of the chair, 'Come on then, lass! You've a lot to learn, an' there's no time like the present to mek a start!'

As Katy marched the surprised Queenie out of the room, Queenie glanced backwards, and she caught sight of Father Riley and Rick trying desperately not to laugh. It was certainly easy to see the funny side of the situation, and Queenie bit her upper lip in an attempt to stem the rising giggles. The exercise was a futile one, and the grin that was pulling at her mouth gave way to the laughter bubbling inside her.

'Control yourself, my girl! Can't think what there is to giggle at!' Katy Forest relaxed not a muscle as she proceeded determinedly towards the kitchen. Hurrying to keep step, Queenie felt happier than she had done for a long time. She felt instinctively that Katy Forest was going to be a good friend.

Chapter Six

The coarse laughter and drunken shouts followed them down Parkinson Street. Queenie felt degraded and humiliated, but she knew where her duty lay, and she wouldn't shirk it to save face in front of a pack of no-good layabouts! There was no mistaking her anger as she addressed the man in her charge. 'George Kenney! You're a disgrace! Your senses befuddled with drink, and no shame in you at all!'

Over the past eighteen months, since she'd started work at the Church-house, Queenie's ever-increasing errands to retrieve George Kenney from the Navigation had become an altogether too common sight, an endless source of amusement to the drunken louts who frequented the bar.

'Good girl! Don't forget to take 'is socks off afore you put 'im to bed.'

'You can take me 'ome an' all if you want! . . . an' put me to bed . . . long as *you* come wi' me.'

Queenie ignored the raucous sneers and lewd suggestions which raked her ears. Goodness knows, she ought to be used to such foul mouths by now. Hadn't she lived under George Kenney's wicked tongue all these years? She'd long since given up trying to talk any sense into his dozy head, convinced that most of the time he wasn't even in his right mind.

Her arms ached from dragging and pushing his near-dead weight down the considerable length of Parkinson Street. And on top of that, he was trampling all over her poor feet in his desperate efforts to shake her off and return to his cronies.

'Geddof! Get your bloody sodding 'ands off me! No-good little bitch!'

If Queenie hadn't developed a very nifty line in ducking out of his way, George Kenney's flailing arms would have knocked her cold. As it was, she was well in command of the situation and his constant stream of abuse and low language offended only her ears.

'Just look at you,' she grumbled, 'a grown man, and you can't even walk straight!'

Queenie decided. There was no sense trying to get him abed. He was in a worse state than she'd ever seen him before and they just couldn't go on like this. When Queenie tumbled into bed half an hour later, she'd left George Kenney sprawled out across the settee with a bucket strategically placed near his head.

Lying there in the dark, Queenie tried every which way to think on a course of action which might save George Kenney from boozing himself to death. But she couldn't see any way which hadn't already been tried, and which hadn't failed miserably.

Father Riley had taken the time to come round on several occasions during George Kenney's rare coherent periods. He'd tried to talk sense into him, reminding him of his responsibility to Queenie. Then the kindly priest had pointed out to George Kenney that he was slowly but surely killing himself, taking his poor soul further away from salvation.

The only thanks he got for all his trouble and genuine concern was a curt loud instruction to 'PISS OFF!' Queenie was horrified, but Father Riley's bland expression conveyed nothing of what he might be feeling.

The plain truth was that George Kenney was beyond anyone's help. It wasn't in Queenie's nature to dwell on things, but many was the time she'd sat in front of the pictures of her loved ones, questioning what it was all about. 'Here I am,' she'd tell them quietly, 'coming up seventeen, and I feel like some old woman as nobody wants!'

But these self-pitying occasions were rare; mostly, Queenie's sense of acceptance and mature resignation would come to the fore and she'd end up counting her blessings.

The one thing which played on her mind in quieter moments, was the fitfulness of Auntie Biddy's sleep when she'd been close to death's door and the delirious words she constantly muttered. These words had magnified in Queenie's puzzled mind, until she found herself thinking of them more and more. 'Queenie will have to know.' 'God help us . . . he's not for her.' Strange meaningless words, which had haunted Auntie Biddy even on her deathbed.

Queenie had never summoned up the courage to question Auntie Biddy, for even in her calmer moments the terrible anguish which tormented her had coloured the few precious, pain-free periods in her illness. Queenie hadn't the heart to lay further cares on her darling Auntie Biddy by asking questions. Instead, she had chosen to assume that the words were born out of stress and fever.

But now, she couldn't get them out of her mind. '*What* don't I know? *Who* isn't for me?' No matter how often she turned the words over in her mind, they represented nothing of which she could make any sense. She had wondered in passing whether George Kenney might have the remotest inkling; but for some inexplicable reason, she dared not ask him. It was almost as though she had grown afraid to know the truth of their meaning.

Deliberately turning her thoughts away, Queenie hoped George Kenney would sleep quietly. She didn't want to start the day by cleaning up the results of his boozing.

She needn't have worried; when she woke next morning, she was gratified to see that he hadn't even moved. The dreadful stench of booze, however, filled the room with a thick pungency. Her face twisted in repugnance, Queenie set about throwing the doors and windows open.

'Come on . . . move yourself, George Kenney.' She gripped one of his dangling feet, shaking and waggling it, until the rhythmic movement set off a vibration through his body and right up to his tousled head.

'Wassat? Eh . . .' He fidgeted about in this awakened discomfort. 'What the 'ell you playing at? Sod off! Go on! Bloody sod off!'

Queenie pushed him hard in the back, ignoring his curses.

'Come on! It's time you got up and washed some of that stench off you. You smell like a pig!'

The effect of her words was immediate and

predictable. Queenie stepped back skilfully as his arm swung backwards to clap her one.

'You little cow! You're nowt but a bloody cow!'

Incensed by the fact that she'd managed to dodge the weight of his blindly aimed blow, George Kenney fumbled and writhed about until he'd managed to sit almost upright. With his broad back wedged supportively in the corner of the settee, and his arms and legs awkwardly spread about, he put Queenie in mind of a rag-doll, devoid of any self-control or discipline. 'Can't you leave a body be?'

Queenie always experienced a sickening helplessness whenever she saw George Kenney in such a state. Her feelings towards this great lump of a man had mellowed and changed with the years. She still hated having to touch him, and sometimes when she caught him looking at her in that strange way he had, an explosion of nausea would rise to her throat, making her want to keck. 'I suppose I'll never forgive him for the way he treated Auntie Biddy,' she'd reasoned.

Now, as she looked on his sulking bloated face, it struck her how strikingly changed he'd become. Oh, he was still the same clumsy hulk he'd always been, and his manner was never anything other than that of a hopeless drunk; but the face, the eyes particularly, had changed. Queenie could remember the times when one look from George Kenney's penetrating eyes had set her shivering in terrible fear. How could she ever forget? But slowly over the passing years, especially since Auntie Biddy's death, the light had gone from his features. The vivid eyes were buried forever beneath a hazy film of fine red blood vessels; and the once springy fair hair hung loose and matted against his forehead. He inspired pity, not fear now.

Queenie had told Rick Marsden quite determinedly, when he'd questioned her 'misplaced loyalty', 'I *don't* love him! I could *never* love George Kenney. But Auntie Biddy, and my Mam, left him in my charge. There's nobody else to watch out for him, is there?'

Rick had no answer to Queenie's straightforward reasoning, but Queenie sensed that he was afraid for her. She'd simply shrugged off his unspoken fears. George Kenney might be a no-good drunk, but she didn't see him as dangerous.

Lighting the single gas-ring was always a frustrating palaver. But at least it was better than waiting for the old cast-iron kettle to boil over the coal-fire. Once the water in the pan reached boiling point, everything else came easy. With the loaded toasting-fork wedged firmly over the cheery blaze in the firegrate, Queenie skilfully bustled up a pint mug of tea and two thick wedges of hot buttered toast.

A quick glance at the mantelpiece clock told her it was nigh on eleven o'clock. Mrs Aspen was moving today, and Queenie had promised to go in and say cheerio. Odd that! She never dreamed that Mrs Aspen would ever leave her beloved Parkinson Street, and somehow it just wouldn't be the same without her.

'I'm just going next door to Mrs Aspen's – I'll not be gone long,' she told George Kenney, sighing resignedly at his prostrate form.

He looked towards her, his bleary bloodshot eyes filled with hatred. When he spoke an inexplicable shiver ran down Queenie's spine. His voice held a strange charge of sober emotion, low and growling, as he told her, 'One o' these days, I'll swing for you, so help me!' His threat was so unexpected and vicious that the usual disarming retorts Queenie had cultivated in self-defence died in a flurry of fear. Her quiet reply was an automatic disguise to cover her real feelings.

'Eat your breakfast!' she told him firmly. 'If you can face it, that is.'

Standing on the flagstones outside the front door, Queenie pondered on his words and on the manner in which he'd spoken them. She couldn't recall his voice ever having been so terrifying, and yet so strangely quiet. It was a statement of evil intent, filled with menace.

Queenie's mouth lifted into a forced smile. 'Silly old fool,' she muttered without conviction, 'an' *I'm* as bad for taking notice!'

Vowing to treat the remark with her usual flippancy, Queenie entered Mrs Aspen's open front door. But she couldn't shake off the deep warning murmur which persisted.

Fat little Mrs Aspen was struggling to peep over a tall cardboard box, which she edged onto a nearby stand-chair beside the paraphernalia she had transported from the far side of the room. 'Hello Queenie lass. Sit thisel' down a minute. I'll stop and mek us a brew.' As usual in Mrs Aspen's little house, the tea was already brewed, and stewing nicely on the gas-stove. 'There you are, lass,' she handed Queenie a huge pint pot, 'get that down you!'

Queenie didn't have the heart to tell her that never in a million years would she ever swallow all that tea, yet she accepted it gratefully.

From under the mighty mound of boxes and artefacts which had been placed by the door ready for flitting, Mrs Aspen pulled out a horse-hair pouffe. A delightful easy pleasure filtered into Queenie's thoughts, as she watched Mrs Aspen settling herself comfortably on the low pouffe. The dear little soul couldn't have been higher than four and a half feet, yet her busy manoeuvres were anything but ladylike.

Queenie had no other direction in which to avert her eyes, so it was with a mixture of acute embarrassment and cheeky amusement that she viewed the short chubbiness of Mrs Aspen's wide-apart legs, and the elastic garters which dug deep into the flesh just above the knees. The bulging rolls of pink fat disappeared beneath the ballooning legs of her pantaloons.

'Are you all ready for off then, Mrs Aspen?' Queenie had to make a quick comment to take her mind off the spectacle afore her. It was all she could do not to burst into unforgiveable laughter.

'Ready for off! The only thing as is ready for off in this 'ouse, is yon Jack Aspen!' She threw a cursory glance at the big old alarm clock standing lonely on the floor. 'Just look at that! Nobbut 'alf past eleven, and he's the first one waiting at the Navigation doors. I tell you, Queenie lass . . . men are down-right useless!'

Queenie smiled. She knew Jack Aspen was anything but useless. After all, hadn't he turned this little house into a comfortable home?

'I never thought you'd leave this house and Parkinson Street,' Queenie ventured.

'Aye well, I didn't neither, Queenie lass.' She looked about, her bright eyes glittering with unshed tears as she sent on, 'But our Doreen's managed to get us a place near 'er . . . a lovely little place. It's even got an *inside* toilet! Well, we just couldn't say no. We're both getting on now, Queenie lass.' She inched herself nearer to Queenie, a furtive expression capturing her plump face. 'I'm glad our Jack's not 'ere. I wanted . . . a word with you, lass, quiet like.' Queenie felt slightly irritated by the inexplicable feelings rising within her at Mrs Aspen's changed mood – as though they had endorsed the odd sensation she'd just experienced on leaving George Kenney.

Mrs Aspen continued in a low intimate voice, the uneasy look on her face reflecting her obvious embarrassment, 'Look, lass, I know I'm not your Auntie Biddy . . . Lord rest 'er soul! but I feel as 'ow she'd want me to keep a weather eye on you, lass.' She cleared the hesitance from her throat, before continuing, 'I don't rightly know 'ow to say this, without you thinking bad o' me . . .' She nodded her head gratefully at Queenie's reassuring smile and, encouraged, went on, 'I think I'd best come right out and say it! You didn't ought to be on yer own in yon 'ouse wi' that divil, George Kenney! We all know 'is mind's going . . . an' I'm not altogether surprised, seeing as the creature's swilled enough o' the 'ard stuff to floor a bloody elephant! But y'see lass, men such as thi' Dad . . . well, they've got un'ealthy ideas about women.' She paused for a moment, her face pink and embarrassed. 'What I'm trying to say, lass, is . . . you've told me yerself as there's times when 'e don't recognize you for 'is own daughter. Mebbe . . . God forbid! there'll come a night when 'e's riddled wi' the drink, an' all 'e'll see is a lovely young woman . . . someone to satisfy a special need . . . if you see what I'm getting at?'

Mrs Aspen broke off, cautioned by the look of disbelief in Queenie's face. 'Well . . . 'appen it's only a silly old woman's wanderings, lass. But I 'ad to speak me mind!' An expression of relief crossed her kindly features 'There! That's the crux of it, lass. I'm right afeared for you, right afeared!'

For just a moment, Mrs Aspen's words reverberated in Queenie's shocked mind. Though she told herself that Mrs Aspen's imagination was far too fertile for her own peace of mind, the light-heartedness with which she had entered this house but a few minutes ago suddenly became weighted by a disturbing mix of alien emotions, which couldn't help but leave her curiously perturbed. Yet, as she mentally examined the awful implications of Mrs Aspen's warning, the whole thing seemed so incredible to her that she had no other course but to dismiss it.

Leaning forward to gently chide at Mrs Aspen's anxious face, she told her, 'Really, Mrs Aspen! Don't think I'm not truly grateful for your concern, because you know that I am, but you've no need to worry yourself. Honest. Me and George Kenney, we're just a burden to each other, that's the crying truth of it. Most of the time, he's off down the Navigation or they're all gathered in one or another's houses, drinking and gambling. When he's steady enough to find his way home, he's either sprawled out sleeping it all off, or he's getting ready for off out again!'

In her efforts to reassure Mrs Aspen and restore the little soul's peace of mind, Queenie *almost* reassured herself; but somehow she couldn't seem able to completely shake a lingering disquiet. 'There's no harm in George Kenney. No *real* harm anyroad,' . . .

certainly not in the way *you* suggest! Queenie's thoughts added.

'Aye well, *I* don't 'appen to agree with you lass.' Now that the subject had been broached openly, Mrs Aspen attacked it with new vigour. 'And there's plenty o' folks as feel the same! They've all seen you dragging 'im 'ome from the pub at all hours o' the morning and night. There's not a single soul as doesn't shame at the way he's treated you, since the day your poor Mam died giving you life. It's 'imself 'e should be punishing. By! That man's got a lot to answer for!' Her voice suddenly changed, taking on a deeper intimacy. 'Your Auntie Biddy never mentioned to you . . . about . . . anything?'

'What, Mrs Aspen?' She felt the need to prompt her. 'Mentioned about what?'

'No. It's nothing, lass. I'm just rambling, feeling a bit mixed up, what with leaving Parkinson Street after all these years. I'm just a silly forgetful old woman.' Changing the subject quickly in order to avoid the questions already forming on Queenie's tongue, she asked, 'How are you doing at the Church-house, lass?' Her laugh was thin and forced. 'Katy Forest's a rum one eh? I'll bet you find 'er a rum one?'

Queenie knew that no amount of questioning on her part would resurrect the subject that Mrs Aspen had broached. It was destined, like so many things, to remain a mystery to her. Churning the question over in her thoughts, Queenie's belief that Auntie Biddy had kept something from her was strengthened. Auntie Biddy's incoherent mutterings ran through her mind. 'The lass should be told.' 'What you did George Kenney, was blasphemous.'

Queenie hadn't forgotten; and now, Mrs Aspen asking if she'd been told! Told what?

She made an attempt at uncovering whatever it was. 'Mrs Aspen, what did you mean about Auntie Biddy telling me something?'

Mrs Aspen struggled to her feet, collecting the mug of cold tea from Queenie, 'I told you lass. It was nothing! Summat and nowt afore you were born . . .' From her tone of voice, Queenie knew the subject was well and truly closed, '. . . Now then! You've let your tea go cold. I'll brew us a fresh lot.'

'No. That's all right, Mrs Aspen. I've a lot to do; so I'd best be off.'

'You still 'aven't said 'ow you manage with yon Katy Forest – been there over a year now, 'aven't you?'

'Yes, just about. I like Katy right well. She's taught me a lot. I can embroider and darn a lot better now . . . and I'm a decent cook now, too.'

Mrs Aspen's chuckle indicated her relief that Queenie didn't appear to be pursuing the matter any further. Things were best left alone to the past.

'Well, I dare say I'll see you afore we go, Queenie. Old Charlie's moving us, and he does like to 'ave everything ready by the door, so I'd best shift meself.'

'Oh, you're 'aving old Charlie to move you, then? Not Maisie?'

'No lass. Maisie's waggon ain't big enough to cart all *my* rubbish, an' anyway, you never know these days whether she's drunk or sober.'

'I shouldn't take too much notice of what folks say, Mrs Aspen,' Queenie said, her loyalty to Maisie obvious.

'No, I don't as a rule, Queenie lass, but I've seen it wi' me own eyes! Ever since that Sheila went off,' her voice dropped to fearful whisper, 'they do say as 'ow the lass is wi' child! an' run off to 'ide the shame!'

Queenie wasn't as shocked as she might have been. Sheila was a rum handful, and anything she did wouldn't surprise Queenie. The next thing Mrs Aspen told her however, did shock. 'Folks reckon as 'er twin brother Raymond's the father! That's why Maisie's tekkin' it so bad!'

Sheila had told Queenie before she went that she'd write to her. There and then, Queenie decided to put the whole matter out of her head till she heard from Sheila. Folks were often wrong.

Later, after Jack Aspen returned from the Navigation where he'd been saying a fond farewell to his drinking pals, Queenie watched from her window as Charlie and the Aspens loaded everything onto his truck. Charlie Ramsbottom's efforts to coax the antique truck into life were proving futile. Several times, a hefty swing of the starting handle spluttered the tired worn engine into life only to cough and hiccup, before finally dying just as Charlie reached the cab.

'Sod and bugger it!' he shouted in exasperation, his thin poker face screwing up into the most frightening contortions. Then he would grab his neb-cap from his head, and proceed to thrash the poor old truck with it. 'Thirty-six quid! Thirty-six bloody quid – and it won't even go!'

Suddenly, as his angry booted foot landed smack on the side of the bonnet, it shook and shuddered before slowly painstakingly rattling into life. Charlie threw his arms across it, bestowing a loud grateful kiss on the corroded paintwork. 'You little beauty! You right little darling!' Then, for fear it might stop just as suddenly as it had started, Charlie jumped in the cab, urging the waiting Aspens to do the same, shouting, 'Make way,' to the multitudes of curious children and grown-ups lining the pavement. They chugged off down the road in noisy jerking fits and starts.

Queenie had waved from her quickly acquired place amongst the wellwishers until the truck was no more than a moving speck down the end of Parkinson Street. Afterwards feeling suddenly lonely, she exchanged the time of day with a few neighbours before taking herself quietly indoors.

'Well she's gone, Auntie Biddy, Mrs Aspen's gone, and the house is empty.'

Auntie Biddy's youthful smiling expression remained immobile under Queenie's sad-eyed gaze, but it helped somehow just to gaze on the picture, and to utter what was in her heart. Slightly cheered, she grabbed her mac from behind the door and let herself out onto the street.

The Saturday market was as good a place as any, she calculated. But she'd need to hurry if she wanted to wander about at leisure. It was already half-past three, and they started packing up at five o'clock. It wasn't far though; only a stone's throw from the end of Parkinson Street.

Queenie entered the busy market square, feeling better already, as the exuberant shouts of the stall-holders penetrated her ears. 'Bananas! Get yer bananas!' 'Quality cloth! Don't tek my word for it, love – come an' feel it!' Everyone shoved and jostled, totally preoccupied as eyes swivelled, stared and stretched in a desperate effort not to miss a single bargain.

Queenie loved it all. She derived the greatest satisfaction and enjoyment from watching and listening to all the familiar sounds which carried her above the mundane loneliness and boredom of her own existence. Queenie had always seen Blackburn market as a magic carpet, and when a body climbed aboard it would be transported to another world . . . a fairytale world where round every corner a new adventure waited. So many times Auntie Biddy had brought her here, and even now, after all this time, the magic was not lost to Queenie. Tossed into the hub of activity and camouflaged beneath the great umbrellas of red and white awnings which covered every stall down every avenue, touching each other until the sky itself was obliterated by this spreading, billowing roof, Queenie took delight in all about her and the cautious step of her feet against the jutting cobbles became a carefree skip.

The hot sticky aroma of candy-floss permeated the air; urgently persuasive voices cut across the atmosphere calling a body to 'Taste this, missus,' 'Try this on, love,' and 'Go on . . . do yourself a treat, darling!' From a distance Queenie could distinguish the familiar clatter of the dray-horses' waggon being loaded up with barrels of best ale outside Thwaites' Brewery, where Queenie knew the two great black shires would be patiently standing, magnificent in their leather harness and polished brass, with plaited manes and the hair of their white fetlocks washed and brushed to a spreading feathery finish.

'Hey, Queenie!' The cry seemed to be coming from behind Tommy's fruit stall. Stretching her neck above the multitude of moving heads, Queenie recognized the tall lithe figure of Rick Marsden emerging from the winkle stall.

Waving his free hand he shouted, 'Stay where you are!' Then, using the considerable weight of his strong frame, he pushed and wended his way towards her, although when he finally made contact, she was suddenly whisked from her feet and propelled by the surging crowd to come to rest some ten yards on.

Since Auntie Biddy's death, Queenie had found little cause for laughter. But now, a helpless fit of giggling gripped hold of her . . . fired now by the appearance out of nowhere of a huge mountainous woman, who pushed past Queenie in full cry with both arms flung into the air as though appealing to someone of a higher authority to make way. 'Hurry up, Tilly!' she screamed. 'There'll be no decent smellin' fish left atime *we* gets there!'

There had been no warning of the woman's gushing approach. Certainly, Rick Marsden had no time to brace himself as she blundered into him, knocking the precious tub of winkles flying from his hand, to splatter itself decoratively over Henshaw's grand display of prizewinning artificial flowers.

Hurrying away from the scene as quickly as possible, Rick looked back, to draw Queenie's attention to poor Henshaw, busily shooing the pack of roving dogs who sought to indulge themselves in the unexpected treat.

'I queued for twenty minutes for those winkles.'

Rick Marsden's feigned indignation reduced them both to fits of hysterical laughter. 'Don't know what we're laughing at,' he continued between spurts of spontaneous giggling, 'if old Henshaw finds out who splattered his precious flowers, he'll have my guts for garters!'

Even the possibility of such an unlikely punishment failed to stem Queenie's laughter. Just being near Rick created within her such an abundance of joy that she felt like singing. She revelled in the welcome company of this happy young man. He was like a much-needed tonic, a breath of fresh air in the staleness of her life.

'Come on,' she told him, 'let's find another winkle stall.'

It didn't take long for them to locate such a stall. Rick took his place in yet another queue, determined that this time he wouldn't be robbed of the succulent delicacy. 'You carry these,' he instructed Queenie, shoving two king-sized tubs into her hands, 'and I'll lead the way, in case of unexpected accidents.'

Queenie walked behind him, holding the winkles almost up the back of his smart tweed jacket as he wended a way through the pushing crowd, the laughter in her heart spilling out compulsively in frequent collapses of helpless tittering.

'Behave yourself woman,' came Rick's mock command, as he responded delightfully to the odd disapproving looks from passing shoppers, 'or you'll get me belt across your buttocks!'

The stone horse-trough in the heart of the market square was raised up on a slight incline. On one side was the open flagstoned area, where the horses stood tethered in easy reach of a refreshing drink. On the other side, a wooden bench offered a resting place for the weary traveller. It was to this bench that Rick led them.

Oddly, the thronging crowds of hurrying shoppers always gave wide berth to the stone horse-trough, very rarely opting to take refuge and comfort from the bench.

'I never could understand it,' Rick told Queenie, his lively eyes dancing into hers, 'you'd have thought they'd be glad to take the weight off their feet.' He reached out to take one of the winkle-tubs from Queenie; extracting a few for the tethered shire behind him, a great monster of a horse with huge soft eyes and a gentle expression.

'Well, I don't think he'll bother us, eh?' Rick assured Queenie with a warm smile.

'He's beautiful.' Queenie thought everything was beautiful right at the moment. Oh how I love you Rick Marsden, she told him silently. Tucking into the delicious winkles with renewed enthusiasm, she reminded herself to know her place, which deep in her heart she was sure was not by Rick's side.

Rick was obviously thoroughly enjoying himself. That is, until the shire decided it wanted a drink! Plunging its great clumsy head into the over-filled trough, it created a tidal wave of water with no place to go but forwards. The flood surged over the side of the trough, swamping Queenie and Rick. Both tubs of winkles landed upside down on the flagstones, leaving Queenie and Rick breathless and dripping. In the second after the initial shock their wide eyes met in surprise, before they collapsed completely into each other's arms, helpless in the laughter which engulfed them. All of this was much to the delight of the highly amused crowd which had gathered around to share in the fun.

'Now we know, don't we?' Rick's voice broke through the laughter; Queenie couldn't contain herself as the tears rolled joyously down her face.

'Know what?' she asked.

'Why nobody ever sits here!' His enlightened comment stimulated the crowd and Queenie into renewed fits of hysterical laughter.

Having decided that they were nearer to Queenie's home, the two of them made a hasty retreat down Parkinson Street to No. 2, where they could towel themselves dry and indulge in a welcome brew of tea.

'You stand side o' the fire an' dry your clothes off,' Queenie said as she threw him a towel, 'I don't think you'll come to any harm if they dry on you.'

As she entered the scullery to light the gas ring, her heart fluttered and bounced at the delicious notion of Rick without his clothes. She flushed pink with embarrassment. Brewing the tea was one of Queenie's accomplished arts. Auntie Biddy had always insisted she could make the finest brew in the whole of Lancashire. Rick Marsden obviously shared that belief.

'Do you know?' he remarked. 'That's the best pot of tea I've ever tasted.'

Queenie smiled gratefully, taking the towel he held towards her, and spreading it out in the grate to dry.

'Are your clothes dry? I think *you* got the better part of the soaking,' she observed.

167

Recalling the incident triggered off a short bout of giggling; then for some inexplicable reason, Queenie suddenly fell silent. She had always felt pleasantly uncomfortable in his presence but now the pit of her stomach kept folding and unfolding in dizzy sickening spasms. She really felt as though she was going to be sick.

Rick seemed to sense her feelings. Taking the mug out of her hand, he placed it, together with his own, down in the grate. Queenie could feel his intense eyes burning into her face, though she dared not look up.

'Queenie!' His voice was soft, his breath fanning her face like the gentle caress of a summer breeze. 'You know I've always loved you . . . don't you?'

The rush of emotion which swamped her heart raised every dream she'd ever dared to dream, and she had to ask herself, Am I hearing right? He loves me? *Loves* me? But still she dared not look up to meet his penetrating gaze.

His hands reached out to touch her face, to stroke her hair lovingly. 'Did you hear me Queenie?' he insisted. 'I love you so very, very much my darling. I've never loved anyone else.'

Queenie raised her hands to cover his fingers. As she slowly lifted to him the innocent beauty of her open grey eyes, the depth and magnitude of her desperate love for him shone brightly in them and the tears ran unheeded down her lovely face.

With a deep heartfelt cry at the open emotions bared to him, Rick grasped her tightly, drawing her fiercely to him. The passion in his voice caused her to tremble. 'Queenie . . . oh, my lovely Queenie! I've *always* loved you . . . always!' His mouth came down on her eager lips, to claim the prize he coveted. The warmth of his kiss sent a shiver of ecstasy through her as he took her to him fiercely, hungrily.

Queenie surrendered to him completely, opening her heart to receive the love she had hardly dared to dream would one day be hers. Powerful new emotions filled her breast, her loins, with urgent demand.

Locked in each other's arms, they didn't heed the entry into the room of George Kenney.

Queenie's instinct of his overpowering presence stabbed her happiness with sharp paralysing fear. Drawing away from the exquisite pleasure of Rick's covetous passion, she looked at her father.

'Oh! Mr Kenney.' Rick's proper upbringing showed in his embarrassment as he got sharply to his feet.

George Kenney, hopelessly drunk, clung to the door staunchings as if for support, his face drained of colour, his eyes staring in disbelief. 'It's him!' His voice was so different that Queenie found it hard to recognize. 'It's Richard Marsden!'

Rick reached out to gather Queenie in his arms. 'We love each other Mr Kenney . . . Queenie and I . . .'

George Kenney's look of horror warped into a smile before becoming a strange high-pitched roar of laughter which bordered on hysteria. 'Richard Marsden!' he shouted, over and over again, before collapsing onto the settee in a smothering of broken sobs.

'I'd better stay awhile, Queenie . . . ' Rick was visibly shocked by George Kenney's behaviour and he feared for Queenie.

Queenie knew however from experience that no one could help her with George Kenney when he chose to be difficult. With a tender expression which conveyed all he wanted to know, Queenie told him quietly, 'Please Rick, it's best that you should go now. I'm used to seeing him like this.'

Reaching down to touch her lips with his own, Rick whispered, 'Oh Queenie. If only you knew how happy I am. I'll never let you go again.'

Queenie wanted to enfold him in her arms and hold him to her heart forever but the moment was cruelly lost. No matter, there would be all the time in the world later. 'I know,' she whispered, the thickness of her voice betraying the depth of her thoughts, 'and I love you.'

With George Kenney seeming to have drifted into a restless half-sleep, Queenie saw Rick to the door; her mood becoming one of concern when she saw how pained his expression had become and how sad were his words when he spoke. 'Queenie . . . I have to go to London with my father . . . business demanding he says. We're leaving first thing in the morning and it'll be some weeks before I see you again, but I'll ring the Church-house. Katy won't mind me talking to you. I'll go and see Father Riley to tell him I have to keep in touch.'

'Father Riley would want you to keep in touch, Rick.' She touched his face lovingly, at the same time assuring him, 'Katy will no doubt be glad to pass on a message, I'm sure, and I'll be waiting for your call.' Their eyes met and as he continued to look on her, Queenie felt a warm blush rising from her neck to the roots of her hair. When his lips came down on hers, Queenie's heart soared with ecstasy.

As she watched him striding away, tall and

handsome, the love in her heart for this man curled into every corner of her being, making her feel reborn, and so wonderfully happy that it took her breath away. 'Rick Marsden,' she whispered aloud, 'I'll make you happy for the rest of your life . . . I promise.'

In her rapt attention on Rick's departing figure, Queenie hadn't perceived George Kenney's presence behind her down the passage.

From here, he had been watching her closely, his face a grotesque study as his gaze travelled from her pretty trim shoulders down the length of her shapely back and over the perfectly slim legs. The look on his face was one usually reserved for the floozies he kept company with. As Queenie closed the door and turned away from it, George Kenney surged forward, violently pinning her against the wall. Then, as Queenie's mouth fell open in astonishment, he brought his face close to hers and in a strange voice growled, 'Like the men, d'you, eh? Got an appetite fer such things 'ave yer?'

Beneath the probing stare of his bulbous eyes and swamped by the stench of his breath, Queenie gasped for air. Pushing both hands hard against his chest and thankful for the strength born in her through carrying this awful creature these many years, she wedged a distance between the two of them. 'You! You're filthy drunk!' she shouted and the forceful vehemence of her accusation seemed for a moment to startle him.

Such a moment was all Queenie needed, and at once she was free of him. Hurriedly, she flung open the door in order to thwart any further thoughts he might have of handling her. She would have thrown him out on the flagstones in the very next instance. But already he was ambling down the passage towards the parlour door, where he turned and laughing in a soft, sinister way said, 'So! You've got an appetite for the men, eh?' Then his face straightened into blankness, as though looking in upon itself, and when he spoke again it was in a voice tearful from the drink. 'My Kathy never 'ad no appetite fer other men!' Now he was looking at Queenie with the old hatred distorting his features. His bleary eyes roved over her as he struggled to steady himself against the door jamb. Now he was laughing again in as cruel a voice as Queenie had ever heard.

'Appetite fer men, eh? Oh! But not with *that* one, it's to be 'oped!' He jerked a thumb towards the open door, adding after a thought, 'Ah! But 'appen it's yer just deserts, eh?' And throwing his head back, he roared with laughter, 'Aye! 'Appen you two deserve each other!'

When George Kenney disappeared into the parlour, still laughing, Queenie leaned against the passage wall, her thoughts in a turmoil. Something would have to be done about George Kenney. He was crazier now than he'd *ever* been! She couldn't make head nor tail of him no more and the way he'd looked at her just now had sickened her.

With a mind to thrash the whole sorry business out with him, she hurried to the parlour, only to find George Kenney draped over the settee, half-conscious and oblivious to all and sundry; the suffocating reek of booze and stale tobacco permeating every corner of that little parlour. Sighing heavily, Queenie realized the futility of trying to reason with him now. What she had to say would have to wait until tomorrow.

'You stinking thing!' she told his prostrate form.

'You can lie in it all you like. I'm off to bed!'

It was barely eight o'clock, but Queenie couldn't abide the thought of sitting in the parlour with him. As the nights were getting too chilly for walking about, she decided to bank the fire up, leave his food prepared and take herself off to bed. Placing a heaped-up pile of pork dripping sandwiches on the table where he could see them on waking, and securing the guard in front of the fire, Queenie lifted his dangling legs to a more comfortable position on the settee; then she quietly closed the parlour door behind her on her way to bed.

Oddly enough, although the hour was not late, Queenie felt unusually tired. 'I expect it's all the excitement,' she told her mother's picture, 'and I *still* can't believe it. Rick loves me . . . really loves me.'

Before sleep closed her tired eyes, she whispered her innermost secrets to Auntie Biddy. 'I know you weren't fond of Rick, Auntie Biddy, but that was because you didn't *know* him . . . not like I've always known him. Oh we'll be happy, you'll see; and I do need him so.'

The gas-lamps were out in the street. Queenie had left the curtains apart, to allow a gentle breeze through. The yawning blackness at the open window told her it was gone midnight. She'd awakened disturbed. Somebody was here in her bedroom!

'Who's there?' she whispered into the dark. 'Who is it?'

Although Queenie felt impelled to ask that question, she was already persuading herself that it was all her imagination. Too much happening all at once, she quietly assured herself. Turning to settle further down the bed, her senses too heightened for comfort, Queenie saw the shadowy figure as it lunged straight for her. She opened her mouth to scream but the sound caught tight in her throat as his broad rough hand covered her face.

Gasping for breath, Queenie fought with every ounce of strength she could summon. But the powerful brutality of her attacker rendered her helpless and the horror which smothered her screaming became unbearable.

Tearing aside her flimsy nightwear and shattering the golden-heart chain about her delicate throat, George Kenney in his brutality took his own child's virgin innocence, with no thought of consequence or compassion, his own lust uppermost in his mind.

In the midst of unbearable pain and the blinding confusion of a nightmare, Queenie's sinking senses registered the pleading words: 'Kathy . . . my lovely, forgive me. Richard Marsden was a sin. Oh . . . don't fight me, Kathy.'

The merciful blackness opened its arms to engulf Queenie. A rush of cold air lifted the curtain end to catch against Kathy's picture, knocking it face down on the dresser as though not to witness the dreadful deed which at once caressed and violated her name.

It was still dark when Queenie's senses rushed her to painful consciousness. Recollections of the horror infiltrated her waking thoughts. The agony of her limbs and body screamed out with every move she made.

The rising vomit soured her mouth as she struggled to the edge of the bed. Only when she stood leaning on the stand-chair for support, and her red-misted eyes scoured the bed which had borne such terror, did she see him. The over-sheet had slithered with her to settle on the floor at her feet. There on the far side of the bed lay the grotesque unclothed figure of George Kenney. Queenie's hand came up to her mouth to stifle the cry within and the torrent of hatred which stormed her heart urgently bubbled her heaving stomach.

Fleeing down the stairs, Queenie located just in time the bucket which she had earlier placed at George Kenney's head. Afterwards the scalding tears ran furiously down her face. But they were born of effort, not of blind hatred nor of shame. For with the physical release of the hard knot which had sat heavily inside her had emerged a strange black calmness. She had to kill the monster who lay upstairs, the evil thing that had invaded her body.

Her head pounding from the acute discomfort which dogged her every step, Queenie stood by the scullery sink and vigorously washed every inch of her poor bruised body. She swept every thought out of her mind other than that of her dark intent, which she allowed to pervade and dominate all other considerations. As though enfolded in the quiet arms of a hypnotic dream, Queenie deliberately made her way back upstairs to unthread the slim leather belt from George Kenney's discarded trousers. Her movements were an automatic execution of the solitary resolution which overrode all her basic gentler instincts.

George Kenney lay on his back, the long heavy arms outsplayed, his thick legs curled towards the swollen ugliness of his booze-swilled stomach.

Queenie's shocked grey eyes swept the bloated face

which sagged repulsively to one side, the wet hanging mouth open and dribbling; then she slid the hard narrow belt underneath the thick redness of his leathery neck. Calmly retrieving the pointed end which reappeared across the pillow, she threaded it through the cold brass buckle, allowing it to slide up tight about George Kenney's neck.

Only vaguely aware of what she was doing, Queenie wondered at the monstrous strength which surged through her. The physical pain and mental anguish which had driven her from the violated sanctity of her bedroom had miraculously disappeared. In their place had emerged an evil as towering and destructive as that which had shattered the quiet of her virgin sleep and dreams of her newly found love.

She watched mercilessly as the hard edges of the belt dug deeper and sharper into his flesh. As she slowly tightened the leather up to its gleaming buckle, the bloated face deepened to an odd blue-tinged purple, and the thick arms swung about with jerky thrashing movements. Queenie's glazed eyes witnessed it all as though in the motions of a nightmare, unable and unwilling to influence the sequence of events.

As George Kenney gyrated on the bed, emitting strange croaking sounds from the base of his throat, the picture of his dead wife Kathy fell from the precarious position on the edge of the dresser.

Startled by the ensuing clatter as it toppled heavily to the floor, Queenie's death-grip on the tightening belt momentarily relaxed. The fresh rush of air into the choking throat of George Kenney shaped out the pleading words which emerged confused and broken into the dark silence of the room.

'Kathy . . . I . . . love . . . you . . .'

Nothing in all of Queenie's experience could have prepared her for the riveting realization that shuddered through her conscious mind. As if awakening from a deep trance, her horror-struck eyes registered the reality before her. The belt end fell heavily from her hands to swing harmlessly over the bed, where it touched the floor and lay still.

The raking spluttering cough of George Kenney rattled and moaned around the room. Gradually, from the far wall into which she had backed, Queenie regained her senses, watching him . . . remembering.

As he struggled to sit up against her pillow, George Kenney's foul mutterings invaded her thoughts. The coldness which had devoured her gave way to bitter raging anger. Collecting the belt which had been shaken free by George Kenney's breathless coughing, Queenie dived at him, screaming her condemnation of his drunken vileness. The violence of her attack upon him as she wielded and slashed with the length of his belt, sent him scurrying in a drunken half-dazed stupor onto the landing, where he fell to the floor and lay unmoving.

Tears now streaming down her face, Queenie gathered up his clothes and threw them over his body. She returned to the bedroom where she dressed herself sobbing fearfully.

Still sobbing, Queenie brought a bowl of boiled water from the scullery, passing the still body of George Kenney, not seeing him and not caring. She threw the sheets and blankets from the bed. Then, with thorough and agitated precision, she scrubbed the mattress and pillows on both sides before standing them against the open window to dry.

Her aching body sore and slow, she lugged the bedclothes down to the scullery, where she immersed them in the water already heating in the boiler. As she bent over her work, Queenie struggled to quell the realization of what George Kenney's moaning words meant to her and Rick. But there was no escaping the awful implications.

Only when the bedclothes hung dripping on the line did the tears and sobbing subside. Then, calmer in herself, Queenie collected the carving knife from the cutlery box in the kitchen. For the remainder of that seemingly endless night, she sat awake in the deep black horse-hair chair, wrapped in her mac and an old coat of Auntie Biddy's. With the carving knife gripped firmly in her small work-worn hands, she listened for any slight movement from upstairs, and watched till the first daylight began to filter in through the window, into the dark corners of that little parlour.

Chapter Seven

'What's the matter, lass? You can tell me.' Katy's broad features were troubled as she carelessly placed the wooden spatula down on the kitchen table and crossed to the big pine cupboard, where Queenie had paused in her polishing. She gently removed the polishing rag and the big old copper plant-pot from the slim nervous hands. Taking Queenie by the shoulders, she gently but firmly propelled her to a stand-chair by the table, where she eased her down.

'Now then, child,' she coaxed, pulling up a chair next to Queenie, and manoeuvering until Queenie had no choice but to meet the kindly soul's questioning gaze, 'you've done nowt but mope about for the last fortnight.' She reached out to lift Queenie's long bedraggled hair out of the sad grey eyes. 'Oh, and just look at you! It's not like you to be slovenly . . . you've allus taken a pride in yourself.'

Queenie listened to Katy, and she knew in her heart that everything Katy was saying was true. But there was nothing left in her to respond. A wave of terrible loneliness and depression engulfed her as the awful riveting truth pierced her heart. Richard Marsden . . . her own brother! She could never wipe out the memory of that dreadful night and what she had learned, would never to able to wash off the sickening feeling of defilement which choked her with its clinging.

'I'm all right, Katy.' Her voice was unconvincing as she went on, 'I just forgot to plait my hair this morning, that's all.'

'Forgot?' Katy Forest searched the dark despair in Queenie's beautiful grey eyes, 'Why, lass, I've never known you to forget *anything*!' She fished about in the enormous cavity of her work-pinnie to produce a handful of hair-grips which she promptly wedged between her teeth as she stood up to plait Queenie's long thick hair. 'There'll be no work done in this kitchen today!' she told Queenie determinedly, 'until I know what's ailing you.'

Queenie had grown very fond of Katy Forest, and normally she would not have hesitated to confide in her. Her face grew uncomfortable from the shame which coloured it, but she could never bring herself to talk about what troubled her now.

'There! That's better.' Katy sat down in the chair, obviously pleased that at least Queenie now looked more like her usual lovely self. She grasped Queenie's hand, at the same time spreading her other palm across the pale high forehead. 'You're not ailing are you, lass? Not been sick or anything?' she asked.

Queenie couldn't cope with all this kindly attention and concern. Her greatest fear was that she should break down and tell Katy what happened, something she could not countenance. She had to convince Katy that everything was all right. Reaching deep inside herself to muster up a semblance of courage, she smiled brightly. 'Yes,' she lied, and hated herself for it

. . . but consoled herself with the fact that there was indeed an element of truth in her words, 'I have been sick, Katy. And I feel terrible.'

'Well!' Katy got to her feet in a flourish, 'I *knew* it! And you thought I wouldn't notice?' Her tone was rapidly becoming one of anger. 'Silly girl! Forcing yourself to turn up for work. Did you think I couldn't manage without you? You should be abed! You look at death's door, child!'

Queenie drank the sour-tasting concoction which Katy pushed under her nose, 'Now get that down you! I'm off to find Father Riley.' She flounced out of the bright cosy kitchen, leaving Queenie to her melancholy thoughts.

She had already pushed the memory of what might have been deep into the most hidden recesses of her mind. She and Rick must never again see each other, or talk to each other again . . . it would be too unbearable and Queenie could not envisage a time when it would not be so. The pain and humiliation she was suffering seemed as nothing compared to the searing grief in having been denied the only love she had ever wanted.

Father Riley lost no time in instructing Katy to collect Queenie's coat and things. 'Really, lass, you should have known better than to bring yourself in to work,' he said, looking at her reproachfully.

'There's no need for me to go home,' Queenie protested. 'I'm all right.'

But Father Riley would hear no more. 'All right? Why Queenie, lass, you're as white as a sheet. And by the looks of you, I can't think when you ate a proper meal?'

'Well, I can tell you that not a morsel's passed 'er lips since she got 'ere this morning! Refused everything, she did!' Katy told him.

On the ride home in Father Riley's ramshackle car Queenie appreciated that they were both extremely concerned, yet for all her gratitude, she couldn't be doing with their worriting and fussing. She would be glad when they bade her cheerio.

'Right then,' Katy Forest made sure that Queenie was settled in the horse-hair armchair by the fire, a steaming drink of hot milk clasped in her fist, 'drink it all up! And then get yourself off to bed. I'll pop round in the morning.'

'Oh, but Katy . . .'

'No buts! You're to stay in bed till I come round. I'll not have you worrying about housework when you're poorly . . . leave that to me! It's nobbut a twopenny tram ride to Parkinson Street.'

Father Riley touched Queenie's hand reassuringly, and said, 'She's right, you know. There's nothing for you to worry about so just concentrate on getting better, eh?'

Queenie found it easier to let them go on believing that she was poorly. Perhaps it was nearer the truth than she was ready to admit but it irked her conscience all the same, to deceive them so. She waited for the front door to close behind them before she visibly relaxed. 'I don't deserve such friends,' she murmured, placing the hot drink on the oilcloth, where it was allowed to go cold.

After a while, Queenie walked across to the mantelpiece and Auntie Biddy's picture. For a long moment she stood, quietly looking into the youthful face. 'You were never beautiful of face, were you Auntie Biddy?' Queenie said, her voice small and broken, 'but all *your* beauty was inside you . . . where it matters.' Reaching up, she plucked the silver-framed picture from its place in the centre of the array of ornaments and held it closer to focus on the detail. 'You always told me that I was beautiful. But I'm not! not inside . . . I'm dirty and ugly, like a festering sore.' Her face took on a savage hatred as she went on, 'And *he* did it! Your brother! He spoiled me – and he spoiled my love for Rick. You knew all along, didn't you, Auntie Biddy? All that crying in your sleep. You never wanted us to be friends, because you knew . . . you *knew*!' Queenie's final words were choked with sobs.

For what seemed an age she gazed on the picture; then she kissed its silent image and placed it back on the mantelpiece. 'George Kenney made you suffer too, I know, more than anybody could realize. But you still loved him, didn't you?' Queenie had never understood Auntie Biddy's vigilant loyalty to her brother; she only knew that if it hadn't been for that little woman's love for her, it would have been an empty world indeed. There was no trace of the anger she had initially felt at Auntie Biddy's deception regarding Rick's background as she now whispered, 'Oh, I wish you had told me . . . we might have been spared such heartache.'

The sharp rattling on the front door startled her. Was it Katy come back? As she manoeuvred herself round the table and towards the window, the noise shook the little house. It crossed Queenie's mind that it might be one of George Kenney's drinking cronies. But then, he was usually with them at this time of day.

Gingerly lifting the corner of the curtain, Queenie peeked out at the figure on the flagstones. It didn't look like one of his illustrious friends. 'Never seen him before,' she observed in a whisper, her curiosity faintly aroused.

He looked to be about nineteen or twenty, of medium height with stocky capable build. His carrot-red hair stood out in leaping armfuls of wild springy curls, and the dark mischievous eyes darted about in quickness, from the door to the window and back again. It was on one of these searching sweeps that the eyes alighted on the half-hidden Queenie, who swiftly stepped back, but too late.

'Aha!' The young man sprang towards the window, where he pushed his face flat against the pane, his nose spreading out in curious grotesque dimensions. 'You'll be the fair Queenie! Am I right?'

Queenie quickly dropped the curtain back over the distorted features and retreated into the relative safety of the parlour. Leaning against the table, she watched the face as it moved across the window, relentlessly pursuing her.

'You might as well let me in, Queenie, because I'm very persistent. I'm your new next-door neighbour. The name's Mike Bedford, and I'm 'ere on strict instructions from me Mam, to introduce meself.'

'Go away!' His rude insistence frightened Queenie.

'Ah! Not only is it beautiful. It also talks!'

'Michael!' The stranger's voice carried a sharp reprimand, 'I said to *introduce* yourself, not frighten the lass 'alf to death! Come away, you gurt gormless dope!'

Queenie assumed her rescuer to be the lad's mam; the voice had a friendly ring about it, in spite of its aggravated tone. All the same, Queenie did not want to be bothered with either of them. 'Wish they'd just clear off and leave me alone,' she thought. Now it seemed that the mother was no less insistent than the boy, for the rat-tatting started again. 'Oh, I'd best see what they want,' Queenie conceded, 'or there'll be no peace!'

The woman was a tiny busy little character, with dark short-cropped hair and bright eyes of mottled green and black.

'Hello, lass,' she said loudly, and without further ado she stepped into the passage. 'Thought we should introduce us-selves, being new neighbours an' all!' As she spoke, her head nodded up and down in a peculiar fashion, which held Queenie captivated, so that the red-headed young man had moved in and closed the door behind him before Queenie had time to realize it.

''Ow do, Queenie,' he winked and his dark eyes danced into hers, 'yer a right little sod, aren't you? I thought you'd never let me in!'

'Hey! Stop being so cheeky, fella-me-lad,' his mam's sharp tongue cut the air, 'less you want a clip o' the bloody ear!'

Queenie thought them a strange pair. Seems they'll not go away satisfied till I've let them in, she mused.

It was usual for new neighbours to make themselves known, but these two were more than a bit moithering, Queenie observed, more amused than irritated at that moment. She led them into the parlour.

'Ooh, look at this, our Mike!' The multi-coloured

185

eyes popped open wide, sweeping the room in blatant scrutiny. 'What a lovely cosy little parlour; oh, an' just see at that mantelpiece . . . all them quaint little pieces.' She turned to look Queenie in the face. 'All your Auntie Biddy's, I expect?' Without waiting for an answer, she scurried over to the mantelpiece, and stretched up on to her toes to examine the array of ornaments collected over the years by Auntie Biddy and treasured now by Queenie. Of a sudden, the woman's eyes fell upon the picture of Auntie Biddy. 'Hmph . . . so that'll be your Auntie Biddy?'

Queenie bristled. She didn't like this woman's downright nosiness. And how did she know her Auntie Biddy? At once, Queenie asked her.

'Mrs Farraday in the corner shop told me all about you and your Auntie Biddy,' came the reply, followed by a disapproving glare as she finished, '*and* that father o' yourn, George Kenney!'

Queenie hadn't felt right since Katy brought her home. Now, at the mere mention of George Kenney's name, her stomach turned somersault, and such was the nausea which rose within her that she had to lean on the table for support.

'Here!' The young man rushed forward and eased her into the nearest chair with surprising gentleness. 'Been at the booze again, 'ave you?' he laughed.

Queenie, feeling impatient with herself and at a disadvantage, smiled weakly at his thoughtless quip. She didn't feel well at all . . . perhaps Katy had been right. A comfortable bed and a good night's sleep seemed very attractive all of a sudden.

'I'm sorry,' she apologized, 'I was fetched home from work just now. I'm glad to have met you and I'm sure you'll like living in Parkinson Street; but I must excuse myself, if you don't mind?'

'Aye,' the woman said as she eyed Queenie up and down, 'I must say you don't look too bright . . . too skinny an' all, if you ask me.' Queenie had not asked her, and she didn't particularly want an opinion.

'Oh, I wouldn't say that, Mam!' The red-haired young man eyed Queenie with unabashed appreciation. 'Looks tasty enough to me.'

'I've told you afore, young Mike! You're too bloody for'ard.' She peered into Queenie's face with a look of apology as she went on, 'The lad means no 'arm, 'e's just like 'is Dad, a bit too much o' what the cat licks its arse with!'

Queenie had only ever heard such talk up the Navigation when she'd fetched George Kenney from his drinking. She hadn't liked it then and she cared less for it in this house. In spite of her tolerance, the disapproval showed in her face.

'Aw, tek no notice of me Mam,' Mike Bedford assured her, 'she's allus 'ad a colourful tongue!'

'You'll mek no excuses for me, my lad,' she said as she smiled sweetly at Queenie, 'if the lass is offended at me outright manner, that's just too bad. Folks tek me as they find me, I say.' She smiled broadly at Queenie. 'I dare say I could watch me P's and Q's, if I'd a mind though. Now then, I'm Gladys . . . Gladys Bedford . . . and this 'ere's my lad, Mike.'

'At your service.' He reached out to take Queenie's hand. Queenie took the extended hand and allowed it to shake hers for the merest second before pulling it away. Startled at the mistrust with which Queenie was regarding him, Mike Bedford told her chastisingly,

'Well, bless me socks! I ain't gonna *rape* you!'

Queenie wished fervently they would leave her be. 'You must excuse me,' she reminded them.

The sound of a key turning in the lock temporarily halted any further insistence on Queenie's part. She stood up, unsure of what to do next. Since George Kenney's violation of her and of all she held precious and decent, she had not been able to come to terms with anything, let alone having to look at his face, and him not even knowing or caring about what he had done.

If Queenie ever had murder eating away at her mind, it had been these last few days, when she'd kept well out of his way, her mind unable to settle. There was no order to her existence and the pattern of her life seemed hopelessly shattered.

George Kenney appeared at the parlour door, his unsteady gait warranting that he should lean heavily on the scruffy brawny strength of the inebriated woman by his side.

Queenie could not bring herself to look at either of them. By his very manner, it was painfully obvious to Queenie that he was oblivious to the dreadful deed he had committed against her. She had been even more sickened by the fact that in the depths of his drunkenness the confusion with what was real and what was imagined had accelerated until, in his own twilight world, the past and present had merged. Any sense of right or wrong had simply ceased to exist for him.

'Looks as if you've got company, Georgie love.' The woman steadied him as best she could, in view of the fact that she was finding difficulty in standing up straight. She cackled and screamed at his futile attempts to focus on the people in the parlour. 'Poor sod! Can't see too straight!'

Queenie cast a cursory glance at George Kenney's companion; the shock she received riveted her to the ground. It was Maisie Thorogood! And the change in her was devastating!

She gawped at Queenie through half-seeing eyes, bloated and deformed by the 'divils' whose company she had kept these last years, and who had finally demanded their pound of flesh and driven her as low as she could go.

Mike Bedford and his mam fidgeted nervously, looking to Queenie for reassurance. 'That your dad, is it?' The young man's voice was not as cocky as before.

'No, it's not! It's George Kenney the drunkard . . . and Maisie Thorogood as was!' Queenie retorted, the coolness of her voice belying the knot of disgust which had tightened her stomach into a fist.

''Course it's 'er dad, you gormless fool!' Mrs Bedford leaned forward to shove him ahead of her, seemingly glad of an excuse to leave. 'Come on, lad, we'd best be off.' She squeezed past Queenie, staying close to her son, her eyes shifty and uneasy as if expecting something untoward to happen.

George Kenney blundered into the room, falling into his armchair and pulling the staggering Maisie on top of him. 'Come 'ere, you bitch!' His roving hands roughly travelled her body, moving faster at her squeals of delight. 'Let's see what you're hiding under them skirts.' His laughter was thick and vulgar, his face growing redder by the minute.

The coarse vulgarity appeared to excite Mike

Bedford, as with a leer on his face he told Queenie, 'Hey – he's a right 'un, your dad, ain't 'e?'

If Queenie could have opened up the ground to swallow her, she would have done. If there had been anywhere she could have fled to escape that parlour, there would have been no holding her. But the ground was solid and there was nowhere to go. Her life, whether she liked it or not, was here. There was no use pretending otherwise. Turning now towards the mantelpiece, she took hold of Auntie Biddy's picture, swept across the room towards the door and told Mrs Bedford and her son, 'I'll see you out.' She did not need to look at George Kenney and his partner. Everything was reflected in Mike Bedford's ogling eyes. And Queenie's shame was complete.

'Er . . . would you like me to stay . . . keep you company for a bit, Queenie?' he asked, the leer still on his face.

'Goodnight!' The inflection of her voice left Mike Bedford in no doubt as to her response to *that* suggestion.

'Goodnight, dear,' Mrs Bedford said as she looked at Queenie with sympathetic eyes, 'get yourself off to bed.' Her glance strayed to the writhing couple on the chair.

Queenie closed the door behind them and made her way upstairs, with Mike Bedford's departing words ringing in her ears. 'See you tomorrow,' he'd said . . . well, he'd be lucky! Standing Auntie Biddy's picture next to her mother's on the dresser, Queenie whispered, 'Couldn't leave you down there to witness those goings-on!'

She glanced at her mother's picture; the glass was

gone and the picture torn in half where Queenie had disposed of George Kenney. How she wished the flesh and blood version could so easily be discarded! Lying in front of the picture, near the old brass crucifix, was Mr Craig's golden heart; its chain snapped in several places, the pieces of which had been carefully retrieved by Queenie. 'I'll get you fixed,' she promised, 'and a new frame for my Mam.'

She turned the big iron key in the lock. Never before had that key secured Auntie Biddy's room from such evil. But now, not a night passed without it being clicked home. Even then, Queenie's sleep was shallow and fitful, racked by horrifying memories.

Queenie had dragged the bed round so that she was nearer the window. She could not rightly say why, but somehow being able to look out over Parkinson Street helped to calm her. If she hitched herself up against the pillow, she could see down the whole length of that familiar endless street . . . she could see herself as a little girl skipping alongside Auntie Biddy. She could see old Mr Craig, and Maisie Thorogood's colourful cart. She had taught herself to try and concentrate on the things that had made her laugh; the times when she had been innocently happy. At these times, she felt peaceful within herself.

Queenie sat doubled up against her pillow, her eyes scouring the street below. It was in this uncomfortable position with her bedroom door securely locked and her ears assailed by the obscene laughter from downstairs, that she fell asleep.

Chapter Eight

'You ought to be ashamed o' yourself, George Kenney!' Queenie stretched her head from the restrictions of the pillow, cocking it attentively to one side. No! she wasn't dreaming, she decided; it *was* Katy Forest's voice, loud and angry, downstairs in the parlour.

George Kenney's answering abuse was promptly put down by the sharp-tongued Katy.

'You're nowt but a pitiful, beer-swilling no-good! And why that lovely child puts up with you, I'll never know! If it were up to me, she'd leave you to fend for yourself. And if you choked to death on your own vomit, George Kenney, it's a sure fact *I* wouldn't lose any sleep over it!' Her loud forceful roars of condemnation left no room for George Kenney's frequent attempts at retaliation.

Not so long ago, Queenie would have intervened, in the unlikely role of patient defender. But the horror of George Kenney's act of desecration towards her still sat ugly and tainted in her darkest nightmares.

Feeling more rested and relaxed after a night of comparatively undisturbed sleep, she lay there listening, deriving the greatest pleasure from hearing

George Kenney being put firmly in his place. Her grey eyes searched to focus on the picture by the brass crucifix. She fixed her gaze on Auntie Biddy's face.

'Can you hear that row downstairs?' said Queenie out loud, a whimsical smile shaping her full rich mouth. 'Sounds like the old days' . . . when Auntie Biddy was strong and full of fight, and life might have been poorer, but much less complicated. The tears clogged in her throat and a long shivering sigh escaped her. Her heart was so full with hopeless love for Rick.

'Go on! Get out George Kenney – and take your floozy with you!' The sharp words pierced Queenie's thoughts. She couldn't ever remember Katy Forest sounding so uncontrollably angry. Her voice rose to a frenzy of rage, 'You don't belong under the same roof as that girl! Clapped in jail, that's where *you* belong. You *and* that trollop! Both of a kind!'

'Don't tell *me* what to do in me own bloody 'ouse! Katy Forest! If anybody's getting out, it'll be you!'

At the ensuing scuffling and shouting, Queenie jumped out of bed, slipping quickly into her skirt and jumper. She knew from experience that George Kenney was capable of anything, and she feared for Katy's safety.

The front door banged shut, amid furious cries of 'If you ever set foot in my 'ouse again, Katy Forest, I'll not answer for my actions!'

Queenie's fearful heart fluttered as she hurried to the bedroom window. But the unexpected scene which greeted her caused her to clap her hand over her mouth in a futile effort to stifle the rising laughter. Then throwing her head back, she laughed out loud.

Poor old Maisie Thorogood was already at a jolly trot halfway down Parkinson Street and bringing up the rear in hot pursuit was the ungainly figure of George Kenney. 'Maisie! Maisie love! Come back . . . I'll kick the old bugger out . . . Come back!' he was shouting.

Katy Forest, satisfied that they were well out of the house, and in no immediate danger of returning, crossed to the foot of the stairs and called Queenie. Queenie, already on her way down, couldn't resist a chuckle. 'Katy, what's all the goings on? Have you really chucked 'em both out?'

The homely face stretched into a wickedly delightful grimace. 'I've always 'ad a right bad temper, lass,' she admitted cheerfully. She led the way into the parlour where her tone of voice changed to one of disgust. 'Just look at this place! Pigs! The pair of 'em. They don't belong in a decent house with decent folks!'

Queenie looked around the room. By the look of it, she thought George Kenney's cronies must have turned up with more booze after she'd gone to sleep. Strewn from one end of the oilcloth to the other, empty bottles and jugs had trickled their last sediments into small pools of dark brown stain. There wasn't an ornament left standing upright anywhere on the sideboard, and somebody's half-hearted attempt at poking the fire had filled the hearth with black cinders and ash, like a thick dirt carpet.

Over by the scullery door, the stand-chair which

normally stood there like a dutiful sentry was toppled over in a most undignified manner. Queenie surmised that some drunken body had made a futile attempt at diving for the back door which led to the outer yard. Futile, because of the considerable deposit of reeking vomit, spread across the chair-legs and surrounding oilcloth.

Queenie had become used to clearing up such a mess. But she knew that Katy Forest had no such undesirable experience; having been raised in the most genteel manner, by strictly moral parents. Her father had been a well-respected clerk to the council.

'I'm sorry Katy,' Queenie said, deeply ashamed that Katy Forest should have to witness such a scene. Her throat tightened with angry emotion. 'I wish you hadn't seen the place like this.' She moved to tackle the job of clearing up.

'Oh no you don't, young lady!' Katy intervened. 'You get yourself back up them stairs to bed, and don't move till I tell you.' Her strong capable hands proceeded to eject Queenie from the room, towards the stairway.

'No. Please Katy?' Queenie could not, in any circumstances, allow the dear lady to forage about in such filth. With startling clarity she suddenly realized how close she'd come to sinking into a state of self-pity and foolish dreams of what could never be. She would have to accept things as they were. There was nothing closer to her heart's desire than to have won and kept the love of Rick. By the self-same token, there was nothing more forbidden, or more ir-refutably impossible. Life had become a lonely bitter road. But it was *her* road, and one that only she could tread.

'Look at the state of you, lass,' Katy's voice grew gentle. Her kind eyes brimmed with concern at Queenie's pale drawn face, and the painful thinness of her form. 'You're not fit to be out o' bed. Go on back and sleep awhile. I'll soon 'ave this lot cleared up and smarter than a barracks!' Her strong broad face creased into a reassuring smile. 'Then I'll fetch us a nice cup o' tea and some cake I brought from 'ome.'

Katy Forest's concern for the waif-like girl before her showed freely in her face; but she had come to know of the inner strength which drove Queenie against all odds. And she had come to love and respect her.

The tears in Queenie's heart rose to mist her sad eyes. Katy was such a friend; such a wonderful person; and it was with regret that Queenie now saw the only possibility left open to her. Because of her impossible love for Rick, and all that had happened, she had no choice but to cut herself off from anything and anyone which might create a link between them, however inadvertently.

Now, as she looked around her to see the awful mess left by George Kenney, the thought of actually clearing up behind him even once more seemed too much of a purgatory. So when Katy began pushing her towards the stairs, saying, 'Now then! I'm not tekkin no for an answer. You take yourself back up yon stairs, make the bed and pinch some roses into them there cheeks, and you can come back down to

give me an 'and, eh?' Queenie offered little resistance. She did exactly as Katy instructed, and when
some time later she returned to the parlour it was to
see Katy with her sleeves rolled up and the parlour
looking a little more like its old self.

With renewed vigour, Queenie got out the dub-
bing rags and polish and in less than no time at all,
between the two of them, the parlour was shining
like a new pin.

'By 'eck lass!' Katy Forest jumped in fright, as the
gas-ring she was lighting backfired vehemently, 'it's
time you 'ad a modern cooker or summat! This
blessed thing's likely to give a body 'eart-attack!'

Queenie collected the matches from the floor
where Katy had dropped them, 'It's all right Katy,'
she smiled. Then turning the gas-tap on slowly, she
carefully fed the lit match towards the hiss of gas,
explaining, 'It's just a knack. Auntie Biddy used to
say it were "temperamental".'

'Aye well, 'appen it's grown more cantankerous
with age, eh?' Katy threw bulbous arms up and
laughed loudly at herself. 'Like me, eh? Old and
cantankerous . . . like old Katy Forest!'

Queenie smiled appreciatively; but there was no
real laughter in her heart.

Katy Forest carried the mugs of tea through to
the parlour, where she settled herself in George
Kenney's horse-hair armchair. Then ruminatively
regarding Queenie across the firegrate, she observed, 'You've not asked about Rick.'

The statement drew no response, and in the wake
of heavy silence, Katy went on. 'He's a grand lad is
that! Grand and proper.' She drew a mouthful of tea

then leaned forward to peer penetratingly into Queenie's blushing face. 'Fond of 'im aren't you lass? And I *know* he's taken with you.' She grinned broadly, as she released the secret she'd been minding. 'He telephoned Father Riley this morning. First thing the lad did was ask after you. Said as 'ow he downright misses you, and can't wait to see you again. Ringing back later he is; 'Course, Father Riley said nowt about you being poorly. Oh, Queenie! 'Appen things is coming right at last, eh?'

Katy's well-meant cascade of words mingled into Queenie's confused thoughts. Rick had asked after her . . . *missed* her! Oh, it couldn't be more than she'd missed *him*. The treasured image of his tall straight figure and fair smiling features lit up her mind, making her resolution falter. *Why* shouldn't they still have each other? The strength of their love was surely all that mattered. But a sense of desolation prevailed, as Queenie realized that nothing in the world could undo the fact that Rick was her brother. They could be united only in the common blood of George Kenney. And that was the worst damnation!

'What's up wi' you, lass?' Katy's persistent voice reached into Queenie's thoughts. 'Miles away you are – *miles* away!'

Queenie looked up, acutely conscious of her intimate line of thought. 'Sorry Katy. I was just thinking. That was kind of Rick to ask after me. When he rings again, please tell him I'm sorry to have missed him . . .'

'Why should *I* tell 'im?' Katy winked cheekily as she spoke. 'When he rings back, *you* can tell 'im.

Oh, it would be grand to see you two wedded. Made for each other, you are; an' there's nobody in this world as could look after you better.'

Queenie knew of no other way to end this painful conversation, 'I think I'll go back to bed for a while, Katy.'

'Good grief!' Katy Forest reprimanded herself. 'You'd think I'd know better than wearing you out. That's right! Get off to your bed. I'll fetch you some soup. It'll do you good.'

Queenie didn't want any soup. But when Katy brought it up to her, she drank it dutifully under those kindly watchful eyes, surprised in herself to realize just how hungry she was.

'Right then, lass. I'll be off. But I'll be back in the morning. Strict instructions from Father Riley!' Katy declared stoutly.

As Queenie gazed through the window watching Katy amble off down Parkinson Street, a terrible sense of loss swamped her. The emotion she'd deliberately suppressed found outlet in the heartfelt tears which streamed unheeded down her face. The resolution she needed to make created a cutting ache within her. She knew there was no other course than to stay away from those she had come to love so dearly. And as her tired voice murmured, 'I must avoid Rick at all costs,' the quiet words echoed against her heart like mighty blows. The torment of the decision could only be likened to the loneliness she had experienced when they had lowered Auntie Biddy into the cold enveloping ground.

She recalled the happiness and laughter she'd enjoyed in Rick's company. Cherishing the memory,

Queenie was convinced that such times would come no more. Nevertheless, she would not go to Father Riley's house again.

Rummaging through the dresser drawer she found a pencil and writing paper. 'It isn't as easy as I thought,' she muttered, searching her mind for the right words to put in the note. All the same, there was a calm determination in the sweeping flow of her writing:

Dearest Father Riley,
I have something to tell you, which I hope you can find it in your wise heart to understand. I will not be coming to the Church-house again. I have a boyfriend and it is my intention to accompany him on a trip connected with his employ.

I'm not certain of the date of my return; but in the event, it would be as well for Katy to find someone to take my place in your house.

I would be very obliged if you could please inform Richard Marsden of my plans; and ask him not to attempt to contact me in any way. Also Katy Forest, who has been my very good friend, and to whom I shall always be grateful for her kindness towards me. I shall be in good hands. My companion is kind and extremely fond of me.
Thank you for everything.

Yours affectionately
Queenie

Queenie was still crying bitterly as she folded the

note and placed it in the envelope. She felt as though she had closed the last friendly door, and in doing so had condemned herself to a cruelly empty existence.

All the way to the Church-house, Queenie felt unbearably guilty, hating herself for doing the only thing she believed to be right.

The sound of Father Riley and Katy Forest having one of their friendly heated discussions as to the value of today's society permeated the night air, as Queenie carefully slipped the note through the letter-box, before making a hasty retreat.

The journey home concluded a sad task. Queenie was thankful that the night hid her tears from view. Closing the bedroom door behind her and turning the heavy key securely, Queenie undressed, turned out the light and slipped between the sheets.

She couldn't even bring herself to look at Auntie Biddy's picture, or that of her dead mother. Her shame and acute sense of sorrow were too pressing. Tonight, for the first time in her life, she had brought herself to lie. And to a priest of God no less! No amount of self-justification could persuade her that it had been the only course; yet she could see no alternative.

The prayer which filled the room with its sincere plea was born from the depths of her wretchedness.

'Dear God in Heaven,

I have no one to turn to, only you. I love Rick with all my heart. I want no other; and so it seems I'm determined to be forever lonely. I can't pretend to understand your ways, God, but I hope You can understand me; and find it in Your heart to forgive me my sin this night.'

Burying her face deep in the pillow, Queenie willed herself to sleep. But sleep eluded her. When George Kenney stumbled into the house in the early hours, she was still awake and wrestling unsuccessfully to shut out the image of the young man she so desperately loved. But Rick Marsden stayed indelibly in her mind, cherished forever in her lonely heart.

Chapter Nine

It had been a fitful night, filled with strange fantasies of gyrating creatures and misshapen faces which disturbed her sleep and made rest impossible. Several times, Queenie had been compelled by driving nausea to go downstairs and outside to the lavvy. But when there was no relief from the upsurging demons in her stomach, she had gone back to her bedroom, where she knelt forlornly by the open window.

The hours dragged on as she scoured the length and breadth of Parkinson Street, searching for she knew not what. In her heart, she fought away from the implications of her sickness. The possibility that her own father's child was growing inside her was too monstrous to contemplate. A shutter in her mind blocked out the dark thought, and for a while no thought but of Rick occupied her.

When the sky finally lightened to herald the start of another day, Queenie was still kneeling by the window. Her legs had grown stiff from their crooked position, and her body ached and protested against her abuse of it. But still, she did not move. She watched the 'knocker-up' as he wended his zig-zag way down the stretching row of houses. His meandering steps took him from one side to the other, following his set pattern so as not to miss a single dwelling. Each house represented the gradely sum of a threepenny piece, for which he returned on a Friday night; it wasn't likely that he'd want to miss any out.

A faint smile whispered across Queenie's lovely mouth as she observed with interest that the loud whistling which accompanied each resounding knock of his long stick on the bedroom window meant that he really had no need to wake the folks at the bottom of the street. By the time he'd whistled and rattled the *top* half awake, there wasn't a soul in the street left asleep.

Straightening the bed, Queenie then gathered her clothes up and moved out onto the landing. Ingrained habit caused her to glance towards George Kenney's bedroom door. The loud broken snores emerged as muffled groans across the span of landing, but the expression on her face revealed nothing of the swirling emotions which confused and tormented her.

She strip-washed at the scullery sink, donned clean clothes, then set about the housework. But there was no eagerness in her heart. She felt herself lost in the strangest of moods, as if her deepest inner self had deserted her. For a long time she sat deep in thought, curled up in the horse-hair chair, whose familiar prickliness brought her small comfort. Persistent images rushed in and out of her mind, of Rick and the hopeless wonderful love which had so cruelly excited their lives, only to plunge them in terrible despair. Then there were other images, of dearest Auntie Biddy and the burdening secret she had so jealously guarded to the grave. And of George Kenney, the foulest, darkest thing that God ever saw fit to create!

She didn't quite know when or how the idea began

to take shape. It was just suddenly there, like an answer to an unspoken prayer. She would go to the Sisters at Nazareth House. They had understood the desperate physical needs which had driven Auntie Biddy to them; Queenie sensed that they could help now, in her tormented search for spiritual guidance. She was lost to everything which had been her anchor. The Sisters were close to God and the understanding of His children, and she had never felt less like one of God's children than she did now. She had grown tired, tired of battling on her own, tired of struggling towards an end she just couldn't see any more, tired of living.

Queenie had hoped that she would never again have to tread the path to Nazareth House. Yet here she was, facing a barrage of conflicting and painful emotions, that left her drained and at the same time filled with dreadful fear. Suddenly, the need to deliver herself to Nazareth House took on a frantic urgency. She would leave no explanation of where she had gone. There was no one here to care. And she would take nothing with her but the pictures of her mother and Auntie Biddy, together with Mr Craig's golden heart.

Stepping from the tram at Cherry-Tree, Queenie hastened towards the path which would take her to Nazareth House and, she hoped, peace of mind.

At the top of the winding path, however, she stopped, half hiding herself behind a tree. Creeping doubts gnawed at her intention, until she considered turning back. But realizing that turning back would steep her again in the terrible darkness which had almost suffocated her, Queenie renewed the last part of her journey with increased determination, in spite of the whispering questions and anxieties which teased and played on her mind. Would the nuns turn her away? Was a mug of tea and a dripping buttie the full extent of their Christian hand? And would they treat her with contempt, because of her own inability to cope with life's increasing pressures? She had no way of knowing. She only knew that emotionally and physically, she was totally void. She prayed with all her heart that God would not desert her.

'Queenie? Do you have a surname?' The black-frocked nun waited for a reply.

Queenie felt small and insignificant beneath the searching gaze of the elderly nun. Perhaps she shouldn't have come after all? The plaguing doubts returned, and she cursed herself for having been so foolish! 'No,' she murmured, 'just Queenie.'

At the nun's instructions, Queenie followed her into the inner hall where, in the cold vastness of that place, a feeling of awe came over her; that same sensation she supposed a body might experience on entering a mighty cathedral.

'If you'd like to wait there,' the elderly nun gestured briskly towards a long wooden settle over to the right of the main doors, 'I'll fetch Mother Superior.'

With the disappearance of the nun, a comforting quiet settled around Queenie, calming her troubled thoughts and relaxing her so that she found herself drawing pleasure from the unfamiliar things around her.

The huge hall, with its half-panelled walls and thick aroma of seasoned and polished wood made a warming impression of richness. The floors were of honey-coloured blocks, worn dull by the door and in front of the settle. Right in the centre of the floor was a circular carpet of brown and gold leaf design, on which stood a magnificent table of huge proportions.

Queenie calculated that the lip of the table-top must be at least ten inches thick. The surface was polished so beautifully that the reflection of the resplendent silver candelabra in the centre shone clearly from its fathomless depths. The reach of table-top was at least twelve foot in length, and five foot across. The whole heavy beautiful thing was supported by two circular legs, one set partly in at each end. The legs were carved into bulbous shapes which first swelled out, then pinched in again at regular intervals. Their diameter was easily that of tree-trunk proportion; but in spite of the obvious weight and cumbersome quality of this beautiful table, it exuded craftsmanship and delicacy of the highest calibre. The same exquisite detail could be seen in the settle upon which Queenie sat patiently waiting. There was no other furniture in the hall. There was no need of it.

The door through which Queenie had entered was solid oak at the bottom. The top half was a full stained glass window, depicting the crucifixion of Christ; where the daylight played upon its back, the silhouettes shone and gleamed in wonderful rich hues of amber, reds and golds, and the crown of thorns piercing His head stood out sharp in pointed blades of opaque black. Above the door, fixed low on the wall, was a picture of the Virgin Mary and the baby Jesus.

The overpowering emotions of great peace and humility convinced Queenie beyond any further doubt that she had done the right thing in coming here.

'Queenie?' The nun was tall and slim, with soft velvet eyes and a full generous mouth. 'Sister Mary said you didn't give your second name?' she asked in a gentle, concerned manner. Her long black habit rustled as she moved towards the settle, and the rosary about her waist peeked and hid in and out of her skirt with each step.

Queenie rose to meet her, the initial flutterings of nervousness quickly allayed by the nun's warm disarming smile.

'I've got no second name,' she said clasping the extended hand of friendship, which propelled her gently back to the settle, 'folks just call me Queenie.'

The nun seated herself beside Queenie. 'I'm the Mother Superior,' she said, her perceptive eyes measuring the sadness in one so young, 'do you need help?'

The question was so outright that it dispersed all the carefully planned answers Queenie had rehearsed while waiting. For the first time, she felt decidedly anxious in the presence of this gentle creature. With equal candour, she replied. 'Yes Mother Superior . . . I need help.'

The Mother Superior clasped Queenie's hand, feeding her own strength into the trembling heart of the girl before her. Her eyes caressed the unhappy face, as she lifted a finger to brush away the tears which careered helplessly from Queenie's sorry grey eyes. 'I don't know whether what you seek is here, with us,' she told Queenie sincerely, 'but I do hope so. Don't tell me anything just yet . . . only if you feel you need to. You don't have to justify your presence here, child.

This is a place where all of God's people are welcome.' She urged Queenie to her feet. 'We *all* of us need sanctuary sometimes, child. And I hope we can quiet the troubles which brought you here.' She started towards the door, through which Sister Mary had disappeared earlier. 'Come on, let's see if we can find Sister Mary. She'll find a place for you.' Her glance swept the surrounds of the wooden settle, as she went on, 'You brought nothing with you?'

Queenie shook her head, at the same time wondering what Auntie Biddy would make of it all. 'No, I brought nothing with me,' she confirmed, following the Mother Superior into the passage and clutching her hand tightly around the pictures in her coat pocket.

'It doesn't matter, Queenie. We have all you'll need.' A mischievous gleam lit up her face as she caught Queenie's eye and added, 'Oh and don't let Sister Mary frighten you. She is a dreadful little monster who bosses everyone. Including me!'

Queenie soon found out that the Mother Superior's account of Sister Mary was painfully accurate. She ordered Queenie about with the energy and ruthlessness of a Sergeant-Major. Having skilfully elicited that Queenie was well versed in the skills of washing and pressing, she promptly installed her in the basement to assist in the busy laundry duties.

The order of the convent was not officially a silent one, but apart from Mother Superior and Sister Mary the nuns rarely spoke although they were polite and helpful enough.

Free to come and go as she pleased, Queenie gladly

gave of her time, and indeed enjoyed laundering the long black flouncing skirts and sparkling white breast yokes, which were starched to such a degree that Queenie marvelled at the will-power required even to wear them. There wasn't all that much difference though, in laundering these unfamiliar iterns, and washing and pressing for folks down Parkinson Street. The small copper boiler and dolly-tub at home might not be a match for the great big boilers used here but at the end of a busy day, the result was the same.

Nazareth House was Queenie's oasis in her sea of troubles. She began to thank the unseen hand which had guided her to this quiet place.

Her days were spent as she willed. Some of the time she would work hard and eager in the bustle and heat of the basement laundry; then she would wander about the magnificent grounds, regularly stopping to sit on the bench where, as a hungry child, she had shared the tramp's crust of bread. Often, when sitting there, with the branches moving and murmuring in the breeze, she would look up at every sound, half expecting to see the tramp; but she never did.

At these times, her heart would cloud over at the memory of her darling Auntie Biddy; and the irrepressible waves of nostalgia would persuade her back to the sheer enjoyment of polishing Auntie Biddy's prized possessions. She would long for the sight and touch of them. But then George Kenney's face would loom into her mind and she would tremble with fear and hatred. And she knew she wasn't yet ready.

In spite of all her efforts to shut him out of her mind, Rick occupied her thoughts more and more, and she accepted completely that she would never be able to forget him, or to stop loving him with every fibre of her being.

Each day started with her quickly adopted routine. At five a.m. when she heard the nuns moving about on the floor beneath where her room was situated, she would rise to tidy the narrow room which was furnished only with the sparest of necessities, consisting of a chest of drawers and a wardrobe, together with a long wooden cross adorning the wall above her bed. After tidying her room, she would wait for the sisters to vacate the little chapel where they gathered for prayers, before filing into the long narrow dining room for breakfast. Then, Queenie would quietly make her way downstairs and into the chapel, where for twenty minutes or so she knelt in thoughts of past happiness and questions for the future.

Queenie rose from the pew, and made her way towards the dining room. The restlessness which had driven her to pace the floor of her tiny room half the night showed clearly in the dark rings under her eyes, and the agitated way she folded and unfolded her hands.

As she entered the breakfast room, the Mother Superior smiled a greeting, 'Good morning, Queenie.'

'Good morning, Mother Superior,' Queenie said as she collected a plate and two slices of toast from the trolley by the door, acknowledging the varied smiles of welcome as she wended her way to the far end of the table, to the place allocated to her.

She poured herself a cup of lukewarm tea, before becoming aware of the Mother Superior standing by her side. 'Queenie, when you've had your breakfast, can you spare me a few moments? I'll be in my study.'

'Of course, Mother Superior.' Queenie replaced the teapot in order to concentrate on the Mother Superior's kindly face. 'There's nothing wrong is there?'

'No Queenie. There's nothing wrong. I'd just be glad of a chat.' She turned to go. 'Whenever you're ready.'

Queenie was ready now, but she finished her breakfast before making her way down to the Mother Superior's office. It was an old dusty office, smelling of books and starch. But the view from the window was breathtaking. Situated at the back of the convent, it commanded sweeping views across the considerable span of landscaped gardens.

'Come in,' the voice raised itself with crisp authority. 'Sit yourself down, Queenie. And don't concern yourself that there is anything wrong. On the contrary, I'm delighted to see how well you're doing.' She looked questioningly at Queenie as she went on, 'You *are*, aren't you?'

Queenie seated herself on the bench over by the window, where she didn't feel quite so hemmed in. 'Yes . . . thank you, I'm happy here.' The ring of her quiet voice wasn't quite as convincing as she would have liked.

Mother Superior came and seated herself by Queenie, reaching out to take the small hand in her own. 'I heard you last night, Queenie. Your room is right above mine. You must have been pacing the floor half the night?'

Queenie felt ashamed, 'I'm sorry. I didn't realize . . .'

'No, Queenie. There is no need for apologies.

You're troubled, aren't you . . . still?'

Queenie couldn't deny it. Inside, she felt restless; although perhaps not as frightened and bitter as when she had first arrived. She had acquired a kind of peace, a degree of self-belief. But there was still something very much amiss.

The Mother Superior seemed to sense the hesitance in Queenie's reply. 'You can stay here as long as you like, Queenie; you know that, don't you?' She waited till Queenie nodded before continuing, 'But you have to be sure. You have to know in your heart exactly what it is you want. Sometimes, when we seek to leave something behind, it clings to us; and even though the elements within it cease to hurt or haunt us, we can't seem to shake it off.' She looked hard at Queenie, anxious that she should understand. 'Life,' she continued quietly, holding Queenie's eyes fast in the strength of her own, 'is a process. It's a gradual process through which we *have* to find the courage to live, because it is that very living which shapes the person we become. We can remove ourselves *physically* from the source of our troubles; but in our hearts and minds, we have to carry it with us.' She placed a gentle hand beneath Queenie's chin and lifted her face to gaze upon it. 'Do you understand what I'm saying, Queenie?'

Queenie *did* understand, and the understanding seemed to lessen the furtive restlessness within her. Her place wasn't here. It was at home, amongst the things she knew and loved – and also amongst the things she hated and feared. But now she didn't hate or fear them anymore. In the place of fear and hatred there had emerged a clearer insight into her own responses, and subsequently, her control of those responses. There was nothing more to be done here at Nazareth House.

Not once did the Mother Superior question her motives for having come to the convent, and Queenie was thankful.

'Thank you. I *do* understand,' she told her, rising to leave, 'and I'm very grateful, Mother Superior.'

Mother Superior was still sitting by the window as Queenie closed the door. She reached up to the hall stand for her mac, which she threw around her shoulders, before wandering outside to sit thoughtfully on the bench.

'You'll catch pneumonia!'

Sister Mary collapsed herself onto the bench next to Queenie, her wrinkled face a mass of pink and blue crevices as she screwed her features up against the cold blasting wind. 'Seems like winter's arriving with a vengeance! What on earth are you doing out here?'

Queenie pulled the collar of her mac up about her neck. She turned to glance at the old nun, whom she had grown to respect. 'Just thinking,' she said simply.

Sister Mary let out a noisy shiver. 'Thinking eh? Thinking of leaving us?' Her voice slid to a quietness, 'I've seen it the last few days. You've only been here a couple of weeks, Queenie; but you've changed a lot in that short time.'

'Changed?' Queenie wondered at that.

'Oh yes. You've grown more . . . self-assured. And stronger.'

Queenie pondered. Stronger? Yes, maybe that was it! She'd grown stronger inside, more able to cope with it all now. She'd certainly grown stronger in her conviction that George Kenney was unanswerable for his actions. If only because he wasn't even aware of them! The knowledge that she had come so close to taking his life tempered her repugnance of him. And at last, she could see him for the weak pitiful thing he was.

She also knew the final futility of her love for Rick. Accepting that had been the hardest thing of all. Yet, at the back of her thoughts, a disturbing insistence had forced recognition of one other aspect of her love for him. After George Kenney's violation of her, Queenie wondered whether she could ever have submitted herself to any man's embrace, however much she loved him. Would her fear have melted away in Rick's arms or would it have spoiled their happiness? She couldn't tell.

'You are thinking of leaving us, aren't you Queenie?'

Queenie thought she perceived the faint glint of a tear in the old nun's fading eyes. She reached out to cover the cold hand which rested exposed on the long black frock. She smiled up into the questioning face, and her eyes shone strong as she squeezed Sister Mary's fingers firmly. 'Yes,' she whispered gently, 'it's time I went home, where I belong.'

Chapter Ten

'It's starting to snow,' Queenie said as she stretched her neck against the window, 'best put your cap and scarf on when you go out.'

'Don't keep talking to me as if I were a two-year-old!' The deterioration in George Kenney was startling. It had been no more than a few weeks since the night Queenie had delivered herself to the convent, and three days since her return to Parkinson Street. But in that short span of time, George Kenney had been reduced to a thin trembling shadow of his former self. His tone was less aggressive, as though the devil in him had burned itself out, and all his inebriated cronies appeared to have deserted him.

On arriving home, Queenie had been stunned by the shocking manner and degree of George Kenney's demise. During the time she had spent at the convent, the frayed threads of her mental and emotional courage had somehow emerged stronger while George Kenney, who was at the very root of her flight to sanctuary, had disintegrated almost beyond recognition.

She still couldn't find it in her heart to completely forgive him; the scars were too deep, too new . . . but now she partly accepted that the evil within him was too strong and ingrained even for him to control, until finally it had turned inward to destroy him with the same merciless intent with which he had sought to destroy her from the day of her birth. Her own salvation had been derived from the strength bestowed on her by beloved Auntie Biddy; and latterly from the unquestioning kindness of the sisters at Nazareth House.

She wondered in passing what George Kenney's salvation might be? Or even whether he indeed wanted any form of redemption. They did say that when a body had sunk beneath a certain level he was in the company of his own kind, and desired it no other way. It seemed to Queenie that his fornication and sins, and the shame and punishment he had brought down on them, had risen up to suffocate him.

But now more immediate problems loomed. Her few savings had all but run out, and she knew there was nothing else for it but to go out and find a 'proper' job. Nobody was setting on till after Christmas now, but Queenie calculated that they would manage well enough till then.

Father Riley and Katy Forest had apparently been to the house several times, looking to talk to her; and according to George Kenney's tauntings he had delighted in informing them that she had 'run off'.

Not a single day or night had gone by without Queenie thinking of Rick. 'Due home for Christmas', Katy had mentioned in a note which she had pushed through the door, and which had lain on the mat until Queenie's return. 'Haven't fooled old Katy,' Queenie mused, 'she knows I wouldn't have no other boyfriend.'

'Who says I'm going out anyway?' George Kenney's demanding tones shattered her thoughts. 'And what about *you*, eh? You never go through that sodding door . . . not since you got back from your tom-cat's wanderings! Never show yer face outside, allus getting that cheeky Bedford fella from next door to do yer running about!'

'No such thing! Mike just pops into Farraday's now and again for me on his way home from work!' Queenie retorted. 'And as for me not going out, where would I go, eh? There's enough in this house to keep me well occupied.

'I don't like that Bedford chap! Cunning bugger if you ask me.' His face fell into itself as he asked quietly, 'Got some'at special, 'as 'e? What's 'is price for doing your errands, eh? A quick thrash in the bed, is it?' He collapsed into a fit of vulgar laughter, then his eyes fixed on Queenie as she busied herself about the room in an effort to control her rising temper, and he asked in a quieter voice, 'Fancied that young Richard, didn't you? Saw yourself as 'is wife, no doubt, eh?' He fell into laughing again, his cruel jibes relentless. 'What 'appened then . . . two peas out of the same pod, was it?'

Queenie brushed past him. She had to get out away from his spiteful tongue. She grabbed her mac and scarf and hurried out into the cold December night. As she left, George Kenney's raised voice filtered into the street after her, 'Sins of the father, is it?' Probably the only coherent thing left about George Kenney was his unique cruelty. Everything else had crumbled into senility.

Queenie slammed the door shut and headed briskly

down Parkinson Street, towards the market square. The snow was coming down thick and heavy now, settling on the ground like a white mantle. 'Hiding the dirt beneath,' thought Queenie bitterly, still smarting from George Kenney's sneer at her love for Rick. She turned her collar up and pulled her belt into a tighter notch.

'Hello there, lass,' Mrs Farraday's friendly greeting arrested Queenie in her tracks, 'thought I'd best throw a bit o' salt down 'ere. Don't want me customers slipping over.'

Queenie blinked the soft fluffy snowflakes from her long lashes, her eyes following the scattering movements of Mrs Farraday's gloved hands. She watched the salt sizzling and bubbling, flattening the considerable layer of soft squashy snow, until the flagstones beneath emerged all clean and wet. 'I thought you'd be shut by now, Mrs Farraday . . . it's gone six o' clock,' Queenie told her.

'Oh aye. We've nobbut this very minute closed,' she clapped her hands together to release the last few pinches of salt, 'but it looks as if it'll snow all night. Best to be prepared, I allus say.' Waggling her head, she declared stoutly, 'I shall spread some sawdust an' all!' Then, looking at Queenie in a strange quizzical way, it seemed she might be about to ask something, but in a moment she had obviously changed her mind.

Queenie wondered if during her two weeks' stay at Nazareth House there had been a degree of speculation as to her whereabouts; then she dismissed the notion. Even when she was at home, she had preferred to stay within the confines of her own four walls, rarely venturing outside; so she was probably not missed at all.

Plunging her hands deep into her mac pocket, the biting cold catching her breath, she shuddered, 'Brr! I thought it was supposed to be warmer if it snowed?'

'Don't you believe it, lass! Snow's cold ain't it? Then it must mek the air cold eh? Stands to reason, does that!' Mrs Farraday waggled a welcoming hand towards the shop door. 'Why don't you come in for a warm?' she asked.

Queenie did not need asking twice, although it did cross her mind that the kind gesture was totally uncharacteristic. It was a well-known fact that Mrs Farraday was a jolly sort in the shop, as helpful as they came, but she had always been most reluctant to expose any of her private life to her customers. In fact, Queenie could not recall anyone who had ever set foot inside the Farradays' living quarters.

Mr Farraday was down on his hands and knees, collecting the strewn cinders from the hearth and chucking them back into the flames. 'Hello there, young Queenie,' he said with a smile. He had a soft spot for this girl who, in his opinion, had been given short shrift of life's simple pleasures. 'Keeping all right are you, lass?' His thin old face was upturned into a permanent grimace, sculptured by the constant effort to prevent his glasses from sliding off the edge of his nose.

Mrs Farraday helped him up. 'Don't know why you bother doing that, love, they'll only keep on spitting out. We'll just have to get a new grate.'

Queenie watched them with interest, a pleasant

smile lighting up her face. What a delightful scene, she thought, and what a lovely couple, happy in each other's company. She looked around the room, and saw that it was a true reflection of their contentment. The rosy flames flickered and danced in the firegrate, warming the room with a comfortable glow. The furniture was not unlike Auntie Biddy's; solid home farm, and just as lovingly cared for. Everywhere Queenie looked there was brass in abundance: brass plates; bellows; slipper boxes . . . and all the fire furniture was made of brass, as golden and brilliant as Aladdin's cave.

'Cold are you?' Mrs Farraday enquired as she toddled off to open the sideboard door. 'I've got summat 'ere to warm you up,' she chuckled, shouting triumphantly as she located a dumpy bottle full of a rich red fluid, 'damson wine! Best ever . . . made to me old Mam's recipe. This 'ere bottle's been sitting in yon cupboard since me sister brought it nigh on five years back.' She reached into the cupboard to produce two glasses. 'I 'ope it don't go off! No! 'course not. They say it improves with age.'

As she tipped the drink into the glass, Queenie put up a staying hand, saying, 'I'd best not, Mrs Farraday, if you don't mind. I've never taken to drinking and I'm afeared it will make me sick.'

Mrs Farraday was having none of it and she chided, 'Get away wi' you, lass! This won't mek you sick. Here!' she pushed the half-full glass into Queenie's hand, 'you just take a little sip. If it don't suit you, I'll eat me words!'

Queenie was pleasantly surprised. The fiery liquid

warmed her right through to the bones. 'It *is* pleasant tasting, Mrs Farraday,' she agreed.

''Course it is! Lovely.' She stared hard at Queenie as she went on, 'Mind you, I'm not a drinking person meself! Oh no! it'll be in that cupboard long after me an' my man are gone. So . . . we might as well mek the most of it, eh?' And to Queenie's question as to whether the shop would be open tomorrow, she replied, 'No, lass. We like three days off over Christmas, and anyway most folks 'ave done their shopping by Christmas Eve.' She sat down next to Queenie, 'If you're wanting summat, you'd best tek it now. You can pay me after the holidays if you like.' Quick to notice Queenie's embarrassment, she suddenly exclaimed, 'But I'll tell you what! I've some perishables left over . . . Good stuff! Be a pity to throw them out. There's a turkey an' a string o' sausages. Oh, aye! An' there's a couple o' trays o' mince tarts. Do me a favour will you, lass? Tek 'em with you.' She patted Queenie's hand as she spoke.

Queenie knew full well that such items of food were unlikely to be leftovers. She told herself that probably everybody in Parkinson Street knew how badly off she and George Kenney were. And her vow to acquire a job after the holidays burned stronger than ever.

'That's kind of you, Mrs Farraday,' Queenie answered politely but firmly. 'I shall pay for them in full – how much will it be?' That would be the first chunk from her paypacket.

Mrs Farraday smiled and shook her head resignedly, 'I should 'ave known better. You've allus been a proud 'un, even when you were little. All right then

. . . that'll cost you nineteen and sixpence. I'll get me man to put 'em in a box.' Of a sudden, she eyed Queenie with concern. 'Where were you off to in this weather?'

Queenie knew that if she was to divulge her reason for being out on such a night, Mrs Farraday would only dig deeper and deeper. It was time to be going. 'Thought I'd get a breath of air,' she answered, then drinking the remainder of the wine, she stretched her long legs and rose to her feet. 'I'd best be going now, Mrs Farraday . . . I expect the fire needs banking up.'

'You mean to say,' interrupted Mrs Farraday sharply, 'as George Kenney leaves that job to you!' Her eyes drew up into a tight narrow line as she went on, 'I expect 'e's off down the Navigation, eh?'

'No . . . he's sitting by the fire or he was when I left him just now. It's safer though if *I* see to the fire.' Queenie had gauged Mrs Farraday's reaction to that titbit of information, and she had to suffer the consequences, as her ears burned beneath the deluge of accusation against George Kenney. She was glad when Mrs Farraday bumbled to her feet.

'Right then! Let's get your goods and chattels.' She led the way into the shop, where Mr Farraday had withdrawn to long before to carry out the 'stocktaking'.

In a moment, Queenie had the box tucked beneath her arm as Mrs Farraday threw open the door for her to step out into the night. 'Mind your footing,' she warned, giggling foolishly, 'an' I think you've 'ad a drop too much to drink!' Queenie gaped at her in surprise. Why! Mrs Farraday was tipsy!

Queenie had to admit that in the rush of night air she too felt more than a little light-headed. Pushing her way home, she began to wish she had not indulged in the wine at all. All efforts to assemble her thoughts into disciplined coherence fell away in an irrational complusion to giggle. How silly, she chided herself, what was there to giggle about? All the way home she fought off a rising nausea, yet, in the midst of it all, she felt warm and cosy inside.

'Where've you been, Kathy love?' George Kenney was hovering by the door as Queenie let herself in. He called her Kathy most of the time now and she had become used to it. At first, she had contradicted him; but the confusion and argument which ensued was far more difficult to handle than just letting him loose in his own make-believe world.

'Get out of the way!' She pushed by him, and even that fleeting contact sickened her.

George Kenney, already dressed to go out, banged his fist hard on the wall, and his voice took on a sickening pettishness as he rebuked her, 'It's *you* as drives me to drink Kathy! You never stop picking fault with me mates . . . an' it pleases you to mek me feel guilty. Well, I don't! D'you 'ear me? I don't feel guilty.' His face began to crumple and from his whining, Queenie knew that he was about to cry. 'Oh, Kathy . . . I do love you! I *do*.'

On another occasion, Queenie would have spoken sharply to him and rushed him away outside. But this time she collapsed into a fit of giggling, in her helplessness letting the box of goodies fall to the floor.

George Kenney's face fell open with surprise, his whining stopped and he looked at her in astonishment. Then with a grunt of disgust, he stormed out into the street.

Mike Bedford must have been waiting outside, because the minute George Kenney had disappeared through the door Mike walked into the house almost before the door had closed.

'Well! Well! Well!' He leaned on the door jamb, with a superiority which would normally have prompted a sharp rebuke from Queenie, 'Better let old Mike in on your little secret, eh? What's tickling your fancy, Queenie me old darling? And where've you been hiding yourself these past weeks?'

Queenie was having difficulty deciphering his words. She felt both furious and foolish at her inability to control these strange moods which suddenly appeared to have a stranglehold on her. A fit of laughter overrode her deeper instincts, and finding herself helpless in this devil-may-care mood, she made no protest when Mike Bedford seized his chance to move in on her and gather her roughly into his arms. 'You know, you're quite an eyeful,' he breathed against her ear, 'drive a man crazy, you could.'

Something emerged from the murkiness clouding her mind to murmur a warning inside Queenie's head. 'Leave me be!' she exclaimed sharply, pulling away from his encircling arms, 'I can't breathe . . . want some fresh air.'

'Quite right! The very thing, Queenie my girl.' He followed her to the front door. 'Well . . . you've already got your coat on, so you've either just been – or you're just going!' he observed with a laugh.

'That's right,' Queenie agreed with an appreciative chuckle, allowing him to close the front door and lead her away.

Halfway down Parkinson Street, Queenie began to

have misgivings about where they were heading. Yet somehow it did not seem to be of paramount importance.

The one and only call to her fading sobriety was the precious face of Rick Marsden. His handsome features swam in and out of her consciousness, powering a force within her which would not be denied, and only the quick realization of past events beckoned the drowning fog to smother her reasoning.

The bright lights shone from the windows of the Navigation, moving the night in weird and wonderful shapes. Inside, the gyrating figures danced to the tuneful voice of Guy Mitchell issuing from the newly installed juke-box and charging the night air with excitement.

'Can you hear that, Queenie lass?' Mike Bedford tapped his feet into a walking dance as they drew nearer to the activity. 'I hope you can dance?'

Blinded by the brilliance of the light, which seemed all the brighter because of the accompanying music, Queenie narrowed her eyes to look at him. 'I don't know,' she said with a nervous chuckle, 'I've never really tried.'

'Never tried!' Mike Bedford was genuinely shocked. 'A smashing looker like you? An' you mean to tell me you've never been to a dance?' He swung her off her feet, drawing her to him tightly. 'Well, you're going to learn tonight, Queenie me darling! Or me name ain't Mike Bedford!'

Pushing and manipulating Queenie in and out of the laughing groups of drinkers, Mike found her a vacant table by the corner of the window. 'Park your arse down there an' I'll get us a drink to start the festivities,' he said as he eased her onto the wooden bench behind the table. 'I'll get you summat to knock your 'ead off!' He moved away, laughing loudly.

From all corners of the bar, shouting above the music, came the voices of men and women loud with the confidence bought with a pint of ale. Queenie's ears were deafened with matters of politics and sport.

Not three feet away from her the discussion swelled into serious debates, following one observation that 'These past few years, since the start o' the break-up of the British Empire, the dark-skinned folk 'ave started trekking into our little island . . . an' it won't be long afore they come a *flooding* in, I'll tell yer!' Back came the reply, 'Aye! well . . . they've every right, tha' knows!' And when a third intervention related, 'If somebody 'ad offered me the bloody Crown Jewels some five years back, against a body swappin' the land o' sunshine to come to Blackburn . . . I'd never 'a tekken the bet! Now would *you* ever 'a thought it? Or *you*, eh?' he asked nodding his head to one and all, 'an' I'll tell you some'at else! They reckon as there's nigh on *fifty* dark-skinned families settled i' Blackburn alone! My youngest came to close quarters wi' a black face in Market Hall for the first time a' Friday . . . an' the missus says 'e set up such a bawling it were 'ard to tell who took fright most, the young 'un or the poor unsuspecting fella!' Then, supping his pint he shook his head, and added, 'It's summat us shall *all* 'ave to get used to, an' that's a fact!' A profound remark, greeted with nods of resignation and a call for another round of pints; after which, that particular subject done with, the conversation turned to the winning prowess of Blackburn Rovers football team.

The booze was flowing fast, and a bitter-sweet pungency filled the atmosphere together with rising clouds of tobacco smoke, blocking Queenie's nostrils and tasting strong in her mouth. The feeling of nausea which she'd fought to keep down brewed and simmered in her stomach like a smouldering volcano until she feared it might spill over.

'All right are you, lass?' The bleary-eyed woman seated opposite Queenie leaned forward to examine her. 'Yer not going to be sick, are you?' Her eyes narrowed in suspicion as she went on, ''Appen yer in the family way?' Pointing to a seat by the Ladies cloakroom she suggested, 'You'd best sit over there – you look as if you might not mek it fro' here!' She rocked back and forth in her seat, loudly cackling until she caught the attention of a group by the bar.

One of the men, a tall gangling fellow wearing a thick black muffler and neb-cap, peered through the foggy atmosphere of the room until his roving eyes alighted on the conspicuous Queenie. 'Hey! Well, I'll be buggered!' His voice carried the length and breadth of the room, 'It's young Queenie . . . George Kenney's lass!' He twisted his neck to stretch in the far direction of the opposite corner, 'I say, Georgey Porgey, did you know as your little lass was paying us a call?' He guffawed loudly, 'Many's the time we've seen 'er fotch you away; but I never thought she'd lower 'erself to *join* us!'

'Young Queenie!' The big blowsy woman reached across the bar where she was serving, and fixing Queenie with a smug expression, she exclaimed, 'Well, I'm blowed! Wonders never cease, eh? By God, if her Auntie Biddy was here, there'd be hell to pay!'

Queenie recognized the vulgar-faced barwoman as 'Fat Molly', one of George Kenney's floozies; with that recognition came the realization of what she herself was up to. As she stared up at the sea of faces turned in her direction, two in particular stood out. One was that of Mike Bedford, returning with a glass in each hand. And only steps behind him came George Kenney, bent on seeing for himself that Queenie was actually drinking in his place of worship.

It was the sight of that familiar figure with its hunched shoulders and expressionless face that brought Queenie to her senses. With every ounce of determination she could muster, she rushed from that place and from the sea of mocking faces.

''Ere! Watch what yer doing!' The woman who had derived such pleasure from taunting her fought to retrieve her wobbling pint, which had set off in a jig as Queenie took flight towards the main door.

'Queenie!' Mike Bedford called as he slammed the drinks down in front of the woman. 'What the bloody hell 'ave you been saying to frighten 'er off?' he demanded, at once pushing and shoving his way out in pursuit of his prize. 'Queenie! You silly little sod! Come back . . .'

'Let 'er go,' George Kenney shouted, falling about drunkenly, 'you don't want no truck wi' 'er. Run off an' left me she did . . . left me!' Then, when the mock cries of 'Shames' and 'Ah, poor old Georgey Porgey' raised up from the onlookers, he bowed his head and went off to sulk in a corner.

The cold air whipped against Queenie's face as she ran down Parkinson Street. The black night, relieved only by the sparse flicker of gas-lamps, threw its cloak about her, and in her panic she knew she would not make it home in time. Looking for the nearest ginnel, Queenie followed its narrow path until she located the communal dustbins and she relieved herself of the nausea which dogged her into the first one. Afterwards, leaning against a wall, she waited for her rapid heartbeats to subside. She felt degraded and indecent; ashamed of her irrational behaviour. What in God's name had come over her this night?

Emerging from the ginnel and back into Parkinson Street, Queenie looked in the direction of the Navigation, and there she saw Mike Bedford running towards her. She had no strength left to flee from him, so, standing her ground, she waited for him to draw level.

'What the 'ell d'you think you're playing at!' he demanded angrily, the words spurting out breathlessly.

Queenie watched his breath vaporize in the cold night air, then facing him with deliberate calm, she answered, 'I'm sorry, Mike . . . Mrs Farraday gave me some wine, and I can only think it stole away my reasoning . . . for I would never have entered the Navigation if I'd been in my right senses.'

'Aye! But you *did* go in there! And you left me looking a right bloody fool!'

'Mike, I said I was sorry. And I am – what more is there to say?' Except that any decent man wouldn't have taken a girl in there in the first place! she thought. Oh, she was angry at him. But mostly at herself.

Mike Bedford had suddenly seen that he would make small headway with Queenie if he continued to abuse her. So he tried changing his attitude, and forcing a smile, he said, 'Aw, that's all right Queenie. I'm sorry an' all, for shouting at you like that.' He slid an arm round her shoulders, and, in a whisper, he suggested, 'Anyroad . . . we don't need no crowd round us, do we, eh?'

Queenie found herself smiling . . . This Mike, he just never gave up, did he? 'You go on back, Mike,' she told him, 'I'm sure you'll find a girl to take home.'

'It's *you* I want to tek home, you cloth'ead! *You*, an' nobody else.'

Queenie knew that she would have to settle this once and for all if she was to get any peace from Mike Bedford's attentions. When she lifted her grey eyes to his, there was a stiffness in them which seemed to have a sobering effect on him, for he moaned, 'You're not gonna bear a grudge, are you?'

'No grudge,' she promised, 'but I have to tell you, Mike . . . I could never love you, or any other man.' His face crumpled and she was quick to assure him, 'Oh, it isn't *you*! It's just that I already love someone else.' Her eyes grew small and sad. 'It can never come to anything, I know that now; but I'll always love him, Mike . . . always.'

The quiet sincerity in her voice appeared to have a calming effect on the young man before her. When he spoke, it was to ask quietly, 'You're not just trying to let me down gently?'

'No, I'm telling you the truth. Please, Mike . . . I don't want to talk about it any more.' He knew she was speaking the truth, because it was written in pain across her lovely face.

'God, Queenie! I've never loved anybody afore and to be honest, I'm not altogether sure that I know what love is. All I know is that it would be the easiest thing in the world for me to take you as me wife. I've never wanted to do that afore . . . not with *any* girl! Look! I don't know who this fella is, but I hope 'e deserves you, and that things *will* work out.'

Queenie was made to feel cruel and spiteful, because, not for the first time, she sensed his genuine affection for her. And the last thing she wanted to do was to hurt him.

'I'll tell you what then, Queenie. I'll mek a deal with you!' he challenged. 'If I'm to be forever denied the pleasure of your lovely company,' his cheeky smile told Queenie that everything would be all right now, 'I ought to be granted one last favour – you know, like a dying man! A kiss, one last kiss from your lovely lips.'

Queenie didn't like that idea at all. 'Better not Mike,' she protested. At once, he was pleading in mock fashion that he would never bother her again.

'Cross me heart,' he declared in a pretend sob.

Queenie relented. 'All right then, you impossible fool! Just one quick kiss.'

With practised panache he drew her to him, lowering his mouth onto hers with slow deliberation.

The touch of his warm moist lips on her mouth sent a spiral of astonishment through her, to stir the sleeping monsters in her mind. His body became that of George Kenney, and the arms which encircled her became a prison from which she madly struggled to escape. Unable to voice the scream which welled up inside her, she pressed at his chest with clawing hands. And of a sudden, her wide eyes were attracted by the movement of someone nearing them. The familiar walk, and the tall manly bearing. It was Rick!

Her frantic attempts to pull away from Mike Bedford seemed to excite him into thinking that she was responding favourably to his advances. But on Rick's desolate cry of 'Oh, Queenie!' he pushed her from him with such surprise that it took Queenie's breath away. Now he was facing Rick to demand through clenched teeth, 'Who the hell might *you* be?'

Queenie would have run to Rick and begged him to hear the truth of the matter. But she knew it would be to no avail. The stricken look in his dark eyes held her immobile. When she took a small step towards him, the accusing glare on his face froze her in her tracks. At once Rick strode angrily away.

'Who's that chap?' snarled Mike Bedford, still smarting from being disturbed.

Queenie felt numb. In her feverish mind, she saw only what Rick had seen and it caused her the same anguish she was sure it had caused him. But surely, she consoled herself, what he must now be feeling couldn't be half as cruel as the truth. He was not aware of their true relationship, that they were destined to be apart, that they were brother and sister. And Queenie did not want him to know. Better that he should think the worst of tonight's episode.

'Aw, let's forget the intruder,' persuaded Mike, attempting once more to encircle her waist, 'now, where were we?'

'Let me be! Just go away. Go away!' she cried, pushing her hands hard against his chest, and taking flight down Parkinson Street.

'Please yourself!' he yelled after her, 'but you'll want me afore I want you!' And with an angry flourish of his fist, he stormed off in the opposite direction.

Letting herself into the house, Queenie slammed the door and ran straight to her bedroom where she threw herself onto the stool in front of the dresser and stared back at her own angry image. 'Well!' she screamed, 'what does it matter if he saw you in the arms of another man? What difference does it make? Oh, you're a fool, Queenie! A fool!'

The quietness she had gained in herself through her stay at Nazareth House evaporated beneath this new anguish.

Snatching up the hairbrush on the dresser, she fetched it high up above her head, then swiftly down, to smash violently against the mirror; shattering her image into tiny fragments which splayed in every direction.

Gripped now by a wild fever and a wrath which knew no bounds, and haunted by the long empty years stretching before her, she was driven to pour a hatred into the destruction of all she had loved; the gentleness of her spirit was devoured as, in a terrible frenzy, she smashed again at things which had brought her pleasure to see. They were only material things, and disposable.

Long after the cessation of her terrible vengeance, Queenie felt drained, and more alone than ever.

With pictures of her mother and Auntie Biddy clutched protectively in her arms, she gave way to the wretchedness which had been anger and was now sorrow. 'Oh Auntie Biddy,' she sobbed, looking around the room, the results of her outburst terrible to see, 'oh, just look what I've done!' She stared at the picture of the woman who had been as a mother to her. 'If you only knew how much I miss you, Auntie Biddy

. . . if you only knew,' she whispered. She wanted to tell her about how she loved Rick Marsden, and how he loved her also. And she wanted an answer as to why it was that when something wonderful had entered her life, fate always stepped in to forbid the pleasure. 'Tell me what to do, Auntie Biddy. Please, please – tell me what to do!'

Her sobbing quieter after a while, Queenie clasped her precious pictures to her heart. Then she fell back into the bed shutting out her dismal thoughts, and slept more soundly than she had done for some long time.

Chapter Eleven

The morning air struck cold and sharp against Queenie's waking face. Lifting her head in a daze, she wondered at the monotonous throbbing which forced her to raise both hands to her temples. As she stared in amazement at the normally tidy room which was now all but devastated, she knew instinctively that it was she who was responsible for its state, but other than that she could not recollect for the moment. When, very gradually, it did dawn on her, she suffered none of the emotions that had caused her to do such a thing, because overriding everything else was a sense of shame and more than a small degree of anger. Inching herself out to perch unsteadily on the edge of the bed, she recalled the wine she had drunk at Mrs Farraday's and immediately following that thought came the realization of what had taken place at the Navigation, then afterwards in the street. Above all else, she remembered the hurt in Rick's eyes as he had seen her and Mike Bedford in what appeared to be a passionate embrace. Oh, what a tangle, she thought bitterly; what a God-forsaken tangle!

With a heavy heart, Queenie set about putting the room in order, wondering what was to become of her. She shook the mat out of the window, feathered up the bed and bolster, replacing the eiderdown with reverence; collected all manner of broken items into an old cardboard box. Then taking the box in her hand, she left the room with a last disdainful glance at the shattered mirror. With a sigh she murmured, 'Never knew you had such a temper, Queenie girl! As your Auntie Biddy would say, "You deserve your arse smacked!"'

As Queenie reached the foot of the stairs, something against the front door mat caught her eye. Coming towards it, she noticed that the manner in which it lay, wedged half-hidden between the wall and the mat, suggested it might have rested there undetected for quite some time. Certainly she had not seen it when she'd shaken and replaced the mat yesterday morning.

It was a small grubby-looking envelope addressed to her and stamped from Blackpool. 'That's funny!' She turned the envelope over and over in her hand, apprehensive about opening it, 'I don't know anybody from Blackpool.' The handwriting was large and scrawly, like that of a child's, and it was not familiar. She tore the envelope open. The letter was from Sheila.

Dear Queenie,
Hey! I'm having a right bloody good time. Got meself a smashing fella – decent sort! Did you know I was pregnant from that lad in David Street? No! 'Course you didn't! Never one for gossip was our Queenie, eh? Well, this fella I've got now don't care whose kid it is, a kid's a kid, he

says. We've got a little place aside o' the front and you can come and set with us awhile if you've a mind?

Oh, Queenie! I'm that happy! Hey, I bet that gorgeous Rick Marsden's been after you, eh? I had a thing going for that one, you know . . . but he were allus crazy after you. Grab him kid! He's all right, and he's worth a bob or two.

I'll have to go now. I want to write to me Mam and see if we can mek friends again. I do love her you know . . . even if she *is* a silly old cow! But she is me Mam, eh?

See you, kid, Sheila

Queenie wandered into the parlour, where she thoughtfully placed the letter on the mantelpiece. She was glad for Sheila, glad too that Mrs Aspen and Maisie had been wrong about Raymond being the father, that Sheila had not forgotten to keep in touch. She would write back soon, she decided. But there was no point in telling her about Rick. Of a sudden, Queenie found herself giggling out loud. 'Can't imagine Sheila with no baby!' she chuckled, and there came into her heart a desire to see the child when it was born, to hold it close and to pray that one day there would be a child for her. She dared not think of Rick in the same moment.

Glancing absent-mindedly at the clock on the mantelpiece, Queenie was shocked to notice that the time was ten-fifteen. 'Half the morning already gone!' she remarked crossly, 'Christmas Eve an' all!' The thought of Christmas brought a rush of pleasure. She would go to Evening Mass and light some candles. The thought cheered her, but at all costs she must avoid Father Riley.

The idea of a bowl of cereals for her breakfast left her cold. Instead, she emptied a Cephos-Powder into a glass of water in the hope that it might help to quieten the waterfall inside her head. Serves me right if it doesn't! she told herself, and thought it might be a good idea to attend confession while she was at the church. It was only the thought of bumping into Katy, and the fact that it would be Father Riley who took the confession, that changed her mind.

Busying herself about the little house, she polished and scrubbed till everything shone brightly. Then she brought the old biscuit-tin out from its home beneath the stairs where it had rested all these long years, as far back as Queenie could remember, and lifted the lid, letting the daylight in for the first time since last Christmas. The glittering stars cut out from silver-paper shone and danced in the light; and the fairy-doll, which Auntie Biddy had made for Queenie's very first Christmas, lit up the room with its bright smile. With warm memories of happier, less lonely Christmasses she strung the hand-made paper garlands around the room. The fondest memory of all brought tears to her eyes . . . that of the first Christmas with Rick and the children from the Ragged School. She recalled how the excited children had queued to collect their tatty secondhand toys, and how afterwards they had gone away clutching them, as if for all the world they had been given some fantastic treasure.

Queenie smiled to herself at the memory she would cherish always. But for now, she had to force her mind to other things. Whether George Kenney rose from his bed or lay there till opening time was of no particular importance to Queenie. She stuck to her routine of making his meal and leaving it by the gas-ring.

It began to appear that he intended staying in his bed till evening. It wouldn't be the first time, she reminded herself. In fact, many was the time Queenie had known him to lie half-unconscious in his bed for days on end.

At two-thirty, Queenie decided she had better make tracks if she was going. She had hardly missed a weekend going to the churchyard since Auntie Biddy died; neither snow nor storm would keep her from this special errand.

The journey wasn't a long or arduous one; just a short brisk walk down Parkinson Street, and on through the market square, to catch the tram to where a little way beyond the Church-house stood the old church and its pretty graveyard. Auntie Biddy's place was far enough away from the Church-house for Queenie not to worry about the possibility of an uncomfortable confrontation with Father Riley or Katy.

By the time Queenie turned in at the arched iron gate the snow was starting to fall again, and the grey skies were already dulled under a twilight mantle.

Entering the storm porch which led to the church entrance, Queenie fished about in her mac pocket until she found two pennies. It was a habit of hers to call in at the church before going into the churchyard; and she always lit *two* penny candles – one for Auntie Biddy, and one for any poor soul who had no friend to light their way to Heaven.

The little church struck exceedingly cold as she

pushed the heavy oaken door shut behind her. She scanned the highbacked pews before coming to rest on the altar, at the same time swinging a wary glance round the perimeter of the church walls, where huge stone slabs carved with the names of the Glorious Dead formed a sombre immobile procession.

A long rippling shiver travelled the slim length of Queenie's back as the penetrating cold reached inside her mac to draw the warmth from her veins. She moved forward to get on with the job of lighting the candles.

Clinking her pennies into the mouth of the tin-box, she reached for two little white candles. For a moment, she thought Father Riley had forgotten to place a new box of matches in the tray, for they were nowhere to be seen.

Growing concerned, she looked for them. 'Can't light them if I've got no matches!' she told the benevolently smiling Virgin Mary above the candle-rack; at which moment, out of the corner of her eye, she spied the blue box on the floor by her feet. With relief she bent to collect them; then giving the Virgin Mary a curious glance, she whispered, 'Oh! playing games is it? You rascal!' straightway thinking that if anyone should overhear her, they'd be sure to say she was crazy.

After lighting the candles, Queenie wedged them firmly into the wrought-iron holders on the highest rack before bowing her head and naming the folks whose beacons they were. Then, Auntie Biddy sitting heavy on her mind, she left for the direction of the churchyard.

The little churchyard was a pleasure to behold. Tall,

stately conifer trees spread their protective branches over the various gravestones, and here and there were laurels and rhododendrons to add various shades of green.

Queenie could have found Auntie Biddy blind-folded. Up the narrow winding footpath and in between the prayer-book and the little angels, and she was there.

Queenie had never forgotten the vow she had made to put 'the loveliest statue in all the world' on Auntie Biddy's resting place; most of her scanty earnings since then had gone into keeping that fervent promise.

Standing proud above the head of Auntie Biddy's grave, the tall and magnificent Sacred Heart statue held out its hand in perpetual blessing. There was even a marble kerbstone surround; the inner well was filled with tiny pieces of green-coloured granite chippings. Right beneath the white marble headstone were carved the words of Queenie's choosing:

> Auntie Biddy Kenney
> Loved more than words can tell.
> Dear God, please keep her safe
> Till we meet again.

There were no dates apart from the date of her death. Queenie never knew Auntie Biddy's real age . . . she even doubted that Auntie Biddy herself knew it. Biddy was reckoned by the older residents of Parkinson Street, to be in her late fifties. It could however be of little importance now that she was gone and placing a date, which she had kept secret, on a headstone for all the world to see, seemed an invasion of Auntie Biddy's privacy. So Queenie let the truth lie quiet with her.

As always, Queenie sat on the cold kerbstone surround. During these visits, she would gaze upon the Sacred Heart, whose gentle eyes seemed to know her deepest most private thoughts, and when she closed her eyes tight, Queenie could see the dear familiar face of her Auntie Biddy as clear as could be. All the love and loneliness in her would reach out until the still face in her mind warmed to life and smiled tenderly upon her, when for a brief moment the two of them were together again.

Queenie always left Auntie Biddy's side with a great sense of calm and peace; her love for mankind strengthened and her toleration of George Kenney stretched to encompass a little more patience and perseverance.

Placing her hand caressingly over Auntie Biddy's name, Queenie whispered her farewell; unaware that a short distance away stood Rick Marsden.

Knowing how much these quiet moments meant to Queenie, he had no wish to intrude; so he stayed his distance, his eyes filled with longing as they followed her every move, yet his whole manner indicating a reluctance to approach her. The memory of Queenie in another man's arms still caused him confusion and pain.

Tightening her headscarf and hunching lower into her mac, Queenie quietly observed, 'Looks like it'll snow for a week!' Then, she closed the iron gate behind her, and trudged her way back to Parkinson Street deep in thought. Would George Kenney be abed . . . or would he have already departed for Fat Molly's place? He did seem to be spending more time there lately, and Queenie gave it little mind. She would have gladly preferred him to clear off and live at Fat Molly's for good.

Thinking on a 'lifetime', Queenie's mood fell into one of frustration. A lifetime of what? she asked herself. Looking into the immediate future at least, she could see nothing to bring her joy. The full sensual mouth which had tasted the warmth of Rick's kisses trembled as she thought of him and of what had been denied them both.

She wondered fleetingly what Mother Superior might have said if she had known the truth; known that the girl she was helping had unwittingly fallen in love with her own brother, and he with her. She reflected on her stay at the convent, and somehow it seemed so far away in the past that it was like a dream. She knew, however, that during her stay in that place she had experienced a wonderful tranquillity which had helped her through a strange frightening insight into herself; through a period when her own store of strength and resolve had fallen away beneath the battery of shock and pain which had devastated her.

As she entered the house, Queenie knew at once that George Kenney had emerged from his bed. She could smell his pungent presence.

Shaking the thick clinging snowflakes from her coat and scarf, she hung them up behind the front door.

'Is that you, woman?' George Kenney's coarse demanding voice called out to her, and Queenie's heart sank as she recognized that he was in one of his 'moods'. Just for once, she wished he would call her by name, but he never did.

'If we had a dog, I bet he'd talk to it better!' she

muttered beneath her breath, the irritation showing in her curt reply, 'What is it now?'

George Kenney lifted his drowning eyes, the bloodvessels standing out like bright purple rivulets running away in meandering multitudes. 'You mind yer bloody tongue!' he yelled, a spasmodic coughing fit preventing further abuse.

Sometimes, when Queenie looked at George Kenney, a feeling of intense loathing would come over her as she remembered that he . . . a monster of filth and vile doings had . . . had . . . Even in the secrecy of her own mind, she could not face the awful truth, and somewhere deep inside her there would sound a warning bell, calling her from the nightmare which threatened to engulf.

Leaving him now to his noisy coughing, she went to put the kettle on. A quick glance told her that he had not touched his food. 'Waster!' she called, 'you wouldn't be so wasteful if it was *you* paying for it!' The last few words were spoken under her breath; but if George Kenney's other faculties had gone, he could still hear when he'd a mind to.

'Talking to your bloody self, is it? I'd watch that if I were you. I've seen folks tekken away for less!' His voice rose to a deafening roar, 'I don't want yer sodding slop! . . . I wants summat *decent* inside o' me. An' if I can't 'ave substantial food I'll bloody well go wi' out, d'you 'ear?'

Queenie had lost count of the number of times they had been through this self-same procedure. Now she stalked back into the parlour to face him defiantly, 'You make me sick, George Kenney! Every day I leave

248

you good food, and every day I have to throw it out. I've a good mind to leave you to your rotting!'

She never looked more like her mother than when her blood was up, and the strong grey eyes were all the more lustrous and beautiful for the passion of anger.

George Kenney sat for a lohg moment in the ensuing hush. His uplifted face, which had daily grown more ugly from the blasphemous life he followed, twisted itself into an expression of genuine confusion. 'Nay, Kathy love,' the tears of remorse traced a path over the bulbous eyes, and down through the hanging folds of his face, as he spoke, 'don't upset yersel' love. I didn't mean to shame you . . . I've disowned the lad, an' I promise I allus will.' He was pathetically ignorant of the terrible effect his words were having on Queenie.

She could not listen to any more. Her heart felt as though it would break in two, and her defiant efforts to stem the threatening tears were ineffective. Rushing into the passage, she collected her mac and scarf, still wet from the churchyard visit, and fled the house as though the devil himself was on her heels.

Once out on the flagstones, she wasn't quite sure what she was doing out there. All she was certain of was that she could not go back in that house . . . not yet.

A small group of carol-singers shuffled their way along Parkinson Street, their bright swinging lanterns making a comforting picture for Queenie's eyes. Wiping the tears from her face, she watched and listened as they eased their voices into a beautiful rendering of 'Silent Night'.

The lovely lilting melody warmed Queenie's heart

and brought a soft smile to her face. So engrossed was she, that the mac which should have protected her from the cold wet evening remained tightly clutched in her hands.

Without warning, the door opened to reveal George Kenney groping his way into the night. 'Kathy,' he called in a piteous voice, 'is that you, Kathy?' He peered towards Queenie, his arm outstretched and his mouth quivering as though ready to cry.

The anger he had provoked within her, had been somewhat dissipated by the exquisite singing of the choristers. 'Go on back in,' she told him, 'stop your blubbering, and take yourself back inside out of the cold!'

Out of the night came a voice she knew only too well. 'Is everything all right, Queenie?' asked Rick. For a moment, Queenie was struck dumb. How foolish she felt, yet how wonderful it was to see him again.

'Rick!' she cried, her voice caressing his name, her every instinct to run to him. But in that initial rush of happiness, there came too a quickening sense of what must be done.

The hardened resolve betrayed itself in the changing tone of her voice. 'I'm just getting him back inside. I can manage, thank you.' It came to her, how strange it was that she could force herself to say one thing, when all the time she wanted to throw herself into his strong arms and feel the caress of his mouth on her own. When suddenly he took a step nearer, she was filled with fright and worried that he might have somehow read her thoughts.

George Kenney's mind was forever wandering. But now, as Rick stood bathed in the light from the hallway, his handsome features took reflection in the deranged man's eyes. And as they stared one to the other, the light of recognition caused George Kenney's eyes to widen in horror, and his voice to thicken with hatred as he called out, 'Richard Marsden!' He lunged forward to grab the startled Rick by the collar, and no amount of struggling on the part of Rick, who was more than equal in strength to his attacker, could release the vice-like grip which clutched him. 'Richard Marsden! It were *your* mother as led me to betray my Kathy! Your *mother* as spawned you from my own loins. A living sin to remind me! To haunt my Kathy. That's what you are, my rotten bastard!' He was half-crazed from the years during which his conscience had eaten away at him, and as he poured forth his loathing such vile and evil abuse fell from his mouth that the group of singers were silenced. They stood shocked, watching and listening, mouths open and eyes disbelieving.

Queenie had heard it all before. But how her heart went out to Rick, who could never have suspected that George Kenney was his rightful father.

Queenie watched the blood drain from Rick's face, as the awful realization of what was being said dawned on his paralysed mind and wrote itself on the expression of slow horror which grew on his face. As he turned towards Queenie, she saw in those tragic brown eyes a desperate plea for her to deny the implications of George Kenney's accusation.

If Queenie had the power to dispel the suffering of this night she would gladly have sacrificed herself to do so. But such a miracle was not in her power, it never had been. The crimes which had shaped her and Rick's path had been committed long ago. And the sins were not of her making, nor of Rick's. They had been fashioned by Rick's mother and this man whom she could never bring herself to call 'father'.

She recognized in Rick the desperate determination to question, to search frantically for a way out, as she herself had done so many times before, all to no avail. As she looked on the scene where George Kenney shook Rick like a rag-doll Queenie's suffering became unbearable. Taking at once to her heels, she fled down Parkinson Street, away from the heartache of what she had been forced to witness. She ran from the horrors of that night, only to sink further into the pit of darkness which threatened to engulf her.

Many lost hours later, Queenie had no way of knowing how long she'd been running, or even where she was.

In her headlong flight into the black night, she had entertained no thought of destination, nor of returning. But running away solved nothing. Neither she nor Rick could be held responsible for the flaw in this man's character; a monstrous flaw which reduced him to a creature of evil intent and immoral purpose. All those years ago, thought Queenie, when her mother had been young, and she herself not even born, George Kenney had committed adultery. Rick was the living proof of that infidelity, a constant reminder of betrayal at the basest level. Had not Kathy Kenney and Auntie Biddy borne the shame too? Above all Queenie could not forgive George Kenney for the pain he must have caused these two women. If he had strived to atone in any way, to be kinder and more generous with Auntie Biddy, it might have been easier to forgive him, but how was it possible to forgive him when he wallowed in every kind of debauchery? Oh, she could not!

Her rampaging mind drained of thought, Queenie shivered violently as she drew to a halt. Ignoring the wet clinging snowflakes which had melted into her clothes through the warmth of her body, she donned the mac and scarf which had been clutched in her hand. It was a futile exercise, for the garments were sopping wet and offered no protection. The deadening cold had already infiltrated her inadequate clothing, dampening her to the bones and chilling her to the marrow.

The gas-lamps were all out, and everywhere was pitch black except for a small flicker of light appearing like a star in the distance. Queenie made her way towards it, and as she drew near, it was easy to recognize the squarefronted grimness of Bent Street Constabulary. Queenie had never been more glad to see it than at that moment.

'Bent Street!' Her cry of astonishment echoed eerily in the surrounding silence. She had wandered four miles and more from Parkinson Street. From a place where lay the only home she had ever really known; and the place where lived the devil's own disciple! Yet return to it she must . . . for she had no place else to go.

The snow was coming down at a furious pace now and the driving wind had begun to whip up a sea of swirling drifts.

Trudging her way carefully along the flagstones, Queenie felt a deep wave of nostalgia for long-ago Christmas Eves when she and Auntie Biddy would sit huddled round the fire, talking and laughing, and looking forward to Christmas Day and its fundamental meaning. 'Folks 'ave already forgotten what Christmas is *really* about!' she would tell Queenie, 'it's only simple folks like us who still remember it has to do with love and sacrifice.'

Bending herself against the wind, Queenie dropped her chin deep into the collar of her mac and pushed her way along. As she came into more familiar surroundings, her heart remained stifled by memories she would have liked to lose. 'Nearly eighteen,' she murmured quietly, her words taken by the air and scattered about until lost, 'nothing to look forward to, and no one to love!' She was not given to self-pity, but as she neared Parkinson Street once more it seemed to Queenie that everything she had ever cherished was gone forever. Her mother whom she had never known but through Auntie Biddy's answering of her questions; poor old Mr Craig . . . and more kind familiar faces. Even Mrs Aspen had moved away, and it crossed Queenie's mind to wonder whether she would ever again see Sheila?

The loneliness which engulfed her found outlet in the rushing tears which spilled onto her frozen cheeks and sped down the stiffness of her face. 'Oh why?' she cried. 'Oh, Rick! *Why* did you have to come into my life?' She felt anger towards him; the same confusing anger which she had suffered at the loss of her Auntie Biddy. It was instantly followed by a kind of pity and an all-consuming love. And oh, how she wanted him! Yes, still wanted his arms about her and the comfort of his murmuring voice in her ear. In her body too, there was a strange hunger for him, even in the knowledge that he was her own flesh and blood.

The blinding snow fused with her tears until it became impossible to see. Drawing herself up, she rested awhile, searching in her mac pocket and retrieving from it a hankie with which she wiped her face and eyes. And all the time, the sobs rose within her, emerging now with a fierceness which shook her and rendered her helpless.

''Ere! What's all this?' Mike Bedford's voice livened the night, and although Queenie felt profusely ashamed to be caught crying so openly, she could do nothing to stop it. 'Christmas Eve, an' 'ere's Queenie crying in the snow!' Stepping closer, he threw his arm about her shoulders. 'Feeling a bit low, are we Queenie, lass?' he enquired.

Queenie gave no answer. Instead, she buried her face in the folds of his coat and drew on the comfort of his closeness; surprised that she could feel warm and secure in his arms. 'Go on Queenie, lass!' Mike Bedford urged, proud of his ability to be in the right place at the right time, 'Cry yer little 'eart out!' Propelling her gently towards home, he urged softly, 'Come on, angel . . . let's get you home and afront o' the fire afore you catch the death!'

No sooner had he moved Queenie two paces than he drew her to a halt, and crooking his finger beneath her chin he lifted her face. Then looking deep into her large tear-filled eyes, he said, 'Queenie – will you marry me? Say yes, an' you'll not regret it.'

Queenie heard his question well enough, and she understood it. Mike Bedford wanted her for his wife. Her heart answered no, but almost without her being conscious of it, she was smiling through her tears and nodding in agreement. No sooner was the deed done than she suddenly felt violently ill, as though everything inside her had collapsed, taking every ounce of her strength with it.

Mike Bedford had not known Queenie long enough to assess the tough capable trait in her character, so when she cried out at the sharp jagged pains which tore through her body, he suspected that she was just another hysterical woman.

As she sank to the ground, her lovely face as white as the snow settling about her, Mike Bedford paused just long enough to know that Queenie was deeply unconscious and desperately ill. Gathering her frail weightless body into his arms, he made haste to his own front door. 'God above!' he exclaimed to the night, 'she's nobbut skin an' bone!' As he hurried along he stole a glance at her face which was still and white as death, and her beauty astounded him. 'You're magnificent!' he whispered, 'do any man proud, you would. I'll not forget that this night you've promised yourself to me!'

Mrs Bedford flung open the door, angry at the loud banging which had disturbed her nap. 'What's the bloody game?' she demanded, her quick eyes instantly assessing the urgency of the situation. ''Ere!' she ran in front of him to the parlour, 'put the lass down 'ere on the settee by the fire.' As her eyes alighted on Queenie's face, she threw her hands up despairingly. 'Lord 'elp an' save us! Wherever did you find the poor creature?'

Mike Bedford rubbed his freezing hands back to life, 'Found 'er crying down Parkinson Street.' He made no mention of the fact that he had proposed to Queenie, and that she had accepted. His mam was a funny woman where such matters were concerned, and she had long told him that his fancy for Queenie would come to grief.

He watched while his mother busied about Queenie's prostrate form, and when she cried out, 'Oh my God!' he feared the worst for Queenie's life. 'Quick Mike!' she cried, 'run up to Mrs Farraday's – ask 'er if you can use the phone to call an ambulance.' She tutted impatiently and propelled him towards the door. 'You gormless twerp! Run I tell you! Queenie's past all I can do for 'er!' And the fear in her voice silenced Mike Bedford's protests as he left Queenie's side to hurry out into the night.

Chapter Twelve

Blackburn Infirmary was a scarred relic of a grand Victorian era. In its heyday, people from all walks of life would marvel at its square strength and ornate façade; suitably impressed also at the wonderful facilities provided by its costly construction and choice personnel.

Now, however, with the fading of its youthful bloom beneath the relentless ravages of time, the building no longer drew a profusion of praise, but a torrent of complaint and abuse. The dampness breathed in the walls, and the wind persistently whistled through the ill-fitting window-jambs. The long snaking corridors, devoid of windows, were dark and dungeon-like. Their shadowy unclean appearance ensured that no one ever lingered in their recesses.

The nurses, though, were of the cheerful, no-nonsense variety – easy to talk to and not so easy to refuse. 'Come on now, Queenie!' The dumpy fair-haired nurse held the glass of medicine under Queenie's nose, 'I'm not budging an inch till you've shifted this!'

Queenie grimaced at the prospect. 'It's awful!' she protested.

'I never said it weren't! I'm just telling you to get it

swallowed.' She pushed it further into Queenie's face. 'Come on! Close your eyes and dive straight in.'

Queenie obeyed, with much coughing and spluttering afterwards.

'Nurse Woods!' Queenie's call brought the departing nurse to turn about. 'I am sorry, but how much longer have I to take it?'

Queenie's face still registered a bitter distaste which made the nurse laugh as she answered, 'You're right, it *is* awful. But you can take heart, love; twice more today and four times tomorrow . . . and that's it.'

'Thank goodness for that!' Queenie's eyes rolled upwards in a gesture of relief.

Nurse Woods smiled patiently, and returned to sit on Queenie's bed; her sharp eyes alert for Sister, who abhorred such practices. 'You know, Queenie,' she said, her voice filled with concern, 'I don't think you realize just how badly ill you've been.' She paused on seeing a look of irritation on Queenie's face, 'Oh, you might not want to talk about it, young lady! but when you first came in here, I wouldn't have given you tuppence for your chances.' She leaned forward, her voice rising on a cheerful edge as she continued, 'But you're all right now, love . . . you *and* your baby.' Getting up from the bed, she wagged a chubby finger at Queenie, 'And you're to take things easy when we send you home! Still, that nice fiancé of yours will look after you, I've no doubt.' She watched as Queenie slithered down the bed and turned her head away into the pillow. 'Here! Don't you be hiding your face, my girl! You're not the first to start a child out of wedlock and you'll not be the last!' Shaking her head, she turned and ambled from the room.

The sound of the church-bells in the distance rang out; 'calling worshippers to Sunday Mass' thought Queenie, allowing the comforting echo to enter her head and to drive out all manner of thought for a while. A gentle smile whispered across the fine lines of her lovely features, each curve accentuated more now by the enervating pneumonia which had brought her close to death's door and kept her there for many a day and night.

The core of George Kenney's sin, which had as she feared taken root in the very heartbeat of her violated body, seemed often to engulf her. Yet try as she might, she could not bring herself to reject that tiny spark of life, which had clung on so tenaciously throughout her illness. It was a poor innocent being, as much a victim as she herself was.

'Like to 'ear them blasted bells donging away, don't you?' The penetrating voice at once drew Queenie from her thoughts. Lifting herself up in bed, she sought out the owner of the voice.

'Oh, it's you, Mrs Lewis!' This eagle-eyed woman was always wandering up and down the ward, moaning about one thing or another. 'Yes . . . I do like to hear the church-bells ringing,' Queenie told her truthfully.

'Hmph! Doesn't surprise me! You young whipper-snappers, noise! noise! noise!' Gathering her long winceyette nightie into her hands, she snorted her disapproval, moved off down the ward, and pounced on yet another bedridden soul.

Queenie couldn't help but laugh. There was something very likeable about poor Mrs Lewis in spite of her miserable ways. She leaned back into the pillow and watched in amusement as Nurse Woods collected the woman and frogmarched her straight back to her own bed, 'Now just you stop bothering everybody! Read a book or something. The visitors will be here soon, and I've got more to do with my time than to follow you about the ward.'

At the mention of visitors, an expression of anxiety filtered into Queenie's smile. The smile quickly fell away and the grey eyes became deep and thoughtful. She had been in this place now for three weeks. The New Year festivities had come and gone without her knowing, and during that period, when she was lost to all awareness, Queenie had been allowed very few visitors. It was afterwards, when Queenie had sought to place the lost pieces of jigsaw loose in her mind, that she had learned of Katy Forest's unselfish love and devotion. Katy had not missed one single day in coming to Queenie's sick bed. There had been little to console Katy, or to relieve her distress at Queenie's lifeless form and thin dead face. There could be no conversation, and for long endless days and nights hardly a flicker of hope. So Katy had just sat quiet by the bed, weeping sometimes, and praying hard for the lass she had come to love as a daughter.

Queenie might have remained unaware of Katy's exceptional dedication had it not been for a burst of angry chastisement from Nurse Woods, when the recovering patient flatly refused to entertain any visitors.

'You're a selfish ungrateful girl!' Queenie had been reprimanded in no uncertain terms, 'and what of old Katy Forest might I ask? Who sat at your bedside day in and day out for more than a fortnight! Aye! and so concerned was she that she slept sitting up, through the long worrying nights.'

Following such a revelation, however much she longed to be left alone, however tired she was, Queenie could not bring herself to deny access to Katy. And, much to Queenie's surprise, she began to look forward to Katy's visits, deriving a degree of comfort and pleasure from having her close. During the course of their conversations not a word was uttered about Queenie's unborn child; although both women held the subject close to their hearts. The unspoken questions weighed the atmosphere. Yet, even as she dreaded the moment, Queenie knew instinctively that the time for answers was looming close.

In the late evening after the visitors had departed and the nurses laid the ward to rest, Queenie would fall to pondering about certain matters. So many things had happened that she was forced to confront. The fear of being with child had become a reality. How could she ever rid from her mind the awful look on Rick's face when he had learned that he'd been made a bastard, by a bastard! And that the outrage was followed by an even more devastating one; forbidding by every law, both moral and legal, further intimate contact with the love of his heart. Even now, though Queenie's mind had dwelt on little else since recovering consciousness, she could not think on it at all without her own heart breaking.

At first, the fact that Rick had made no attempt to see her, even when she was at death's door, had hurt Queenie more than she could tell. But gradually she had accepted that he had obviously decided, as she had, that no other course was open to him. She wondered, too, how in a moment of weakness she could have agreed to become Mike Bedford's wife. For days now, she had pondered on ways to tell him that it had all been a mistake, brought about by loneliness and fear of the future. Because of his regular and prolonged visits and his special cosseting of her, Queenie could see more clearly now how the doctors and nurses had assumed that he was the father of the child she was carrying.

And somehow, bombarded by his roguish charm and persistence and the conspicious absence of Rick, she had allowed herself to be persuaded into agreeing to an early marriage. 'For the child's sake,' Mike had said . . . and because he loved her so very much. And wasn't it the case, he demanded, that it was obvious she would get no support from the real father? Whom he suspected was that 'bloke what come across us 'aving a cuddle!' It was plain as a pikestaff to Mike that there had been something special between Queenie and that big bloke. And where was the fellow now, eh? Some men were like that! Run clean away from responsibility they would. Oh, but not him! He would give Queenie and the child a home; and if she still hankered after that 'big bloke' well, he'd put up with that, because he knew Queenie would come round to loving his good self in time.

Queenie knew that even though Rick could not now figure in her life, she would always love him, and she told Mike as much. But he would have none of it, assuring her that she would get over the other fellow and come to see him for what he was. After all, what kind of a man could desert the woman who loved him and who carried his child? And how many times had he come to see her at the Infirmary? Not once!

The ordeal and humiliation of having to confess the true indentity of the child's father had shamed Queenie into silence. She could not go through with such a prospect. If, as Mike claimed, he was happy for people to think the child was his, and if he was so eager to provide both herself and the child with a home and name, then on what grounds could she refuse? She had been as honest with Mike as was possible, and still he wanted her. So, in a fit of gratitude, she had said yes to him, deliberately hardening her heart to the memory of Rick and what might have been. It was not an easy thing, for often in an unguarded moment his laughing handsome face would fill her dreams and warm her heart, afterwards leaving a great void within her.

Time and time again she would assure herself that these painful memories would pass, and only by constantly reminding herself of this was she able to grow stronger in both mind and body.

George Kenney had not been to the Infirmary, but that was no wonder to Queenie, and no loss. He was a dark stranger who invaded only her most terrible nightmares.

'You look a right scalawag!' Nurse Woods called, summoning Queenie's attention. 'Oh, I tell you – if I had your bewitching face and beautiful hair, I'd spend half my life in front of a looking-glass!'

Queenie smiled in that old-fashioned manner which was part of her charm. 'Don't you know it doesn't matter how the good Lord made you *outside*?' she said. 'It's the quality of what's *inside* that really matters.' Auntie Biddy's philosophies had settled deep.

'You're an odd one, Queenie,' Nurse Woods said as she grunted and groaned in her efforts to lift the head-rest out, 'talk about an old head on young shoulders! Anybody would be forgiven for thinking you were ninety-nine!'

As Nurse Woods' voice faded out of earshot Queenie wondered just how much could be squeezed into ninety-nine years? Certainly not worse than I've known, she mused. In answer to Nurse Woods' comment, she declared, 'Well! I sometimes *feel* as if I'm ninety-nine!'

Nurse Woods might have responded with a sharp reprimand, but there were things about this poor young girl she'd learned from Katy Forest which had caused her to count her own blessings. On impulse, she gave Queenie a cuddle. 'Now then, young lady . . . let's get you sitting up!' she chided gently. Between them they eased Queenie from down the bed to a half-sitting position.

'Stronger and stronger by the minute, eh?' Nurse Woods laughed.

'Thank you,' Queenie replied, adding hopefully, 'it won't be long before you let me home, will it?' It surprised her to find that she was still thinking of Parkinson Street as 'home'. She and Mike would be returning under George Kenney's roof as man and wife – strangely enough, he had not protested. Only quite recently Queenie had discovered that Mike's mother had disowned him, after demanding to know the truth concerning Queenie's condition. Mike had admitted that he was not the father. But he would say no more than that. His mother was furious with her son for taking on another man's responsibilities. The whole business had made Queenie feel guilty, and even more obliged not to refuse Mike's kind offer of marriage.

'Hey! Penny for them?' asked Nurse Woods, chucking Queenie under the chin. 'And as for you going home, well . . . that's not for me to say. You'll have to ask Dr Foley tomorrow. But don't be too surprised if he's not too quick to let you go.' She brushed Queenie's hair from her brow and went on, 'You're lucky to be alive, and you're not eating enough to keep a sparrow lively!'

Queenie's grey eyes fired with a spark of defiance.

'That's no reason to keep me here!' she declared sternly, 'I've never had a big appetite, and I've always been skinny!'

Nurse Woods rolled her eyes in mock anguish, clapping her hands heavily on her well-padded thighs. 'Well! It's all right for some, I must say! What I wouldn't give to shed some of this.' She twisted her mouth into a posture of pondering, 'I expect it's 'cause you're so tall . . . elegant like? How tall are you, Queenie?'

The last thing Queenie felt like was discussing her height; but she seemed obliged to humour the nurse. 'Haven't ever measured myself,' she said thoughtfully, 'but I'm a bit shorter than Father Riley and he's five foot eight. He told me once when I remarked on the material in his frock.'

'Frock?' Nurse Woods looked puzzled.

'Yes, you know! He wears a long black frock, like all Catholic priests.'

'Oh, that's right! I remember. He came to see you a couple of times when you were really badly.' She came back to her original question. 'So that makes you about five foot six?'

'I expect so.' Queenie had grown tired of this conversation. Hadn't Nurse Woods got anything better to do? 'How long is it to visiting?' she asked, changing the subject.

Nurse Woods picked up the little watch which hung upside down on her lapel, 'Lord! Ten minutes!' she exclaimed, and already she was halfway down the ward.

As the big hand on the clock over the door straightened up to register seven o' clock, the double glass doors swung open, and the flower-bedecked visitors poured in; the orderly lines opening out to disperse in all directions. Queenie found it heartening that her sick colleagues should have been blessed with such an abundance of attentive friends and relatives. The pale sickly faces about her were at once wreathed in smiles, and it did her a power of good.

'Katy!' Queenie spotted the old woman at the door. There was no way that Katy could have known of Queenie's move up the ward; a treat for progressing so well of late. 'Katy . . . up here!' Queenie waved her hands to catch Katy's attention and smiled appreciatively when Katy spotted her.

With her face crinkled in relief, Katy hurried up the ward to Queenie's side, where she caught Queenie into her arms and kissed her soundly. 'Thought I'd lost you, lass! she grinned. Dropping onto the chair, she rummaged in her bag to retrieve all manner of paraphernalia.

Queenie's heart turned over as she took quiet stock of Katy Forest. At first glance, she'd seemed no different from the cantankerous housekeeper who had flatly denied that she needed Queenie to help her at the Church-house. Now, however, it suddenly dawned on Queenie, that Katy really *did* look close to her seventieth year. The grey hair had settled about her worn face like a soft cloud, and the worry-lines were etched deeper into the mould of her homely features. Queenie knew that at least a degree of this transformation had been brought about by her own illness, and she wished it had not been so. 'Oh, Katy,' she said now, with profound sincerity, 'I do love you coming to see me.'

Katy placed her gifts on the locker-top before gathering Queenie's hands in both of hers. As she looked up, the deep love she felt for Queenie shone through the ready smile in her eyes. 'Queenie lass,' she said, slowly shaking her head from side to side, 'I'm an old woman, with few pleasures left in life, and coming to see you is the brightest spot in my day.' Their eyes met in mutual understanding and affection. 'So we'll have no more silly talk, eh?' she concluded firmly.

'If you say so,' agreed Queenie, 'but I'm hoping you won't be needing to come for much longer, Katy, because I'm asking Dr Foley if he'll let me home tomorrow. There's a lot to see to before Mike gets back,' she added more soberly. Her change of tone was not lost on Katy.

There then followed a short discussion of how Mike had landed a good job a week or so back, labouring on a new road construction down south. He would be back in a few weeks' time, with money in his pocket for him and Queenie to be married.

'And have you in mind to stay with George Kenney, the two of you?' Katy asked, horrified at the thought.

'It's not *his* house! It's me Aunt Biddy's,' replied Queenie defiantly, 'and left to him, it would go to rack and ruin! Anyway, Katy, we've got no choice seeing as how Mike's mother doesn't want us there.' She saw no point in explaining that Mike had been thrown out by Mrs Bedford, and that there was now bad blood between them, on account of her.

'Oh, lass!' Katy gently clapped her hands together in a gesture of helplessness, 'I know I shouldn't say it . . . but truth be told, I've to shame the divil an' say that I had hoped as how the babby you're carrying might not be Mike Bedford's but Rick's. Oh, I'm sorry, lass, it's just an old woman's fancy. But I could see you and Rick wed one o' these fine days!' She would have pursued the matter, because she felt in her heart that all was not as it seemed here. But Queenie had dropped her head to her chest in a forlorn manner, and now, looking up, she told Katy not to let her imagination run away with her. 'Mike is the man I'm to wed. Rick . . . well, he's part of the past, and best left there. Believe me, Katy.' Her crisp dismissive words belied her heavy heart. So, Rick had kept George Kenney's secret close. Perhaps it was just as well, when all was said and done.

In the next breath, Katy apologized and explained that anyway, Rick had gone away to take prior instruction before entering the priesthood; on hearing this, Queenie prayed that he would find contentment with his life and remember her now and then in a kindly manner. As for herself, she could never forget him, nor did she want to. In her most secret heart those wonderful moments with Rick brought her a measure of comfort.

At that moment, Queenie's attention was distracted by the scurryings and shouting at the entrance to the ward, where Nurse Woods and the ward sister were involved in a scuffle with an aggressive figure who was obviously the worst for drink.

'Why! Lord help us! It's George Kenney!' Katy's cry was wrung from her as she got to her feet and went quickly down the ward, with the intention of assisting the intruder right back out of the door and away from Queenie. But as she neared the struggling bodies, the ward sister cried out to Katy to go quickly and fetch Dr Lane from the next ward.

As Katy hurried off, not exactly sure as to the location of the next ward, the fighting drunken weight of George Kenney proved too much for the two women in uniform. Shaking himself loose, he glanced rapidly down the ward to where Queenie sat, shocked and bolt upright in her bed. Then, with a low growl and a half-smile that was terrible to see, he headed straight for her, his broad head hanging down and his gait unsteady. His eyes though, were true and sinister, fixed on Queenie without a falter.

It had been the case since Queenie was barely large enough to stand that the close presence of George Kenney triggered off a frightening revulsion in the pit of her stomach. It was no different now when she saw him bearing hard down on her. But nothing of her fear showed, when she raised her face and challenged his piercing stare with her own.

George Kenney towered over her, his booze-loose face swollen and twisted with hatred. For a long weighted moment he continued to stare at her and she at him; until in a quiet driving voice, he hissed, 'You little cow! You trollop!' Had he shouted the words they might have appeared less menacing, but his face was so close to Queenie's that she felt faint from the pungency of his foul breath, his voice but a heavy rasping whisper which echoed like thunder in her head. 'You don't fool me,' he sneered, 'your own brother! Lying abed with your own brother! An' 'im fathering your child! Dirty filthy pair . . .' He laughed low, the sound spurting out on the bed of spittle which ran down his chin.

Queenie thought the strangling sensation in her throat would surely choke her as George Kenney's vile words pierced her gentle heart; it broke her to see that he was taking such pleasure in it all. It served to magnify her loathing of this man – this scum! Her rejection of him in every way filled her being like a giant tidal wave until beyond all human control it burst open to swallow him in its vehemence.

'May God in His mercy forgive me, George Kenney!' Her voice scraped low and hard in its bitterness, 'But I've never hated you more than at this moment! Oh! I despise the very air you breathe . . . and *you*!' The outrage within her lifted the tone of her voice, 'It's *you* who's the scum! You, the filth who violated me and got me with child! It's *your* sin . . . *yours*! . . . do you understand? Yours! Yours! Yours!' Her fury burned like a beacon in the darkness of her eyes, holding him riveted; until with a great roar, he backed away.

Throughout the ward there was a deathly hush, as

wide disbelieving eyes all fell on George Kenney. As Katy re-entered the ward with the doctor and the two of them joined forces with Nurse Woods and the sister, all became still in the wake of an eerie silence.

His face drained white, tongue struck silent, George Kenney stood like a man of stone. His expression had emptied, his eyes loosened wide, and his thick arms were hanging lifeless by his sides. And still, Queenie felt no compassion in the torrent of her hatred.

Slowly and deliberately, he moved down the ward through a silent gauntlet of accusers. As he wrenched open the double doors, George Kenney turned but once. His defiant eyes swept the length of the ward, accepting the stares of disgust with the resignation of a man condemned. Then lowering his head, he dragged himself away, out of sight.

'There, there, lass,' Katy comforted the shaking sobbing girl in her arms, 'nobody inherited such a bad lot as you did, child!' She repeatedly kissed Queenie's head. 'Old Katy's here . . . don't fret.'

As the sobs raked Queenie's body, she felt as though her whole being was pouring out of her. 'Oh, Katy! Katy! Why does he haunt me so?' she pleaded.

Katy snifled and swallowed the painful core of emotion filling her throat. ''Cause he's a divil!' came the vehement reply. 'A divil as can't be reasoned with!' She commenced to rock Queenie back and forth, as one might pacify a babe, as all the while her anger rose. What manner of man, she asked herself, would come into an Infirmary drunk and looking for fight? And why? Well, there was one thing for certain. Queenie must never live under George Kenney's roof again!

Like as not, her very life could be in danger at the mercy of such a low creature.

No! Katy decided resolutely. Until Mike Bedford got back to look after his responsibilities, Queenie would come home to the Church-house.

Chapter Thirteen

Queenie was relieved to be out of the Infirmary at long last. Her stay there had been just short of three weeks but it had seemed like a lifetime. Now, travelling home with Katy in a taxi on this bright January morning when her mood should have been lighter at having been discharged, Queenie was made to feel apprehensive because of Katy's ill-disguised anxiety. To make matters worse, Katy had skilfully avoided any of Queenie's questions; although she had assured Queenie that no harm had come to either Rick or Mike.

Queenie was left with no choice but to imagine that George Kenney had been up to some manner of evil mischief. Surely to God, she reasoned, he would not have gone to Father Riley or to Mr Marsden with his malicious stories?

Obviously Rick had chosen not to confide in anyone concerning the news imparted to him by George Kenney. Queenie understood and applauded the decision. Rick would not want to open up old wounds for his mother, nor cause distress to the man he had always known as father. Yet Queenie was left in no doubt that if George Kenney had his way, no one would be spared the pain he had in his power to cause.

Katy had been right when she'd said that George
Kenney was 'a divil who can't be reasoned with'. But
she would not let him drive her away from Auntie
Biddy's little house, the place where all those years she
had been blessed with the love and friendship of that
dear woman. All the spite of George Kenney had
never been able to overshadow that special bond
between her and Auntie Biddy.

But what now? Would George Kenney find pleasure
in taunting her and Mike about this child in her body?
This new being that she so much wanted to hate, but
could not. She had no doubt that if he could create
further upheaval in her life, he most certainly would.
But somehow she could not see George Kenney
risking a possible jail sentence. Even he, in a rare sober
moment, must now realize the awful enormity of what
he had done. Yet every instinct in her body told her
that the news Katy was concealing from her was
somehow linked to George Kenney.

It suddenly struck Queenie that, for once, George
Kenney might be afraid of her. She had it in her power
to see that he was locked away for his wickedness. She
enjoyed the possibility; until her thoughts turned to
Auntie Biddy, who had loved her hapless brother in
spite of all his faults. If George Kenney was put to rot
in some jail, the whole world would know of her own
shame. How would she ever be able to hold her head
up, and how on this earth would she ever find
contentment in the new beginning that Mike had
offered her?

No. Rather that Mike should go on believing the
man he had seen in the shadows that night was the

father of this child. The man he knew as 'the big bloke' and whom, to Queenie's relief, he could not easily identify. It was better for things to be kept as they were.

More than once over the last week, Queenie had toyed with the idea that maybe she and Mike should move right away from Parkinson Street. A further consideration was the strain of Mike's mother having disowned him, yet still living so close. It was an awful thing, and Queenie blamed herself. She could see that a move to a new area might be for the best. Yet in her heart, she knew that she could not leave. And as for the break-up between Mike and his mother, maybe with patience and tact there would be a way to bring about a reconciliation. She hoped so, for Mike had been good to her, and had asked for nothing but that she might in time come to love him.

As the taxi pulled into the grounds of the Church-house, Queenie stole a glance at old Katy, and she knew by the manner of her fidgeting that whatever had happened, it was decidedly not pleasant.

Katy, aware that Queenie was watching her, turned her head and gave a nervous smile, at the same time covering Queenie's hand with her own and saying, 'We're here now, Queenie. Father Riley will be waiting to see you.' She made a special effort to lighten her voice and lift the smile on her face, but deception was not one of Katy's strong points. It was particularly distressing to her that she should have been unable to hide her anxiety from the ever-perceptive Queenie, the last person in the world she would want to alarm. Queenie's quick senses had always amazed her, as had the girl's quiet strength and gentle ways. For one so young, not eighteen for several more weeks, there was something wonderfully wise about Queenie, and though she'd been cursed with more than her fair share of bad things, she'd been blessed with rare understanding and loveliness; such striking beauty as might cause any other girl to be arrogant and unduly proud. Taking quiet stock of Queenie's plain brown shoes and shapeless cream mackintosh, and exquisite face enclosed in broad plaits of soft shining hair, Katy's biggest regret was in never having had a daughter such as Queenie. Yet she loved the girl as though she was her own. She would have said as much, had it not been for the tightness of her throat, which would only allow her to say brokenly, 'Come on then, lass, let's get you in the warm!'

Katy alighted from the taxi first, then fussed and fretted until she had Queenie safe by her side. 'Look,' she cried, the relief heavy in her voice, 'here's Father Riley now.' She glanced towards the familiar sight of his black-clothed figure hurrying towards them. 'He'll see to the driver. We'll get off inside,' she told Queenie, hustling her across the open ground to the front door, 'don't want you catching cold, my gel!' She propelled Queenie past Father Riley, into the house and straight through to the library.

Father Riley returned just as Queenie was taking off her mac. 'Queenie,' he said, his eyes soft with concern, 'let Katy take your coat.' He looked at her thin drawn face and wondered how to break the news that her father, George Kenney, had suddenly departed this world. For all George Kenney had been a tyrant to his daughter, he was after all her last remaining flesh and blood; with the exception of the child not yet born.

Katy Forest was attentively hovering, her arm outstretched to collect Queenie's outdoor clothes. When Father Riley asked, 'Katy, perhaps a sandwich and a hot drink?' she scuttled into the sanctuary of her kitchen with such haste that Queenie suspected Father Riley had previously asked Katy to leave them alone, so that he could impart certain news.

Queenie was not deterred by Father Riley's obvious discomfort, evident in every line of his thoughtful face. 'I knew as soon as I saw Katy this morning that something was wrong, Father Riley. Please tell me at once.'

When he remained hesitant, she stepped closer, pinning his anxious eyes under the inquiring strength of her own. 'Please!'

Father Riley placed his hands on her slim shoulders. 'Of course,' he conceded. 'It's bad news; and I had no intention of keeping it from you.' His face softened, and he continued, 'It's just that you've been through so much . . . I was looking for the *right* way to tell you.'

He eased her gently into the armchair, attempting at the same time to relieve Queenie of the bulky brown paper bag clutched so tightly in her hand. The bag contained pictures of Auntie Biddy and her mother; Katy had brought them to the Infirmary for her and Queenie grasped them tight for comfort. Father Riley's anxious face tightened to a half-smile as he sat in the chair opposite, his eyes searching Queenie's expression. 'It's your father, Queenie . . . He's dead. I'm very sorry.'

As the quiet words filtered through to her, Queenie experienced a wave of inexplicable emotion which numbed her mind and stifled her heart. George Kenney? Dead? The words stood out tall and powerful in her mind but, somehow, Queenie couldn't recognize what they were saying. Slowly, their message sank in to her consciousness. There was no sorrow. George Kenney was dead, Father Riley had told her, so she accepted it to be the truth. But there was nothing in her to respond, no sense of loss at all. It seemed to Queenie at that moment that the name 'George Kenney' belonged to a stranger, to someone who had passed through her life, but played no real part in it. And now she had none to play in his death.

'I know George Kenney failed in his duty towards you as a father, Queenie,' Father Riley's voice went on, 'there was never anything to be done about *that*, I'm afraid.' He leaned back in his chair, his eyes intent on her face, 'But I know too that *you* have always committed yourself to the responsibilities left to you. So I thought we ought to let your father know of the arrangements for you to spend a short period of convalescence here, with Katy and me . . .' He paused, then reached into the folds of his long black frock, to draw out an envelope. 'I found George Kenney slumped in a chair. They told me his heart had given out.' He held out the letter.

'This envelope was on the floor by his feet. The letter from it was clutched tight in his hand.' Father Riley lowered his voice to a reassuring softness, 'The letter is addressed to *you*, Queenie. I put it back into the envelope. No one else has touched it . . . but I recognized the writing as Rick's.'

Queenie's voice caught silently in her throat as she reached out to take the letter from Father Riley. Rick's writing? she mused. Strange, I've never seen his writing. I know every line of his dear face, and every wish in his heart, and that's all I ever really want to know.

As her fingers closed around the envelope a ripple of warmth spread through her being. *He* had touched this letter; held it close and thought of her. A great sense of closeness cradled her to him. She didn't hear Father Riley close the door, as he left her alone.

Queenie put her brown paper bag down on the floor before grasping the letter and holding it lovingly to her face. She wanted to read the letter with all speed; but at the same time she felt a little afraid to know its contents. Bracing herself to face whatever new heartbreak Rick's words might carry, Queenie took the letter from the already-opened envelope and read:

My darling Queenie,
I know you'll find it in your heart to forgive my behaviour, for you are the kindest, gentlest of creatures. Before I met you, there was no other desire in my heart than to become a priest.

The honest love and truth in your quiet grey eyes and the beauty of your nature drove away all my desires for a life in the church. I love you, my little Queenie. I have always loved you, and shall do so to the end of my days.

Since the night George Kenney proclaimed me to be his son from an illicit affair with my mother, I haven't been able to think of anything else. I can only assume, from the way you ran into the night, that you were just as deeply shocked as I was.

For hours, I wandered the streets looking for

you; but even if I'd found you my darling, I couldn't have eased your pain, any more than I could ease my own. I thought that coming to Dorset, and an old friend of Father Riley's, might give me the quiet I needed, to work things out for us. But it is not to be. If there was any right way in this world for us to be together, nothing would ever part us again. But you must know, as I now do, that we can never be together in the sanctity of marriage. I pray with all my heart that you will find happiness, for no one deserves it more than you. You'll be forever in my thoughts and in my heart, my lovely Queenie.

I only know one thing for certain. If I can't spend my life with you, then I want no other woman. I may, after all, enter the church. At least in the employment of helping others, my life will have some purpose.

God bless you Queenie, and take care of you. You'll always be in my heart,

Rick

The storm of emotions raged through Queenie mingled great joy and deepest unhappiness. Through the fog of confused feelings emerged a stabbing anger and bitterness. Why had they been punished so? How could it happen that two innocent people should suffer and be made to pay for their father's sins? The questions insisted. But Queenie could find no answer. Things were as they were, and she in all her deep distress and anger could do nothing to change them.

She read the letter again and again; each time told her more surely than the last that the love they cherished for each other, the pleasure in its memory, would last strong and true. Nothing would ever belittle that.

Queenie sat, head bowed despondently, her sad eyes raking comfort from the heartfelt words before her. Suddenly, the wave of emotion so bravely suppressed erupted uncontrollably into raking sobs which broke the surrounding quietness.

Katy Forest made little sound as she entered the room to slide a comforting arm around Queenie's shoulders. 'What is it, lass? Is it the news about your father?'

Queenie shook her head in denial of Katy's assumption. Strange, how in the depths of her sorrow there had been no room for the memory of George Kenney. She supposed, deep down, she had hated him all her life; long before his monstrous image had stalked her dreams since the night of her violation. It was with a small shock that Queenie realized she actually experienced pleasure at his demise. Somewhere, beyond her own consciousness, a dam had opened up to flood her with relief that never again would she suffer at the hands of George Kenney.

Katy squeezed her shoulders lovingly, 'Take heart love . . . take heart,' she kept saying over and over. And Queenie did. Yet in her short life she had always managed to cope somehow or another, had prided herself on her independence until desperation and fear had driven her to Nazareth House; now Queenie's inner strength had deserted her completely, so that Katy became the mother Queenie had never known but always craved. In old Katy at this moment there seemed to be an essence of Auntie Biddy, and Queenie clung to her readily, eagerly, burying her face in the ample comfort of Katy's encircling arms.

After a while, Queenie allowed herself to be eased to her feet. When Katy told her, 'You're tuckered out, lass. We'd best settle you in your room,' it suddenly struck her just how tired she was. She felt the hard reality of the crumpled letter still in her hand, and when a fleeting image of George Kenney's jeering face crossed her mind she was glad that he no longer had the power to hurt her. He was gone from her world, and perhaps, after all, he was the lucky one.

As she moved up the stairs with Katy, she had already made a decision. She would not go to George Kenney's funeral. The forgiving that was needed was not in her to give, nor would she be a hypocrite for appearances' sake.

'There you are then!' Katy had chosen a lovely room for Queenie's stay. The wide bay windows trapped the light of day, sending it echoing round the room, highlighting the floral bedspread and cheery pink emulsion of the walls. The large, comfortably furnished room was a world away from her own little hideaway at Auntie Biddy's house. Queenie particularly liked the brown polished wardrobe and matching dresser with its large oval mirror, and the floral patterned oilcloth which shone rich and warm. Although she thought it all very grand and beautiful, a spiral of nostalgia wormed its way through her wandering thoughts, as she pictured Auntie Biddy's little house, now standing empty. She supposed she was feeling a bit homesick.

Thoughts of returning there, even as Mike's wife, somehow restored her feeling of belonging. The prospect brought no particular joy with it. But then neither did it bring an intolerable measure of sorrow. The best thing she could do now was to heed an old saying of Auntie Biddy's: 'You must always make the best of what you've got, my gel!'

Katy bustled about, turning the bedcover and half closing the pretty pink curtains. 'You get yourself to bed, love,' she suggested determinedly, 'a couple of hours' rest; that's just what you need . . . then we'll have a nice little chat, if you feel you want to talk.'

Queenie didn't.

Katy turned on her exit to ask, 'Do you want a snack or anything?'

Queenie didn't want anything. 'No Katy, thank you but I'll do as you say. I'll have a couple of hours' sleep . . . you won't let me sleep any longer though, will you?' she pleaded.

'It's only natural you feel tired lass! You've been right poorly, bless you. You 'ave a sleep. I'll not forget to waken you,' she promised.

Queenie crossed to kiss her on the cheek. 'You're a real friend, Katy. Will you thank Father Riley, and tell him I'll see him when I come down?'

Katy laughed, 'Don't you worry about Father Riley! If I know him, he'll be waiting at the foot of the stairs to greet you when you wake. 'Course I'll tell 'im!' She called as she closed the door behind her, 'Now you get some rest!'

Queenie slipped her shoes off and lay back on the bed. In the quietness it was inevitable that her thoughts should turn to Rick. All their dreams, all their plans . . . all come to nothing! They had glimpsed a wealth of beauty and happiness only to have it cruelly snatched from them. She closed her eyes and saw clearly Rick's face, his warm strong mouth, the reliable squareness of his jaw, and the lively passion in his dark eyes.

With enormous effort, Queenie drove the image from her mind and forced into its place a picture of Mike's homely face, with its cheeky grin and mop of hair the colour of ripe tomatoes.

But it would not stay. Aching for sleep, Queenie relaxed into it so that for a precious while all thoughts were still.

Chapter Fourteen

'What's got into you, son?' Mr Marsden was a big man given to plumpness, yet there was a stiff uprightness about him and a forthright manner which suggested he was a man of responsibility, a man who knew his way about the corridors of business.

At one time, he had owned four thriving cotton mills, two textile firms, and a number of haberdashery shops in the High Street of Wigan. But in more recent years he had converted most of the properties into hard cash which he then wisely invested. It was said of Mr Marsden that he was not 'short of a bob or two'. And he had a vested interest in the slum-clearance and rebuilding programme underway hereabouts.

Some eighteen years back he had brought his wife and son here to this place where nobody knew him, and where he could regain what he had so nearly lost.

Over the years his marriage had grown stronger, and so too had the love of his wife Rita for him. Nothing meant more to Mr Marsden than his family. Everything he did was for Rita and young Richard; and the fact that Richard was not his own blood-child made not the slightest difference. He loved the boy! Maybe that was why he had not found the courage to tell him the truth about his tragic background. Had it not been for the fact that Rita had stepped in where he himself failed to do so, then God alone knows what might have befallen the lad. Richard was adopted by himself and Rita, and since that day when those papers had been signed, it was as though the lad had always been his own son. He had given thanks for that little lost wide-eyed boy, who had since found a very special place in his heart.

All these years, he and Rita had been most careful to keep the dreadful truth from Richard. And now, if he was to insist on entering the church, his documents and background would have to be made available. There had been love enough for that other little fellow, Rita's son . . . but that had been George Kenney's child, and such a thing was not so easily forgotten. All the same, when the illness took the youngster, that too had been equally hard to bear. With Rick's arrival, in spite of the reason for it, had come new hope, and a second chance.

But God help the day when the lad should have to be told that his own demented mother had been locked away these past eighteen years for the brutal murder of his father; and that on the days when Rita was gone for hours it was not, as she claimed, to see an old friend, but to spend a while in a closed cell with her own sister; the woman who by her violent action had made it possible for Rita and Richard to take on the blessing of raising the boy in their own name.

Mr Marsden rubbed his fingers across his forehead as though he might erase the thoughts of guilt which plagued him. Not once since his wife's sister had been committed, and the adoption papers signed, had he been able to bring himself to pay her a visit. Oh, he told himself that the reason was one of deep anger that she should have callously taken a man's life and as a consequence orphaned her only child; but if that had been the true reason at the beginning, it was not what had continually kept him away. The boy had come into his and Rita's life like a ray of sunshine after a storm. Richard was his son now . . . his and Rita's, and he didn't even want to acknowledge the existence of a woman whose claim on Richard was so much stronger than his own. All these years the truth had been kept close; if it was in his power to keep it silent forever, then he would do so.

He was proud that his son had grown into a fine young man; and even though he was disappointed that Richard had shown little interest in the two remaining cotton mills, he never lost faith that it was only a matter of time before the lad took up his rightful and proper place at the helm. All this talk of becoming a priest . . . well, it would pass. Richard was too worldly, too aware of the pleasures in life ever to give them up completely. Oh yes, he was a man after his own heart, a man of commercial enterprise. Hadn't he proved as much last summer when there was that crisis in the Chorley Mill? He had the men eating out of his hand. In no time at all, Richard had put together a sensible deal; it was put to the workers, and the threatened strike averted. Mr Marsden looked around the room, at its fashionable paintings and expensive walnut furniture. To him, these material belongings spelt success, but to Rick, they were merely items of furniture, things which could not compare with essential human qualities, such as love, kindness and a sense of fair play. The same measure of fair play which had endeared him to his father's workers.

Stretching his back away from the heat of the fire, Mr Marsden rammed his hands deep into his jacket pockets and took a step forward. Then, pursing his lips to a concentrated pucker, he lifted his chin high and directed his gaze across the richly patterned carpet to where his wife Rita sat, feigning to decipher a knitting-pattern. Sensing his eyes on her, she looked up, her expression one of helplessness. This appealing glance settled momentarily on her husband, before finding its way to where Rick stood gazing out of the window. She watched him for a while, her heart aching at the forlorn droop of his broad shoulders and at how, deep in thought, he was absent-mindedly running his finger around the perimeter of the window-pane.

Something was heavy on his mind, she knew that; and so did his father. But Rick was not the kind of man to unburden his troubles onto others. He had a strong streak of independence in him which demanded that he work out his own problems. He had always been that way, and Rita Marsden loved him for it. Now, however, she would have given anything if only he would seek her help.

Rita Marsden sensed that Rick was deeply in love and that for some reason it was causing him a deal of heartache. Sitting up straight in the chair, she quietly addressed his back, 'Rick. Your father's talking to you.'

For a moment, it seemed as though he had not heard; then just as his mother braced herself to call him again, Rick straightened up and swung round to face his parents, 'Sorry, Dad, I was miles away,' he apologized.

As Mr Marsden launched into a long explanation of his intention to step down and let Rick take on the responsibility for overall running of the cotton mills, Rick was still miles away. Fourteen miles to be exact. That was the physical distance between him and Queenie at that moment; yet in truth, she was no further than his own heart. Only this very morning, on his return from Dorset, he had learned through Father Riley that Queenie, who was with child, had been in the Infirmary but was now discharged into Katy's care, until her future husband came to collect her. The added news of George Kenney's death had taken him completely by surprise, and his reactions were a mixture. He had wanted to first of all dash to Queenie's side and to tell her that no other man would ever lay claim to her; not while he had a breath in his body. But then, he was reminded of two things; firstly, Queenie was his half-sister. Secondly, and equally shattering, was the revelation that Queenie was with child. He knew it was not his, because as much as he had wanted to, and as close as they had come to loving each other in that way, Queenie's wonderful shyness and virgin innocence had persuaded him to be patient. What now? He recalled the night when he had discovered Mike Bedford and Queenie locked in each other's arms. Dear God! That man had better deserve her. For if he didn't he would have Rick Marsden to deal with.

Yet it seemed that Mike Bedford was not attempting to evade his responsibilities. Didn't Father Riley say that Queenie and Mike Bedford were to be married in a few weeks' time? Oh, it didn't bear thinking on!

His Queenie, married to another man.

Before talking to Father Riley this morning Rick had remained uncertain as to what direction his life should take. Now he was in no doubt at all. But there was one more thing to be done, distressing though it would prove. He had it in mind to question his mother about George Kenney. He needed to have confirmation from her own lips which could convince him that the late un-lamented George Kenney had been telling the truth.

'Have you been listening to a word I've said?' Mr Marsden demanded, a hint of impatience in his voice. 'Will you take it on, eh? After all, it's what I've always planned . . . and now you're almost twenty-one, it's time!'

Rick came to his father and clapped a hand on his shoulder as he asked, 'Will it wait till later, Dad? I'd like a word with Mother . . . alone.'

'Well, I'll be buggered!' Mr Marsden rarely brought his shop-floor language into his home, but now he blew out his cheeks in exasperation and ran a hand over his thinning hair as he gave an impatient half-smile and started towards the door. 'You *didn't* hear a word I've said! Well, whatever you need to get off your chest it'll be better said and done with. Then perhaps we can get back to matters of business, eh?' He directed a crafty wink at Rita; he too thought there must be a woman at the root of Rick's preoccupation. Oh, there had been girls before; but you could always tell when that special one came along, the one that knocked you right between the eyes and took hold of your heart with both hands. Just like Rita had with him, all those years back. Well, it would be a grand thing to see Rick wed. And oh, what problems it would solve, for the time being at least.

Seated in the chair opposite his mother, Rick wished for all the world that he could spare her the anxiety he was about to cause. The dilemma within him showed clearly on his face, and before he could make a start at his questions, his mother reached out a hand and coupled it with his own, saying with a cautious smile, 'Do you love her so much that her name sticks in your throat, son?' She watched until Rick visibly relaxed, then she went on to persuade him that things were never as bad as they might seem.

As he listened to her well-meaning and revealing words, Rick was horrified; because far from comforting him, they only endorsed his worst fears.

Rita Marsden confided to her son, that years ago she too had been faced with a dilemma of the heart, when her attraction to a particular man had all but broken up two marriages. Had it not been for the absolute love and devotion of her husband, she might have given in to her own selfish feelings. 'You see, Rick,' she explained, 'sometimes you're dazzled into believing that what you feel is really love, when it's nothing more than fascination. I found out that this man's wife was expecting his child; and I believed for a long time that *that* was the reason I gave him up . . . at a bad time for me too.' She lowered her eyes and squeezed his hand, before going on in a tremulous voice, 'It was a time when I desperately needed the strength and support he was offering me. I'm grateful that it didn't take me long to realize that it was not love I felt for him. I was attracted by his tall strong physique, and his laughing blue eyes. But things can change with time, Rick, and so often infatuation can really seem like a torment of love. You have to be *sure*, don't you see? You must take the time to be sure of your true feelings.' She paused to look up, and Rick was moved by the anguish in her eyes.

Then, almost in a whisper, and as though speaking to herself, she uttered the name he had not wanted to hear. 'I never loved George. I only thought I did. It was a foolish irresponsible encounter . . . all in the name of love!' Drawing herself up straight, she brightened her face with a smile, and with a small laugh she told him, 'Oh, Rick! I don't know if any of that helped you? But I think you know what I'm trying to say – be sure!'

'Don't concern yourself, Mother,' came the reply, and though Rick felt compelled to reassure her he was devastated by her revelation, although glad in his heart that he had not been made to question her, for she had voluntarily given him the answers he sought. The 'bad time' she talked about must have been when she was expecting George Kenney's child: himself.

He felt drained of emotion. There was no denying the truth of it all. When he saw his mother's anxious face looking to him for further reassurance, he told her with a misleading smile, 'You're right of course, Mother. Infatuation *can* so easily be mistaken for love.' Oh, but in this instance, he thought, there could never be any such mistake! Queenie was entangled hopelessly around his heart and every nerve inside him strained for her. He loved her, like he would never love another.

Now he was certain of two things. One was that he had lost Queenie forever. The other was that he must inform his father of his decision to enter the church.

Chapter Fifteen

'Well, lass, you're saying I can't keep you here no longer, eh?' Katy clapped her hands together over her baking, brushed off the remaining flour on her pinnie, and carried the tray of pies across the kitchen, where she put them into the oven. 'Now then, what else does he have to say?'

Queenie came into the room and sat down on the big wooden rocker by the fire. These last few weeks under Katy's fussing had brought about a remarkable change in Queenie. She had kept to her decision not to attend George Kenney's funeral; and she had given her blessing for him to be laid to rest beside his sister, Biddy. Queenie knew it would have been Biddy's wish.

Since the funeral, and in the days that followed, Queenie had seemed to grow quickly self-assured; she had learned to smile again, and the long rambling walks in the lovely gardens had brought a healthy glow to her hitherto pale complexion.

There was an old thatched cottage in the grounds and whenever Queenie went missing, Katy would know exactly where to look. The cottage had been Katy's home for many years, where she had spent the happiest time of her life with her beloved husband, now some twelve years departed. After Katy gave in to Father Riley's insistence that she should move into the main house the cottage was never lived in again and, sadly, it became very neglected. Queenie had come across it one morning, and in spite of its deterioration she had thought the cottage the most beautiful place she had ever seen. Some days she would toil at the overgrown garden, trimming back the shrubbery and fetching back a semblance of order where there had been chaos. Other times, she would go inside and bide on the deep window-seat where she would peep out of the leaded criss-cross of light strips to watch the birds pecking at the food she'd scattered. It was a peaceful, lovely place, where Queenie could gather her strength and well-being.

Queenie quickly scanned the letter in her hand, then looking up with bright clear eyes she replied, 'Nothing much, Katy . . . just that I'm to get my skates on, polish up the little house on Parkinson Street, and expect him home Friday week.' She raised the letter to look again, saying, 'This was posted on 24 February, the same day he said he got my letter. Today's Thursday, so that means he'll be back a week tomorrow.'

Katy returned to her baking, 'Hmm. I expect that means I'll have no option now but to give you the key to the house on Parkinson Street?' She paused for a moment and turned to look at Queenie. These last few weeks having Queenie here had been just grand. She'd watched the heaviness lift from the lass's shoulders, and she'd seen a quiet contentment replace the terrible lost look in her soulful grey eyes.

It were true that a woman with child grew brighter, and more contented in herself, and mebbe that was it. There was no doubt Queenie's world was a happier place without George Kenney. Or mebbe Queenie really *was* looking forward to marrying this Mike Bedford; though Katy would never be convinced of that. She wasn't no expert on young love, but she'd seen enough to know that Rick and Queenie had struck it off right from the very first, so much so that she would have staked a year's supply of snuff on the two of them together. Well, now it seemed as though Rick had decided on a future in the church. Mr Marsden was coming to see Father Riley about the very matter sometime next week. On the surface, it would seem that Rick had made a straightforward choice, but somehow Katy believed there was more to it. And she'd sensed for some time that Queenie hadn't fully confided in her. Still an' all! Whatever it was that had brought a little brightness into Queenie's face, Katy was grateful for it.

'Will *you* come to Parkinson Street with me, Katy?' Queenie could not disguise the apprehension in her voice. On Katy's advice, she hadn't been to Parkinson Street since leaving the Infirmary. Now the prospect seemed more than a little daunting.

Katy wagged a finger. 'We'll not set foot out o' this house if there's going to be any nonsense about you staying there on your own!'

Nothing was further from Queenie's mind. She couldn't face being there alone. 'Promise,' she assured Katy.

Katy set about warming up the home-made soup.

'We'll catch the three-thirty tram . . . that is, if it's still running! It seems every blessed time I set foot outside they've replaced yet another tram-service with one o' them awful buses! Too many things changing too fast, lass, and that's a fact. There'll not be a tram left at all afore so long! Any road, we'll not be going nowhere till you've swallowed that soup.'

It was about quarter past four when Queenie and Katy arrived at the top end of Parkinson Street; already, the dusk of day's end was gathering in the sky.

Queenie had never liked this time of year. Too bleak and quiet, she pondered. All the special things like Christmas and New Year had passed, leaving little to look forward to, except perhaps her imminent eighteenth birthday, which she thought didn't warrant a fuss anyway.

With a lurch of sadness, she recalled other, more enjoyable birthdays; like the special one when she was ten, and Mr Craig had given her that beautiful golden heart. She turned to Katy, who was beginning to puff and pant at the long trek up Parkinson Street. 'Katy where can I get a necklace mended?' she asked.

Tackling the endless journey and answering Queenie's question all at one and the same time was too much to ask of poor old Katy. She brought herself to a grateful halt, her chest heaving in and out like a great puffing bellow.

'Queenie! I must be older than I give meself credit for,' she gasped as she threw her head back and snatched at the air, 'or you're forcing too fast a pace on an old worn-out lady. What necklace?'

Queenie reached into her mac pocket to draw out the golden heart, still hanging from the chain which George Kenney had viciously snapped. 'Old Mr Craig gave me this,' she said tenderly, placing it in Katy's outstretched hand, 'he loved it more than anything else in the world.'

Katy turned the beautiful necklace over and over, her eyes bright with amazement. 'I'm not surprised,' she murmured, 'it's lovely! How did it get broken lass?'

'I can't remember,' Queenie lied, blushing fiercely, 'but I *have* to get it mended.'

'Can you trust me with it a day or two, Queenie?'

''Course I can . . .' Her heart bumped a little faster at even the remotest possibility that it might get lost. 'But you will be careful with it, won't you Katy?' she asked hesitantly.

Katy laughed heartily, and pulled Queenie affectionately towards her. 'Seems like it might be more than me life's worth to lose it, eh? Bless your 'eart, lass; you put more store by an old man's treasured gift than you do by your own welfare!' She looked deep into Queenie's anxious grey eyes. 'Ey, lass! I'll guard this 'ere necklet like it were the Crown Jewels!' she said earnestly, releasing Queenie to place the necklace carefully into her purse. Setting off again, she urged, 'Come on, then! There's a fair way to go yet!'

Queenie slowed down her pace. Her long youthful legs found it no difficult task to cover the length of Parkinson Street. She repeated the name to herself. It had a comforting sound about it. Here, on this street, she'd grown up. She had known small happiness and experienced emotions that had left her scarred, but it would always be home to her. How often had she and Auntie Biddy trod these very same flagstones? Even at that moment, Queenie convinced herself she could feel Auntie Biddy close by.

As they walked further down Parkinson Street, and drew nearer to No. 2, it was as though each step took Queenie not into the past, but away from it.

It was an odd inexplicable feeling, but she knew in her heart of hearts that the time for looking back was long gone. She had accepted the loss of Rick, and in doing so had formed a measure of quietness in herself. In the past lay only heartache and pain. Perhaps there wasn't much more ahead either, she told herself, but what else could she do but look forward with faith and belief in her own strength. Yet, even as she contemplated her future with Mike, and with the child not of her choosing, she could find little in it to excite her.

'Here we are, Queenie.' The house key had been placed in Katy's care by Father Riley, and now she drew it from her pocket and turned it in the lock.

As she followed Katy along the passage and through to the parlour, Queenie thought the house was chillingly cold. Hostile even. She had the strongest instinct that it was alive and angry with her.

'I don't know if we should light a fire. What do you think, Queenie? Feels damp doesn't it?'

Queenie shivered. 'No. Don't light a fire Katy,' she replied.

Katy shrugged her shoulders in acknowledgement. 'All right, I'll just check round, and make sure everything's as it should be.' She ambled off to the scullery.

Queenie couldn't understand the strangeness of her feelings. She looked around. Nothing had changed. The furniture shone beneath its fine film of dust, and the ornaments stood where they had always stood. So what was it? she demanded of herself. And the answer came back, it's him! It's George Kenney!

As she looked wonderingly over all the familiar things her eyes came to rest on George Kenney's armchair. A flutter of fear, or perhaps a weird sort of pleasure, disturbed Queenie's heart. So *that* was where he had read Rick's letter? Her letter! And that was where he had died. A great wave of emotion surged through her, and deliberately turning her back on George Kenney's chair, she ran her fingers along the sideboard. The pleasure she always experienced at the touch of Auntie Biddy's furniture was still there, but the house itself had become a forbidding stranger.

Queenie felt afraid. This little house had always been her anchor in times of storm and now it seemed as though she had lost that security. She searched for reasons. Perhaps the house was sulking? Or maybe George Kenney's tortured soul had seeped into it? Queenie couldn't rightly say but suddenly, quite inexplicably, she felt the urge to run from that place and never come back. It was a startling revelation to her, making her both guilty and sad. So many memories tied her to this house, but, somehow, the good ones and the awful ones had intermingled into a suffocating whole. It was plain to Queenie that she could not easily separate the ties of the past. She must let them all go, the good memories and the bad. Only in that way could she ever hope to go on with a brave heart.

When Katy called that it was time for them to leave, Queenie was more than ready. They called in at Mrs Farraday's before they left Parkinson Street; and although the dear soul rattled on about anything and nothing, Queenie thoroughly enjoyed the visit.

Later, when she sat on the tram pretending to look out of the window and nodding occasionally at Katy's general remarks, she sought reassurance within herself. She wondered whether growing up really meant growing away? And did a body shed the past in the same way that a butterfly sheds its chrysalis?

But then, she'd never felt anything *but* grown-up! Even at school in the playground, or down Parkinson Street, she'd never mixed with the other children. Why should she? They all had mothers and fathers, friends and relatives. Some even had nice new clothes and pennies to spend. None of these things had ever figured in her childhood. She had nothing in common with any of the children.

Queenie sighed inwardly, wondering whether these things had really been so important. Childhood should be something you enjoy; something you could look back on with pleasure. She wasn't able to do that, except perhaps for just a few isolated precious memories of times spent with Auntie Biddy. She *did* miss what she had never had: she missed not having a real father; and she would much rather have had a mother to talk to instead of a picture.

Her eyes closed momentarily . . . how she wished with all her heart that she and Rick could have been free to love each other, free to build cherished memories for themselves and their children. Strange how she'd never responded to other boys' persuasions, yet when Rick first spoke to her she felt she had known him all her life. Now the love she felt for Rick weighed her down and dominated her every thought. It could not go on! Not now. She was about to be married and in several months' time, there would be a child, a real baby to care for. If it took every ounce of her will-power, she would inwardly deny her love for Rick. She must.

Chapter Sixteen

On 14 March 1963 Mike Bedford and Queenie stood in St Mary's Church before Father Riley, and reverently exchanged their marriage vows.

Mike made an additional vow to himself that if by chance he ever found out the identity of the 'big bloke' who had deserted Queenie, he'd flatten him to the ground; although his fury was tempered by the fact that the circumstances had brought about his own opportunity to take Queenie as his wife. For it was plain enough fact that she would not otherwise have wed him. He knew she didn't love him in the way he would have liked. But she would in time. He'd make sure of that!

In the midst of the ceremony, Queenie had silently asked that the Good Lord should help her to be a loyal wife to this man in both thought and deed. Father Riley, too, appealed to the Lord to understand and accept his act of joining these two young people here in the church. Tradition could sometimes be a hard master, and surely the fact that Queenie offered herself as a new bride already with child should not be a sufficient cause to deny them God's blessing.

It was a simple service, with only Katy and Mrs Farraday as guests, and Mr Farraday to give away the bride. Afterwards, Katy took a snap or two of the newlyweds; Mike looking stiff and uncomfortable in a borrowed suit, and Queenie quiet and lovely in a blue loose-fitting twopiece.

It had been a wild March day, with a keen spiteful wind which after the service hurried everybody away to their respective homes. In the following weeks the weather had grown steadily worse, its monotony broken only by the constant radio broadcasts about the scandal involving John Profumo, the Secretary of State for War. It was a revelation which had rocked the country and kept the men of Blackburn muttering into their beer for many a night.

Queenie worked hard in her new role as Mike Bedford's wife, and every morning she saw him off to care for the Corporation's roads and highways with his snap-tin packed with wholesome sandwiches and freshly baked pies. On his return home, she would have a hot filling meal ready and a banked-up fire to cheer the little parlour; in which, in spite of her every effort, she could not feel wholly comfortable.

Queenie had wanted to throw out George Kenney's black horse-hair chair, but Mike would have none of it, arguing, 'Don't be bloody daft, woman! You don't throw away good solid stuff like that.' So it stayed. And she polished the furniture around it and kept the whole house shining like a new pin. She washed her husband's muddy clothes and saw to it that he had a warm comfortable home, and a full belly. But the one thing he craved, she could not bring herself to give.

On that first night when they were man and wife Queenie had lain beside her husband, praying that

Mike's strong passion for her would infuse her own heart with love. When in all his warm nakedness he had taken her into his arms, however, two images rose to fill her mind. One was Rick's familiar smile, and the other was the devilish form of George Kenney on that awful night. It was this apparition which spread to blacken her mind and to freeze all hope of responding to the urgent demands of the man beside her.

Mike had sensed her reluctance, and, throwing her from him, angrily declared, 'I'll take no woman against her will! Not even me own wife!' In a fit of temper, he had stormed from the room to sleep downstairs. But for Queenie there was no sleep. Going on tiptoe, she had carried a blanket down to him and quietly draped it over his sleeping form. Then just as silently she had returned to the bedroom, where she spent most of the night pacing up and down.

In the long empty weeks that followed, Queenie was desperate to make amends and to fulfil her wifely duties. Mike was no fool, and he recognized her efforts for what they were, rejecting them with the words, 'I'll put it down to the fact that you're with child. But if I could be sure that it was its father you were craving after, I'd tear you apart, so help me, God!' Then he had taken her roughly by the shoulders and shaken her so hard that she thought her neck would surely snap. And in a threatening voice, he had demanded to know the truth. *Was* she pining after the man who'd filled her with child! Queenie, in all truth, was able to assure him that as God was her judge, she would *never* pine for that man.

Seeing the truth in her eyes, Mike Bedford had quietly taken her into his arms and told her that much as he wanted her body, he would leave her be until after the child was born. But then, by God, she'd better be ready to give herself to him as a wife should or face the consequences.

Queenie had forced herself to face many things, and to come to terms with them. But lying in Mike's arms while he invaded her body, however lovingly, was not one of them.

These last few weeks, she had grown surprisingly closer in spirit to the tiny helpless being inside her. She had often lain quiet and still in the hush of early morning, and marvelled at the movements that quickened inside her. It was a strange and wondrous experience, which never failed to make her feel both humble and guilty, that she should ever have thought to lay the blame for George Kenney's evil doings at this innocent babe's door. Up until the day of Mike's angry outburst, Queenie had begun to look forward to the child's birth. Now, in the wake of his ultimatum, she dreaded it.

'Fares please!' The bus conductor's intrusive address brought Queenie back to the moment, as she dug into her purse for her fare, which she offered in exchange for a ticket.

'Looks like I'll be charging half-fare as well, afore long, eh?' he laughed, looking at the slight bulge beneath her flowered dress. Queenie smiled and hated the pink flush that ran up her neck to suffuse her face.

'Not yet awhile,' she replied, regretting the fact that she had chosen to seat herself right by the platform where he stood throughout the journey.

There was one more stop before Queenie would

alight for the Church-house, so she settled back into the seat and gazed out of the bus window. It was a lovely morning, the first day of May, and after the unusually long winter the countryside had come alive at last. The fields looked fresh and green; in the distance, Queenie could see the lambs skipping and diving at each other in playful occupation. Everything was so peaceful and lovely, with the chimneys and mills of Blackburn Town seeming a million miles away. Queenie thought how delightful it would be to live in the country, and suddenly she found herself thinking of the pretty thatched cottage which had once been Katy's home. She wondered, too, whether Katy might not return there when she retired from her work.

A quiet smile lit up Queenie's grey eyes as she thought on Katy and the idea of her ever 'retiring'. Katy would be up in arms at the very idea! And anyway, by the look of the cottage when she saw it last, Queenie thought it must be beyond repair. That was a sad thing, to be sure.

Queenie was so glad that Katy was back home. Almost two weeks she'd been gone, since getting word that an old friend of her late husband had been taken gravely ill, with no one to fend for him. In spite of Katy's tender care the old fellow had died, so after seeing to all the formalities, Katy had hurried back to Father Riley. One of the first things she did on her return was to telephone Mrs Farraday's shop, and leave a message for Queenie, saying that she was back and would be out to see Queenie sometime in the next few days.

But bored and restless, Queenie couldn't wait. So here she was, all done up in the smart brown sandals which Mike had bought her, a matching brown beret over her shining braided hair and the pretty, flowered smockdress she had made herself.

Next stop the Church-house, thought Queenie, as the bus shuddered to a halt at Chantry Cross. There were not many houses here, and usually not many people waiting for the bus. But it looked as though the lovely sunny day had persuaded people from their parlours, for there were eight or nine folk heavily laden with bunches of flowers, already clambering onto the bus, bound for the churchyard, thought Queenie, to remember departed loved ones.

Most of the passengers went straight upstairs, and the conductor followed them. Queenie watched as the last two got on, a woman and a boy. The woman was a quick, busy little person with a hard-set face and, judging by the number of times she threatened to clout the lad's ear, a quick temper. 'Move yerself!' she instructed him, 'get on. An' tek yersel' upstairs after yon conductor. Ask 'im if it's all right to fetch this 'ere bike on!' The boy ran away upstairs and the woman lost no time in yanking what Queenie took to be the boy's bicycle on board.

'Little sod won't go nowhere wi' out this bloody great contraption!' she told Queenie. Then quickly aware of Queenie's condition, she added with a knowing grin, 'Kids is trouble! You'll find out soon enough. You'll see.' Just then the boy returned with the conductor sharply on his heels.

''E says we can't tek me bike, Mam!' the boy protested, his bottom lip protruding in a sulk.

'I'm sorry, missus. It's the rules! No bikes.'

'What kind o' bloody rules is them eh?' the woman

retorted as she glared at him. When the conductor stood his ground and continued to shake his head, she turned her anger on the boy, and fetched him down a resounding clap to his ear, shouting, 'I told yer to leave the bloody thing at 'ome, didn't I? Yer little sod! Why can't yer ever do as yer told?'

The boy promptly broke out crying. And to this tune, the woman added her own loud abuse, of the boy, of children in general, and particularly of the conductor, whose help she vehemently refused as she and the boy wrestled the bike off the bus.

Once the bus started to move away she set up a fresh volley of complaint at which the boy, with surprising suddenness, stopped crying, and vigorously shook his fist as he yelled at the conductor, 'I'll not come on yer rotten bus again! So yer can stick it right up yer arse! An' I 'ope it chokes yer!'

Open-mouthed, the conductor turned and saw Queenie in the grip of helpless laughter, so he came and sat beside her. 'It's the rules, you see. The rules,' he explained. Of a sudden, he too was laughing.

Then the other passengers saw the funny side of it all. And all the way to the next stop the bus rang to the sound of helpless laughter. Amidst his roars of delight, the conductor paused to assure one and all, 'It's the rules! These buses aren't as big as the trams. It's change, you see, change!'

'Aye, mebbe,' yelled a kind-faced woman, 'but the biggest change i' Blackburn these last five years 'ave been you Indians choosing to live 'ere!' At this, the laughter was renewed, no one enjoying the observation more than the jolly black-eyed conductor.

Half an hour later saw Queenie at the door of the

Church-house, and once Katy caught sight of her, she was whisked into the kitchen, set down by the table and confronted by a mug of tea and a great wedge of cherrycake. 'Huh! I can see you've been neglecting yourself since I've been gone, my girl!' Katy declared, tucking into her own generous slice.

'I have not!' protested Queenie. 'I've been eating very sensibly, Katy.' Just to please Katy, she nibbled at the cherry-slice.

Then followed from Katy a short account of the old fellow and how at eighty-two, he'd lived to 'a good old age'. Queenie genuinely expressed her sympathy, telling Katy of how she had missed her regular visits, and of how she was glad to have her back.

'Oh, that's nice, lass. And I'm glad to *be* back.' She tutted and shook her head as she said, 'It's just as well an' all. Father Riley . . . an' *all* men, I've no doubt, doesn't have the first idea how to look after himself! I arranged for a lass to come in daily from the village. But she's been neither use nor ornament!' Suddenly a quietness came over her, and leaning forward to look Queenie deep in the eye, she asked, 'How've you been, lass? Really?'

Queenie's gaze was unfaltering as she looked into Katy's wise old eyes. Was there *nothing* she could hide from this dear old lady? she wondered. Yet all she said was, 'I'm fine, Katy, thank you.' Adding as an afterthought, 'I am a bit bored though. The longest I can make the housework stretch is two hours. Then I'm at a loose end.'

At once, Katy was fired with enthusiasm, 'Well now – you like children, don't you? An' you've a way with 'em. I know for a fact as Father Riley's finding the work at the Ragged School a bit too much on top of his parish demands. How would you feel about helping him out . . . say for the Wednesday club? An' mebbe weekends?'

Queenie didn't need asking twice. It was settled. Katy would tell Father Riley the minute he got back from his visits, 'Or better still, Queenie . . . *you* wait an' tell him yourself.'

'No, Katy. I'd best not stay too long, on account of Mike likes me to be in, with his meal all ready, when he gets home. And I've to get some shopping yet.'

That brought Katy back onto the subject of Mike. Was he treating her well? Did he give her enough money? And had he made matters up with his mother?

Queenie quickly answered 'yes' to the first two. But on the last question she could not disguise her despair. No, Mike and his mother had not spoken a word since the wedding. If she saw Queenie on the street or in the shop, Mrs Bedford would stare right through her, and hurry away.

'Well, if she wants to be like that, you take no notice, d'you hear me, Queenie?' Queenie nodded her agreement, but in all truth she did not altogether blame Mrs Bedford, and she would have liked them to be friends. She and Mike owed his mother for respecting Mike's wish that she should not tell people he was not the father of Queenie's child. There was no doubt that Mrs Bedford had her own reasons for keeping the truth to herself, but all the same Queenie was grateful.

Queenie stayed chatting to Katy for the best part of the morning. Then after returning from a stroll through the gardens to the cottage, Queenie voiced her intention to leave. It had been on the tip of her tongue to ask after Rick, but somehow she had kept the urge under control.

As they neared the door, however, Katy suddenly stopped and said, 'Wouldn't you like to stay and say hello to Rick?'

It was like a bolt out of the blue. The flush of excitement that coloured Queenie's face did not escape Katy's sharp eyes. 'You hadn't forgotten that Rick was coming to work with Father Riley? I thought I told you?'

'Yes. You did, Katy. But I've had so much on my mind lately . . . what with the baby coming and everything,' she lied. During her visits to Parkinson Street, Katy had not lost a single opportunity to keep Queenie informed of Rick's activities, and Queenie had kept close every snippet of information. That Rick and his father had clashed about Rick's decision to turn his back on the Marsden business and make his future in the church; and that because of the love and respect Rick had for his father, he had agreed to two particular requests.

One was to spend a few weeks at the heart of Mr Marsden's 'new baby' as he called the lately acquired cotton mill in Chorley. Badly run-down and on the market cheap as it was, he had been unable to resist the challenge it presented. Katy had declared her belief that Mr Marsden was hoping such a venture might appeal to the businessman in Rick, and persuade him away from the church. What was more, she claimed, it was also her belief that Rick was indeed cut out for commercial enterprise. He had a sharp mind and a natural way of handling people. But then, it was true that these very qualities would make him an excellent priest; although somehow, Katy sensed that his heart was in neither venture.

Queenie had offered no comment, so Katy had gone on to explain that the wily old Mr Marsden had cleverly hedged his bets by pointing out to Rick and Father Riley that perhaps it would be best if Rick came to stay at the Church-house for a year, during which time he could work closely with Father Riley and consider his intended commitment. Rick had resented the implication that he had not already given the matter a great deal of thought. But Father Riley, on the other hand, thought it an excellent idea. So it was arranged.

'And he'll be here any minute! Oh, Queenie . . . you will stay a while longer, won't you?' Katy pleaded.

Queenie kissed the old lady on the cheek, collected her shopping bag from the hall table and stepped out through the open doorway, saying, 'You give him my regards, and tell Father Riley I'm sorry I missed him.'

'Tell him yourself, lass!' cried Katy, her eyes growing wide as they looked past Queenie to the path beyond. 'It's Father Riley – an' he's got Rick with him!' As Katy rushed to greet them, Queenie felt frozen to the spot, unable for a moment to turn round. Then with determined effort she swallowed the hardness which had paralysed her throat, put on a smile and turned to greet them.

Rick had taken Katy into such a hug that threatened to lift her from the ground. As he put her down his eyes met Queenie's. For a moment they stood, each aware only of the other, and both helpless in the emotions sweeping through them.

As Father Riley engaged Katy in conversation Rick

came slowly towards Queenie, his gaze locked into hers. Queenie would have drawn her eyes from him, but she could not. It was some months now, since their last meeting, and though she had quietly carried him in her heart Queenie was not ready for the reality of actually being in his presence. He was strikingly handsome in light-coloured flannels and blue sweater, with that familiar lock of hair brushing his eyes. But he was thinner, thought Queenie, and more serious of feature. When he took her outstretched hands in his, murmuring, 'Oh Queenie . . . Queenie!' the warmth of his skin burned through her. In that moment she would have given the world for him to take her in his arms and never let her go. Instead, she refused the threatening tears, and summoning every remaining ounce of strength, she told him quietly, 'Hello, Rick. You look well.' It struck her as being extraordinary that her heart could be turning somersaults while her voice managed to sound so cool and polite.

For what seemed a lifetime, Rick gave no reply. Holding her hands fast in his own, he continued to regard her, to take his fill of this lovely creature who would always be the centre of his every thought. He marvelled at her shining beauty and at the innocence there. And he marvelled at his own ability to constrain that driving urge within him to gather her close to him and tell her that in all these long empty months, he had loved her stronger by the day. He had fought to accept the circumstances of their parting, and he had roared his protest at the cruelty of it all. Then, spent of searching for an answer which could not be found, he had learned to come to terms with a situation over which neither he nor Queenie could have control. It had crossed his mind more than once to wonder whether Queenie was the stronger of them both. For hadn't she taken a husband and wasn't she now heavy with child? Oh, God, that it was *his*! That *she* was his! The awful agony of his love for her spilled out to draw itself on his face and to materialize in a small cry which threatened to crumble his restraint.

Acutely aware of his every thought, for they were the same as her own, Queenie took it upon herself to save them both further heartache. Swiftly drawing her hands away she stepped aside, then deliberately lowering her gaze, she told him, 'I must be going, Rick . . . I'll see you again, no doubt.' Without looking back she quickly crossed to bid Father Riley and Katy goodbye before hurrying away.

Rick watched Queenie out of sight, his thoughts a turmoil. He had read the love in her eyes. Yet she had been so decisive in her attitude. Had this husband of hers taken *everything* that had been his own? He wanted to chase after her, to annihilate the barrier between them. And he cursed the sins that had brought about their despair.

So too did Queenie, as, heavy-hearted, she stumbled along the narrow lane to the bus-stop. The tears she had earlier stifled ran unchecked down her face, and more than ever she dreaded the bleak empty years that loomed up before her.

Katy, too, was deeply moved by the scene she had purposely witnessed between Rick and Queenie. She knew – as she had known all along – that these two belonged together. They *did* love each other. It was there in their eyes for all the world to see, although Father Riley, bless him, was too wrapped up in other things to see what was under his nose. Yet for some reason known only to them, Rick was turning his back on Queenie's world. She meanwhile had become another man's wife, and mother to his child. Oh, 'twas all very odd, thought Katy. How could *she* interfere? By what right could she go questioning two grown people who had made a choice with their eyes wide open? But surely, she thought, alarmed at her own wickedness, there would be no harm in taking advantage of any small opportunity that might present itself?

When such an opportunity did present itself, in the form of Father Riley's deliberations about what specific duties to allocate to Rick, Katy was smartly in with her suggestion that Rick would 'make a grand job of the Ragged School!'

'Why of course! Katy, that's a marvellous idea. The very thing to bring Rick close to the children, and to the heart of the community,' declared Father Riley.

And close to Queenie, thought Katy, conveniently omitting to inform Rick and Father Riley of Queenie's agreement to contribute to the self-same project.

'How do you feel about taking on the Ragged School, Rick?' asked Father Riley.

When, his mind still on Queenie, Rick nodded his acceptance, Katy put his tea before him, smiled into his sad eyes and said, 'Cheer up, me lad! There's a silver lining behind every cloud . . . and the sunshine not far behind!'

Chapter Seventeen

'Here's your mam, Tommy, come to fetch you.' Queenie bent to hug the round-faced boy, who threw his arms around her neck in a vice-like grip, causing her almost to lose her balance. As she prised him from her she laughed, 'Well, it's nice to be loved, darling . . . but I'm not really fit for wrestling!' Then the boy settled for nestling his hand in hers, and Queenie led him towards the plump little woman making her way towards them. 'There you are, Mrs Craig. One little boy all tired and ready for his bed.'

'Aye! An' I'll be bound 'e's not the *only* one!' Mrs Craig remarked, her face a broad smile as she collected her son. 'This 'ere club on a Wednesday night and Saturday is a right blessing to the kids 'ereabouts, Queenie. You couldn't keep my Tommy from it if you tried. Oh, but just look at you, lass! Wi' child an' tiring yersel' out wi' other folk's young 'uns.'

'But *I* enjoy it as much as they do,' Queenie replied, smiling at Mrs Craig's continued chastisement as she walked the boy towards the door.

'I know you do lass,' came the reply. 'An' it's for sure us mothers is grateful, bless yer 'eart. You're a grand 'un!'

Mrs Craig had echoed Rick's quiet thoughts as he witnessed the scene from the rear of the hall. He'd never known anyone to be so natural with children as was Queenie. Thanks to her, this Ragged School had become a resounding success. She'd introduced a new element of excitement for the children by organising surprises, competitions and impromptu talent shows and parties. The mothers, worn-out from struggling to make ends meet with little money or time to spend on their countless offspring, trusted Queenie implicitly, and loved her as much as did the children, who sensed Queenie's natural affection for them.

Father Riley had remarked that there were more youngsters coming to the Ragged School now than he had ever known. Because of Queenie's insistence that even more children would come if only there wasn't the stigma of the name, he was in the throes of seeking approval to take up Queenie's suggestion that it should be renamed 'Blackburn Children's Club'.

As Queenie came towards him now, Rick thought how tired and spent she looked, and his heart went out to her. But over these last weeks he had learned to control his emotions and to confine his love for Queenie to words and gestures. And he had grown increasingly grateful for the wonderful moments spent in her company here at the Ragged School. They were all he had come to live for; other demanding church-duties and parish-work with Father Riley paled into insignificance besides them. As for Queenie, he dared not wonder how she felt, and he dared not ask. Yet occasionally, in the midst of laughing together with the children, he would look at her and see the sad reflection of his own love in her eyes. At such times, he would question the mercy of this God whom he had professed to serve.

Always at this hour on Wednesday evenings, Rick felt down in spirit because he knew that around eight o'clock when the last child had gone, he and Queenie would depart in separate directions, he to the bus-stop for Church-house and she on foot to Parkinson Street. On each occasion, he would return to the Church-house with a heavy heart, impatient for the days to pass swiftly until he would see her again.

Rick watched Queenie now as she came closer, her long shining hair loose about her trim shoulders and those marvellous grey eyes alive and smiling. It struck him how graceful were Queenie's movements in spite of her advanced pregnancy. Then at once, she was within arm's length and such was the strong urge within him to put his arms about her and bring his mouth down on those rich smiling lips that he quickly turned away on the pretence of having forgotten to lock the back door. As though having read his thoughts, Queenie didn't wait for his return. Instead she flung her cardigan about her shoulders and hurried to the front exit, calling as she did so, 'I'd best be away, Rick . . . I'm late as it is.' When Rick came back, she was gone. For a while he stood alone in that quiet place, his dark eyes fixed on the door, still ajar after Queenie's hasty departure.

Out in the warm sunshine of a beautiful summer

evening Queenie began to wonder whether continuing at the Ragged School was a wise thing to do. Of course, she knew it was not. But how could she give up the very light of her existence? The only escape she had found from the prison that was Mike Bedford and Parkinson Street? So many times in these last few weeks she had asked herself the very same questions. Always, the answer came back that she could not, *would* not give up the measure of happiness she had found. Oh, she had been forced to steel herself in those unguarded moments when she and Rick, engrossed in the antics of a demanding child, were drawn so close that she might feel the warmth of his breath or brush his hand with her own. Her conscience told her that these moments were forbidden, and her heart drew both sorrow and happiness from them. Yet, because of the inner strength they gave her, she could not deny them. Was it not enough that she and Rick had learned to command their emotions? Should they then be made to sacrifice the small pleasures found in each other's company? No, Queenie answered herself. And yet, deep inside her, she knew that soon it must stop. For the happiness she derived from working with Rick was lately in danger of being swamped by the lengthening periods of regret. Yet for now, these times of depression were a small price to pay for her snatches of joy.

Through her work at the Ragged School, Queenie had become a popular and familiar figure to those hitherto unknown to her. Now, as she wended her way down the alleys then across the market square, greetings were called out to her from men, women and children alike. Cheered, she turned into Parkinson Street with a lighter step.

Mike Bedford caught sight of Queenie before she saw him. Anxious at her being some fifteen minutes late, he had started out to meet her. Now, at the sound of his voice as he called her name, Queenie looked up. Seeing Mike striding towards her, his copper-coloured hair a thick profusion jutting out from beneath his hastily donned cap, and a deep scowl darkening his face, she groaned inwardly. Mike as a rule was not quick to temper and was easily placated. But where she was concerned, he was impossibly possessive and jealous of every moment she spent away from him. And such was his anger at her devotion to the Ragged School that he vehemently refused to set foot inside it.

'Where the hell have you been?' he demanded, taking her arm and propelling her at a brisker pace down the street. 'You know I get worried when you're late!'

'I'm sorry, Mike,' she told him, breathless from the force of pace after her long walk. 'It were little Tommy Craig. He's always the last . . .'

'Aye, well! I don't care what the reason is. If you're late again, I'll stop you going altogether!'

By the time they had got home, and come to rest in the parlour, Queenie had diffused her husband's black mood by skilfully switching from herself and on to the Corporation, his employer. While she brewed him a pot of tea, he related to her all the traumas of his working day.

'An' I've missed you, sweetheart,' he told her, 'I *allus* miss you. Every bloody minute I'm away!'

As Queenie came back into the parlour, with the teapot, Mike came up behind her. Slapping her heartily on the rear, he caught her to him as she straightened up from setting the teapot on the table. Wiping his mouth down the silky warmth of her neck, he whispered hoarsely, 'Sometimes I think I'll go mad if I've to wait one more second for you.' Then as Queenie stiffened against him he suddenly stepped away, saying in a hard voice, 'Oh, don't worry! I'm a man o' me word. I can bide me time till it's born.' He prodded an impatient finger at her bulging middle. 'It's got summat to answer for, 'as that brat! What wi' one thing an' another.'

'Please, Mike,' Queenie pleaded. They had gone through all this before, and she felt too tired to endure it tonight.

'Aw come 'ere, sweetheart,' he said as he grabbed her to him, then he took a handful of her hair and gently forced her head back to kiss her full on the mouth.

Queenie did her best to respond, but tight in his arms and acutely aware of the hardness of his body against her, she could not escape the truth. Not even in the farthest reaches of her imagination could she ever see herself submitting to his advances. She knew that before such a thing could happen, her gratitude to him would turn into hatred.

She did not want that. So what to do? It had crossed her mind to run away; but where could she run with a baby due, no money and no visible means of supporting herself, let alone a child! Anyway there was no doubt at all in her mind that if she did leave this man, who was her husband in every sense but the real one, he would search to the ends of the earth to find her, and she would never know peace.

Unwilling to release her, Mike Bedford swayed Queenie in his arms, feeling the softness of her body against his fevered loins. 'D'you want me, sweetheart?' he murmured 'as much as I want you, eh?' When Queenie dropped her head and gave no reply, he laughed out loud, 'Oh! Shy, is it?' Then he came to an abrupt stop, put his hand beneath Queenie's chin and raised her face to his. In a voice thick with passion, he cried, 'God! You're so beautiful, Queenie. But you're my wife! And soon – oh, soon you'll *really* be mine!' As though he could contain himself no longer, he turned from her and in a moment he was at the door. 'I'm off to the pub,' he told her, 'is there owt you want?'

'No nothing,' replied Queenie, glad to see the door close behind him, yet at the same time feeling ashamed. Something akin to pity for him surged through her body. In turn it became a boundless energy, which drove all the tiredness from her and launched her into a deluge of house-cleaning which occupied her mind and took all fearsome thoughts away.

This same determined tide of energy carried Queenie over the next few weeks and into her eighth month of pregnancy. She had felt remarkably well and given thanks for her good health. But now, of a sudden, she felt uncomfortably heavy and every effort, however small, left her drained of energy. So too did the niggling pains down her left side, and the spasmodic attacks of breathlessness.

'An' what does the doctor have to say about it?' demanded an anxious Katy, having arrived early this Friday afternoon to find Queenie in an exhausted condition, after hanging out the considerable load of washing done that morning.

Queenie sipped at the mug of tea which the kindly woman had thrust into her hands, then smiled gratefully, saying, 'You are an old fusspot, Katy . . . but I'm glad you're here. The doctor said the baby must be lying on a nerve and there's nothing to be done, except wait for it to shift.'

'Is that so? Well all I can say is, it'll be a blessing when it shifts right out o' there altogether!' Katy took stock of Queenie's unusually high colouring and weariness of face, and she sensed that the birth was not far away. 'It's a miserable business carrying a child late in this hot weather. I've never known such a muggy summer . . . fair suffocates a body!' she declared, adding as an afterthought, 'I can't understand that husband o' yours, lass. Whatever prompted him to take on a Saturday shift an' you nobbut a few weeks from your time?'

'We could do with the extra money, Katy,' Queenie said. She wasn't lying. But neither was she telling the full truth. Mike *had* let her down, though she could hardly admit to Katy that in all truth she felt more than relieved.

He seemed to have become more and more possessive of late, always on her heels whenever she moved from the parlour to the kitchen or upstairs. And since Wednesday evening when she'd returned from the Ragged School, where Rick and the children had surprised her with a little farewell party, Mike had taken every opportunity to remind her that it wouldn't be long now before he could make her 'his real wife'.

Queenie was left in no doubt as to what he meant. Last night while undressing for bed, Queenie had suddenly sensed Mike watching her. When she had turned to see him staring at her, a look of smiling satisfaction on his face, she had experienced a deep feeling of fear and humiliation. When she grabbed her housecoat about her Mike had got from the bed and crossed to the dresser where he snatched her into his arms. Peeling the housecoat from her body, he had stroked his hands all over her, touching her face, her long silky hair and her breasts. Then standing astride before her, he ran the palm of his hand up and down the bulge of her stomach, his voice a caressing murmur as he told her, 'This 'ere brat won't be a barrier for much longer, eh?' With a chuckle, he turned away, his voice growing hard as he growled, 'I'm working tomorrow, sweet'eart . . . shan't be finished till eight.'

'Eight o'clock?' Queenie had groaned inwardly, 'Oh, Mike! You promised – I've told them you'll be there.'

'Well you can bloody well *un*tell 'em then, can't you! I should never have let you talk me into it in the first place . . . What do I want to go mixing with *your* cronies for? We've got nowt in common!' He had not looked at her as he'd climbed back into bed, adding quietly, 'An' you're not to go neither. I won't have it! I want my wife here when I get home from work. D'you hear?'

Queenie heard, and she knew from the tone of his voice that it would be no good arguing. Mike had lied to her before, and he had broken promises without conscience. Since their marriage, he had proven himself to be a man of fickle persuasion and easy deceit. But for all that, Queenie didn't doubt for one moment that he loved her. Yet his love was not a tender caring, but a suffocating single-mindedness that drove her ever further away from him.

When Rick had asked that she come to his twenty-first birthday party and extended that invitation to Mike, Queenie had feared that on meeting, Mike might recognize Rick as being the 'big bloke' who had disturbed them on a particular night many months ago. When Mike had accepted the invitation, remarking, 'It's about time I gave this 'ere would-be priest the once-over,' Queenie's fear deepened. So now his sudden refusal to go was a source of relief to her. But his insistence that she should stay at home infuriated her; at times like this she wondered whether she had not merely exchanged one George Kenney for another.

Fearful as George Kenney had been, she had stood up to him fair and square, even when her heart shrank at the sight of him and her body trembled uncontrollably in horror of the consequences. And by God! she could just as well challenge *this* bully! Mike Bedford could stay away from Rick's party if he had a mind to, but *she* was going, with or without his permission.

Later, when the quiet darkness of the room was disturbed only by the rhythmic breathing of her sleeping husband, Queenie thought of how very much she was looking forward to Rick's party. She had long since given up trying to delude herself that her excitement stemmed from any other source than the prospect of seeing Rick again.

The thought of actually going into Mrs Marsden's home and coming face to face with her, had at first seemed rather daunting to Queenie. She recalled the one occasion on which she and Rick's mother had met; it was when she and Rick had been collecting toys for the children and Mrs Marsden had brought a collection of Rick's childhood playthings. The two women had done no more than exchange glances across a room. Queenie had not been aware, at the time, that Mrs Marsden and George Kenney had been lovers many years before, nor that the consequences of their illicit relationship would have such a drastic bearing on her own future happiness and that of the man she adored.

Since George Kenney had taunted her with the revelation of his wickedness, Queenie had forced herself to consider other matters closely related to the facts. She thought of her mother, Kathy, and wondered at the degree of suffering George Kenney had caused his wife. And a great sadness had overwhelmed her. Queenie was concerned also that Mrs Marsden must know her to be George Kenney's daughter.

That being so, would not Queenie's presence at Rick's party cause old wounds to reopen? Then try as she would, Queenie could not quell a sense of outrage towards the woman, who together with George Kenney had been the root cause of so much unhappiness.

Queenie had voiced all of these anxieties to Rick and together they had talked them through. 'No amount of wishing it away can ever make a difference,' he had insisted. Beneath Rick's power of persuasion and strength of mind, Queenie had found within herself a measure of forgiveness and understanding she had not thought possible.

Yet this inner strength had been rendered helpless when Rick had taken her hands in his; the dark passion in his gaze drawing the innermost secrets of her heart into her own eyes for all the world to see. For what seemed an endless moment, they had held each other's gaze and become painfully aware of that which was theirs, but which was ever denied to them.

There had been no such intimate moment since that Wednesday evening. Queenie at once erected that invisible barrier which could help to diminish the pain of awareness. She had to keep her relationship with Rick on a careful footing, if she was to go on with a degree of sanity. Things might be easier now, she thought, with her not able to keep on at the Ragged School; she wouldn't be seeing Rick so often and there'd be a baby to keep her occupied. Yet even as she took small comfort in these possibilities, Queenie was not fooling herself. She'd miss being with Rick, even in the presence of a dozen or so children.

It was seven o'clock when Father Riley's little black car drew up outside No. 2, Parkinson Street. Queenie had been watching out of the window, but it was Katy who spotted him first. 'Quick, lass,' she called, 'get your things. We're off!' And in a moment, she was down the passage, out of the front door and into the rear of Father Riley's car.

Queenie took a minute to check that everything was ready for Mike's tea when he got home. There was a small fish pie and a dish of vegetables. Queenie had filled her largest pan to the brim with water, and placing the cooked dishes on a plate she had put the plate over the pan and left it quietly simmering on a low light. She had never done that before, but Katy assured her that it would be perfectly safe and keep the meal fresh and hot for more than the hour needed. There were also freshly baked scones which Katy had prepared, so Mike would have a welcoming meal waiting for him.

Scribbling a short note, explaining that she had gone to Mrs Marsden's with Katy and Father Riley, Queenie left it propped up on the mantelpiece where Mike was bound to see it. He would be angry, she knew that. But she was not his prisoner, yet, and it was not right that he should think she was!

Having satisfied herself that everything was all right Queenie came out of the house and shut the door.

As she turned towards the car, a quick movement in the window opposite told Queenie that Mike's mother was watching. It was an easy thing to read the woman's thoughts: Mike working all day and coming home to find his wife gallivanting out and no meal on the table! In spite of herself, Queenie felt a pang of conscience, then just as quickly she chided herself for being silly. After tonight, Mike would have her home all the time. And whatever Mrs

Bedford might choose to think, her son was well fed and cared for.

'C'mon, lass!' Katy urged, 'else it'll be finished afore we get there.'

In a moment, Father Riley was out of the car and holding the front passenger door open. 'You'll find it more comfortable in the front seat,' he told Queenie, then with a chuckle, he added, 'there's room for two.'

As the car sped away from Parkinson Street, and towards the Marsden home in Wigan, Queenie felt as though she was slipping the shackles of imprisonment. With every mile that brought her closer to Rick, a lightness flooded her heart. And where there had been pain and guilt, there came a wonderful sense of joy which made her want to laugh out loud.

This last hour or so, Rita Marsden had noticed the same lighter mood in her son. Now as he anxiously paced from the fireplace to the window and back again, she would have gone to him to satisfy her curiosity as to his restless behaviour had not her duties as a hostess prevented her.

Rick had insisted that his party should not be a fancy affair. He had wanted only family and close friends. His father had protested, but Rick was adamant, and eventually it was agreed that the number of guests would not exceed ten.

Rita Marsden was an accomplished hostess whose experienced touch reflected itself throughout the room. It was an elegant room, bedecked with Regency furniture and heavy tapestry curtains, all skilfully set out to create a rich effect. The polished mahogany piano by the window lent an air of culture although in truth it had not been played since its arrival in the house. It had been Rita Marsden's intention to learn but as yet, she had not found the time nor the incentive. The carpet's deep red colours created just the right blend with the raised red and pink roses in the curtains. And the gold dralon upholstery of the deep-buttoned chairs found an echo in the numerous lampshades, all gracefully shaped and festooned with tassles of silk.

At the far end of the room stood a long curved sideboard, its top laid over by a white cloth upon which stood a splendid array of huge plates, all displaying succulent food: hams, cheeses, fish cutlets and desserts of all manner and description. To the right of it was a small curved bar, heavy with decanters of sherry, bottles of wine and spirits and the finest of crystal glasses.

In the centre of the room a small dancing area had been cleared. Now, as Queenie followed Father Riley and Katy into the room, soft music from the radiogram was playing in the background.

Queenie was visibly taken aback by the grandness of the room. As she cast her eyes from one group of guests to another, all smartly dressed and obviously well-off, she felt sadly conscious of the burgundy-coloured smock which had taken her many days to make, and which still didn't feel entirely comfortable. But the material had cost more than she'd ever paid before, and it was her best ever effort. Up until now, she had felt proud of her achievement in making it.

Of a sudden, Mr and Mrs Marsden appeared

before them. Mr Marsden was the first to speak. 'Queenie, isn't it?' he asked, stepping forward to grasp her small hand with his two fists. 'I've heard so much about you from my son I feel I know you.' Turning to Katy, he welcomed her warmly and nodded to Father Riley. His manner was brisk, almost offhand and Queenie felt decidedly uncomfortable beneath his scrutinous eyes. She knew of this man only what Rick told her, that as a businessman he was clever and successful and, as a father, there could be no better. By all accounts, he made friends easily. But somehow Queenie sensed he was in no hurry to make friends with her. A thought crossed her mind; was he holding her in contempt because she was George Kenney's daughter? How much, she wondered, did Mr Marsden know of the truth concerning his wife's affair with George Kenney? Had she confessed all to him? Did he know that Rick, whom he idolized, was not his son? If that was the case, then she could understand his feelings of resentment towards her. Strange, wasn't it, she thought cynically, how George Kenney could still create hostility after his demise!

'Queenie!' Rick pushed his way through to her side and Queenie had never been more thankful to see him. 'I thought you'd changed your mind!' he told her, 'but you're here now. That's all that matters.' His brown eyes danced into hers.

Mr Marsden thumped Rick playfully. 'Now then, son! Don't you allow this lovely creature to monopolize you all evening.' And to Queenie, 'I'm surprised your husband lets you out of his sight, with you so near your time, child.' He wore a smile. But Queenie recognized the undercurrent of his words, and there was no mistaking the meaning in his reproachful stare as he moved away with Father Riley.

Mrs Marsden stepped forward, exquisite in a straight pale-blue dress, her fair hair softly curled and a bright smile in her gentle blue eyes. Taking Katy's hand in her left and Queenie's in her right, she kissed each of them in turn, saying, 'Oh, I'm so glad you're here. I appear to be outnumbered by the male element . . .' Turning her head slightly to indicate the truth of her remark, she caught sight of her husband in deep conversation with Father Riley and returning her gaze to Rick, she laughed, 'Your father never gives up!' Then, with a warm smile to Queenie she went on, 'I gather you have done wonders with the Ragged School, Queenie. I know Rick will miss you. But it's lovely that you're expecting your first child. It'll bring you a great deal of joy.'

'An' a heap o' sleepless nights too, I'll be bound,' interrupted Katy with a great beaming smile.

'Maybe . . . but that's the price we all have to pay,' returned Rita Marsden. 'Oh, but look at her, Katy. She's positively blooming! And what a clever choice of colour, Queenie, that smock is lovely.'

'Thank you, Mrs Marsden,' Queenie replied, her confidence boosted. She had taken an instant liking to Rick's mother, drawn by Mrs Marsden's genuine warmth and open welcome. Somewhere behind the smile in those soft blue eyes, Queenie had sensed a degree of sacrifice and unhappiness and was forced to think again on George Kenney's selfish past.

As Rita Marsden took stock of Queenie, whose quiet loveliness had taken her by surprise, she too was forced to think on her youth and her passion for the girl's father. When she recalled how Katy once told her of George Kenney's rejection of the girl, her heart was pained and she unquestioningly accepted part of the blame. There had been so much unhappiness. Not least of all was the loss of that beautiful baby boy, created in sin by her and George Kenney, and taken from her as though in punishment. It was all such a long time ago, she thought, but never forgotten.

Now, as she looked at Rick, so good and confident, she gave thanks for this young man who had come into her life to replace the son she had lost. 'Rick, take charge of Queenie will you? While I introduce Katy to our guests.'

With Rick's appearance, Queenie had eyes for no one else. Without a word he took her hand in his; she was so afraid of the emotions awakened in her that she wanted to put as much space between them as was humanly possible, so that in the span of their lifetimes, they would not meet again. Oh, but how could she? How devastating such a prospect seemed.

If she had been nervous at first, Queenie soon warmed to the festivities. Rick took her round the room, introducing her to the 'well-off' people she had been wary of, but whom she now saw as friendly and warm. There was Mr Marsden's brother Harold, a short stocky man of bald pate and red face, which grew even redder as he took his fill of the lovely Queenie. Harold's wife and daughter, Patricia, were as alike as two peas in a pod, tall, skinny and red-haired; the daughter Patricia, whom Queenie assessed to be a little older than herself, was a giggly shy person, obviously overwhelmed by Rick's presence. Then came two business colleagues of Mr Marsden, dressed in severe pin-stripe suits complete with identical silver watch chains and black shiny shoes. Queenie thought them to be more suited to a funeral than a birthday celebration and the odd secretive way they huddled together made her chuckle to herself. They put her in mind of coffin-bearers. But they were friendly enough and made her feel comfortable.

The two remaining guests were the ones who intrigued Queenie the most. One was a gentleman by the name of Mr Snowdon. He had the kindest face and the mildest of manners, and Queenie could not help but notice that both Mr and Mrs Marsden went out of their way to see that he was being looked after. Rick introduced Mr Snowdon as being 'Uncle Rodney'. But afterwards he confided to Queenie that Mr Snowdon was not his real uncle, just a long-standing friend of the family, and one who had watched him grow from a child.

As Irish as the shamrock, Father O'Malley was a darling, out of all the guests he was the one who made Queenie laugh out loud. Tall and ungainly in his smart suit and white neck collar, he had the most riotous laugh, and the largest ears Queenie had ever seen. Compared to Father Riley's priestly mannerisms, Father O'Malley might just as well have been a bricklayer's navvy.

'Now then, Rick me boy,' he smiled, 'shall I take

this little darlin' twice round the floor?' Even as he spoke Father O'Malley had whisked Queenie into his arms, and with a certain style that would have shamed a ballroom champion, he led her into a slow foxtrot.

Queenie had never learned to dance properly, and she felt somewhat cumbersome with the weight of her child, but the light skilful steps of her partner hid her mistakes. When the other guests took to the floor, the evening was really started.

At one point, Katy leaned out of Mr Snowdon's arms to confide in Queenie, 'This is all very grand, Queenie. But me feet are killing me. Oh, give us me old kitchen, with a freshly brewed mug o' tea, hot muffin an' me old baggy slippers, eh?'

Then came the waltz in Rick's arms. And Queenie thought she would never be nearer to paradise. She was held so close that she imagined his heart beating within her own. Until the music drew to a close, Queenie dared not trust herself to look up at him. Only when they were standing still did she lift her eyes to his.

In that same instant, Rita Marsden knew what she had suspected ever since Queenie had arrived that evening. The girl was in love with Rick, and he with her.

In God's name! What were they thinking of? Queenie married and heavy with child and Rick paving the way for his career in the church. Rita Marsden was not in favour of her son becoming a priest because she had long suspected his reasons. But this! Yet in her instinctive condemnation Rita Marsden was reminded that when Queenie was not yet born, she herself had committed the same for-bidden mistakes with George Kenney.

Just as abruptly as it had stopped, the music started up again. Rita Marsden watched as her son escorted Queenie and Katy Forest to the buffet table, and as she followed their movements, her gaze fell upon the figure of her husband. Mr Marsden had been deep in conversation with his two business colleagues. But now he had walked away from them and was standing against the bar, his eyes intent on Rick and Queenie.

Rita Marsden knew at once that her husband had witnessed the affection between his son and George Kenney's daughter. And the look on his face as he continued to stare after Queenie struck her rigid. Never before had she seen such animosity there.

Chapter Eighteen

'She's nowt but a trollop, I tell you!' Mrs Bedford proclaimed, wagging a finger at her son, Mike. 'If you were a man, you'd get yourself out to the Marsden place and fetch that wife o' yourn 'ome!'

'Oh, I'm a man right enough!' Mike Bedford retorted as he took his mother by the arm and marched her down the passage to the front door, 'man enough to throw you out an' all!' Wrenching the door open, he deposited her on the doorstep.

'Yer a bloody fool, my lad! Can't see what's under yer own nose. I saw 'er get in that car . . . all full o' the joys o' spring. An' you comin' 'ome to an empty 'ouse!'

'It's *my* business! An' I'll thank you to keep yer nose out!' Ignoring her protests, Mike Bedford closed the door in his mother's face and returned to the parlour where he sat in the black horse-hair chair, his mind churning with anger. So Queenie had defied him, eh? Gone to that bloody do after he'd forbidden it! His mam was right; what sort of man would he be if she was allowed to get away wi' making a fool of him? An' what was so precious about this bloody party that she couldn't keep away, eh?

For a long time, he paced up and down the floor, torn two ways and unsure as to how to deal with the matter.

343

All the nagging suspicions came creeping back. He'd never found out the identity of the big bloke who'd fathered Queenie's child. 'Appen the bastard was after worming his way back into Queenie's favour. Aye! Well, if that was the case, there'd be more trouble than the bugger 'ad ever dreamed of.

Driven by his insane jealousy and the thought that Queenie was deceiving him, Mike Bedford came to the conclusion that there was only one way to settle this business. If he hurried, he might just catch the eight-thirty bus out to Wigan and the Marsden place; a big house on Brewers Hill as couldn't be missed, according to his mother. Lord knows where she got 'er information from, but she always were a nosey bugger! Still an' all, it were a good thing as somebody knew what was going on.

Brewers Hill was easily found and, once there, the Marsden place rose up before him. Mike Bedford leaned against the iron-railings which ran across the front of the house. The evening air had turned chilly with the coming of dusk and he cursed himself for not putting a warm jumper beneath his jacket. Pulling the corded jacket about him, he fastened up the buttons and stood awhile to get his breath back. The long uphill walk from the bus stop through the town-centre and out again towards Brewers Hill had left him fair wheezing. But for all that pushing along and fresh air, the raging anger inside him had not died down. The last bus returned to Blackburn at quarter past ten, according to yon conductor. Well! Him an' Queenie would be on it. She owed him a deal of explanation.

When he had composed himself enough, Mike

Bedford followed the drive up to the house and knocked against the front door with three resounding thumps. Judging by the music and laughter emanating from inside, he would *need* to thump hard, he thought, in order for them to hear.

In a moment, the door was opened by Rita Marsden, and, upon identifying himself, Mike Bedford was immediately made welcome. 'Did Queenie know you were coming? She didn't say anything,' Rita Marsden enquired as she led the way through the hall and into the living room. So this is Queenie's husband she mused, feeling more than a little surprised that the two of them could find anything in common. Yet for all that, she was filled with a sense of relief that he had turned up.

The effects of daring to dance in her advanced condition had begun to show on Queenie. When Mike Bedford's searching gaze located her, she was seated with Katy by the window, awaiting Rick's return from the bar where he had gone to collect her a glass of orange juice.

'I think you're ready for home, lass. You should never have allowed yersel' to be danced round that floor at all!' scolded Katy.

Queenie would have answered that she was not yet ready to go and besides, a couple of slow rounds on the dance floor was not really excessive. What was more, she was thoroughly enjoying herself. But when she saw Mike Bedford striding across the room towards her, the words froze in her mouth. When he stood before her, his eyes broad and staring as he instructed in a gruff voice, 'Get yer things. You're coming with me!' her heart sank.

Queenie realized that Mike was furious and, she reasoned, maybe he had every right to be. Hoping to avoid any embarrassing scenes she got to her feet and, turning to Katy, she said, 'You're right, Katy. It *is* time I was off home.'

'Aye . . . but wait on. I'll get Father Riley to run you both back, eh?' She was already on her feet.

'No thank you!' Mike Bedford snapped as he waited for Queenie to collect her bag from the window-sill, 'I'm not after anybody's favours. We'll mek us way back on the bus!' Cupping his hand beneath Queenie's elbow, he urged her forward. As he did so, Rick returned from the bar to position himself in front of them.

'Mike, isn't it?' he asked, placing Queenie's glass of orange on top of the piano and extending his hand out in greeting. 'Glad to meet you at last. I'm Rick . . . Rick Marsden.'

'Rick Marsden, eh?' The smaller man stood back to eye up this fellow who seemed to command so much of Queenie's time and respect. He decided two things straight away; he didn't like him and he believed that they had met somewhere before.

Queenie had seen a glint of recognition in her husband's eyes and she prayed he would not remember. But her fears were allayed as Mike pushed her forward ignoring Rick's outstretched hand. 'Goodnight one an' all. Can't stay . . . got a bus to catch,' he called out in a mocking fashion. Of a sudden, everyone's eyes were on Queenie and this strange little man who looked totally out of place.

Queenie had found herself forced to an abrupt halt as Rick barred their way. His face darkened by the

anger he felt at seeing Queenie pushed unceremoniously across the room, he asked with forced
politeness, 'You surely don't intend walking Queenie
all the way to the bus stop in her condition, and with
no outdoor coat?'

'Should a' thought o' that, shouldn't she?'

Rick stood his ground, his fury mounting until he
could have lifted Mike Bedford from the floor. 'I'm
sorry. I can't let you do that!' he said, with a calmness
which belied the challenge in his eyes.

'You can't what!' exploded Mike, whose tightening
grip on her arm caused Queenie to wince. 'You'll get
outta me bloody way if you know what's good for
you . . .'

Queenie did not like the way Mike and Rick were
already squaring up to each other and she was painfully
conscious of the fact that everyone had begun to move
in on them. She had it in mind to step forward and
hurry Mike from the room. But at this point Mrs
Marsden reached in between the two men to hand
Queenie a lightweight mackintosh. 'Here, Queenie,'
she said, 'this might be of some use to you?'

Queenie was grateful for the timely intervention.
'Thank you, Mrs Marsden,' she said, taking the coat
and wrapping it round her shoulders. Then with
deliberation she stepped between her husband and
Rick, at the same time telling Mike, 'If we're to catch
the last bus, we'd best be off.' With a disarming smile,
she turned to Rick, saying, 'Goodnight, Rick . . .
thank you. It's a lovely party.'

'Look, Mike . . . Queenie . . .' Father Riley pushed
in between Rick and his mother, 'let me run you back
in the car?'

'Thanks all the same. But I'm capable of seeing Queenie back!' retorted Mike, edging himself and Queenie forward. At the door, he looked back to where Mr Marsden appeared to be arguing with Rick and, raising his voice, he called, 'As for you, Rick Marsden, you might do well to remember that it's bad manners to interfere between a fella an' his wife. If I've a mind to run 'er stark naked through the town, I'd not need your *bloody* permission!'

Throughout the room, there were gasps of surprise and what followed happened so swiftly that no one could have prevented it. With a cry of 'You bastard!' Rick sprang forward to grab Mike Bedford by the throat and the sheer weight of his lunging body catapulted the two of them into the hall. Relieving his grip on the surprised Mike Bedford just long enough to throw open the front door, Rick hoisted him into the air and out onto the porch, where the two of them fought and grappled until Mike Bedford broke loose and escaped down the steps to the drive. 'You're a bloody maniac!' he shouted, 'an' I'll tell you this much, Marsden . . . you'll not be setting eyes on my Queenie again!' He raked his glaring eyes over the figures watching from the porch snarling, 'She's mine! D'you 'ear? She'll be 'aving nowt to do wi' any o' you buggers!'

Rick would have gone for him again. But in a moment Mr Marsden and Father Riley had him by the shoulders.

'No, son, the man's right. It's not for you to interfere,' cautioned Mr Marsden. And as Queenie quickly descended the steps to Mike's side he told her, 'Get your husband off home.'

Katy, down the steps in a flash, was asking Queenie anxiously, 'Will you be all right, lass?'

For answer, Queenie kissed Katy on the cheek. 'Take them back to the party,' she urged, 'we'll be all right.' She felt Rick's eyes on her and she knew what was in his heart, because it was in her own. It seemed like a lifetime that they all stood there in deathly silence when in fact it was but a matter of seconds. In those seconds, something happened that brought a new kind of fear to Queenie.

She saw the dawning on Mike Bedford's face as he stared back at Rick being held in the fists of the two men. They were at the forefront of the porch and, in the gathering darkness, there was no mistaking Rick's strong broad frame and the tall pride with which he held himself. Only Queenie heard the whisper that fell from Mike's bruised lips, 'It's the big-bloke!'

Taking swift advantage of the fact that Mike was dazed from the fight and his unexpected discovery Queenie grabbed his arm and hurried him away.

All the way home on the bus and even after they had arrived back at No. 2, Mike Bedford maintained a stony silence, as though unable to cope with this new and devastating piece of knowledge. Queenie attended to Mike's swollen mouth and as she did so, she was painfully aware of his eyes following her every move. The minute they had returned, he had thrown himself into the black horse-hair chair, his face a study of hatred. She had thought it wisest to let him make the first move, yet she dreaded the moment when he would. Just once she had glanced at him and the granite set of his face had frightened her.

Now, as she placed the bowl of hot water on a stool

before him, he murmured something under his breath
and when she ignored his mutterings, he gave a great
roar, at the same time lashing out with his foot against
the bowl.

The bowl flew up into the air, its steaming hot
contents splattering Queenie's eyes and face. When
she jumped to her feet with a scream of pain, he
fastened his hands about her throat, his fury like a
dozen tigers let loose. 'You an' that Marsden. All this
time be'ind my back! Laughing at me, the pair o' you!'

With her closed eyes on fire and her throat squeezed
tight beneath his fingers, Queenie was at his mercy.
When he drew her down to the floor, she could do
nothing to stop him.

'You're mine!' he repeated over and over, all the
while kissing her, viciously at first and then with
tenderness. Now, he was wiping her eyes. 'I'll kill you
both afore I let him have you! Oh . . . an' you've been
giving Rick Marsden what's rightfully mine! Ain't
you? Tell me the truth!'

Queenie could feel the clothes being peeled off her
back. In an instant he was on top of her and the weight
of his thrusting body sent her swollen stomach into her
chest, squeezing out the breath and causing such
unbearable pain inside her that she thought she would
faint dead away. Yet she made no sound, nor did she
resist. Afterwards, when he helped her to her feet, she
avoided his glance, gathered her clothes and disappeared into the scullery. Instinct, and the gripping
pains which raked her, told Queenie that the child had
started before its time.

In the scullery she bathed herself and half dressed,
then went on upstairs as Mike watched her silently

from the parlour, changed into a clean nightdress and climbed into bed.

Strange, she thought, how there was no emotion inside her. No shame or anger, just this searing pain which came and went in spasms, and a deadness of heart.

Chapter Nineteen

'It's a good job I felt the need to come an' see if you were all right, my gel!' Katy gently rubbed the small of Queenie's back, pausing now and then to allow Queenie the luxury of shifting her sitting position in the stiff upright stand-chair. 'All that dreadful business at the party! I knew no good would come of it!'

Queenie let Katy rant on. She had no heart or stomach for argument this morning, for hadn't they both been emptied into the lavatory during the night? In between when she had fallen into sleep, the dreams which denied her proper rest seemed worse than reality.

She had been awakened by the noise of rain battering against the window. There was no sign of Mike Bedford and no indication that he had come to his bed. On going downstairs, Queenie discovered him gone, without his snap-tin and nothing left to say when he would be back. But whether he came back or stayed away made no difference to Queenie. He had the right to come and go as he pleased.

During the early part of the morning, two or three of the neighbours had called in with presents for the baby; little things made by their own hands and for which Queenie thanked them profusely. There was

Mrs Bradford from three doors down and the two old ladies who had some time back come to live next door. Queenie liked them all well enough, but they were very old and kept themselves to themselves. Mrs Bradford hardly ever came out of her house and when she did, she had little to say to anyone.

Queenie had never dreamed that she could ever be lonely on Parkinson Street, but there were few young people here now and, since Maisie Thorogood and her brood had left for newer parts, the street didn't seem the same. Often Queenie thought of Sheila Thorogood and would have loved to hear from her. But there had been no word now for some time. The last letter she sent off had come back marked 'gone away'.

The loud rat-tat-tatting on the front door gave Queenie a start.

'Now, who can that be?' asked Katy, already on her way down the passage to the front door. There came the sound of the sneck being lifted and Katy's surprised cry 'Oh! It's you. Well . . . I suppose you'd best come in. But only for a few minutes, mind!'

Queenie's eyes were on the parlour doorway which a moment later was filled with Rick's broad frame. Her heart gave such a skip that for a fleeting moment the pain in her body was gone. She opened her mouth to speak, but nothing came out.

'Are you all right, Queenie?' He spoke with great tenderness and, Queenie thought, a degree of apology. He came forward to grab a stand-chair from the table and when he was seated opposite, his face so close to hers that Queenie felt the colour flooding into her own, she saw the dark cups beneath his eyes and with aching heart she knew that he too had taken little sleep last night.

'I'm fine, Rick, really, she assured him, 'but it isn't wise for you to come here.'

'My very sentiments exactly!' Katy exclaimed, standing before them, hands on hips and a look of exasperation on her face, 'as if there ain't been enough upset!'

'I'm sorry, Katy . . . but I had to know that Queenie was all right.'

'Yes, if you can call being in labour all right!' snorted Katy.

'In labour?' Rick reached out and drew Queenie's hand into his own. 'Oh, Queenie . . . Queenie.' How he wished that Katy would go, for then he could take Queenie into his arms, he could smother that pale tortured face with kisses and he could tell her that in spite of them having the same blood in their veins, he wanted her to come away with him right now.

'Look, my boy . . . I'll be but a minute in the scullery. When I come out, I want you gone!' Katy flounced off and Rick wondered if in her wisdom she had sensed his desperate need to be alone with Queenie.

He leaned forward, his gaze searching deep into those soulful grey eyes that had the power to reduce him to jelly. His voice a mere whisper, he asked, 'Queenie, my love. Will you tell me one thing? One thing I must know for sure. You married Mike . . . you're expecting his child, so it might be a foolish question to ask. But dear God. I have to know. Do you love him? I mean really love him?'

The throbbing started up in the small of Queenie's back again and, had Rick not been there, she would have borne it less bravely. But there was something else, something much more important that demanded her courage. Here was Rick, a man she would follow to the ends of the earth, if only things were different. And it could not be. They were brother and sister. She was married and about to birth their father's child. Too much had happened; too much to be undone now. There was no hope of redemption for her, she knew that and she must accept it. Oh, but there was at least something for Rick. There *had* to be and, in time, he might forgive her for what she must now do. She would not see him cheated of a chance at life because of her. He had asked a question. And she must give him the only answer she could.

'Yes, Rick,' she murmured, holding his gaze, yet despising herself for the pain which she must cause him, 'I *do* love Mike. And now I think it's best that you go.' She watched his eyes widen in disbelief, then grow bright with tears. It was then that she tore her gaze away. When he slowly got to his feet, she thought her heart would break.

Suddenly he bent to grip her shoulders. 'I don't believe you,' he cried, the tears spilling down his face, 'you're lying! Tell me you're lying.'

'I'm not lying,' she answered in a clear bold voice; and again, as she lifted her eyes to his, 'I love him. Now please . . . *please*, just go.'

'I think you'd best be off, lad.' Katy's eyes too, were bright with tears, for she had witnessed the whole thing. For the life of her, she could not understand this situation; not for one minute. But she'd known all along that these young 'uns loved each other and she also knew that if she didn't get Rick out of that house, there was no telling what the consequences might be.

So, putting on her best airs and graces, she clamped a chubby hand on Rick's arm and fairly pushed him to the front door and out onto the pavement. Seeing that Rick had come to Parkinson Street in Mr Marsden's car, she urged him to return to the Church-house. She sensed his hesitation and with a determined shake of her grey head, she told him, 'You mustn't think o' going back in there, son. Tell Father Riley I'll see Queenie right. Then I'll catch the tram back – there's no point in him coming for me like we arranged, 'cause I don't know how long I'll be with Queenie already started.'

'Oh, Katy . . . take good care of her.'

Katy was torn in two by the anguish in Rick's eyes. 'Aw, lad. O' course I will, you know that.'

They heard the noise before it was possible to distinguish the huddle of figures moving towards them.

'Go on lad!' Katy urged Rick, urgently nodding her head, 'get yourself off then.' Something warned her that Mike Bedford was one of the approaching figures. In a moment her fear was confirmed.

'Well now! Some buggers just never learn, do they?' Mike Bedford stood a pace in front of his two burly colleagues, who occasionally took his weight as he swayed back onto them. It was clear that they were all the worse for drink. 'A bit different now, ain't it,

Marsden? There's *three* on us for you to contend with this time!' He bunched his fists in front of his face and jabbing them towards Rick, he demanded, 'Come on! Let's see what yer made of!'

It took Katy but a moment to regain her composure. And now, as Rick squared himself up to the three men, who had drawn themselves into a straight solid line blocking his path, she thrust herself before Mike Bedford. 'There'll be no fighting!' she told him, her eyes raking from one man to the other, before coming to rest in contempt on Mike Bedford. '*You* get yoursel' inside – your wife's got need of you!' When he dropped his fists and stared at her, she turned to the larger of his two companions. 'Mrs Bedford's inside an' she's started in labour. So you'd do well to get yersel's off home.' Such news was all that was needed to send the two men away down the street, arm in arm and singing 'Roll out the Barrel', at the top of their voices.

Their rowdiness brought several curious neighbours to their doorsteps; when they saw Mr Bedford unsteady on his feet and looking to cause trouble, they made no attempt to return to the quiet of their parlours.

'If you've a mind to claim what you think is yours, Marsden, you'd best think again. There's *nowt* o' yours under my roof! So piss off! Go on, piss off!'

Rick gave no answer. Instead he stared at the other man, his face set as though in stone and the urge strong within him to argue that there was indeed something under this man's roof that *was* his. But then he recalled Queenie's declaration of love for Mike Bedford. 'All right Bedford,' he said through tight lips, 'I'll go. But let me tell you this: I'll be watching every move you make. And so help me, if you ever harm a hair on Queenie's head, I'll swing for you.' His icy glare held Mike Bedford's mocking eyes for a long moment until the challenge fell from them and in its place came a look of realization. Then turning to Katy, he said again, 'Take good care of her, Katy. I'll make my way back to Father Riley and tell him the way of things here.'

'An' *you* can take yourself with 'im!' Mike Bedford straightened himself up as he looked at Katy, and cocked a thumb over his shoulder to the car parked by the kerb. 'I want *none* of you in my bloody 'ouse!'

'Well now young man, that's too bad!' snapped Katy, ''cause that girl's like my own . . . an' you'll not shift me till I know she's all right!'

Mike Bedford did not answer, but with a grunt he pushed past Katy into the house.

Katy exchanged a quiet smile with Rick, who had mighty faith in Katy's ability and felt easier because of it. Without a word he turned away, climbed into the car and disappeared down the road. Katy watched him turn the corner then, with a wise old smile which swept over the watching neighbours, she squared her shoulders and returned to the parlour and Queenie.

The next three hours saw Queenie's labour pains accelerate with a vengeance and Mike Bedford hurry from the bedroom to the parlour, where he sought out a bottle of the hard stuff and proceeded to blot out the sight of Queenie in pain. He wondered what that Forest woman would say if she knew that he had forced himself on Queenie last night. No doubt she'd blame him for having brought on the pains afore time! Well to buggery with it all! Yet for all that, he was sorry for what he'd done and he knew that in doing it he had driven Queenie further away from him. On top of that, he'd probably lost his job for staying away from it today . . . there was many a chap waiting to pick up the bones of another.

He counted his troubles and with every one he took another generous swig from the bottle. As the liquid vanished, his boldness swelled. His mam was right . . . Queenie *was* a trollop! He'd show her and that fellow Marsden who was the boss around here. An' if he'd lost his job, so what? He'd take Queenie right away from these parts, an' then by God, just let any of 'em search him an' Queenie out.

Twice in his new-found courage Mike Bedford mounted the stairs to the bedroom where Queenie was deep in the throes of labour. Twice Katy had left her vigil by Queenie's side to chase him from the room. 'What sort of man d'you call yoursel', to come in here the worse for drink, Mike Bedford?' she had demanded. And when as he retreated he had retorted, 'I'll tell you what sort of man! The sort as teks on a woman carrying another man's brat, 'cause he loves her. That's what sort o' man!' Katy was stopped in her tracks. All the suspicions that had murmured inside her these last months reared up to worry her. Was this true; or was it the drink that was speaking? Yes, it was the drink. It must be.

Yet as Katy bolted the bedroom door against him, she could not rid herself of the suspicion that Mike Bedford was telling the truth. If the child wasn't his, whose was it? Large in her mind came the image of

Rick. But if that were the case, Rick an' Queenie would have wed, she was sure. Oh, 'twas a very puzzling business. She *would* get to the bottom of it, but right now, there was a babby on its way, an' needing all her attention. She would have sent Queenie's husband to summon the doctor but Mike Bedford was incapable and she dared not leave Queenie's side. Still an' all, everything seemed to be progressing normally.

Queenie gave birth to a son some short time after six p.m. When he fought his way into the world, taking with him all the agony that had racked Queenie's body these past hours, she cried hard tears of relief for the ending of such an ordeal. During that last hour preceding the birth, when she'd felt her body cracking in a million places and she had prayed for its ending, Queenie had likened the awful experience to the nightmare invasion of her body by George Kenney. Then, in that first moment when she had looked on the boy-child held in Katy's arms, she had found herself to be deeply shocked by its startling likeness to him.

Katy had also been shocked to see that the child was a detailed miniature of Queenie's father. Even though she silently assured herself that it was a natural enough thing for a child to carry some of its grandfather's colouring or features, she could never recall ever seeing a child set so painstakingly in an exact replica. All manner of things that had been said came flooding into her mind, and others that had not, yet were conveyed to her now by other suggestions. She thought of two young people desperately in love; she fought with the reasons why Queenie had married another and why she had denied herself the man she really loved. A strange light began to dawn in Katy's mind. As it lit up so many questions, she cast her thoughts back to that day in the Church-house kitchen, when Queenie had been taken ill and for a long time after had seemed to hate herself, not caring about her appearance or any other hitherto important matter.

'Can I hold him, Katy?' Queenie had seen the questions written across Katy's face and she knew that Katy was a worrit who liked to know all the answers.

'Aye, child, 'course you can.' Katy put the child into Queenie's arms and it struck her as strange that Queenie made no comment on her son's uncanny likeness to George Kenney. But then, she thought, the lass has every reason to want to shut that dreadful monster out of her thoughts. Mebbe more reason than a body knew.

Katy would have braved herself to question Queenie on the matter that had now begun to haunt. But she reasoned that there'd be time enough for all that when the lass had gained her strength and was on her feet again.

'You're tired, Katy, you go home now. I'll be all right,' Queenie urged.

'Aye . . . 'appen I will, lass. But I've to be sure that the doctor's on his way first. That husband o' yourn rallied himself enough to fetch his mam to watch you for a while.' Katy leaned down, kissed the child and then asked Queenie in a whisper, 'She's downstairs, now. Will you be all right with her?'

Queenie reached out her free arm and drew Katy into her embrace. 'Oh, I do love you, Katy,' she said, 'and I'm glad Mrs Bedford's here. I want to see her and Mike friends again.'

Katy straightened up, 'Right then!' she declared, gathering the child into her arms. 'I'll see the child comfortable, then I'll tek me leave.' She first went over to the cot where she carefully wrapped the child up warm. As she halted at the door, she told Queenie, 'I'll be back first thing in the morning, lass.'

Queenie nodded and watched Katy close the door behind her. Soon after came the sound of voices below in the parlour, shortly followed by the click of the front door closing and the ensuing taps of Katy's footsteps receding down Parkinson Street.

With Katy's departure, Queenie felt lost. Downstairs were her husband and her mother-in-law; inside the cot at the foot of her bed was her newly born son. To most people, thought Queenie, all of that would bring a sense of security and belonging. But to her, it brought fear and uncertainty.

She could hear them now, Mike Bedford and his mother, engaged in argument. He demanding that she stay and look after Queenie. She vehemently protesting that she would not be told what to do. Let him look after his own mistakes for she wanted no part of 'that trollop – or her little bastard!'

The row raged on for some time, during which Queenie crawled to the foot of her bed where she knelt to gaze into the cot at the small sleeping face of her son. Reaching in, she tenderly lifted the tiny fingers into her own and a great swell of love surged through her. 'You're a little innocent,' she murmured, 'and I won't hold you to blame for my father's sins.'

For a while, the child seemed to sleep soundly, only

occasionally snuffling as though fighting an irritation in its nose. Queenie lifted him over on to his side, and, when the snuffling ceased, she moved back up the bed and got beneath the clothes. Of a sudden she had the strongest desire for sleep.

Queenie had no idea how long she had slept. But when she awoke, it was to see Dr Noel bending over her and at once she knew by the uncanny stillness in the room that something was wrong. It took a few seconds for her agitated brain to register what Doctor Noel was taking such kindness to explain.

'I'm sorry, child, there was nothing anyone could have done. It looks to me as though it was a respiratory failure. We'll know soon enough. I'll have him taken straight away . . . your husband has signed the necessary papers.'

In a sudden movement, Queenie was bolt upright, her dazed eyes roving the room. What was he saying? That the baby was dead? But he couldn't be! Her eyes searched the doctor's face and without being consciously aware of the movement, she shook her head from side to side saying 'no' over and over. Then fighting against Dr Noel's restraining hands, she would have dragged herself from the bed and grabbed her son from his cot. But she was weak and something in the doctor's face told her that he was speaking the truth.

The last thing that Queenie saw before feeling the sedating needle slip into her arm was Mrs Bedford seated on the rush chair in the corner of the room. She sat perfectly motionless, her eyes boring into Queenie and her mouth set in a thin grim line.

There was a look of satisfaction on her face as she sat thinking her dark thoughts. This woman who had taken her son from her, had now lost her own. And she was glad that she had been here to witness Queenie's suffering. It was through her that Mike was as lost to her as though he too were dead. Through this woman, there had grown such anger and bitterness between her and Mike that it could never be mended. He was a changed man. Oh, he'd always liked a drop o' the hard stuff, that was true. But after signing the papers for the doctor to take this woman's bastard away, he'd fallen into such terrible despair that anybody would think he was responsible for its untimely death. Then draining the contents of the bottle he'd cradled all afternoon, he had taken himself away down Parkinson Street, no doubt in search of the nearest pub. 'Respiratory failure,' the doctor had said; but she knew better. It were an act of God, that's what it were!

'Keep an eye on her, Mrs Bedford,' instructed Dr Noel, 'she should sleep soundly for a few hours.' He glanced at his watch, 'It's almost nine p.m . . . I'll call back first thing tomorrow. Meanwhile if she wakes, make her a hot drink and get her to take two of these.' He placed a small bottle into her hand. 'I'll instruct the undertaker to collect the child within the hour.'

Yes, and that was as long as she intended to stay in this house, thought Mrs Bedford. If the doctor expected her to sit and watch over this woman all night, he'd got another think coming. She would see the undertaker away because she'd been left with no choice. But she would be damned if she'd stay another minute longer!

* * *

The light of a new day was already dawning when Constable Green stepped from his car and hurried across the pavement to No. 2. He was surprised to find the door unlocked and off the sneck. However, in this particular instance, he had to admit that he was grateful for it. The news he brought to this house was bad enough without having to knock the whole street awake.

Cautiously feeling his way into the passage, the constable located the light switch and clicked it on. It was but a few steps more to the parlour where he tapped on the door calling out, 'Mrs Bedford? Hello!' When there came no reply, he pushed open the door and peered into the darkness. There, seated in the black horse-hair chair, her bent outline just visible in the half-light from the window, was Queenie.

'Good Lord!' exclaimed the constable, shocked. 'Mrs Bedford, is it?' He switched on the light and came towards her. 'I did knock at the door . . . I'm sorry, I hope I've not alarmed you?'

Queenie looked up; on seeing the uniformed man, she suspected he had come about the child. 'He's gone,' she said, slowly turning her gaze away to rest it once again on the fender, 'they've all gone.'

'Mrs Bedford . . . are you all right, love?' Constable Green took off his helmet and took the liberty of seating himself so that he had Queenie full in his sights. He didn't care for the way she was just sitting there, her head bent and eyes staring as though under the weight of some terrible grief. She couldn't know that he was the bearer of bad news . . . he'd only just been given the details of it himself. She'd probably been

366

sitting up half the night, waiting for her husband to come home and imagining all manner of things, the way wives did. But this was one time when a wife's worries had justification and he would have given anything not to have brought the awful tidings to her door. But he had, and the sooner they were delivered the better.

In the gentlest manner possible, Constable Green related to Queenie how her husband had fallen beneath the wheels of a coal-lorry. It had all been instantaneous, so he had suffered no pain. 'I'm dreadfully sorry, Mrs Bedford, but it will be necessary for you to identify him.'

Queenie had taken the news in total silence, not moving a muscle in acknowledgment. But now she was speaking and her voice was quiet and still as was her empty heart. 'Thank you, constable . . . I'm sure this was not an easy thing for you to do.'

For a while the constable talked to her, in comforting words, which for Queenie held no meaning at all. She listened and gave him small response, until eventually he got to his feet and left, murmuring his sincere apologies again.

Outside, he stood by the door and replaced his helmet. He could not get the young woman's face out of his mind. Such beautiful eyes, he thought, beautiful and tragic. Yet in those eyes he had seen a strength which almost frightened him. He wished she had not refused his offer to stay awhile. He would gladly have stayed for he had children of his own, who were not much younger than she was. He had the feeling that Queenie Bedford was no stranger to sorrow, yet she would cope. There *were* women like that, women who were born with a cross to bear, and who by their very nature rose above the adversities of this world, with an instinctive determination to survive.

Chapter Twenty

The street was just beginning to awaken as Queenie came out of the house. In the distance could be seen the milkman's horse and cart and at thc far end of Parkinson Street there came the slamming of doors and hurrying feet as the early shift-workers left for the cotton mills.

These sounds were all very familiar to Queenie and the knowledge that she would never hear them again in this street brought a mingling of joy and sadness to her.

Dressed in the brown gaberdine mackintosh that she had not been able to wear for many months, and her hair neatly braided into place, she looked painfully thin and devoid of colour. The shadowy circles beneath her eyes told that she had slept very little since Constable Green's departure some four hours back.

During those four hours, Queenie had not moved from her chair. Her body had been too exhausted by recent events, and her mind too alive with confusion, to let her sleep soundly. But she had slept. Her weary body had occasionally demanded that she close her eyes and drift into quietness.

For what had seemed an endless time to Queenie, she had flitted in and out of this strange fitful sleep, like a lost thing tossed first this way, then that.

Until, in the last hour, she had been startled awake by something within herself that grew in such strength that she could no longer deny it. She must go from this place where she had spent all of her life. There were things in this house that would not willingly let her go, which clawed at her like so many hands, seeking to drown her forever. And if she did not now find the resolve to shake free, then she never would.

After bathing herself and putting on a clean set of clothes, Queenie had written three letters; one to Katy, saying that she would get in touch and not to worry over her; and a second to Mike's mother, which read:

Dear Mrs Bedford,
Please forgive me if you can. I would have shared your sorrow, but I know you despise me for having shared your son's life. I honestly did my best by him, believe me.
   Here, in this envelope, is the rent-book and house-key. Everything in the house is yours to sell . . . perhaps for Mike's funeral?
   God be with you

Queenie

The third letter was addressed to Mrs Farraday, asking that she please see that the notes were given over, but that the one to Mrs Bedford should be withheld until certain news had been delivered; and could Mrs Farraday please contact Constable Green of the local constabulary, with reference to that particular matter. At the mention of Mrs Bedford's name, he would take it all in hand. Also, would she please oversee that the enclosed golden locket be sold, to provide a resting-place for her child, by the side of his father, George Kenney?

Queenie went on to thank Mrs Farraday for her concern and kindness over the years. She had not written any word for Rick. Sometimes a body had to be cruel to be kind.

The three envelopes, together with Mr Craig's golden heart, she had placed in a larger envelope. Then, collecting Auntie Biddy's picture from the mantelpiece, Queenie had packed it into her small portmanteau alongside only the barest essentials she might need.

Now, without looking back, she set off down Parkinson Street to Mrs Farraday's shop, where she put the letter through the door. She hoped that Mr Craig would understand that his beautiful locket had been used in an act of love.

''Ello there! After me job, are you?' The postman's cheery greeting took Queenie by surprise, and it was only when she swung round that she realized just how drained of strength she was. But there was no going back . . . not now.

'Now, would I do a thing like that?' she smiled. Then seeing him look at the portmanteau which she had rested on the pavement, she quickly added, 'I'm away to relatives for a while. Mrs Farraday will keep an eye on things for me.'

'Aye . . . allus a good idea to let folks know when you're away.' His eyes widened in recognition. 'Aren't you from No.2?' he asked, 'Mrs Bedford?' When Queenie nodded, he fished in his shoulder-bag and withdrew a letter. 'There you are . . . save me the bother now, won't it?' And setting up a merry whistle, he gave her the letter, posted a batch through Mrs Farraday's door and went on his way.

Queenie glanced at the writing. It was from Sheila . . . oh, the letter was from Sheila, and it gladdened her heart. Quickly she opened the envelope and scanned the note inside. She could read it again when she had made her escape from Parkinson Street, before Mrs Farraday or anyone else stopped her. But she could not resist a quick look at Sheila's letter which read:

Queenie, my darling!
I expect you thought I were dead, eh?
Well, I'm not. But things 'ave changed. Me old man's done a bunk . . . rotten sod! But I'm well shot of 'im, 'cause I've found meself a merchant captain, an' we're all off to sail the seven seas! What d'you think o' that, Queenie me love? An' me sick on a merry-go-round!

This fella's not short of a bob or two neither . . . he's set me Mam up in a guest house in Lytham. Can you imagine that, for Christ's sake?

Me brother's gone off to find his fortune an' all's well with the world.

Tek care o' yourself, Queenie . . . I'll keep in touch, gel,

Sheila

She's a card, thought Queenie, a broad smile on her face as she folded the letter into her pocket. Just then, something warm and soft brushed against her leg. When she looked down, she was relieved to see that it was Mrs Farraday's ginger tom, and his sudden appearance put her in mind of a day some years back, when Auntie Biddy chased Fountain Crossland from the house, trouserless and in mortal fear for his life. Queenie found herself looking back down the years to realize that there had been plenty of laughter amidst the tears, 'Oh . . . you little darling,' she told the ginger tom, bending to fondle it, 'you gave me a fright, but I think your old man gave Fountain Crossland a bigger one!'

She remembered that Mike had a fondness for cats, and just for a moment she felt herself being drawn back down that long road.

With new resolve, she picked up her portmanteau, together with the handbag which carried the eight pound notes she had carefully saved, and took herself determinedly to the top of Parkinson Street.

Here she stopped and turned around to take one last look at her beloved street. In her mind's eye, she could see the children playing, like they used to when she was also a child. She could see old Mr Craig sitting outside his door. She warmed to the wonderful memories of the times with Auntie Biddy, and the tears filled her scarred grey eyes. It was all gone, and now she was going, never to return. She would leave the bad memories and take only the good ones with her.

Blinking the tears from her eyes, Queenie turned her back on Parkinson Street, and, with a stronger pace, she set off walking.

A smile lit up her face as she thought on Sheila's letter. 'All's well with the world,' she had said, and happen it was, yes, happen it was.

There was no doubt in Queenie's mind that one day

she would seek out Maisie Thorogood, and Sheila, her dear friend. But not yet. Not for a long while.

Queenie had no thought of any particular destination in mind; she would keep going until there was space enough for her to breathe. Somewhere out there was happiness and peace of heart – there must be, she told herself. And with the help of God she would find it.